THE AUTHOR

RALPH CONNOR was born Charles William Gordon in Indian Lands, Glengarry County, Canada West (later Ontario) in 1860. He graduated from the University of Toronto in 1883 and received his B.D. from Knox College in Toronto in 1887. Three years later he was ordained in Calgary a minister of the Presbyterian Church, and then moved to Banff where he served as missionary to the lumbercamps and mining villages of the area. In 1894 he moved to Winnipeg's Saint Stephen's Church, where he was pastor for the rest of his life.

Seeking financial assistance for his missionary work, the Reverend Charles William Gordon wrote fictional sketches for the Presbyterian magazine *The Westminster*. Under the pseudonym of Ralph Connor, he soon became Canada's best-selling author both at home and abroad. His earliest sketches were collected as *Black Rock* (1898), and this novel, along with his next two novels, *The Sky Pilot* (1899) and *The Man from Glengarry* (1901), sold five million copies.

Connor's fiction originated in his "outdoor" Christianity. His heroes are often churchmen, among other representatives of established civilization, who minister to the needs of a frontier society.

Ralph Connor died in Winnipeg, Manitoba, in 1937.

THE NEW CANADIAN LIBRARY

General Editor: David Staines

THE MAN FROM GLENGARRY

A TALE OF THE OTTAWA

RALPH CONNOR

AFTERWORD BY
ALISON GORDON

Reprinted 1993.
This New Canadian Library edition 2009.

Library and Archives Canada Cataloguing in Publication

Connor, Ralph
The man from Glengarry / Ralph Connor ; afterword by Alison Gordon.

(New Canadian library)
Originally published: Toronto: Westminster Company Limited, 1901.
ISBN 978-0-7710-9385-2

I. Gordon, Alison II. Title.
PS8463.O58 M34 2009 C813'.52 C2009-901273-1

We acknowledge the financial support of the Government of Canada through the Book Publishing Industry Development Program and that of the Government of Ontario through the Ontario Media Development Corporation's Ontario Book Initiative. We further acknowledge the support of the Canada Council for the Arts and the Ontario Arts Council for our publishing program.

Typeset in Garamond by M&S, Toronto
Printed and bound in Canada

McClelland & Stewart Ltd.
75 Sherbourne Street
Toronto, Ontario
M5A 2P9
www.mcclelland.com/NCL

1 2 3 4 5 13 12 11 10 09

DEDICATION

TO THE MEN OF GLENGARRY
WHO IN PATIENCE, IN COURAGE
AND
IN THE FEAR OF GOD
ARE HELPING TO BUILD THE EMPIRE OF
THE CANADIAN WEST
THIS BOOK IS HUMBLY DEDICATED

CONTENTS

PREFACE

The solid forests of Glengarry have vanished, and with the forests the men who conquered them. The manner of life and the type of character to be seen in those early days have gone too, and forever. It is part of the purpose of this book to so picture these men and their times that they may not drop quite out of mind. The men are worth remembering. They carried the marks of their blood in their fierce passions, their courage, their loyalty; and of the forest in their patience, their resourcefulness, their self-reliance. But deeper than all, the mark that reached down to their hearts' core was that of their faith, for in them dwelt the fear of God. Their religion may have been narrow, but no narrower than the moulds of their lives. It was the biggest thing in them. It may have taken a somber hue from their gloomy forests, but by reason of a sweet, gracious presence dwelling among them it grew in grace and sweetness day by day.

In the Canada beyond the Lakes, where men are making empire, the sons of these Glengarry men are found. And there such men are needed. For not wealth, not enterprise, not energy, can build a nation into sure greatness but men, and only men with the fear of God in their hearts, and with no other. And to make this clear is also a part of the purpose of this book.

THE OPEN RIVER

The winter had broken early and the Scotch River was running ice-free and full from bank to bank. There was still snow in the woods, and with good sleighing and open rivers every day was golden to the lumbermen who had stuff to get down to the big water. A day gained now might save weeks at a chute farther down, where the rafts would crowd one another and strive for right of way.

Dan Murphy was mightily pleased with himself and with the bit of the world about him, for there lay his winter's cut of logs in the river below him snug and secure and held tight by a boom across the mouth, just where it flowed into the Nation. In a few days he would have his crib made, and his outfit ready to start for the Ottawa mills. He was sure to be ahead of the big timber rafts that took up so much space, and whose crews with unbearable effrontery considered themselves the aristocrats of the river.

Yes, it was a pleasant and satisfying sight, some three solid miles of logs boomed at the head of the big water. Suddenly Murphy turned his face up the river.

"What's that now, d'ye think, LeNware?" he asked.

LeNoir, or "LeNware," as they all called it in that country, was Dan Murphy's foreman, and as he himself said, "for haxe, for hit (eat), for fight de boss on de reever Hottawa! by Gar!" Louis LeNoir was a French-Canadian, handsome, active, hardy, and powerfully built. He had come from the New Brunswick woods some three years ago, and had wrought and fought his way, as he thought, against all rivals to the proud position of "boss on de reever," the topmost pinnacle of a lumberman's ambition. It was something to see LeNoir "run a log" across the river and back; that is, he would balance himself upon a floating log, and by spinning it round, would send it whither he would. At Murphy's question LeNoir stood listening with bent head and open mouth. Down the river came the sound of singing. "Don-no me! Ah oui! be dam! Das Macdonald gang for sure! De men from Glengarrie, les diables! Dey not hout de reever yet." His boss went off into a volley of oaths –

"They'll be wanting the river now, an' they're divils to fight."

"We give em de full belly, heh? Bon!" said LeNoir, throwing back his head. His only unconquered rival on the river was the boss of the Macdonald gang.

Ho ro, mo nighean donn bhoidheach,
Hi-ri, mo nighean donn bhoidheach,
Mo chaileag, laghach, bhoidheach,
Cha phosainn ach thu.

Down the river came the strong, clear chorus of men's voices, and soon a "pointer" pulled by six stalwart men with a lad in the stern swung round the bend into view. A single voice took up the song –

'S ann tha mo run's na beanntaibh,
Far bheil mo ribhinn ghreannar,
Mar ros am fasach shamhraidh
An gleann fad o shuil.

After the verse the full chorus broke forth again –

Ho ro, mo nighean, etc.

Swiftly the pointer shot down the current, the swaying bodies and swinging oars in perfect rhythm with the song that rose and fell with melancholy but musical cadence. The men on the high bank stood looking down upon the approaching singers. "You know dem fellers?" said LeNoir. Murphy nodded. "Ivery divil iv thim – Big Mack Cameron, Dannie Ross, Finlay Campbell – the redheaded one – the next I don't know, and yes! be dad! there's that blanked Yankee, Yankee Jim, they call him, an' bad luck till him. The divil will have to take the poker till him, for he'll bate him wid his fists, and so he will – and that big black divil is Black Hugh, the brother iv the boss Macdonald. He'll be up in the camp beyant, and a mighty lucky thing for you, LeNoir, he is."

"Bah!" spat LeNoir, "Dat beeg Macdonald I mak heem run like one leetle sheep, one tam at de long Sault, bah! No good!" LeNoir's contempt for Macdonald was genuine and complete. For two years he had tried to meet the boss Macdonald, but his rival had always avoided him.

Meantime, the pointer came swinging along. As it turned the point the boy uttered an exclamation – "Look there!" The song and the rowing stopped abruptly; the big, dark man stood up and gazed down the river, packed from bank to bank with the brown saw-logs; deep curses broke from him. Then he caught sight of the men on the bank. A word of command and the pointer shot into the shore, and the next moment Macdonald Dubh, or Black Hugh, as he was sometimes called, followed by his men, was climbing up the steep bank.

"What the blank, blank, do these logs mean, Murphy?" he demanded, without pause for salutation.

"Tis a foine avenin' Misther Macdonald," said Murphy, blandly offering his hand, "an' Hiven bliss ye."

Macdonald checked himself with an effort and reluctantly shook hands with Murphy and LeNoir, whom he slightly knew. "It is a fery goot evening, indeed," he said, in as quiet a voice as he could command, "but I am inquiring about these logs."

"Shure, an' it is a dhry night, and onpolite to kape yez talking here. Come in, wid yez," and much against his will Black Hugh followed Murphy to the tavern, the most pretentious of a group of log buildings – once a lumber camp – which stood back a little distance from the river, and about which Murphy's men, some sixty of them, were now camped.

The tavern was full of Murphy's gang, a motley crew, mostly French Canadians and Irish, just out of the woods and ready for any devilment that promised excitement. Most of them knew by sight, and all by reputation, Macdonald and his gang, for from the farthest reaches of the Ottawa down the St. Lawrence to Quebec the Macdonald gang of Glengarry men was famous. They came, most of them, from that strip of country running back from the St. Lawrence through Glengarry County, known as the Indian Lands – once an Indian reservation. They were sons of the men who had come from the highlands and islands of Scotland in the early years of the last century. Driven from homes in the land of their fathers, they had set themselves with indomitable faith and courage to hew from the solid forest homes for themselves and their children that none might take from them. These pioneers were bound together by ties of blood, but also by bonds stronger than those of blood. Their loneliness, their triumphs, their sorrows, born of their common life-long conflict with the forest and its fierce beasts, knit them in bonds close and enduring. The sons born to them and reared in the heart of the pine forests grew up to witness that heroic struggle with stern nature and to take their part in it. And mighty men they were. Their life bred in them hardiness of frame, alertness of sense, readiness of resource, endurance, superb self-reliance, a courage that grew with peril, and withal a certain wildness which at times deepened into ferocity. By their fathers the forest was dreaded and hated, but the sons, with rifles in hand, trod its pathless stretches without fear, and with their broad-axes they took toll of their ancient foe. For while in spring and summer they farmed their narrow fields, and rescued new lands from the *brûlé*; in winter they sought the forest, and back on their own farms or in "the shanties" they cut saw-logs, or made square timber, their only source of wealth. The shanty life of the early fifties of last century was not the luxurious thing of to-day. It was full of privation, for the men were poorly housed and fed, and of peril, for the making of the timber and the getting it down the smaller rivers to the big water was a work of hardship and danger. Remote from the restraints of law and of society, and living in wild surroundings and in hourly touch with danger, small wonder that often the shanty-men were wild and reckless. So that many a poor fellow in a single wild carouse in Quebec, or more frequently in some river town, would fling into the hands of sharks and harlots and tavern-keepers, with whom the bosses were sometimes in league, the earnings of his long winter's work, and would wake to find himself sick and penniless, far from home and broken in spirit.

Of all the shanty-men of the Ottawa the men of Glengarry, and of Glengarry men Macdonald's gang were easily first, and of the gang Donald Bhain Macdonald, or Macdonald More, or the Big Macdonald, for he was variously known, was not only the "boss" but best and chief. There was none like him. A giant in size and strength, a prince of broad-axe men, at home in the woods, sure-footed and daring on the water, free with his wages, and always ready to drink with friend or fight with foe, the whole river admired, feared, or hated him, while his own men followed him into the woods, on to a jam, or into a fight with equal joyousness and devotion. Fighting was like wine to him, when the fight was worth while, and he went into the fights his admirers were always arranging for him with the easiest good humor and with a smile on his face. But Macdonald Bhain's carousing, fighting days came to an abrupt stop about three years before the opening of this tale, for on one of his summer visits to his home, "The word of the Lord in the mouth of his servant Alexander Murray," as he was wont to say, "found him and he was a new man." He went into his new life with the same whole-souled joyousness as had marked the old, and he announced that with the shanty and the river he was "done for ever more." But after the summer's work was done, and the logging over, and when the snap of the first frost nipped the leaves from the trees, Macdonald became restless. He took down his broad-axe and spent hours polishing it and bringing it to an edge, then he put it in its wooden sheath and laid it away. But the fever was upon him, ten thousand voices from the forest were shouting for him. He went away troubled to his minister. In an hour he came back with the old good humor in his face, took down the broad-axe again, and retouched it, lovingly, humming the while the old river song of the Glengarry men –

Ho ro mo nighean, etc.

He was going back to the bush and to the biggest fight of his life. No wonder he was glad. Then his good little wife began to get ready his long, heavy stockings, his thick mitts, his homespun smock, and other gear, for she knew well that soon she would be alone for another winter. Before long the word went round that Macdonald Bhain was for the shanties again, and his men came to him for their orders.

But it was not to the old life that Macdonald was going, and he gravely told those that came to him that he would take no man who could not handle his axe and hand-spike, and who could not behave himself. "Behaving himself" meant taking no more whiskey than a man could carry, and refusing all invitations to fight unless "necessity was laid upon him." The only man to object was his own brother, Macdonald Dubh, whose temper was swift to blaze, and with whom the blow was quicker than the word. But after the second year of the new order even Black Hugh fell into line. Macdonald soon became famous on the Ottawa. He picked only the best men, he fed them well, paid them the highest wages, and cared for their comfort, but held them in strictest discipline. They would drink but kept sober, they would spend money but knew how much was coming to them. They feared no men even of "twice their own heavy and big," but would never fight except under necessity. Contracts began to come their way. They made money, and what was better, they brought it home. The best men sought to join them, but by rival gangs and by men rejected from their ranks they were hated with deepest heart hatred. But the men from Glengarry knew no fear and sought no favor. They asked only a good belt of pine and an open river. As a rule they got both, and it was peculiarly maddening to Black Hugh to find two or three miles of solid logs between his timber and the open water of the Nation. Black Hugh had a temper fierce and quick, and when in full flame he was a man to avoid, for from neither man nor devil would he turn. The only man who could hold him was his brother Macdonald Bhain, for strong man as he was, Black Hugh knew well that his brother could with a single swift grip bring him to his knees.

It was unfortunate that the command of the party this day should have been Macdonald Dubh's. Unfortunate, too, that it was Dan Murphy and his men that happened to be blocking the river mouth. For the Glengarry men, who handled only square timber, despised the Murphy gang as sawlog-men; "log-rollers" or "mushrats" they called them, and hated them as Irish "Papishes" and French "Crapeaux," while between Dan Murphy and Macdonald Dubh there was an ancient personal grudge, and to-day Murphy thought he had found his time. There were only six of the enemy, he had ten times the number with him, many of them eager to pay off old scores; and besides there was Louis LeNoir as the "Boss Bully" of the river. The Frenchman was not only a powerful man, active with hands and feet, but he was an adept in all kinds of fighting tricks. Since coming to the Ottawa he had heard of the big Macdonald, and he sought to meet him. But Macdonald avoided him once and again till LeNoir, having never known any one avoiding a fight for any reason other than fear, proclaimed Macdonald a coward, and himself "de boss on de reever." Now there was a chance of meeting his rival and of forcing a fight, for the Glengarry camp could not be far away where the big Macdonald himself would be. So Dan Murphy, backed up with numbers, and the boss bully LeNoir, determined that for these Macdonald men the day of settlement had come. But they were dangerous men, and it would be well to take all precautions, and hence his friendly invitation to the tavern for drinks.

Macdonald Dubh, scorning to show hesitation, though he suspected treachery, strode after Murphy to the tavern door and through the crowd of shanty-men filling the room. They were as ferocious looking a lot of men as could well be got together, even in that country and in those days – shaggy of hair and beard, dressed out in red and blue and green jerseys, with knitted sashes about their waists, and red and blue and green *tuques* on their heads. Drunken rows were their delight, and fights so fierce that many a man came out battered and bruised to death or to life-long decrepitude. They were sitting on the benches that ran round the room, or lounging against the bar singing, talking, blaspheming. At the sight of Macdonald Dubh and his men there fell a dead silence, and then growls of recognition, but Murphy was not yet ready, and roaring out "Dh-r-r-i-n-k-s," he seized a couple of his men leaning against the bar, and hurling them to right and left, cried, "Ma-a-ke room for yer betthers, be the powers! Sthand up, bhoys, and fill yirsilves!"

Black Hugh and his men lined up gravely to the bar and were straightway surrounded by the crowd yelling hideously. But if Murphy and his gang thought to intimidate those grave Highlanders with noise, they were greatly mistaken, for they stood quietly waiting for their glasses to be filled, alert, but with an air of perfect indifference. Some eight or ten glasses were set down and filled, when Murphy, snatching a couple of bottles from the shelf behind the bar, handed them out to his men, crying, "Here, ye bluddy thaves, lave the glasses to the gintlemen!"

There was no mistaking the insolence in his tone, and the chorus of derisive yells that answered him showed that his remark had gone to the spot.

Yankee Jim, who had kept close to Black Hugh, saw the veins in his neck beginning to swell, and face to grow dark. He was longing to be at Murphy's throat. "Speak him fair," he said, in a low tone, "there's rather a good string of 'em raound." Macdonald Dubh glanced about him. His eye fell on his boy, and for the first time his face became anxious. "Ranald," he said, angrily, "take yourself out of this. It is no place for you whatever." The boy, a slight lad of seventeen, but tall and well-knit, and with his father's fierce, wild, dark face, hesitated.

"Go," said his father, giving him a slight cuff.

"Here, boy!" yelled LeNoir, catching him by the arm and holding the bottle to his mouth, "drink." The boy took a gulp, choked, and spat it out. LeNoir and his men roared. "Dat good whiskey," he cried, still holding the boy. "You not lak dat, hey?"

"No," said the boy, "it is not good at all."

"Try heem some more," said LeNoir, thrusting the bottle at him again.

"I will not," said Ranald, looking at LeNoir straight and fearless.

"Ho-ho! mon brave enfant! But you have not de good mannere. Come, drink!" He caught the boy by the back of the neck, and made as if to pour the whiskey down his throat. Black Hugh, who had been kept back by Yankee Jim all this time, started forward, but before he could take a second step Ranald, squirming round like a cat, had sunk his teeth into LeNoir's wrist. With a cry of rage and pain LeNoir raised the bottle and was bringing it down on Ranald's head, when Black Hugh, with one hand, caught the falling blow, and with the other seized Ranald, and crying, "Get out of this!" he flung him towards the door. Then turning to LeNoir, he said, with surprising self-control, "It is myself that is sorry that a boy of mine should be guilty of biting like a dog."

"Sa-c-r-ré le chien!" yelled LeNoir, shaking off Macdonald Dubh; "he is one dog, and the son of a dog!" He turned and started for the boy. But Yankee Jim had got Ranald to the door and was whispering to him. "Run!" cried Yankee Jim, pushing him out of the door, and the boy was off like the wind. LeNoir pursued him a short way and returned raging.

Yankee Jim, or Yankee, as he was called for short, came back to Macdonald Dubh's side, and whispering to the other Highlanders, "Keep your backs clear," sat up coolly on the counter. The fight was sure to come and there were seven to one against them in the room. If he could only gain time. Every minute was precious. It would take the boy fifteen minutes to run the two miles to camp. It would be half an hour before the rest of the Glengarry men could arrive, and much fighting may be done in that time. He must avert attention from Macdonald Dubh, who was waiting to cram LeNoir's insult down his throat. Yankee Jim had not only all the cool courage but also the shrewd, calculating spirit of his race. He was ready to fight, and if need be against odds, but he preferred to fight on as even terms as possible.

Soon LeNoir came back, wild with fury, and yelling curses at the top of his voice. He hurled himself into the room, the crowd falling back from him on either hand.

"Hola!" he yelled, "*Sacré bleu!*" He took two quick steps, and springing up into the air he kicked the stovepipe that ran along some seven feet above the floor.

"Purty good kicking," called out Yankee, sliding down from his seat. "Used to kick some myself. Excuse *me.*" He stood for a moment looking up at the stovepipe, then without apparent effort he sprang into the air, shot up his long legs, and knocked the stovepipe with a bang against the ceiling. There was a shout of admiration.

"My damages," he said to Pat Murphy, who stood behind the counter. "Good thing there ain't no fire. Thought it was higher. Wouldn't care to kick for the drinks, would ye?" he added to LeNoir.

LeNoir was too furious to enter into any contest so peaceful, but as he specially prided himself on his high kick, he paused a moment and was about to agree when Black Hugh broke in, harshly, spoiling all Yankee's plans.

"There is no time for such foolishness," he said, turning to Dan Murphy. "I want to know when we can get our timber out."

"Depinds intoirly on yirsilf," said Murphy.

"When will your logs be out of the way?"

"Indade an' that's a ha-r-r-d one," laughed Murphy.

"And will you tell me what right hev you to close up the river?" Black Hugh's wrath was rising.

"You wud think now it wuz yirsilf that owned the river. An' bedad it's the thought of yir mind, it is. An' it's not the river only, but the whole creation ye an' yir brother think is yours." Dan Murphy was close up to Macdonald Dubh by this time. "Yis, blank, blank, yir faces, an' ye'd like to turn better than yirsilves from aff the river, so ye wud, ye black-hearted thaves that ye are."

This, of course, was beyond all endurance. For answer Black Hugh smote him sudden and fierce on the mouth, and Murphy went down.

"Purty one," sang out Yankee, cheerily. "Now, boys, back to the wall."

Before Murphy could rise, sprang LeNoir over him and lit upon Macdonald like a cat, but Macdonald shook himself free and sprang back to the Glengarry line at the wall.

"Mac an' Diabhoil," he roared, "Glengarry forever!"

"Glengarry!" yelled the four Highlanders beside him, wild with the delight of battle. It was a plain necessity, and they went into it with free consciences and happy hearts.

"Let me at him," cried Murphy, struggling past LeNoir towards Macdonald.

"Non! He is to me!" yelled LeNoir, dancing in front of Macdonald.

"Here, Murphy," called out Yankee, obligingly, "help yourself this way." Murphy dashed at him, but Yankee's long arm shot out to meet him, and Murphy again found the floor.

"Come on, boys," cried Pat Murphy, Dan's brother, and followed by half a dozen others, he flung himself at Yankee and the line of men standing up against the wall. But Yankee's arms flashed out once, twice, thrice, and Pat Murphy fell back over his brother; two others staggered across and checked the oncoming rush, while Dannie Ross and big Mack Cameron had each beaten back their man, and the Glengarry line stood unbroken. Man for man they were far more than a match for their opponents, and standing shoulder to shoulder, with their backs to the wall, they taunted Murphy and his gang with all the wealth of gibes and oaths at their command.

"Where's the rest of your outfit, Murphy?" drawled Yankee. "Don't seem's if you'd counted right."

"It is a cold day for the parley voos," laughed Big Mack Cameron. "Come up, lads, and take a taste of something hot."

Then the Murphy men, clearing away the fallen, rushed again. They strove to bring the Highlanders to a clinch, but Yankee's voice was high and clear in command.

"Keep the line, boys! Don't let 'em draw you!" And the Glengarry men waited till they could strike, and when they struck men went down and were pulled back by their friends.

"Intil them, bhoys!" yelled Dan Murphy, keeping out of range himself. "Intil the divils!" And again and again his men crowded down upon the line against the wall, but again and again they were beaten down or hurled back bruised and bleeding.

Meantime LeNoir was devoting himself to Black Hugh at one end of the line, dancing in upon him and away again, but without much result. Black Hugh refused to be drawn out, and fought warily on defense, knowing the odds were great and waiting his chance to deliver one good blow, which was all he asked.

The Glengarry men were enjoying themselves hugely, and when not shouting their battle-cry, "Glengarry forever!" or taunting their foes, they were joking each other on the fortunes of war. Big Mack Cameron, who held the center, drew most of the sallies. He was easy-tempered and good-natured, and took his knocks with the utmost good humor.

"That was a good one, Mack," said Dannie Ross, his special chum, as a sounding whack came in on Big Mack's face. "As true as death I will be telling it to Bella Peter." Bella, the daughter of Peter McGregor, was supposed to be dear to Big Mack's heart.

"What a peety she could not see him the now," said Finlay Campbell. "Man alive, she would say the word queeck!"

"'Tis more than she will do to you whatever, if you cannot keep off that *crapeau* yonder a little better," said Big Mack, reaching for a Frenchman who kept dodging in upon him with annoying persistence. Then Mack began to swear Gaelic oaths.

"'Tain't fair, Mack!" called out Yankee from his end of the line, "bad language in English is bad enough, but in Gaelic it must be uncommon rough." So they gibed each other. But the tactics of the enemy were exceedingly irritating, and were beginning to tell upon the tempers of the Highlanders.

"Come to me, ye cowardly little devil," roared Mack to his persisting assailant. "No one will hurt you! Come away, man! A-a-ah-ouch!" His cry of satisfaction at having grabbed his man ended in a howl of pain, for the Frenchman had got Mack's thumb between his teeth, and was chewing it vigorously.

"Ye would, would you, ye dog?" roared Big Mack. He closed his fingers into the Frenchman's gullet, and drew him up to strike, but on every side hands reached for him and stayed his blow. Then he lost himself. With a yell of rage he jambed his man back into the crowd, sinking his fingers deeper and deeper into his enemy's throat till his face grew black and his head fell over on one side. But it was a fatal move for Mack, and overcome by numbers that crowded upon him, he went down fighting wildly and bearing the Frenchman beneath him. The Glengarry line was broken. Black Hugh saw Mack's peril, and knew that it meant destruction to all. With a wilder cry than usual, "Glengarry! Glengarry!" he dashed straight into LeNoir, who gave back swiftly, caught two men who were beating Big Mack's life out, and hurled them aside, and grasping his friend's collar, hauled him to his feet, and threw him back against the wall and into the line again with his grip still upon his Frenchman's throat.

"Let dead men go, Mack," he cried, but even as he spoke LeNoir, seeing his opportunity, sprang at him and with a backward kick caught Macdonald fair in the face and lashed him hard against the wall. It was the terrible French *lash* and was one of LeNoir's special tricks. Black Hugh, stunned and dazed, leaned back against the wall, spreading out his hands weakly before his face. LeNoir, seeing victory within his grasp, rushed in to finish off his special foe. But Yankee Jim, who, while engaged in cheerfully knocking back the two Murphys and others who took their turn at him, had been keeping an eye on the line of battle, saw Macdonald's danger, and knowing that the crisis had come, dashed across the line, crying "Follow me, boys." His long arms swung round his head like the sails of a wind-mill, and men fell back from him as if they had been made of wood. As LeNoir sprang, Yankee shot fiercely at him, but the Frenchman, too quick for him, ducked and leaped upon Black Hugh, who was still swaying against the wall, bore him down and jumped with his heavy "corked" boots on his breast and face. Again the Glengarry line was broken. At once the crowd surged about the Glengarry men, who now stood back to back, beating off the men leaping at them from every side, as a stag beats off dogs, and still chanting high their dauntless cry, "Glengarry forever," to which Big Mack added at intervals, "To hell with the Papishes!" Yankee, failing to check LeNoir's attack upon Black Hugh, fought off the men crowding upon him, and made his way to the corner where the Frenchman was still engaged in kicking the prostrate Highlander to death.

"Take that, you blamed cuss," he said, catching LeNoir in the jaw and knocking his head with a thud against the wall. Before he could strike again he was thrown against his enemy, who clutched him and held like a vice.

VENGEANCE IS MINE

The Glengarry men had fought their fight, and it only remained for their foes to wreak their vengeance upon them and wipe out old scores. One minute more would have done for them, but in that minute the door came crashing in. There was a mighty roar, "Glengarry! Glengarry!" and the great Macdonald himself, with the boy Ranald and some half-dozen of his men behind him, stood among them. On all hands the fight stopped. A moment he stood, his great head and shoulders towering above the crowd, his tawny hair and beard falling around his face like a great mane, his blue eyes gleaming from under his shaggy eyebrows like livid lightning. A single glance around the room, and again raising his battle-cry, "Glengarry!" he seized the nearest shrinking Frenchman, lifted him high, and hurled him smashing into the bottles behind the counter. His men, following him, bounded like tigers on their prey. A few minutes of fierce, eager fighting, and the Glengarry men were all freed and on their feet, all except Black Hugh, who lay groaning in his corner. "Hold, lads!" Macdonald Bhain cried, in his mighty voice. "Stop, I'm telling you." The fighting ceased.

"Dan Murphy!" he cried, casting his eye round the room, "where are you, ye son of Belial?"

Murphy, crouching at the back of the crowd near the door, sought to escape.

"Ah! there you are!" cried Macdonald, and reaching through the crowd with his great, long arm, he caught Murphy by the hair of the head and dragged him forward.

"R-r-r-a-a-t! R-r-r-a-a-t! R-r-r-a-a-t!" he snarled, shaking him till his teeth rattled. "It is yourself that is the cause of this wickedness. Now, may the Lord have mercy on your soul." With one hand he gripped Murphy by the throat, holding him at arm's length, and raised his huge fist to strike. But before the blow fell he paused.

"No!" he muttered, in a disappointed tone, "it is not good enough. I will not be demeaning myself. Hence, you r-r-a-a-t!" As he spoke he lifted the shaking wretch as if he had been a bundle of clothes, swung him half round and hurled him crashing through the window.

"Is there no goot man here at all who will stand before me?" he raged in a wild, joyous fury. "Will not two of you come forth, then?" No one moved. "Come to me!" he suddenly cried, and snatching two of the enemy, he dashed their heads together, and threw them insensible on the floor.

Then he caught sight of his brother for the first time lying in the corner with Big Mack supporting his head, and LeNoir standing near.

"What is this? What is this?" he cried, striding toward LeNoir. "And is it you that has done this work?" he asked, in a voice of subdued rage.

"Oui!" cried LeNoir, stepping back and putting up his hands, "das me; Louis LeNoir! by Gar!" He struck himself on the breast as he spoke.

"Out of my way!" cried Macdonald, swinging his open hand on the Frenchman's ear. With a swift sweep he brushed LeNoir aside from his place, and ignoring him stooped over his brother. But LeNoir was no coward, and besides his boasted reputation was at stake. He thought he saw his chance, and rushing at Macdonald as he was bending over his brother, delivered his terrible *lash*. But Macdonald had not lived with and fought with Frenchmen all these years without knowing their tricks and ways. He saw LeNoir's *lash* coming, and quickly turning his head, avoided the blow.

"Ah! would ye? Take that, then, and be quate!" and so saying, he caught LeNoir on the side of the head and sent him to the floor.

"Keep him off awhile, Yankee!" said Macdonald, for LeNoir was up again, and coming at him.

Then kneeling beside his brother he wiped the bloody froth that was oozing from his lips, and said in a low, anxious tone:

"Hugh, bhodaich (old man), are ye hurted? Can ye not speak to me, Hugh?"

"Oich-oh," Black Hugh groaned. "It was a necessity – Donald man – and – he took me – unawares – with his – keeck."

"Indeed, and I'll warrant you!" agreed his brother, "but I will be attending to him, never you fear."

Macdonald was about to rise, when his brother caught his arm.

"You will – not be – killing him," he urged, between his painful gasps, "because I will be doing that myself some day, by God's help."

His words and the eager hate in his face seemed to quiet Macdonald.

"Alas! alas!" he said, sadly, "it is not allowed me to smite him as he deserves – 'Vengeance is mine saith the Lord,' and I have solemnly promised the minister not to smite for glory or for revenge! Alas! alas!"

Then turning to LeNoir, he said, gravely: "It is not given me to punish you for your coward's blow. Go from me!" But LeNoir misjudged him.

"Bah!" he cried, contemptuously, "you tink me one baby, you strike me on de head side like one little boy. Bon! Louis LeNware, de bes bully on de Hottawa, he's not 'fraid for hany man, by Gar!" He pranced up and down before Macdonald, working himself into a great rage, as Macdonald grew more and more controlled.

Macdonald turned to his men with a kind of appeal – "I hev given my promise, and Macdonald will not break his word."

"Bah!" cried LeNoir, spitting at him.

"Now may the Lord give me grace to withstand the enemy," said Macdonald, gravely, "for I am greatly moved to take vengeance upon you."

"Bah!" cried LeNoir again, mistaking Macdonald's quietness and self-control for fear. "You no good! Your brother is no good! Beeg sheep! Beeg sheep! Bah!"

"God help me," said Macdonald as if to himself. "I am a man of grace! But must this dog go unpunished?"

LeNoir continued striding up and down, now and then springing high in the air and knocking his heels together with blood-curdling yells. He seemed to feel that Macdonald would not fight, and his courage and desire for blood grew accordingly.

"Will you not be quate?" said Macdonald, rising after a few moments from his brother's side, where he had been wiping his lips and giving him water to drink. "You will be better outside."

"Oui! you strike me on the head side. Bon! I strike you de same way! By Gar!" so saying he approached Macdonald lightly, and struck him a slight blow on the cheek.

"Ay," said Macdonald, growing white and rigid. "I struck you twice, LeNoir. Here!" he offered the other side of his face. LeNoir danced up carefully, made a slight pass, and struck the offered cheek.

"Now, that is done, will it please you to do it again?" said Macdonald, with earnest entreaty in his voice. LeNoir must have been mad with his rage and vanity, else he had caught the glitter in the blue eyes looking through the shaggy hair. Again LeNoir approached, this time with greater confidence, and dealt Macdonald a stinging blow on the side of the head.

"Now the Lord be praised," he cried, joy breaking out in his face. "He has delivered my enemy into my hand. For it is the third time he has smitten me, and that is beyond the limit appointed by Himself." With this he advanced upon LeNoir with a glad heart. His conscience was clear at last.

LeNoir stood up against his antagonist. He well knew he was about to make the fight of his life. He had beaten men as big as Macdonald, but he knew that his hope lay in keeping out of the enemy's reach. So he danced around warily. Macdonald followed him slowly. LeNoir opened with a swift and savage reach for Macdonald's neck, but failed to break the guard and danced out again, Macdonald still pressing on him. Again and again LeNoir rushed, but the guard was impregnable, and steadily Macdonald advanced. That steady, relentless advance began to tell on the Frenchman's nerves. The sweat gathered in big drops on his forehead and ran down his face. He prepared for a supreme effort. Swiftly retreating, he lured Macdonald to a more rapid advance, then with a yell he doubled himself into a ball and delivered himself head, hands, and feet into Macdonald's stomach. It is a trick that sometimes avails to break an unsteady guard and to secure a clinch with an unwary opponent. But Macdonald had been waiting for that trick. Stopping short, he leaned over to one side, and stooping slightly, caught LeNoir low and tossed him clear over his head. LeNoir fell with a terrible thud on his back, but was on his feet again like a cat and ready for the ever-advancing Macdonald. But though he had not been struck a single blow he knew that he had met his master. That unbreakable guard, the smiling face with the gleaming, unsmiling eyes, that awful unwavering advance, were too much for him. He was pale, his breath came in quick gasps, and his eyes showed the fear of a hunted beast. He prepared for a final effort. Feigning a greater distress than he felt, he yielded weakly to Macdonald's advance, then suddenly gathering his full strength he sprang into the air and lashed out backward at that hated, smiling face. His boot found its mark, not on Macdonald's face, but fair on his neck. The effect was terrific. Macdonald staggered back two or three paces, but before LeNoir could be at him, he had recovered sufficiently to maintain his guard, and shake off his foe. At the yell that went up from Murphy's men, the big Highlander's face lost its smile and became keen and cruel, his eyes glittered with the flash of steel and he came forward once more with a quick, light tread. His great body seemed to lose both size and weight, so lightly did he step on tiptoe. There was no more pause, but lightly, swiftly, and eagerly he glided upon LeNoir. There was something terrifying in that swift, cat-like movement. In vain the Frenchman backed and dodged and tried to guard. Once, twice, Macdonald's fists fell. LeNoir's right arm hung limp by his side and he staggered back to the wall helpless. Without an instant's delay, Macdonald had him by the throat, and gripping him fiercely, began to slowly bend him backward over his knee. Then for the first time Macdonald spoke:

"LeNoir," he said, solemnly, "the days of your boasting are over. You will no longer glory in your strength, for now I will break your back to you."

LeNoir tried to speak, but his voice came in horrible gurgles. His face was a ghastly greenish hue, lined with purple and swollen veins, his eyes were standing out of his head, and his breath sobbing in raucous gasps. Slowly the head went back. The crowd stood in horror-stricken silence waiting for the sickening snap. Yankee, unable to stand it any longer, stepped up to his chief, and in a most matter of fact voice drawled out, "About an inch more that way I guess'll do the trick, if he ain't double-jointed."

"Aye," said Macdonald, holding grimly on.

"Tonald," – Black Hugh's voice sounded faint but clear in the awful silence – "Tonald – you will not – be killing – him. Remember that now. I will – never forgive you – if you will – take that – from my hands."

The cry for vengeance smote Macdonald to the heart, and recalled him to himself. He paused, threw back his locks from his eyes, then relaxing his grip, stood up.

"God preserve me!" he groaned, "what am I about?"

For some time he remained standing silent, with head down as if not quite sure of himself. He was recalled by a grip of his arm. He turned and saw his nephew, Ranald, at his side. The boy's dark face was pale with passion.

"And is that all you are going to do to him?" he demanded. Macdonald gazed at him.

"Do you not see what he has done?" he continued, pointing to his father, who was still lying propped up on some coats.

"Why did you not break his back? You said you would! The brute, beast!"

He hurled out the words in hot hate. His voice pierced the noise of the room. Macdonald stood still, gazing at the fierce, dark face in solemn silence. Then he sadly shook his head.

"My lad, 'Vengeance is mine saith the Lord.' It would have pleased me well, but the hand of the Lord was laid upon me and I could not kill him."

"Then it is myself will kill him," he shrieked, springing like a wildcat at LeNoir. But his uncle wound his arms around him and held him fast. For a minute and more he struggled fiercely, crying to be set free, till recognizing the uselessness of his efforts he grew calm, and said quietly, "Let me loose, uncle; I will be quiet." And his uncle set him free. The boy shook himself, and then standing up before LeNoir said, in a high, clear voice:

"Will you hear me, LeNoir? The day will come when I will do to you what you have done to my father, and if my father will die, then by the life of God [a common oath among the shanty-men] I will have your life for it." His voice had an unearthly shrillness in it, and LeNoir shrank back.

"Whist, whist, lad! be quate!" said his uncle; "these are not goot words." The lad heeded him not, but sank down beside his father on the floor. Black Hugh raised himself on his elbow with a grim smile on his face.

"It is a goot lad whatever, but please God he will not need to keep his word." He laid his hand in a momentary caress upon his boy's shoulder, and sank back again, saying, "Take me out of this."

Then Macdonald Bhain turned to Dan Murphy and gravely addressed him:

"Dan Murphy, it is an ungodly and cowardly work you have done this day, and the curse of God will be on you if you will not repent." Then he turned away, and with Big Mack's help bore his brother to the pointer, followed by his men, bloody, bruised, but unconquered. But before he left the room LeNoir stepped forward, and offering his hand, said, "You mak friends wit' me. You de boss bully on de reever Hottawa."

Macdonald neither answered nor looked his way, but passed out in grave silence.

Then Yankee Jim remarked to Dan Murphy, "I guess you'd better git them logs out purty mighty quick. We'll want the river in about two days." Dan Murphy said not a word, but when the Glengarry men wanted the river they found it open.

But for Macdonald the fight was not yet over, for as he sat beside his brother, listening to his groans, his men could see him wreathing his hands and chanting in an undertone the words, "Vengeance is mine saith the Lord." And as he sat by the camp-fire that night listening to Yankee's account of the beginning of the trouble, and heard how his brother had kept himself in hand, and how at last he had been foully smitten, Macdonald's conflict deepened, and he rose up and cried aloud:

"God help me! Is this to go unpunished? I will seek him to-morrow." And he passed out into the dark woods.

After a few moments the boy Ranald slipped away after him to beg that he might be allowed to go with him to-morrow. Stealing silently through the bushes he came to where he could see the kneeling figure of his uncle swaying up and down, and caught the sounds of words broken with groans:

"Let me go, O Lord! Let me go!" He pled now in Gaelic and again in English. "Let not the man be escaping his just punishment. Grant me this, O, Lord! Let me smite but once!" Then after a pause came the words, "'Vengeance is mine saith the Lord!' Vengeance is mine! Ay, it is the true word! But, Lord, let not this man of Belial, this Papish, escape!" Then again, like a refrain would come the words, "Vengeance is mine. Vengeance is mine," in ever-deeper agony, till throwing himself on his face, he lay silent a long time.

Suddenly he rose to his knees and so remained, looking steadfastly before him into the woods. The wind came sighing through the pines with a wail and a sob. Macdonald shuddered and then fell on his face again. The Vision was upon him. "Ah, Lord, it is the bloody hands and feet I see. It is enough." At this Ranald slipped back awe-stricken to the camp. When, after an hour, Macdonald came back into the firelight, his face was pale and wet, but calm, and there was an exalted look in his eyes. His men gazed at him with wonder and awe in their faces.

"Mercy on us! He will be seeing something," said Big Mack to Yankee Jim.

"Seein' somethin'? What? A bar?" inquired Yankee.

"Whist now!" said Big Mack, in a low voice. "He has the sight. Be quate now, will you? He will be speaking."

For a short time Macdonald sat gazing into the fire in silence, then turning his face toward the men who were waiting, he said: "There will be no more of this. 'Vengeance is mine saith the Lord!' It is not for me. The Lord will do His own work. It is the will of the Lord." And the men knew that the last word had been said on that subject, and that LeNoir was safe.

THE MANSE IN THE BUSH

Straight north from the St. Lawrence runs the road through the Indian Lands. At first its way lies through open country, from which the forest has been driven far back to the horizon on either side, for along the great river these many years villages have clustered, with open fields about them stretching far away. But when once the road leaves the Front, with its towns and villages and open fields, and passes beyond Martintown and over the North Branch, it reaches a country where the forest is more a feature of the landscape. And when some dozen or more of the crossroads marking the concessions which lead off to east and west have been passed, the road seems to strike into a different world. The forest loses its conquered appearance, and dominates everything. There is forest everywhere. It lines up close and thick along the road, and here and there quite overshadows it. It crowds in upon the little farms and shuts them off from one another and from the world outside, and peers in through the little windows of the log houses looking so small and lonely, but so beautiful in their forest frames. At the nineteenth cross-road the forest gives ground a little, for here the road runs right past the new brick church, which is almost finished, and which will be opened in a few weeks. Beyond the cross, the road leads along the *glebe*, and about a quarter of a mile beyond the corner there opens upon it the big, heavy gate that the members of the Rev. Alexander Murray's congregation must swing when they wish to visit the manse. The opening of this gate, made of upright poles held by auger-holes in a frame of bigger poles, was almost too great a task for the minister's seven-year-old son Hughie, who always rode down, standing on the hind axle of the buggy, to open it for his father. It was a great relief to him when Long John Cameron, who had the knack of doing things for people's comfort, brought his ax and big auger one day and made a kind of cradle on the projecting end of the top bar, which he then weighted with heavy stones, so that the gate, when once the pin was pulled out of the post, would swing back itself with Hughie straddled on the top of it.

It was his favorite post of observation when waiting for his mother to come home from one of her many meetings. And on this particular March evening he had been waiting long and impatiently.

Suddenly he shouted: "Horo, mamma! Horo!" He had caught sight of the little black pony away up at the church hill, and had become so wildly excited that he was now standing on the top bar frantically waving his Scotch bonnet by the tails. Down the slope came the pony on the gallop, for she knew well that soon Lambert would have her saddle off, and that her nose would be deep into bran mash within five minutes more. But her rider sat her firmly and brought her down to a gentle trot by the time the gate was reached.

"Horo, mamma!" shouted Hughie, clambering down to open the gate.

"Well, my darling! have you been a good boy all afternoon?"

"Huh-huh! Guess who's come back from the shanties!"

"I'm sure I can't guess. Who is it?" It was a very bright and very sweet face, with large, serious, gray-brown eyes that looked down on the little boy.

"Guess, mamma!"

"Why, who can it be? Big Mack?"

"No!" Hughie danced delightedly. "Try again. He's not big."

"I am sure I can never guess. Whoa, Pony!" Pony was most unwilling to get in close enough to the gate-post to let Hughie spring on behind his mother.

"You'll have to be quick, Hughie, when I get near again. There now! Whoa, Pony! Take care, child!"

Hughie had sprung clean off the post, and lighting on Pony's back just behind the saddle, had clutched his mother round the waist, while the pony started off full gallop for the stable.

"Now, mother, who is it?" insisted Hughie, as Lambert, the French-Canadian man-of-all-work, lifted him from his place.

"You'll have to tell me, Hughie!"

"Ranald!"

"Ranald?"

"Yes, Ranald and his father, Macdonald Dubh, and he's hurted awful bad, and –"

"Hurt, Hughie," interposed the mother, gently.

"Huh-huh! Ranald said he was hurted."

"Hurt, you mean, Hughie. Who was hurt? Ranald?"

"No; his father was hurted – hurt – awful bad. He was lying down in the sleigh, and Yankee Jim –"

"Mr. Latham, you mean, Hughie."

"Huh-huh," went on Hughie, breathlessly, "and Yankee – Mr. Latham asked if the minister was home, and I said 'No,' and then they went away."

"What was the matter? Did you see them, Lambert?"

"Oui" ("Way," Lambert pronounced it), "but dey not tell me what he's hurt."

The minister's wife went toward the house, with a shadow on her face. She shared with her husband his people's sorrows. She knew even better than he the life-history of every family in the congregation. Macdonald Dubh had long been classed among the wild and careless in the community, and it weighed upon her heart that his life might be in danger.

"I shall see him to-morrow," she said to herself.

For a few moments she stood on the doorstep looking at the glow in the sky over the dark forest, which on the west side came quite up to the house and barn.

"Look, Hughie, at the beautiful tints in the clouds, and see the dark shadows pointing out toward us from the bush." Hughie glanced a moment.

"Mamma," he said, "I am just dead for supper."

"Oh, not quite, I hope, Hughie. But look, I want you to notice those clouds and the sky behind them. How lovely! Oh, how wonderful!"

Her enthusiasm caught the boy, and for a few moments he forgot even his hunger, and holding his mother's hand, gazed up at the western sky. It was a picture of rare beauty that lay stretched out from the manse back door. Close to the barn came the pasture-field dotted with huge stumps, then the *brûlé* where the trees lay fallen across one another, over which the fire had run, and then the solid wall of forest here and there overtopped by the lofty crest of a white pine. Into the forest in the west the sun was descending in gorgeous robes of glory. The treetops caught the yellow light, and gleamed like the golden spires of some great and fabled city.

"Oh, mamma, see that big pine top! Doesn't it look like windows?" cried Hughie, pointing to one of the lofty pine crests through which the sky quivered like molten gold.

"And the streets of the city are pure gold," said the mother, softly.

"Yes, I know," said Hughie, confidently, for to him all the scenes and stories of the Bible had long been familiar. "Is it like that, mamma?"

"Much better, ever so much better than you can think."

"Oh, mamma, I'm just awful hungry!"

"Come away, then; so am I. What have you got, Jessie, for two very hungry people?"

"Porridge and pancakes," said Jessie, the minister's "girl," who not only ruled in the kitchen, but, using the kitchen as a base, controlled the interior economy of the manse.

"Oh, goody!" yelled Hughie; "just what I like." And from the plates of porridge and the piles of pancakes that vanished from his plate no one could doubt his word.

Their reading that night was about the city whose streets were of pure gold, and after a little talk, Hughie and his baby brother were tucked away safely for the night, and the mother sat down to her never-ending task of making and mending.

The minister was away at Presbytery meeting in Montreal, and for ten days his wife would stand in the breach. Of course the elders would take the meeting on the Sabbath day and on the Wednesday evening, but for all other ministerial duties when the minister was absent the congregation looked to the minister's wife. And soon it came that the sick and the sorrowing and the sin-burdened found in the minister's wife such help and comfort and guidance as made the absence of the minister seem no great trial after all. Eight years ago the minister had brought his wife from a home of gentle culture, from a life of intellectual and artistic pursuits, and from a circle of loving friends of which she was the pride and joy, to this home in the forest. There, isolated from all congenial companionship with her own kind, deprived of all the luxuries and of many of the comforts of her young days, and of the mental stimulus of that conflict of minds without which few can maintain intellectual life, she gave herself without stint to her husband's people, with never a thought of self-pity or self-praise. By day and by night she labored for her husband and family and for her people, for she thought them hers. She taught the women how to adorn their rude homes, gathered them into Bible classes and sewing circles, where she read and talked and wrought and prayed with them till they grew to adore her as a saint, and to trust her as a leader and friend, and to be a little like her. And not the women only, but the men, too, loved and trusted her, and the big boys found it easier to talk to the minister's wife than to the minister or to any of his session. She made her own and her children's clothes, collars, hats, and caps, her husband's shirts and neckties, toiling late into the morning hours, and all without frown or shadow of complaint, and indeed without suspicion that any but the happiest lot was hers, or that she was, as her sisters said, "just buried alive in the backwoods." Not she! She lived to serve, and the where and how were not hers to determine. So, with bright face and brave heart, she met her days and faced the battle. And scores of women and men are living better and braver lives because they had her for their minister's wife.

But the day had been long, and the struggle with the March wind pulls hard upon the strength, and outside the pines were crooning softly, and gradually the brave head drooped till between the stitches she fell asleep. But not for many minutes, for a knock at the kitchen door startled her, and before long she heard Jessie's voice rise wrathful.

"Indeed, I'll do no such thing. This is no time to come to the minister's house."

For answer there was a mumble of words.

"Well, then, you can just wait until morning. She can go in the morning."

"What is it, Jessie?" The minister's wife came into the kitchen.

"Oh, Ranald, I'm glad to see you back. Hughie told me you had come. But your father is ill, he said. How is he?"

Ranald shook hands shyly, feeling much ashamed under Jessie's sharp reproof.

"Indeed, it was Aunt Kirsty that sent me," said Ranald, apologetically.

"Then she ought to have known better," said Jessie, sharply.

"Never mind, Jessie. Ranald, tell me about your father."

"He is very bad indeed, and my aunt is afraid that –" The boy's lip trembled. Then he went on: "And she thought perhaps you might have some medicine, and –"

"But what is the matter, Ranald?"

"He was hurted bad – and he is not right wise in his head."

"But how was he hurt?"

Ranald hesitated.

"I was not there – I am thinking it was something that struck him."

"Ah, a tree! But where did the tree strike him?"

"Here," pointing to his breast; "and it is sore in his breathing."

"Well, Ranald, if you put the saddle on Pony, I shall be ready in a minute."

Jessie was indignant.

"You will not stir a foot this night. You will send some medicine, and then you can go in the morning."

But the minister's wife heeded her not.

"You are not walking, Ranald?"

"No, I have the colt."

"Oh, that's splendid. We'll have a fine gallop – that is, if the moon is up."

"Yes, it is just coming up," said Ranald, hurrying away to the stable that he might escape Jessie's wrath and get the pony ready.

It was no unusual thing for the minister and his wife to be called upon to do duty for doctor and nurse. The doctor was twenty miles away. So Mrs. Murray got into her riding-habit, threw her knitted hood over her head, put some simple medicines into her hand-bag, and in ten minutes was waiting for Ranald at the door.

THE RIDE FOR LIFE

The night was clear, with a touch of frost in the air, yet with the feeling in it of approaching spring. A dim light fell over the forest from the half-moon and the stars, and seemed to fill up the little clearing in which the manse stood, with a weird and mysterious radiance. Far away in the forest the long-drawn howl of a wolf rose and fell, and in a moment sharp and clear came an answer from the bush just at hand. Mrs. Murray dreaded the wolves, but she was no coward and scorned to show fear.

"The wolves are out, Ranald," she said, carelessly, as Ranald came up with the pony.

"They are not many, I think," answered the boy as carelessly; "but – are you – do you think – perhaps I could just take the medicine – and you will come –"

"Nonsense, Ranald! bring up the pony. Do you think I have lived all this time in Indian Lands to be afraid of a wolf?"

"Indeed, you are not afraid, I know that well!" Ranald shrank from laying the crime of being afraid at the door of the minister's wife, whose fearlessness was proverbial in the community; "but maybe –" The truth was, Ranald would rather be alone if the wolves came out.

But Mrs. Murray was in the saddle, and the pony was impatient to be off.

"We will go by the Camerons' clearing, and then take their wood track. It is a better road," said Ranald, after they had got through the big gate.

"Now, Ranald, you think I am afraid of the swamp, and by the Camerons' is much longer."

"Indeed, I hear them say that you are not afraid of the – of anything," said Ranald, quickly, "but this road is better for the horses."

"Come on, then, with your colt"; and the pony darted away on her quick-springing gallop, followed by the colt going with a long, easy, loping stride. For a mile they kept side by side till they reached the Camerons' lane, when Ranald held in the colt and allowed the pony to lead. As they passed through the Camerons' yard the big black dogs, famous bear-hunters, came baying at them. The pony regarded them with indifference, but the colt shied and plunged.

"Whoa, Liz!" Liz was Ranald's contraction for Lizette, the name the French horse-trainer and breeder, Jules La Rocque, gave to her mother, who in her day was queen of the ice at L'Original Christmas races.

"Be quate, Nigger, will you!" The dogs, who knew Ranald well, ceased their clamor, but not before the kitchen door opened and Don Cameron came out.

Don was about a year older than Ranald and was his friend and comrade.

"It's me, Don – and Mrs. Murray there."

Don gazed speechless.

"And what –" he began.

"Father is not well. He is hurted, and Mrs. Murray is going to see him, and we must go."

Ranald hurried through his story, impatient to get on.

"But are you going up through the bush?" asked Don.

"Yes, what else, Don?" asked Mrs. Murray. "It is a good road, isn't it?"

"Oh, yes, I suppose it is good enough," said Don, doubtfully, "but I heard –"

"We will come out at our own clearing at the back, you know," Ranald hurried to say, giving Don a kick. "Whist, man! She is set upon going." At that moment away off toward the swamp, which they were avoiding, the long, heart-chilling cry of a mother wolf quavered on the still night air. In spite of herself, Mrs. Murray shivered, and the boys looked at each other.

"There is only one," said Ranald in a low voice to Don, but they both knew that where the she wolf is there is a pack not far off. "And we will be through the bush in five minutes."

"Come, Ranald! Come away, you can talk to Don any time. Good night, Don." And so saying she headed her pony toward the clearing and was off at a gallop, and Ranald, shaking his head at his friend, ejaculated:

"Man alive! what do you think of that?" and was off after the pony.

Together they entered the bush. The road was well beaten and the horses were keen to go, so that before many minutes were over they were half through the bush. Ranald's spirits rose and he began to take some interest in his companion's observations upon the beauty of the lights and shadows falling across their path.

"Look at that very dark shadow from the spruce there, Ranald," she cried, pointing to a deep, black turn in the road.

For answer there came from behind them the long, mournful hunting-cry of the wolf. He was on their track. Immediately it was answered by a chorus of howls from the bush on the swamp side, but still far away. There was no need of command; the pony sprang forward with a snort and the colt followed, and after a few minutes' running, passed her.

"Whow-oo-oo-oo-ow," rose the long cry of the pursuer, summoning help, and drawing nearer.

"Wow-ee-wow," came the shorter, sharper answer from the swamp, but much nearer than before and more in front. They were trying to head off their prey.

Ranald tugged at his colt till he got him back with the pony.

"It is a good road," he said, quietly; "you can let the pony go. I will follow you." He swung in behind the pony, who was now running for dear life and snorting with terror at every jump.

"God preserve us!" said Ranald to himself. He had caught sight of a dark form as it darted through the gleam of light in front.

"What did you say, Ranald?" The voice was quiet and clear.

"It is a great pony to run whatever," said Ranald, ashamed of himself.

"Is she not?"

Ranald glanced over his shoulder. Down the road, running with silent, awful swiftness, he saw the long, low body of the leading wolf flashing through the bars of moonlight across the road, and the pack following hard.

"Let her go, Mrs. Murray," cried Ranald. "Whip her and never stop." But there was no need; the pony was wild with fear, and was doing her best running.

Ranald meantime was gradually holding in the colt, and the pony drew away rapidly. But as rapidly the wolves were closing in behind him. They were not more than a hundred yards away, and gaining every second. Ranald, remembering the suspicious nature of the brutes, loosened his coat and dropped it on the road; with a chorus of yelps they paused, then threw themselves upon it, and in another minute took up the chase.

But now the clearing was in sight. The pony was far ahead, and Ranald shook out his colt with a yell. He was none too soon, for the pursuing pack, now uttering short, shrill yelps, were close at the colt's heels. Lizette, fleet as the wind, could not shake them off. Closer and ever closer they came, snapping and snarling. Ranald could see them over his shoulder. A hundred yards more and he would reach his own back lane. The leader of the pack seemed to feel that his chances were slipping swiftly away. With a spurt he gained upon Lizette, reached the saddle-girths, gathered himself in two short jumps, and sprang for the colt's throat. Instinctively Ranald stood up in his stirrups, and kicking his foot free, caught the wolf under the jaw. The brute fell with a howl under the colt's feet, and next moment they were in the lane and safe.

The savage brutes, discouraged by their leader's fall, slowed down their fierce pursuit, and hearing the deep bay of the Macdonalds' great deerhound, Bugle, up at the house, they paused, sniffed the air a few minutes, then turned and swiftly and silently slid into the dark shadows. Ranald, knowing that they would hardly dare enter the lane, checked the colt, and wheeling, watched them disappear.

"I'll have some of your hides some day," he cried, shaking his fist after them. He hated to be made to run.

He had hardly set the colt's face homeward when he heard something tearing down the lane to meet him. The colt snorted, swerved, and then dropping his ears, stood still. It was Bugle, and after him came Mrs. Murray on the pony.

"Oh, Ranald!" she panted, "thank God you are safe. I was afraid you – you –" Her voice broke in sobs. Her hood had fallen back from her white face, and her eyes were shining like two stars. She laid her hand on Ranald's arm, and her voice grew steady as she said: "Thank God, my boy, and thank you with all my heart. You risked your life for mine. You are a brave fellow! I can never forget this!"

"Oh, pshaw!" said Ranald, awkwardly. "You are better stuff than I am. You came back with Bugle. And I knew Liz could beat the pony whatever." Then they walked their horses quietly to the stable, and nothing more was said by either of them; but from that hour Ranald had a friend ready to offer life for him, though he did not know it then nor till years afterward.

FORGIVE US OUR DEBTS

Macdonald Dubh's farm lay about three miles north and west from the manse, and the house stood far back from the cross-road in a small clearing encircled by thick bush. It was a hard farm to clear, the timber was heavy, the land lay low, and Macdonald Dubh did not make as much progress as his neighbors in his conflict with the forest. Not but that he was a hard worker and a good man with the ax, but somehow he did not succeed as a farmer. It may have been that his heart was more in the forest than in the farm. He was a famous hunter, and in the deer season was never to be found at home, but was ever ranging the woods with his rifle and his great deerhound, Bugle.

He made money at the shanties, but money would not stick to his fingers, and by the time the summer was over most of his money would be gone, with the government mortgage on his farm still unlifted. His habits of life wrought a kind of wildness in him which set him apart from the thrifty, steady-going people among whom he lived. True, the shanty-men were his stanch friends and admirers, but then the shanty-men, though well-doing, could hardly be called steady, except the boss of the Macdonald gang, Macdonald Bhain, who was a regular attendant and stanch supporter of the church, and indeed had been spoken of for an elder. But from the church Macdonald Dubh held aloof. He belonged distinctly to the "careless," though he could not be called irreligious. He had all the reverence for "the Word of God, and the Sabbath day, and the church" that characterized his people. All these held a high place in his esteem; and though he would not presume to "take the books," not being a member of the church, yet on the Sabbath day when he was at home it was the custom of the household to gather for the reading of the Word before breakfast. He would never take his rifle with him through the woods on the Sabbath, and even when absent from home on a hunting expedition, when the Sabbath day came round, he religiously kept camp. It is true, he did not often go to church, and when the minister spoke to him about this, he always agreed that it was a good thing to go to church. When he had no better excuse, he would apologize for his absence upon the ground "that he had not the clothes." The greater part of the trouble was that he was shy and proud, and felt himself to be different from the church-going people of the community, and shrank from the surprised looks of members, and even from the words of approving welcome that often greeted his presence in church.

It was not according to his desire that Ranald was sent to the manse. That was the doing of his sister, Kirsty, who for the last ten years had kept house for him. Not that there was much housekeeping skill about Kirsty, as indeed any one might see even without entering Macdonald Dubh's house. Kirsty was big and strong and willing, but she had not the most elemental ideas of tidiness. Her red, bushy hair hung in wisps about her face, after the greater part of it had been gathered into a tight knob at the back of her head. She was a martyr to the "neuralagy," and suffered from a perennial cold in the head, which made it necessary for her to wear a cloud, which was only removed when it could be replaced by her nightcap. Her face always bore the marks of her labors, and from it one could gather whether she was among the pots or busy with the baking. But she was kindhearted, and, up to her light, sought to fill the place left empty by the death of the wife and mother in that home, ten years before.

When the minister's wife opened the door, a hot, close, foul smell rushed forth to meet her. Upon the kitchen stove a large pot of pig's food was boiling, and the steam and smell from the pot made the atmosphere of the room overpoweringly fetid. Off the kitchen or living-room were two small bedrooms, in one of which lay Macdonald Dubh.

Kirsty met the minister's wife with a warm welcome. She helped her off with her hood and coat, patting her on the shoulder the while, and murmuring words of endearment.

"Ah, M'eudail! M'eudail bheg! and did you come through the night all the way, and it is ashamed that I am to have sent for you, but he was very bad and I was afraid. Come away! come away! I will make you a cup of tea." But the minister's wife assured Kirsty that she was glad to come, and declining the cup of tea, went to the room where Macdonald Dubh lay tossing and moaning with the delirium of fever upon him. It was not long before she knew what was required.

With hot fomentations she proceeded to allay the pain, and in half an hour Macdonald Dubh grew quiet. His tossings and mutterings ceased and he fell into a sleep.

Kirsty stood by admiring.

"Mercy me! Look at that now; and it is yourself that is the great doctor!"

"Now, Kirsty," said Mrs. Murray, in a very matter-of-fact tone, "we will just make him a little more comfortable."

"Yes," said Kirsty, not quite sure how the feat was to be achieved. "A little hot something for his inside will be good, but indeed, many's the drink I have given him," she suggested.

"What have you been giving him, Kirsty?"

"Senny and dandylion, and a little whisky. They will be telling me it is ferry good whatever for the stomach and bow'ls."

"I don't think I would give him any more of that; but we will try and make him feel a little more comfortable."

Mrs. Murray knew she was treading on delicate ground. The Highland pride is quick to take offense.

"Sick people, you see," she proceeded carefully, "need very frequent changes – sheets and clothing, you understand."

"Aye," said Kirsty, suspiciously.

"I am sure you have plenty of beautiful sheets, and we will change these when he wakes from his sleep."

"Indeed, they are very clean, for there is no one but myself has slept in them since he went away last fall to the shanties."

Mrs. Murray felt the delicacy of the position to be sensibly increased.

"Indeed, that is right, Kirsty; one can never tell just what sort of people are traveling about nowadays."

"Indeed, and it's true," said Kirsty, heartily, "but I never let them in here. I just keep them to the bunk."

"But," pursued Mrs. Murray, returning to the subject in hand, "it is very important that for sick people the sheets should be thoroughly aired and warmed. Why, in the hospital in Montreal they take the very greatest care to air and change the sheets every day. You see so much poison comes through the pores of the skin."

"Do you hear that now?" said Kirsty, amazed. "Indeed,

I would be often hearing that those French people are just full of poison and such, and indeed, it is no wonder, for the food they put inside of them."

"O, no," said Mrs. Murray, "it is the same with all people, but especially so with sick people."

Kirsty looked as doubtful as was consistent with her respect for the minister's wife, and Mrs. Murray went on.

"So you will just get the sheets ready to change, and, Kirsty, a clean night-shirt."

"Night-shirt! and indeed, he has not such a thing to his name." Kirsty's tone betrayed her thankfulness that her brother was free from the effeminacy of a night-shirt; but noting the dismay and confusion on Mrs. Murray's face, she suggested, hesitatingly, "He might have one of my own, but I am thinking it will be small for him across the back."

"I am afraid so, Kirsty," said the minister's wife, struggling hard with a smile. "We will just use one of his own white shirts." But this scandalized Kirsty as an unnecessary and wasteful luxury.

"Indeed, there is plenty of them in the chist, but he will be keeping them for the communion season, and the funerals, and such. He will not be wearing them in his bed, for no one will be seeing him there at all."

"But he will feel so much better," said Mrs. Murray, and her smile was so sweet and winning that Kirsty's opposition collapsed, and without more words both sheets and shirt were produced.

As Kirsty laid them out she observed with a sigh: "Aye, aye, she was the clever woman – the wife, I mean. She was good with the needle, and indeed, at anything she tried to do."

"I did not know her," said Mrs. Murray, softly, "but every one tells me she was a good housekeeper and a good woman."

"She was that," said Kirsty, emphatically, "and she was the light of his eyes, and it was a bad day for Hugh when she went away."

"Now, Kirsty," said Mrs. Murray, after a pause, "before we put on these clean things, we will just give him a sponge bath."

Kirsty gasped.

"Mercy sakes! He will not be needing that in the winter, and he will be getting a cold from it. In the summer-time he will be going to the river himself. And how will you be giving him a bath whatever?"

Mrs. Murray carefully explained the process, again fortifying her position by referring to the practices of the Montreal hospital, till, as a result of her persuasions and instructions, in an hour after Macdonald had awakened from his sleep he was lying in his Sabbath white shirt and between fresh sheets, and feeling cleaner and more comfortable than he had for many a day. The fever was much reduced, and he fell again into a deep sleep.

The two women watched beside him, for neither would leave the other to watch alone. And Ranald, who could not be persuaded to go up to his loft, lay on the bunk in the kitchen and dozed. After an hour had passed, Mrs. Murray inquired as to the nourishment Kirsty had given her brother.

"Indeed, he will not be taking anything whatever," said Kirsty, in a vexed tone. "And it is no matter what I will be giving him."

"And what does he like, Kirsty?"

"Indeed, he will be taking anything when he is not seek, and he is that fond of buckwheat pancakes and pork gravy with maple syrup over them, but would he look at it! And I made him new porridge to-night, but he would not touch them."

"Did you try him with gruel, Kirsty?"

"Mercy me, and is it Macdonald Dubh and gruel? He would be flinging the *feushionless* stuff out of the window."

"But I am sure it would be good for him if he could be persuaded to try it. I should like to try him."

"Indeed, and you may try. It will be easy enough, for the porridge are still in the pot."

Kirsty took the pot from the bench with the remains of the porridge that had been made for supper still in it, set it on the fire, and pouring some water in it, began to stir it vigorously. It was thick and slimy, and altogether a most repulsive-looking mixture, and Mrs. Murray no longer wondered at Macdonald Dubh's distaste for gruel.

"I think I will make some fresh, if you will let me, Kirsty – in the way I make it for the minister, you know."

Kirsty, by this time, had completely surrendered to Mrs. Murray's guidance, and producing the oatmeal, allowed her to have her way; so that when Macdonald awoke he found Mrs. Murray standing beside him with a bowl of the nicest gruel and a slice of thin dry toast.

He greeted the minister's wife with grave courtesy, drank the gruel, and then lay down again to sleep.

"Will you look at that now?" said Kirsty, amazed at Macdonald Dubh's forbearance. "He would not like to be offending you."

Then Mrs. Murray besought Kirsty to go and lie down for an hour, which Kirsty very unwillingly agreed to do.

It was not long before Macdonald began to toss and mutter in his sleep, breaking forth now and then into wild cries and curses. He was fighting once more his great fight in the Glengarry line, and beating back LeNoir.

"Back, ye devil! Would ye? Take that, then. Come back, Mack!" Then followed a cry so wild that Ranald awoke and came into the room.

"Bring in some snow, Ranald," said the minister's wife; "we will lay some on his head."

She bathed the hot face and hands with ice-cold water, and then laid a snow compress on the sick man's head, speaking to him in quiet, gentle tones, till he was soothed again to sleep.

When the gray light of the morning came in through the little window, Macdonald woke sane and quiet.

"You are better," said Mrs. Murray to him.

"Yes," he said, "I am very well, thank you, except for the pain here." He pointed to his chest.

"You have been badly hurt, Ranald tells me. How did it happen?"

"Well," said Macdonald, slowly, "it is very hard to say."

"Did the tree fall on you?" asked Mrs. Murray.

Macdonald glanced at her quickly, and then answered: "It is very dangerous work with the trees. It is wonderful how quick they will fall."

"Your face and breast seem very badly bruised and cut."

"Aye, yes," said Macdonald. "The breast is bad whatever."

"I think you had better send for Doctor Grant," Mrs. Murray said. "There may be some internal injury."

"No, no," said Macdonald, decidedly. "I will have no doctor at me, and I will soon be round again, if the Lord will. When will the minister be home?"

But Mrs. Murray, ignoring his attempt to escape the subject, went on: "Yes, but, Mr. Macdonald, I am anxious to have Doctor Grant see you, and I wish you would send for him to-morrow."

"Ah, well," said Macdonald, not committing himself, "we will be seeing about that. But the doctor has not been in this house for many a day." Then, after a pause, he added, in a low voice, "Not since the day she was taken from me."

"Was she ill long?"

"Indeed, no. It was just one night. There was no doctor, and the women could not help her, and she was very bad – and when it came it was a girl – and it was dead – and then the doctor arrived, but he was too late." Macdonald Dubh finished with a great sigh, and the minister's wife said gently to him:

"That was a very sad day, and a great loss to you and Ranald."

"Aye, you may say it; she was a bonnie woman whatever, and grand at the spinning and the butter. And, oich-hone, it was a sad day for us."

The minister's wife sat silent, knowing that such grief cannot be comforted, and pitying from her heart the lonely man. After a time she said gently, "She is better off."

A look of doubt and pain and fear came into Macdonald's eyes.

"She never came forward," he said, hesitatingly. "She was afraid to come."

"I have heard of her often, Mr. Macdonald, and I have heard that she was a good and gentle woman."

"Aye, she was that."

"And kind to the sick."

"You may believe it."

"And she loved the house of God."

"Aye, and neither rain nor snow nor mud would be keeping her from it, but she would be going every Sabbath day, bringing her stockings with her."

"Her stockings?"

"Aye, to change her feet in the church. What else? Her stockings would be wet with the snow and water."

Mrs. Murray nodded. "And she loved her Saviour, Mr. Macdonald."

"Indeed, I believe it well, but she was afraid she would not be having 'the marks.'"

"Never you fear, Mr. Macdonald," said Mrs. Murray. "If she loved her Saviour she is with him now."

He turned around to her and lifted himself eagerly on his elbow. "And do you really think that?" he said, in a voice subdued and anxious.

"Indeed I do," said Mrs. Murray, in a tone of certain conviction.

Macdonald sank back on his pillow, and after a moment's silence, said, in a voice of pain: "Oh, but it is a peety she did not know! It is a peety she did not know. For many's the time before – before – her hour came on her, she would be afraid."

"But she was not afraid at the last, Mr. Macdonald?"

"Indeed, no. I wondered at her. She was like a babe in its mother's arms. There was a light on her face, and I mind well what she said." Macdonald paused. There was a stir in the kitchen, and Mrs. Murray, glancing behind her, saw Ranald standing near the door intently listening. Then Macdonald went on. "I mind well the words, as if it was yesterday. 'Hugh, my man,' she said, 'am no feared' (she was from the Lowlands, but she was a fine woman); 'I haena the marks, but 'm no feared but He'll ken me. Ye'll tak' care o' Ranald, for, oh, Hugh! I ha' gi'en him to the Lord. The Lord help you to mak' a guid man o' him.'" Macdonald's voice faltered into silence, then, after a few moments, he cried, "And oh! Mistress Murra', I cannot tell you the often these words do keep coming to me;

and it is myself that has not kept the promise I made to her, and may the Lord forgive me."

The look of misery in the dark eyes touched Mrs. Murray to the heart. She laid her hand on Macdonald's arm, but she could not find words to speak. Suddenly Macdonald recalled himself.

"You will forgive me," he said; "and you will not be telling any one."

By this time the tears were streaming down her face, and Mrs. Murray could only say, brokenly, "You know I will not."

"Aye, I do," said Macdonald, with a sigh of content, and he turned his face away from her to the wall.

"And now you let me read to you," she said, softly, and taking from her bag the Gaelic Bible, which with much toil she had learned to read since coming to this Highland congregation, she read to him from the old Psalm those words, brave, tender, and beautiful, that have so often comforted the weary and wandering children of men, "The Lord is my Shepherd," and so on to the end. Then from psalm to psalm she passed, selecting such parts as suited her purpose, until Macdonald turned to her again and said, admiringly:

"It is yourself that has the bonnie Gaelic."

"I am afraid," she said, with a smile, "it is not really good, but it is the best a south country woman can do."

"Indeed, it is very pretty," he said, earnestly.

Then the minister's wife said, timidly, "I cannot pray in the Gaelic."

"Oh, the English will be very good," said Macdonald, and she knelt down and in simple words poured out her heart in prayer. Before she rose from her knees she opened the Gaelic Bible, and turned to the words of the Lord's Prayer.

"We will say this prayer together," she said, gently.

Macdonald, bowing his head gravely, answered: "It is what she would often be doing with me."

There was still only one woman to this lonely hearted man, and with a sudden rush of pity that showed itself in her breaking voice, the minister's wife began in Gaelic, "Our Father which art in heaven."

Macdonald followed her in a whisper through the petitions until they came to the words, "And forgive us our debts as we forgive our debtors," when he paused and would say no more. Mrs. Murray repeated the words of the petition, but still there was no response. Then the minister's wife knew that she had her finger upon a sore spot, and she finished the prayer alone.

For a time she sat silent, unwilling to probe the wound, and yet too brave to flinch from what she felt to be duty.

"We have much to be forgiven," she said, gently. "More than we can ever forgive." Still there was silence.

"And the heart that cannot forgive an injury is closed to the forgiveness of God."

The morning sun was gleaming through the treetops, and Mrs. Murray was worn with her night's vigil, and anxious to get home. She rose, and offering Macdonald her hand, smiled down into his face, and said: "Good by! We must try to forgive."

As he took her hand, Macdonald's dark face began to work, and he broke forth into a bitter cry.

"He took me unawares! And it was a coward's blow! and I will not forgive him until I have given him what he deserves, if the Lord spares me!" And then he poured forth, in hot and bitter words, the story of the great fight. By the time he had finished his tale Ranald had come in from the kitchen, and was standing with clenched fists and face pale with passion at the foot of the bed.

As Mrs. Murray listened to this story her eyes began to burn, and when it was over, she burst forth: "Oh, it was a cruel and cowardly and brutal thing for men to do! And did you beat them off?" she asked.

"Aye, and that we did," burst in Ranald. And in breathless haste and with flashing eye he told them of Macdonald Bhain's part in the fight.

"Splendid!" cried the minister's wife, forgetting herself for the moment.

"But he let him go," said Ranald, sadly. "He would not strike him, but just let him go."

Then the minister's wife cried again: "Ah, he is a great man, your uncle! And a great Christian. Greater than I could have been, for I would have slain him then and there." Her eyes flashed, and the color flamed in her face as she uttered these words.

"Aye," said Macdonald Dubh, regarding her with deep satisfaction. His tone and look recalled the minister's wife, and turning to Ranald, she added, sadly:

"But your uncle was right, Ranald, and we must forgive even as he did."

"That," cried Ranald, with fierce emphasis, "I will never do, until once I will be having my hands on his throat."

"Hush, Ranald!" said the minister's wife. "I know it is hard, but we must forgive. You see we *must* forgive. And we must ask Him to help us, who has more to forgive than any other."

But she said no more to Macdonald Dubh on that subject that morning. The fire of the battle was in her heart, and she felt she could more easily sympathize with his desire for vengeance than with the Christian grace of forgiveness. But as they rode home together through the bush, where death had trailed them so closely the night before, the sweet sunlight and the crisp, fresh air, and all the still beauty of the morning, working with the memory of their saving, rebuked and soothed and comforted her, and when Ranald turned back from the manse door, she said softly: "Our Father in heaven was very good to us, Ranald, and we should be like him. He forgives and loves, and we should, too."

And Ranald, looking into the sweet face, pale with the long night's trials, but tinged now with the faintest touch of color from the morning, felt somehow that it might be possible to forgive.

But many days had to come and go, and many waters flow over the souls of Macdonald Dubh and his Ranald, before they were able to say, "Forgive us our debts as we forgive our debtors."

A NEW FRIEND

The night race with the wolves began a new phase of life for Ranald, for in that hour he gained a friend such as it falls to few lads to have. Mrs. Murray's high courage in the bush, her skill in the sick-room, and that fine spiritual air she carried with her made for her a place in his imagination where men set their divinities. The hero and the saint in her stirred his poetic and fervent soul and set it aglow with a feeling near to adoration. To Mrs. Murray also the events of that night set forth Ranald in a new light. In the shy, awkward, almost sullen lad there had suddenly been revealed in those moments of peril the cool, daring man, full of resource and capable of self-sacrifice. Her heart went out toward him, and she set herself to win his confidence and to establish a firm friendship with him; but this was no easy matter.

Macdonald Dubh and his son, living a half-savage life in their lonely back clearing, were regarded by their neighbors with a certain degree of distrust and fear. They were not like other people. They seldom mingled in the social festivities of the community, and consequently were more or less excluded from friendship and free intercourse with their neighbors.

Ranald, shy, proud, and sensitive, felt this exclusion, and in return kept himself aloof even from the boys, and especially from the girls, of his own age. His attendance at school was of a fragmentary and spasmodic nature, and he never really came to be on friendly terms with his fellow-pupils. His one friend was Don Cameron, whom the boys called "Wobbles," from his gait in running, whose father's farm backed that of Macdonald Dubh. And though Don was a year older, he gave to Ranald a homage almost amounting to worship, for in all those qualities that go to establish leadership among boys, Ranald was easily first. In the sport that called for speed, courage, and endurance Ranald was chief of all. Fleet of foot, there was no runner from the Twelfth to the Twentieth that could keep him in sight, and when he stood up to fight, the mere blaze of his eyes often won him victory before a blow was struck. To Don, Ranald opened his heart more than to any one else; all others he kept at a distance.

It was in vain that Mrs. Murray, in her daily visits to Macdonald Dubh, sought to find out Ranald and to come to speech with him. Aunt Kirsty never knew where he was, and to her calls, long and loud, from the back door and from the front, no response ever came. It was Hughie Murray who finally brought Ranald once more into touch with the minister's wife.

They had come one early morning, Hughie with Fido "hitched" in a sled driving over the "crust" on the snow banks by the roadside, and his mother on the pony, to make their call upon the sick man. As they drew near the house they heard a sound of hammering.

"That's Ranald, mother!" exclaimed Hughie. "Let me go and find him. I don't want to go in."

"Be sure you don't go far away, then, Hughie; you know we must hurry home to-day"; and Hughie faithfully promised.

But alas for Hughie's promises! when his mother came out of the house with Kirsty, he was within neither sight nor hearing.

"They will just be at the camp," said Kirsty.

"The camp?"

"Aye, the sugaring camp down yonder in the sugar bush. It is not far off from the wood road. I will be going with you."

"Not at all, Kirsty," said the minister's wife. "I think I know where it is, and I can go home that way quite well. Besides, I want to see Ranald." She did not say she would rather see him alone.

"Indeed, he is the quare lad, and he is worse since coming back from the shanties." Kirsty was evidently much worried about Ranald.

"Never mind," said the minister's wife, kindly; "we must just be patient. Ranald is going on fast toward manhood, and he can be held only by the heart."

"Aye," said Kirsty, with a sigh, "I doubt his father will never be able any more to take a strap to him."

"Yes," said Mrs. Murray, smiling, "I'm afraid he is far beyond that."

"Beyond it!" exclaimed Kirsty, astonished at such a doctrine. "Indeed, and his father and his uncle would be getting it then, when they were as beeg as they will ever be, and much the better were they for it."

"I don't think it would do for Ranald," said the minister's wife, smiling again as she said good by to Kirsty. Then she took her way down the wood road into the bush. She found the camp road easily, and after a quarter of an hour's ride, she heard the sound of an ax, and soon came upon the sugar camp. Ranald was putting the finishing touches to a little shanty of cedar poles and interwoven balsam brush, and Hughie was looking on in admiration and blissful delight.

"Why, that's beautiful," said Mrs. Murray; "I should like to live in a house like that myself."

"Oh, mother!" shouted Hughie, "isn't it splendid? Ranald and Don are going to live in it all the sugaring time, and Ranald wants me to come, too. Mayn't I, mother? Aw, do let me."

The mother looked down upon the eager face, smiled, and shook her head. "What about the night, Hughie?" she said. "It will be very dark in the woods here, and very cold, too. Ranald and Don are big boys and strong, but I'm afraid my little boy would not be very comfortable sleeping outside."

"Oh, mother, we'll be inside, and it'll be awful warm – and oh, you might let me!" Hughie's tears were restrained only by the shame of weeping before his hero, Ranald.

"Well, we will see what your father says when he comes home."

"Oh, mother, he will just say 'no' right off, and –"

A shadow crossed his mother's face, but she only answered quietly, "Never mind just now, Hughie; we will think of it. Besides," she added, "I don't know how much Ranald wants to be bothered with a wee boy like you."

Ranald gave her a quick, shy glance and answered: "He will be no trouble, Mrs. Murray"; and then, noticing Hughie's imploring face, he ventured to add, "and indeed, I hope you will let him come. I will take good care of him."

Mrs. Murray hesitated.

"Oh, mother!" cried Hughie, seeing her hesitation, "just one night; I won't be a bit afraid."

"No, I don't believe you would," looking down into the brave young face. "But what about your mother, Hughie?"

"Oh, pshaw! you wouldn't be afraid." Hughie's confidence in his mother's courage was unbounded.

"I don't know about that," she replied; and then turning to Ranald, "How about our friends of the other night?" she said. "Will they not be about?" Hughie had not heard about the wolves.

"Oh, there is no fear of them. We will keep a big fire all night, and besides, we will have our guns and the dogs."

"Guns!" cried Mrs. Murray. This was a new terror for her boy. "I'm afraid I cannot trust Hughie where there are guns. He might –"

"Indeed, let me catch him touching a gun!" said Ranald, quickly, and from his tone and the look in his face, Mrs. Murray felt sure that Hughie would be safe from self-destruction by the guns.

"Well, well, come away, Hughie, and we will see," said Mrs. Murray; but Hughie hung back sulking, unwilling to move till he had got his mother's promise.

"Come, Hughie. Get Fido ready. We must hurry," said his mother again.

Still Hughie hesitated. Then Ranald turned swiftly on him. "Did ye hear your mother? Come, get out of this." His manner was so fierce that Hughie started immediately for his dog, and without another word of entreaty made ready to go. The mother noted his quick obedience, and smiling at Ranald, said: "I think I might trust him with you for a night or two, Ranald. When do you think you could come for him?"

"We will finish the tapping to-morrow, and I could come the day after with the *jumper*," said Ranald, pointing to the stout, home-made sleigh used for gathering the sap and the wood for the fire.

"Oh, I see you have begun tapping," said Mrs. Murray; "and do you do it yourself?"

"Why, yes, mother; don't you see all those trees?" cried Hughie, pointing to a number of maples that stood behind the shanty. "Ranald and Don did all those, and made the spiles, too. See!" He caught up a spile from a heap lying near the door. "Ranald made all these."

"Why, that's fine, Ranald. How do you make them? I have never seen one made."

"Oh, mother!" Hughie's voice was full of pity for her ignorance. He had seen his first that afternoon.

"And I have never seen the tapping of a tree. I believe I shall learn just now, if Ranald will only show me, from the very beginning."

Her eager interest in his work won Ranald from his reserve. "There is not much to see," he said, apologetically. "You just cut a natch in the tree, and drive in the spile, and –"

"Oh, but wait," she cried. "That's just what I wanted to see. How do you make the spile?"

"Oh, that is easy," said Ranald. He took up a slightly concave chisel or gouge, and slit a thin slab from off a block of cedar about a foot long.

"This is a spile," he exclaimed. "We drive it into the tree, and the sap runs down into the trough, you see."

"No, I don't see," said the minister's wife. She was too thoroughgoing to do things by halves. "How do you drive this into the tree, and how do you get the sap to run down it?"

"I will show you," he said, and taking with him a gouge and ax, he approached a maple still untapped. "You first make a gash like this." So saying, with two or three blows of his ax, he made a slanting notch in the tree. "And then you make a place for the spile this way." With the back of his ax he drove his gouge into the corner of the notch, and then fitted his spile into the incision so made.

"Ah, now I see. And you put the trough under the drip from the spile. But how do you make the troughs?"

"I did not make them," said Ranald. "Some of them father made, and some of them belong to the Camerons. But it is easy enough. You just take a thick slab of basswood and hollow it out with the adze."

Mrs. Murray was greatly pleased. "I'm very much obliged to you, Ranald," she said, "and I am glad I came down to see your camp. Now, if you will ask me, I should like to see you make the sugar." Had her request been made before the night of their famous ride, Ranald would have found some polite reason for refusal, but now he was rather surprised to find himself urging her to come to a sugaring-off at the close of the season.

"I shall be delighted to come," cried Mrs. Murray, "and it is very good of you to ask me, and I shall bring my niece, who is coming with Mr. Murray from town to spend some weeks with me."

Ranald's face fell, but his Highland courtesy forbade retreat. "If she would care," he said, doubtfully.

"Oh, I am sure she would be very glad! She has never been outside of the city, and I want her to learn all she can of the country and the woods. It is positively painful to see the ignorance of these city children in regard to all living things – beasts and birds and plants. Why, many of them couldn't tell a beech from a basswood."

"Oh, mother!" protested Hughie, aghast at such ignorance.

"Yes, indeed, it is dreadful, I assure you," said his mother, smiling. "Why, I know a grown-up woman who didn't know till after she was married the difference between a spruce and a pine."

"But you know them all now," said Hughie, a little anxious for his mother's reputation.

"Yes, indeed," said his mother, proudly; "every one, I think, at least when the leaves are out. So I want Maimie to learn all she can."

Ranald did not like the idea any too well, but after they had gone his thoughts kept turning to the proposed visit of Mrs. Murray and her niece.

"Maimie," said Ranald to himself. "So that is her name." It had a musical sound, and was different from the names of the girls he knew – Betsy and Kirsty and Jessie and Marget and Jinny. It was finer somehow than these, and seemed to suit better a city girl. He wondered if she would be nice, but he decided that doubtless she would be "proud." To be "proud" was the unpardonable sin with the Glengarry boy. The boy or girl convicted of this crime earned the contempt of all self-respecting people. On the whole, Ranald was sorry she was coming. Even in school he was shy with the girls, and kept away from them. They were always giggling and blushing and making one feel queer, and they never meant what they said. He had no doubt Maimie would be like the rest, and perhaps a little worse. Of course, being Mrs. Murray's niece, she might be something like her. Still, that could hardly be. No girl could ever be like the minister's wife. He resolved he would turn Maimie over to Don. He remembered, with great relief, that Don did not mind girls; indeed, he suspected Don rather enjoyed playing the "forfeit" games at school with them, in which the penalties were paid in kisses. How often had he shuddered and admired from a distance, while Don and the others played those daring games! Yes, Don would do the honors for Maimie. Perhaps Don would even venture to play "forfeits" with her. Ranald felt his face grow hot at this thought. Then, with sudden self-detection, he cried, angrily, aloud: "I don't care; let him; he may for all I care."

"Who may what?" cried a voice behind him. It was Don himself.

"Nothing," said Ranald, blushing shamefacedly.

"Why, what are you mad about?" asked Don, noticing his flushed face.

"Who is mad?" said Ranald. "I am not mad whatever."

"Well, you look mighty like it," said Don. "You look mad enough to fight."

But Ranald, ignoring him, simply said, "We will need to be gathering the sap this evening, for the troughs will be full."

"Huh-huh," said Don. "I guess we can carry all there is to-day, but we will have to get the colt to-morrow. Got the spiles ready?"

"Enough for to-day," said Ranald, wondering how he could tell Don of the proposed visit of Mrs. Murray and her niece. Taking each a bundle of spiles and an ax, the boys set out for the part of the sugar bush as yet untapped, and began their work.

"The minister's wife and Hughie were here just now," began Ranald.

"Huh-huh, I met them down the road. Hughie said he was coming day after to-morrow."

"Did Mrs. Murray tell you –"

"Tell me what?"

"Did she tell you she would like to see a sugaring-off?"

"No; they didn't stop long enough to tell me anything. Hughie shouted at me as they passed."

"Well," said Ranald, speaking slowly and with difficulty, "she wanted bad to see the sugar-making, and I asked her to come."

"You did, eh? I wonder at you."

"And she wanted to bring her niece, and – and – I let her," said Ranald.

"Her niece! Jee-roo-sa-*lem!*" cried Don. "Do you know who her niece is?"

"Not I," said Ranald, looking rather alarmed.

"Well, she is the daughter of the big lumberman, St. Clair, and she is a great swell."

Ranald stood speechless.

"That does beat all," pursued Don; "and you asked her to our camp?"

Then Ranald grew angry. "And why not?" he said, defiantly. "What is wrong about that?"

"O, nothing much," laughed Don, "if I had done it, but for you, Ranald! Why, what will you do with that swell young lady from the city?"

"I will just do nothing," said Ranald. "There will be you and Mrs. Murray, and –"

"Oh, I say," burst in Don, "that's bully! Let's ask some of the boys, and – your aunt, and – my mother, and – some of the girls."

"Oh, shucks!" said Ranald, angrily. "You just want Marget Aird."

"You get out!" cried Don, indignantly; "Marget Aird!" Then, after a pause, he added, "All right, I don't want anybody else. I'll look after Mrs. Murray, and you and Maimie can do what you like."

This combination sounded so terrible to Ranald that he surrendered at once; and it was arranged that there should be a grand sugaring-off, and that others besides the minister's wife and her niece should be invited.

But Mrs. Murray had noticed the falling of Ranald's face at the mention of Maimie's visit to the camp, and feeling that she had taken him at a disadvantage, she determined that she would the very next day put herself right with him. She was eager to follow up the advantage she had gained the day before in establishing terms of friendship with Ranald, for her heart went out to the boy, in whose deep, passionate nature she saw vast possibilities for good or ill. On her return from her daily visit to Macdonald Dubh, she took the camp road, and had the good fortune to find Ranald alone, "rigging up" his kettles preparatory to the boiling. But she had no time for kettles today, and she went straight to her business.

"I came to see you, Ranald," she said, after she had shaken hands with him, "about our sugaring-off. I've been thinking that it would perhaps be better to have no strangers, but just old friends, you and Don and Hughie and me."

Ranald at once caught her meaning, but found himself strangely unwilling to be extricated from his predicament.

"I mean," said Mrs. Murray, frankly, "we might enjoy it better without my niece; and so, perhaps, we could have the sugaring when I come to bring Hughie home on Friday. Maimie does not come till Saturday."

Her frankness disarmed Ranald of his reserve. "I know well what you mean," he said, without his usual awkwardness, "but I do not mind now at all having your niece come; and Don is going to have a party." The quiet, grave tone was that of a man, and Mrs. Murray looked at the boy with new eyes. She did not know that it was her own frank confidence that had won like confidence from him.

"How old are you, Ranald?" she said, in her wonder.

"I will be going on eighteen."

"You will soon be a man, Ranald." Ranald remained silent, and she went on earnestly: "A strong, good, brave man, Ranald."

The blood rushed to the boy's face with a sudden flood, but still he stood silent.

"I'm going to give you Hughie for two days," she continued, in the same earnest voice; and leaning down over her pony's neck toward him: "I want him to know strong and manly boys. He is very fond of you, Ranald. He thinks you are better than any man in the world." She paused, her lips parting in a smile that made Ranald's heart beat quick. Then she went on with a shy hesitancy: "Ranald, I know the boys sometimes drop words they should not and tell stories unfit to hear"; the blood was beginning to show in her cheek; "and I would not like my little boy –" Her voice broke suddenly, but recovering quickly she went on in grave, sweet tones: "I trust him to you, Ranald, for this time and afterward. He looks up to you. I want him to be a good, brave man, and to keep his heart pure." Ranald could not speak, but he looked steadily into Mrs. Murray's eyes as he took the hand she offered, and she knew he was pledging himself to her.

"You'll come for him to-morrow," she said, as she turned away. By this time Ranald had found his voice.

"Yes, ma'am," he replied. "And I will take good care of him."

Once more Mrs. Murray found herself looking at Ranald as if seeing him for the first time. He had the solemn voice and manner of a man making oath of allegiance, and she rode away with her heart at rest concerning her little boy. With Ranald, at least, he would be safe.

Those two days had been for Hughie long and weary, but at last the great day came for him, as all great days will come for those who can wait. Ranald appeared at the manse before the breakfast was well begun, and Hughie, with the unconscious egoism of childhood, was for rushing off without thought of preparation for himself or of farewell for those left behind. Indeed, he was for leaving his porridge untasted, declaring he "wasn't a bit hungry," but his mother brought him to his senses.

"No breakfast, no sugar bush to-day, Hughie," she said; "we cannot send men out to the woods that cannot eat breakfast, can we, Ranald?"

Hughie at once fell upon his porridge with vigor, while Ranald, who was much too shy to eat at the minister's table, sat and waited.

After breakfast was over, Jessie was called in for the morning worship, without which no day was ever begun in the manse. At worship in the minister's house every one present took part. It was Hughie's special joy to lead the singing of the psalm. His voice rose high and clear, even above his mother's, for he loved to sing, and Ranald's presence inspired him to do his best. Ranald had often heard the psalm sung in the church –

> I to the hills will lift mine eyes,
> From whence doth come mine aid;

and the tune was the old, familiar "French," but somehow it was all new to him that day. The fresh voices and the crisp, prompt movement of the tune made Ranald feel as if he had never heard the psalm sung before. In the reading he took his verse with the others, stumbling a little, not because the words were too big for him, but because they seemed to run into one another. The chapter for the day contained Paul's injunction to Timothy, urging him to fidelity and courage as a good soldier of Jesus Christ.

When the reading was done, Mrs. Murray told them a story of a young man who had shed his blood upon a Scottish moor because he was too brave to be untrue to his lord, and then, in a few words, made them all see that still some conflict was being waged, and that there was still opportunity for each to display loyal courage and fidelity.

In the prayer that followed, the first thing that surprised Ranald was the absence of the set forms and tones of prayer, with which he was familiar. It was all so simple and real. The mother was telling the great Father in heaven her cares and anxieties, and the day's needs for them all, sure that he would understand and answer. Every one was remembered – the absent head of the family and those present; the young man worshiping with them, that he might be a true man and a good soldier of Jesus Christ; and at the close, the little lad going away this morning, that he might be kept from all harm and from all evil thoughts and deeds. The simple beauty of the words, the music in the voice, and the tender, trustful feeling that breathed through the prayer awakened in Ranald's heart emotions and longings he had never known before, and he rose from his knees feeling how wicked and how cruel a thing it would be to cause one of these little ones to stumble.

After the worship was over, Hughie seized his Scotch bonnet and rushed for the jumper, and in a few minutes his mother had all the space not taken up by him and Ranald packed with blankets and baskets.

"Jessie thinks that even great shanty-men like you and Don and Hughie will not object to something better than bread and pork."

"Indeed, we will not," said Ranald, heartily.

Then Hughie suddenly remembered that he was actually leaving home, and climbing out of the jumper, he rushed at his mother.

"Oh, mother, good by!" he cried.

His mother stooped and put her arms about him. "Good by, my darling," she said, in a low voice; "I trust you to be a good boy, and, Hughie, don't forget your prayers."

Then came to Hughie, for the first time, the thought that had been in the mother's heart all the morning, that when night came he would lie down to sleep, for the first time in his life, without the nightly story and her good-night kiss.

"Mother," whispered the little lad, holding her tight about the neck, "won't you come, too? I don't think I like to go away."

He could have said no more comforting word, and the mother, whose heart had been sore enough with her first parting from her boy, was more than glad to find that the pain was not all on her side; so she kissed him again, and said, in a cheery voice: "Now have a good time. Don't trouble Ranald too much, and bring me back some sugar." Her last word braced the lad as nothing else could.

"Oh, mother, I'll bring you heaps!" he cried, and with the vision of what he would bring home again shining vividly before his eyes, he got through the parting without tears, and was soon speeding down the lane beside Ranald, in the jumper.

The mother stood and watched the little figure holding tight to Ranald with one hand, and with the other waving frantically his bonnet by the tails, till at last the bush hid him from her sight. Then she turned back again to the house that seemed so empty, with her hand pressed hard against her side and her lip quivering as with sharp pain.

"How foolish!" she said, impatiently to herself; "he will be home in two days." But in spite of herself she went again to the door, and looked long at the spot where the bush swallowed up the road. Then she went upstairs and shut her door, and when she came down again there was that in her face that told that her heart had had its first touch of the sword that, sooner or later, must pierce all mothers' hearts.

MAIMIE

Before Hughie came back from the sugar camp, the minister had returned from the presbytery, bringing with him his wife's niece, Maimie St. Clair, who had come from her home in a Western city to meet him. Her father, Eugene St. Clair, was president of Raymond and St. Clair Lumber Company. Nineteen years before this time he had married Mrs. Murray's eldest sister, and established his home with every prospect of a prosperous and happy life, but after three short, bright years of almost perfect joy, his young wife, his heart's idol, after two days' illness, fluttered out from her beautiful home, leaving with her broken-hearted husband her little boy and a baby girl two weeks old. Then Eugene St. Clair besought his sister to come out from England and preside over his home and care for his children; and that he might forget his grief, he gave himself, heart and mind, to his business. Wealth came to him, and under his sister's rule his home became a place of cultured elegance and a center of fashionable pleasure.

Miss Frances St. Clair was a woman of the world, proud of her family-tree, whose root disappeared in the depths of past centuries, and devoted to the pursuit and cultivation of those graces and manners that are supposed to distinguish people of birth and breeding from the common sort. Indeed, from common men and things she shrank almost with horror. The entrance of "trade" into the social sphere of her life she would regard as an impertinent intrusion. It was as much as she could bear to allow the approach of "commerce," which her brother represented. She supposed, of course, there must be people to carry on the trades and industries of the country – very worthy people, too – but these were people one could not be expected to know. Miss St. Clair thanked heaven that she had had the advantages of an English education and upbringing, and she lamented the stubborn democratic opinions of her brother, who insisted that Harry should attend the public school. She was not surprised, therefore, though greatly grieved, that Harry chose his friends in school with a fine disregard of "their people." It was with surprise amounting to pain that she found herself one day introduced by her nephew to Billie Barclay, who turned out to be the son of Harry's favorite confectioner. To his aunt's remonstrance it seemed to Harry a sufficient reply that Billy was a "brick" and a shining "quarter" on the school Rugby team.

"But, Harry, think of his people!" urged his aunt.

"Oh, rot!" replied her irreverent nephew; "I don't play with his people."

"Yes, but Harry, you don't expect to make him your friend?"

"But he *is* my friend, and I don't care what his people are. Besides, I think his governor is a fine old boy, and I know he gives us jolly good taffy."

"But, Harry," answered his aunt, in despair, "you are positively dreadful. Why can't you make friends in your own set? There is Hubert Evans and the Langford boys."

"Evans!" snorted Harry, with contempt; "beastly snob, and the Langfords are regular Mollies!" Whereupon Miss St. Clair gave up her nephew as impossible. But Billie did not repeat his visit to his friend Harry's home. Miss Frances St. Clair had a way of looking through her *pince-nez* that even a boy could understand and would seek to avoid.

With Maimie, Miss St. Clair achieved better results. She was a gentle girl, with an affectionate, yielding disposition, tending towards indolence and self-indulgence. Her aunt's chief concern about her was that she should be frocked and mannered as became her position. Her education was committed to a very select young ladies' school, where only the daughters of the first families ever entered. What or how they were taught, her aunt never inquired. She felt quite sure that the lady principal would resent, as indeed she ought, any such inquiry. Hence Maimie came to have a smattering of the English poets, could talk in conversation-book French, and could dash off most of the notes of a few waltzes and marches from the best composers, her *pièce de résistance*, however, being "*La Prière d'une Vierge.*" She carried with her from school a portfolio of crayons of apparently very ancient and very battered castles; and water-colors of landscapes, where the water was quite as solid as the land. True, she was quite unable to keep her own small accounts, and when her father chanced to ask her one day to do for him a simple addition, he was amazed to find that only after the third attempt did she get it right; but, in the eyes of her aunt, these were quite unimportant deficiencies, and for young ladies she was not sure but that the keeping of accounts and the adding of figures were almost vulgar accomplishments. Her father thought otherwise, but he was a busy man, and besides, he shrank from entering into a region strange to him, but where his sister moved with assured tread. He contented himself with gratifying his daughter's fancies and indulging her in every way allowed him by her system of training and education. The main marvel in the result was that the girl did not grow more selfish, superficial, and ignorant than she did. Something in her blood helped her, but more, it was her aunt's touch upon her life. For every week a letter came from the country manse, bringing with it some of the sweet simplicity of the country and something like a breath of heaven.

She was nearing her fifteenth birthday, and though almost every letter brought an invitation to visit the manse in the backwoods, it was only when the girl's pale cheek and languid air awakened her father's anxiety that she was allowed to accept the invitation to spend some weeks in the country.

When Ranald and Hughie drove up to the manse on Saturday evening in the jumper the whole household rushed forth to see them. They were worth seeing. Burned black with the sun and the March winds, they would have easily passed for young Indians. Hughie's clothes were a melancholy and fluttering ruin; and while Ranald's stout homespun smock and trousers had successfully defied the bush, his dark face and unkempt hair, his rough dress and heavy shanty boots, made him appear, to Maimie's eyes, an uncouth, if not pitiable, object.

"Oh, mother!" cried Hughie, throwing himself upon her, "I'm home again, and we've had a splendid time, and we made heaps of sugar, and I've brought you a whole lot." He drew out of his pockets three or four cakes of maple sugar. "There is one for each," he said, handing them to his mother.

"Here, Hughie," she replied, "speak to your cousin Maimie."

Hughie went up shyly to his cousin and offered a grimy

hand. Maimie, looking at the ragged little figure, could hardly hide her disgust as she took the dirty, sticky little hand very gingerly in her fingers. But Hughie was determined to do his duty to the full, even though Ranald was present, and shaking his cousin's hand with great heartiness, he held up his face to be kissed. He was much surprised, and not a little relieved, when Maimie refused to notice his offer and turned to look at Ranald.

She found him scanning her with a straight, searching look, as if seeking to discover of what sort she was. She felt he had noticed her shrinking from Hughie, and was annoyed to find herself blushing under his keen gaze. But when Mrs. Murray presented Ranald to her niece, it was his turn to blush and feel awkward, as he came forward with a triangular sort of movement and offered his hand, saying, with an access of his Highland accent, "It is a fine day, ma'am." It required all Maimie's good manners to keep back the laugh that fluttered upon her lips.

Slight as it was, Ranald noticed the smile, and turning from her abruptly to Mrs. Murray, said: "We were thinking that Friday would be a good day for the sugaring-off, if that will do you."

"Quite well, Ranald," said the minister's wife; "and it is very good of you to have us."

She, too, had noted Maimie's smile, and seeing the dark flush on Ranald's cheek, she knew well what it meant.

"Come and sit down a little, Ranald," she said, kindly; "I have got some books here for you and Don to read."

But Ranald would not sit, nor would he wait a moment. "Thank you, ma'am," he said, "but I will need to be going."

"Wait, Ranald, a moment," cried Mrs. Murray. She ran into the next room, and in a few moments returned with two or three books and some magazines. "These," she said, handing him the books, "are some of Walter Scott's. They will be good for week-days; and these," giving him the magazines, "you can read after church on Sabbath."

The boy's eyes lighted up as he thanked Mrs. Murray, and he shook hands with her very warmly. Then, with a bow to the company, and without looking at Maimie again, he left the room, with Hughie following at his heels. In a short time Hughie came back full of enthusiastic praise of his hero.

"Oh, mother!" he cried, "he is awful smart. He can just do anything. He can make a splendid bed of balsam brush, and porridge, and pancakes, and – and – and – everything."

"A bed of balsam brush and porridge! What a wonderful boy he must be, Hughie," said Maimie, teasing him. "But isn't he just a little queer?"

"He's not a bit queer," said Hughie, stoutly. "He is the best, best, best boy in all the world."

"Indeed! how extraordinary!" said Maimie; "you wouldn't think so to look at him."

"I think he is just splendid," said Hughie; "don't you, mother?"

"Indeed, he is fery brown whatever," mocked Maimie, mimicking Ranald's Highland tongue, a trick at which she was very clever, "and – not just fery clean."

"You're just a mean, mean, red-headed snip!" cried Hughie, in a rage, "and I don't like you one bit."

But Maimie was proud of her golden hair, so Hughie's shot fell harmless.

"And when will you be going to the sugaring-off, Mistress Murray?" went on Maimie, mimicking Ranald so cleverly that in spite of herself Mrs. Murray smiled.

It was his mother's smile that perfected Hughie's fury. Without a word of threat or warning, he seized a dipper of water and threw it over Maimie, soaking her pretty ribbons and collar, and was promptly sent upstairs to repent.

"Poor Hughie!" said his mother, after he had disappeared; "Ranald is his hero, and he cannot bear any criticism of him."

"He doesn't look much of a hero, auntie," said Maimie, drying her face and curls.

"Very few heroes do," said her aunt, quietly. "Ranald has noble qualities, but he has had very few advantages."

Then Mrs. Murray told her niece how Ranald had put himself between her and the pursuing wolves. Maimie's blue eyes were wide with horror.

"But, auntie," she cried, "why in the world do you go to such places?"

"What places, Maimie?" said the minister, who had come into the room.

"Why, those awful places where the wolves are."

"Indeed, you may ask why," said the minister, gravely. He had heard the story from his wife the night before. "But it would need a man to be on guard day and night to keep your aunt from 'those places.'"

"Yes, and your uncle, too," said Mrs. Murray, shaking her head at her husband. "You see, Maimie, we live in 'those places'; and after all, they are as safe as any. We are in good keeping."

"And was Hughie out all night with those two boys in those woods, auntie?"

"Oh, there was no danger. The wolves will not come near a fire, and the boys have their dogs and guns," said Mrs. Murray; "besides, Ranald is to be trusted."

"Trusted?" said the minister; "indeed, I would not trust him too far. He is just wild enough, like his father before him."

"Oh, papa, you don't know Ranald," said his wife, warmly; "nor his father either, for that matter. I never did till this last week. They have kept aloof from everything, and really –"

"And whose fault is that?" interrupted the minister. "Why should they keep aloof from the means of grace? They are a godless lot, that's what they are." The minister's indignation was rising.

"But, my dear," persisted Mrs. Murray, "I believe if they had a chance –"

"Chance!" exclaimed the minister; "what more chance do they want? Have they not all that other people have? Macdonald Dubh is rarely seen at the services on the Lord's day, and as for Ranald, he comes and goes at his own sweet will."

"Let us hope," said his wife, gently, "they will improve. I believe Ranald would come to Bible class were he not so shy."

"Shy!" laughed the minister, scornfully; "he is not too shy to stand up on the table before a hundred men after a logging and dance the Highland fling, and beautifully he does it, too," he added.

"But for all that," said his wife, "he is very shy."

"I don't like shy people," said Maimie; "they are so awkward and dreadful to do with."

"Well," said her aunt, quietly, "I rather like people who are not too sure of themselves, and I think all the more of Ranald for his shyness and modesty."

"Oh, Ranald's modesty won't disable him," said the minister. "For my part, I think he is a daring young rascal; and indeed, if there is any mischief going in the countryside you may be sure Ranald is not far away."

"Oh, papa, I don't think Ranald is a *bad* boy," said his wife, almost pleadingly.

"Bad? I'm sure I don't know what you call it. Who let off the dam last year so that the saw-mill could not run for a week?

Who abused poor Duncie MacBain so that he was carried home groaning?"

"Duncie MacBain!" exclaimed his wife, contemptuously; "great, big, soft lump, that he is. Why, he's a man, as big as ever he'll be."

"Who broke the Little Church windows till there wasn't a pane left?" pursued the minister, unheeding his wife's interruption.

"It wasn't Ranald that broke the church windows, papa," piped Hughie from above.

"How do you know, sir? Who did it, then?" demanded his father.

"It wasn't Ranald, anyway," said Hughie, stoutly.

"Who was it, then? Tell me that," said his father again.

"Hughie, go to your room and stay there, as I told you," said his mother, fearing an investigation into the window-breaking episode, of which Hughie had made full confession to her as his own particular achievement, in revenge for a broken window in the new church.

"I think," continued Mr. Murray, as if closing the discussion, "you'll find that your Ranald is not the modest, shy, gentle young man you think him to be, but a particularly bold young rascal."

"Poor Ranald," sighed his wife; "he has no mother, and his father has just let him grow up wild."

"Aye, that's true enough," assented her husband, passing into his study.

But he could have adopted no better means of awakening Maimie's interest in Ranald than by the recital of his various escapades. Women love good men, but are interested in men whose goodness is more or less impaired. So Maimie was determined that she would know more of Ranald, and hence took every opportunity of encouraging Hughie to sing the praises of his hero and recount his many adventures. She was glad, too, that her aunt had fixed the sugaring-off for a time when she could be present. But neither at church on Sunday nor during the week that followed did she catch sight of his face, and though Hughie came in with excited reports now and then of having seen or heard of Ranald, Maimie had to content herself with these; and, indeed, were it not that the invitation had already been given, and the day fixed for her visit to the camp, the chances are that Maimie's acquaintance with Ranald would have ended where it began, in which case both had been saved many bitter days.

THE SUGARING-OFF

The sugar time is, in many ways, the best of all the year. It is the time of crisp mornings, when "the crust bears," and the boys go crunching over all the fields and through the woods; the time, too, of sunny noons and chilly nights. Winter is still near, but he has lost most of his grip, and all his terror. For the earth has heard the call of spring from afar, and knows that soon she will be seen, dancing her shy dances, in the sunny spaces of the leafless woods. Then, by and by, from all the open fields the snow is driven back into the fence corners, and lies there in soiled and sullen heaps. In the woods it still lies deep; but there is everywhere the tinkle of running water, and it is not long till the brown leaf carpet begins to show in patches through the white. Then, overhead, the buds begin to swell and thrill with the new life, and when it is broad noon, all through the woods a thousand voices pass the glad word that winter's day is gone and that all living things are free. But when night draws up over the treetops, and the shadows steal down the forest aisles, the jubilant voices die down and a chill fear creeps over all the gleeful, swelling buds that they have been too sure and too happy; and all the more if, from the northeast, there sweeps down, as often happens, a stinging storm of sleet and snow, winter's last savage slap. But what matters that? The very next day, when the bright, warm rays trickle down through the interlacing branches, bathing the buds and twigs and limbs and trunks and flooding all the woods, the world grows surer of its new joy. And so, in alternating hope and fear, the days and nights go by, till an evening falls when the air is languid and a soft rain comes up from the south, falling all night long over the buds and trees like warm, loving fingers. Then the buds break for very joy, and timid green things push up through the leaf-mold; and from the swamps the little frogs begin to pipe, at first in solo, but soon in exultant chorus, till the whole moist night is vocal, and then every one knows that the sugar time is over, and troughs and spiles are gathered up, and with sap-barrels and kettles, are stored in the back shed for another year.

But no rain came before the night fixed for the sugaring-off. It was a perfect sugar day, warm, bright, and still, following a night of sharp frost. The long sunny afternoon was deepening into twilight when the Camerons drove up to the sugar-camp in their big sleigh, bringing with them the manse party. Ranald and Don, with Aunt Kirsty, were there to receive them. It was one of those rare evenings of the early Canadian spring. The bare woods were filled with the tangled rays of light from the setting sun. Here and there a hillside facing the east lay in shadow that grew black where the balsams and cedars stood in clumps. But everywhere else the light fell sweet and silent about the bare trunks, filling the long avenues under the arching maple limbs with a yellow haze.

In front of the shanty the kettles hung over the fire on a long pole which stood in an upright crutch at either end.

Under the big kettle the fire was roaring high, for the fresh sap needed much boiling before the syrup and taffy could come. But under the little kettle the fire burned low, for that must not be hurried.

Over the fire and the kettles Ranald presided, black, grimy, and silent, and to Don fell the duty of doing the honors of the camp; and right worthily did he do his part. He greeted his mother with reverence, cuffed his young brother, kissed his little sister Jennie, tossing her high, and welcomed with warm heartiness Mrs. Murray and her niece. The Airds had not yet come, but all the rest were there. The Finlaysons and the McKerachers, Dan Campbell's boys, and their sister Betsy, whom every one called "Betsy Dan," redheaded, freckled, and irrepressible; the McGregors, and a dozen or more of the wildest youngsters that could be found in all the Indian Lands. Depositing their baskets in the shanty, for they had no thought of fasting, they crowded about the fire.

"Attention!" cried Don, who had a "gift of the gab," as his mother said. "Ladies and gentlemen, the program for this evening is as follows: games, tea, and taffy, in the order mentioned. In the first, all *must* take part; in the second, all *may* take part; but in the third, none *need* take part."

After the laughter and the chorus of "Ohs" had subsided, Don proceeded: "The captains for the evening are, Elizabeth Campbell, better known as 'Betsy Dan,' and John Finlayson, familiar to us all as 'Johnnie the Widow,' two young people of excellent character and, I believe, slightly known to each other."

Again a shout went up from the company, but Betsy Dan, who cared not at all for Don's banter, contented herself with pushing out her lower lip at him with scorn, in that indescribable manner natural to girls, but to boys impossible.

Then the choosing began. Betsy Dan, claiming first choice by virtue of her sex, immediately called out, "Ranald Macdonald."

But Ranald shook his head. "I cannot leave the fire," he said, blushing; "take Don there."

But Betsy demurred. "I don't want Don," she cried. "Come on, Ranald; the fire will do quite well." Betsy, as indeed did most of the school-girls, adored Ranald in her secret heart, though she scorned to show it.

But Ranald still refused, till Don said, "It is too bad, Betsy, but you'll have to take me."

"Oh, come on, then!" laughed Betsy; "you will be better than nobody."

Then it was Johnnie the Widow's choice: "Maimie St. Clair."

Maimie hesitated and looked at her aunt, who said, "Yes, go, my dear, if you would like."

"Marget Aird!" cried Betsy, spying Marget and her brothers coming down the road. "Come along, Marget; you are on my side – on Don's side, I mean." At which poor Marget, a tall, fair girl, with sweet face and shy manner, blushed furiously, but, after greeting the minister's wife and the rest of the older people, she took her place beside Don.

The choosing went on till every one present was taken, not even Aunt Kirsty being allowed to remain neutral in the coming games. For an hour the sports went on. Racing, jumping, bear, London bridge, crack the whip, and lastly, forfeits.

Meantime Ranald superintended the sap-boiling, keeping on the opposite side of the fire from the ladies, and answering in monosyllables any questions addressed to him. But when it was time to make the tea, Mrs. Cameron and Kirsty insisted on taking charge of this, and Mrs. Murray, coming round to Ranald, said: "Now, Ranald, I came to learn all about sugar-making, and while the others are making tea, I want you to teach me how to make sugar."

Ranald gladly agreed to show her all he knew. He had been feeling awkward and miserable in the noisy crowd, but especially in the presence of Maimie. He had not forgotten the smile of amusement with which she had greeted him at the manse, and his wounded pride longed for an opportunity to pour upon her the vials of his contempt. But somehow, in her presence, contempt would not arise within him, and he was driven into wretched silence and self-abasement. It was, therefore, with peculiar gratitude that he turned to Mrs. Murray as to one who both understood and trusted him.

"I thank you for the books, Mrs. Murray," he began, in a low, hurried voice. "They are just wonderful. That Rob Roy and Ivanhoe, oh! they are the grand books." His face was fairly blazing with enthusiasm. "I never knew there were such books at all."

"I am very glad you like them, Ranald," said Mrs. Murray, in tones of warm sympathy, "and I shall give you as many as you like."

"I cannot thank you enough. I have not the words," said the boy, looking as if he might fall down at her feet. Mrs. Murray was greatly touched both by his enthusiasm and his gratitude.

"It is a great pleasure to me, Ranald, that you like them," she said, earnestly. "I want you to love good books and good men and noble deeds."

Ranald stood listening in silence.

"Then some day you will be a good and great man yourself," she added, "and you will do some noble work."

The boy stood looking far away into the woods, his black eyes filled with a mysterious fire. Suddenly he threw back his head and said, as if he had forgotten Mrs. Murray's presence, "Yes, some day I will be a great man. I know it well."

"And good," softly added Mrs. Murray.

He turned and looked at her a moment as if in a dream. Then, recalling himself, he answered, "I suppose that is the best."

"Yes, it is the best, Ranald," she replied. "No man is great who is not good. But come now and give me my lesson."

Ranald stepped out into the bush, and from a tree near by he lifted a trough of sap and emptied it into the big kettle.

"That's the first thing you do with the sap," he said.

"How? Carry every trough to the kettle?"

"Oh, I see," laughed Ranald. "You must have every step."

"Yes, indeed," she replied, with determination.

"Well, here it is."

He seized a bucket, went to another tree, emptied the sap from the trough into the bucket, and thence into the barrel, and from the barrel into the big kettle.

"Then from the big kettle into the little one," he said, catching up a big dipper tied to a long pole, and transferring the boiling sap as he spoke from one kettle to another.

"But how can you tell when it is ready?" asked Mrs. Murray.

"Only by tasting. When it is very sweet it must go into the little kettle."

"And then?"

Her eager determination to know all the details delighted him beyond measure.

"Then you must be very careful indeed, or you will lose all your day's work, and your sugar besides, for it is very easy to burn."

"But how can you tell when it is ready?"

"Oh, you must just keep tasting every few minutes till you think you have the syrup, and then for the sugar you must just boil it a little longer."

"Well," said Mrs. Murray, "when it is ready what do you do?"

"Then," he said, "you must quickly knock the fire from under it, and pour it into the pans, stirring it till it gets nearly cool."

"And why do you stir it?" she asked.

"Oh, to keep it from getting too hard."

"Now I have learned something I never knew before," said the minister's wife, delightedly, "and I am very grateful to you. We must help each other, Ranald."

"Indeed, it is little I can do for you," he said, shyly.

"You do not know how much I am going to ask you to do," she said, lightly. "Wait and see."

At that moment a series of shrieks rose high above the shouting and laughter of the games, and Maimie came flying down toward the camp, pursued by Don, with the others following.

"Oh, auntie!" she panted, "he's going to – going to –" she paused, with cheeks burning.

"It's forfeits, Mrs. Murray," explained Don.

"Hoot, lassie," said Mrs. Cameron; "it will not much hurt you, anyway. They that kiss in the light will not kiss in the dark."

"She played, and lost her forfeit," said Don, unwilling to be jeered at by the others for faint-heartedness. "She ought to pay."

"I'm afraid, Don, she does not understand our ways," said Mrs. Murray, apologetically.

"Be off, Don," said his mother. "Kiss Marget there, if you can – it will not hurt her – and leave the young lady alone."

"It's just horrid of them, auntie," said Maimie, indignantly, as the others went back to their games.

"Indeed," said Mrs. Cameron, warmly, "if you will never do worse than kiss a laddie in a game, it's little harm will be coming to you."

But Maimie ignored her.

"Is it not horrid, auntie?" she said.

"Well, my dear, if you think so, it is. But not for these girls, who play the game with never a thought of impropriety and with no shock to their modesty. Much depends on how you think about these things."

But Maimie was not satisfied. She was indignant at Don for offering to kiss her, but as she stood and watched the games going on under the trees – the tag, the chase, the catch, and the kiss – she somehow began to feel as if it were not so terrible after all, and to think that perhaps these girls might play the game and still be nice enough. But she had no thought of going back to them, and so she turned her attention to the preparations for tea, now almost complete. Her aunt and Ranald were toasting slices of bread at the big blazing fire, on forks made out of long switches.

"Let me try, auntie," she said, pushing up to the fire between her aunt and Ranald. "I am sure I can do that."

"Be careful of that fire," said Ranald, sharply, pulling back her skirt, that had blown dangerously near the blaze. "Stand back further," he commanded.

Maimie looked at him, surprise, indignation, and fear struggling for the mastery. Was this the awkward boy that had blushed and stammered before her a week ago?

"It's very dangerous," he explained to Mrs. Murray, "the wind blows out the flames."

As he spoke he handed Maimie his toasting stick and retired to the other side of the fire, and began to attend to the boiling sap.

"He needn't be such a bear," pouted Maimie.

"My dear," replied her aunt, "what Ranald says is quite true. You cannot be too careful in moving about the fire."

"Well, he needn't be so cross about it," said Maimie. She had never been ordered about before in her life, and she did not enjoy the experience, and all the more at the hands of an uncouth country boy. She watched Ranald attending to the fire and the kettles, however, with a new respect. He certainly had no fear of the fire, but moved about it and handled it with the utmost *sang-froid*. He had a certain grace, too, in his movements that caught her eye, and she wished he would come nearer so that she could speak to him. She had considerable confidence in her powers of attraction. As if to answer her wish, Ranald came straight to where her aunt and she were standing.

"I think it will be time for tea now," he said, with a sudden return of his awkward manner, that made Maimie wonder why she had ever been afraid of him. "I will tell Don," he added, striding off toward the group of boys and girls, still busy with their games under the trees.

Soon Don's shout was heard: "Tea, ladies and gentlemen; take your seats at the tables." And speedily there was a rush and scramble, and in a few moments the great heaps of green balsam boughs arranged around the fire were full of boys and girls pulling, pinching, and tumbling over one another in wild glee.

The toast stood in brown heaps on birch-bark plates beside the fire, and baskets were carried out of the shanty bulging with cakes; the tea was bubbling in the big tin tea-pail, and everything was ready for the feast. But Ranald had caught Mrs. Murray's eye, and at a sign from her, stood waiting with the tea-pail in his hand.

"Come on with the tea, Ranald," cried Don, seizing a plate of toast.

"Wait a minute, Don," said Ranald, in a low tone.

"What's the matter?"

But Ranald stood still, looking silently at the minister's wife. Then, as all eyes turned toward her, she said, in a gentle, sweet voice, "I think we ought to give thanks to our Father in heaven for all this beauty about us and for all our joy."

At once Ranald took off his hat, and as the boys followed his example, Mrs. Murray bowed her head and in a few, simple words lifted up the hearts of all with her own in thanksgiving for the beauty of the woods and sky above them, and all the many gifts that came to fill their lives with joy.

It was not the first time that Ranald had heard her voice in prayer, but somehow it sounded different in the open air under the trees and in the midst of all the jollity of the sugaring-off. With all other people that Ranald knew religion seemed to be something apart from common days, common people, and common things, and seemed, besides, a solemn and terrible experience; but with the minister's wife, religion was a part of her every-day living, and seemed to be as easily associated with her pleasure as with anything else about her. It was so easy, so simple, so natural, that Ranald could not help wondering if, after all, it was the right kind. It was so unlike the religion of the elders and all the good people in the congregation. It was a great puzzle to Ranald, as to many others, both before and since his time.

After tea was over the great business of the evening came on. Ranald announced that the taffy was ready, and Don, as master of ceremonies, immediately cried out: "The gentlemen will provide the ladies with plates."

"Plates!" echoed the boys, with a laugh of derision.

"Plates," repeated Don, stepping back to a great snowbank, near a balsam clump, and returning with a piece of "crust." At once there was a scurry to the snowbank, and soon every one had a snow plate ready. Then Ranald and Don slid the little kettle along the pole off the fire, and with tin dippers began to pour the hot syrup upon the snow plates, where it immediately hardened into taffy. Then the pulling began. What fun there was, what larks, what shrieks, what romping and tumbling, till all were heartily tired, both of the taffy and the fun.

Then followed the sugar-molding. The little kettle was set back on the fire and kept carefully stirred, while tin dishes of all sorts, shapes, and sizes – milk-pans, pattie-pans, mugs, and cups – well greased with pork rind, were set out in order, imbedded in snow.

The last act of all was the making of "hens' nests." A dozen or so of hens' eggs, blown empty, and three goose eggs for the grown-ups, were set in snow nests, and carefully filled from the little kettle. In a few minutes the nests were filled with sugar eggs, and the sugaring-off was over.

There remained still a goose egg provided against any mishap.

"Who wants the goose egg?" cried Don, holding it up.

"Me!" "me!" "me!" coaxed the girls on every side.

"Will you give it to me, Don, for the minister?" said Mrs. Murray.

"Oh, yes!" cried Maimie, "and let me fill it."

As she spoke, she seized the dipper, and ran for the kettle.

"Look out for that fire," cried Don, dropping the egg into its snowbed. He was too late. A little tongue of flame leaped out from under the kettle, nipped hold of her frock, and in a moment she was in a blaze. With a wild scream she sprang back and turned to fly, but before she had gone more than a single step Ranald, dashing the crowd right and left, had seized and flung her headlong into the snow, beating out the flames with his bare hands. In a moment all danger was over, and Ranald lifted her up. Still screaming, she clung to him, while the women all ran to her. Her aunt reached her first.

"Hush, Maimie; hush, dear. You are quite safe now. Let me see your face. There now, be quiet, child. The danger is all over."

Still Maimie kept screaming. She was thoroughly terrified.

"Listen to me," her aunt said, in an even, firm voice. "Do not be foolish. Let me look at you."

The quiet, firm voice soothed her, and Maimie's screams ceased. Her aunt examined her face, neck, and arms for any signs of fire, but could find none. She was hardly touched, so swift had been her rescue. Then Mrs. Murray, suddenly putting her arms round about her niece, and holding her tight, cried: "Thank God, my darling, for his great kindness to you and to us all. Thank God! thank God!"

Her voice broke, but in a moment, recovering herself, she went on, "And Ranald, too! noble fellow!"

Ranald was standing at the back of the crowd, looking pale, disturbed, and awkward. Mrs. Murray, knowing how hateful to him would be any demonstrations of feeling, went to him, and quietly held out her hand, saying: "It was bravely done, Ranald. From my heart, I thank you."

For a moment or two she looked steadily into his face with tears streaming down her cheeks. Then putting her hands upon his shoulders, she said, softly: "For her dear, dead mother's sake, I thank you."

Then Maimie, who had been standing in a kind of stupor all this while, seemed suddenly to awake, and running swiftly toward Ranald, she put out both hands, crying: "Oh, Ranald, I can never thank you enough!"

He took her hands in an agony of embarrassment, not knowing what to do or say. Then Maimie suddenly dropped his hands, and throwing her arms about his neck, kissed him, and ran back to her aunt's side.

"I thought you didn't play forfeits, Maimie," said Don, in a grieved voice. And every one was glad to laugh.

Then the minister's wife, looking round upon them all, said: "Dear children, God has been very good to us, and I think we ought to give him thanks."

And standing there by the fire, they bowed their heads in a new thanksgiving to Him whose keeping never fails by day or night. And then, with hearts and voices subdued, and with quiet good nights, they went their ways home.

But as the Cameron sleigh drove off with its load, Maimie looked back, and seeing Ranald standing by the fire, she whispered to her aunt: "Oh, auntie! Isn't he just splendid?"

But her aunt made no reply, seeing a new danger for them both, greater than that they had escaped.

A SABBATH DAY'S WORK

The Sabbath that followed the sugaring-off was to Maimie the most remarkable Sabbath of her life up to that day. It was totally unlike the Sabbath of her home, which, after the formal "church parade," as Harry called it, in the morning, her father spent in lounging with his magazine and pipe, her aunt in sleeping or in social gossip with such friends as might drop in, and Harry and Maimie as best they could.

The Sabbath in the minister's house, as in the homes of his people, was a day so set apart from other days that it had to be approached. The Saturday afternoon and evening caught something of its atmosphere. No frivolity, indeed no light amusement, was proper on the evening that put a period to the worldly occupations and engagements of the week. That evening was one of preparation. The house, and especially the kitchen, was thoroughly "redd up." Wood, water, and kindlings were brought in, clothes were brushed, boots greased or polished, dinner prepared, and in every way possible the whole house, its dwellers, and its belongings, made ready for the morrow. So, when the Sabbath morning dawned, people awoke with a feeling that old things had passed away and that the whole world was new. The sun shone with a radiance not known on other days. He was shining upon holy things, and lighting men and women to holy duties. Through all the farms the fields lay bathed in his genial glow, at rest, and the very trees stood in silent worship of the bending heavens. Up from stable and from kitchen came no sounds of work. The horses knew that no wheel would turn that day in labor, and the dogs lay sleeping in sunny nooks, knowing as well as any that there was to be no hunting or roaming for them that day, unless they chose to go on a free hunt; which none but light-headed puppies or dissipated and reprobate dogs would care to do.

Over all things rest brooded, and out of the rest grew holy thoughts and hopes. It was a day of beginnings. For the past, broken and stained, there was a new offer of oblivion and healing, and the heart was summoned to look forward to new life and to hope for better things, and to drink in all those soothing, healing influences that memory and faith combine to give; so that when the day was done, weary and discouraged men and women began to feel that, perhaps after all they might be able to endure and even to hope for victory.

The minister rose earlier on Sabbath than on other days, the responsibility of his office pressing hard upon him. Breakfast was more silent than usual, ordinary subjects of conversation being discouraged. The minister was preoccupied and impatient of any interruption of his thoughts. But his wife came to the table with a sweeter serenity than usual, and a calm upon her face that told of hidden strength. Even Maimie could notice the difference, but she could only wonder. The secret of it was hidden from her. Her aunt was like no other woman that she knew, and there were many things about her too deep for Maimie's understanding.

After worship, which was brief but solemn and intense, Lambert hurried to bring round to the front the big black horse, hitched up in the carryall, and they all made speed to pack themselves in, Maimie and her aunt in front, and Hughie on the floor behind with his legs under the seat; for when once the minister was himself quite ready, and had got his great meerschaum pipe going, it was unsafe for any one to delay him a single instant.

The drive to the church was an experience hardly in keeping with the spirit of the day. It was more exciting than restful. Black was a horse with a single aim, which was to devour the space that stretched out before him, with a fine disregard of consequence. The first part of the road up to the church hill and down again to the swamp was to Black, as to the others, an unmixed joy, for he was fresh from his oats and eager to go, and his driver was as eager to let him have his will.

But when the swamp was reached, and the buggy began to leap from log to log of the corduroy, Black began to chafe in impatience of the rein which commanded caution. Indeed, the passage of the swamp was always more or less of an adventure, the result of which no one could foretell, and it took all Mrs. Murray's steadiness of nerve to repress an exclamation of terror at critical moments. The corduroy was Black's abomination. He longed to dash through and be done with it; but, however much the minister sympathized with Black's desire, prudence forbade that his method should be adopted. So from log to log, and from hole to hole, Black plunged and stepped with all the care he could be persuaded to exercise, every lurch of the carryall bringing a scream from Maimie in front and a delighted chuckle from Hughie behind. His delight in the adventure was materially increased by his cousin's terror.

But once the swamp was crossed, and Black found himself on the firm road that wound over the sandhills and through the open pine woods, he tossed his great mane back from his eyes, and getting his head set off at a pace that foreboded disaster to anything trying to keep before him, and in a short time drew up at the church gates, his flanks steaming and his great chest white with foam.

"My!" said Maimie, when she had recovered her breath sufficiently to speak, "is that the church?" She pointed to a huge wooden building about whose door a group of men were standing.

"Huh-huh, that's it," said Hughie; "but we will soon be done with the ugly old thing."

The most enthusiastic member of the congregation could scarcely call the old church beautiful, and to Maimie's eyes it was positively hideous. No steeple or tower gave any hint of its sacred character. Its weather-beaten clapboard exterior, spotted with black knots, as if stricken with some disfiguring disease, had nothing but its row of uncurtained windows to distinguish it from an ordinary barn.

They entered by the door at the end of the church, and proceeded down the long aisle that ran the full length of the building, till they came to a cross aisle that led them to the minister's pew at the left side of the pulpit, and commanding a view of the whole congregation. The main body of the church was seated with long box pews with hinged doors. But the gallery that ran round three sides was fitted with simple benches. Immediately in front of the pulpit was a square pew which was set apart for the use of the elders, and close up to the pulpit, and indeed as part of this structure, was a precentor's desk. The pulpit was, to Maimie's eyes, a wonder. It was an octagonal box placed high on one side of the church on a level with the gallery, and reached by a spiral staircase. Above it hung the highly ornate and altogether extraordinary sounding-board and canopy. There was no sign of paint anywhere, but the yellow pine, of which seats, gallery, and pulpit were all made, had deepened with age into a rich brown, not unpleasant to the eye.

The church was full, for the Indian Lands people believed in going to church, and there was not a house for many miles around but was represented in the church that day. There they sat, row upon row of men, brawny and brown with wind and sun, a notable company, worthy of their ancestry and worthy of their heritage. Beside them sat their wives, brown, too, and weather-beaten, but strong, deep-bosomed, and with faces of calm content, worthy to be mothers of their husbands' sons. The girls and younger children sat with their parents, modest, shy, and reverent, but the young men, for the most part, filled the back seats under the gallery. And a hardy lot they were, as brown and brawny as their fathers, but tingling with life to their finger-tips, ready for anything, and impossible of control except by one whom they feared as well as reverenced. And such a man was Alexander Murray, for they knew well that, lithe and brawny as they were, there was not a man of them but he could fling out of the door and over the fence if he so wished; and they knew, too, that he would be prompt to do it if occasion arose. Hence they waited for the word of God with all due reverence and fear.

In the square pew in front of the pulpit sat the elders, hoary, massive, and venerable. The Indian Lands Session were worth seeing. Great men they were, every one of them, excepting, perhaps, Kenneth Campbell, "Kenny Crubach," as he was called, from his halting step. Kenny was neither hoary nor massive nor venerable. He was a short, grizzled man with snapping black eyes and a tongue for clever, biting speech; and while he bore a stainless character, no one thought of him as an eminently godly man. In public prayer he never attained any great length, nor did he employ that tone of unction deemed suitable in this sacred exercise. He seldom "spoke to the question," but when he did people leaned forward to listen, and more especially the rows of the careless and ungodly under the gallery. Kenny had not the look of an elder, and indeed, many wondered how he had ever come to be chosen for the office. But the others all had the look of elders, and carried with them the full respect and affection of the congregation. Even the young men under the gallery regarded them with reverence for their godly character, but for other things as well; for these old men had been famous in their day, and tales were still told about the firesides of the people of their prowess in the woods and on the river.

There was, for instance, Finlay McEwen, or McKeowen, as they all pronounced it in that country, who, for a wager, had carried a four-hundred-pound barrel upon each hip across the long bridge over the Scotch River. And next him sat Donald Ross, whose very face, with its halo of white hair, bore benediction with it wherever he went. What a man he must have been in his day! Six feet four inches he stood in his stocking soles, and with "a back like a barn door," as his son Danny, or "Curly," now in the shanty with Macdonald Bhain, used to say, in affectionate pride. Then there was Farquhar McNaughton, big, kindly, and good-natured, a mighty man with the ax in his time. "Kirsty's Farquhar" they called him, for obvious reasons. And a good thing for Farquhar it was that he had had Kirsty at his side during these years to make his bargains for him and to keep him and all others to them, else he would never have become the substantial man he was.

Next to Farquhar was Peter McRae, the chief of a large clan of respectable, and none too respectable, families, whom all alike held in fear, for Peter ruled with a rod of iron, and his word ran as law throughout the clan. Then there was Ian More Macgregor, or "Big John Macgregor," as the younger generation called him, almost as big as Donald Ross and quite as kindly, but with a darker, sadder face. Something from his wilder youth had cast its shadow over his life. No one but his minister and two others knew that story, but the old man knew it himself, and that was enough. One of those who shared his secret was his neighbor and crony, Donald Ross, and it was worth a journey of some length to see these two great old men, one with the sad and the other with the sunny face, stride off together, staff in hand, at the close of the Gaelic service, to Donald's home, where the afternoon would be spent in discourse fitting the Lord's day and in prayer.

The only other elder was Roderick McCuiag, who sat, not in the elders' pew, but in the precentor's box, for he was the Leader of Psalmody. "Straight Rory," as he was called by the irreverent, was tall, spare, and straight as a ramrod. He was devoted to his office, jealous of its dignity, and strenuous in his opposition to all innovations in connection with the Service of Praise. He was especially opposed to the introduction of those "new-fangled ranting" tunes which were being taught the young people by John "Alec" Fraser in the weekly singing-school in the Nineteenth, and which were sung at Mrs. Murray's Sabbath evening Bible class in the Little Church. Straight Rory had been educated for a teacher in Scotland, and was something of a scholar. He loved school examinations, where he was the terror of pupils and teachers alike. His acute mind reveled in the metaphysics of theology, which made him the dread of all candidates who appeared before the session desiring "to come forward." It was to many an impressive sight to see Straight Rory rise in the precentor's box, feel round, with much facial contortion, for the pitch – he despised a tuning-fork – and then, straightening himself up till he bent over backwards, raise the chant that introduced the tune to the congregation. But to the young men under the gallery he was more humorous than impressive, and it is to be feared that they waited for the precentor's weekly performance with a delighted expectation that never flagged and that was never disappointed. It was only the flash of the minister's blue eye that held their faces rigid in preternatural solemnity, and forced them to content themselves with winks and nudges for the expression of their delight.

As Maimie's eye went wandering shyly over the rows of brown faces that turned in solemn and steadfast regard to the minister's pew, Hughie nudged her and whispered: "There's Don. See, in the back seat by the window, next to Peter Ruagh yonder; the red-headed fellow."

He pointed to Peter McRae, grandson of "Peter the Elder." There was no mistaking that landmark.

"Look," cried Hughie, eagerly, pointing with terrible directness straight at Don, to Maimie's confusion.

"Whisht, Hughie," said his mother softly.

"There's Ranald, mother," said the diplomatic Hughie, knowing well that his mother would rejoice to hear that bit of news. "See, mother, just in front of Don, there."

Again Hughie's terrible finger pointed straight into the face of the gazing congregation.

"Hush, Hughie," said his mother, severely.

Maimie knew a hundred eyes were looking straight at the minister's pew, but for the life of her she could not prevent her eye following the pointing finger, till it found the steady gaze of Ranald fastened upon her. It was only for a moment, but in that moment she felt her heart jump and her face grow hot, and it did not help her that she knew that the people were all wondering at her furious blushes. Of course the story of the sugaring-off had gone the length of the land and had formed the subject of conversation at the church door that morning, where Ranald had to bear a good deal of chaff about the young lady, and her dislike of forfeits, till he was ready to fight if a chance should but offer. With unspeakable rage and confusion, he noticed Hughie's pointing finger. He caught, too, Maimie's quick look, with the vivid blush that followed. Unfortunately, others besides himself had noticed this, and Don and Peter Ruagh, in the seat behind him, made it the subject of congratulatory remarks to Ranald.

At this point the minister rose in the pulpit, and all waited with earnest and reverent mien for the announcing of the psalm.

The Rev. Alexander Murray was a man to be regarded in any company and under any circumstances, but when he stood up in his pulpit and faced his congregation he was truly superb. He was above the average height, of faultless form and bearing, athletic, active, and with a "spring in every muscle." He had coal-black hair and beard, and a flashing blue eye that held his people in utter subjection and put the fear of death upon evil-doers under the gallery. In every movement, tone, and glance there breathed imperial command.

"Let us worship God by singing to His praise in the one hundred and twenty-first psalm:

'I to the hills will lift mine eyes,
From whence doth come mine aid.'"

His voice rang out over the congregation like a silver bell, and Maimie thought she had never seen a man of such noble presence.

After the reading of the psalm the minister sat down, and Straight Rory rose in his box, and after his manner, began feeling about for the first note of the chant that would introduce the noble old tune "St. Paul's." A few moments he spent twisting his face and shoulders in a manner that threatened to ruin the solemnity of the worshipers under the gallery, till finally he seemed to hit upon the pitch desired, and throwing back his head and closing one eye, he proceeded on his way. Each line he chanted alone, after the ancient Scottish custom, after which the congregation joined with him in the tune. The custom survived from the time when psalm-books were in the hands of but few and the "lining" of the psalm was therefore necessary.

There was no haste to be done with the psalm. Why should there be? They had only one Sabbath in the week, and the whole day was before them. The people surrendered themselves to the lead of Straight Rory with unmistakable delight in that part of "the exercises" of the day in which they were permitted to audibly join. But of all the congregation, none enjoyed the singing more than the dear old women who sat in the front seats near the pulpit, their quiet old faces looking so sweet and pure under their snow-white "mutches." There they sat and sang and quavered, swaying their bodies with the tune in an ecstasy of restful joy.

Maimie had often heard St. Paul's before, but never as it was chanted by Straight Rory and sung by the Indian Lands congregation that day. The extraordinary slides and slurs almost obliterated the notes of the original tune, and the "little

PRECENTOR.
CONGREGATION.
I to the hills will lift mine eyes, I....... to.......
the..... hills... will...... lift...... mine eyes;
PRECENTOR.
CONGREGATION.
From whence doth come mine aid, From.... whence
PRECENTOR.
doth... come... mine..... aid.... My safe - ty
CONGREGATION.
com - eth from the Lord. My.... safe - ty.... com-
PRECENTOR.
eth from the Lord. Who heav'n and earth hath made.
CONGREGATION.
Who.... heav'n and... earth..... hath.... made.

kick," as Maimie called it, at the end of the second line, gave her a little start.

"Auntie," she whispered, "isn't it awfully queer?"

"Isn't it beautiful?" her aunt answered, with an uncertain smile. She was remembering how these winding, sliding, slurring old tunes had affected her when first she heard them in her husband's church years ago. The stately movement, the weird quavers, and the pathetic cadences had in some mysterious way reached the deep places in her heart, and before she knew, she had found the tears coursing down her cheeks and her breath catching in sobs. Indeed, as she listened to-day, remembering these old impressions, the tears began to flow, till Hughie, not understanding, crept over to his mother, and to comfort her, slipped his hand into hers, looking fiercely at Maimie as if she were to blame. Maimie, too, noticed the tears and sat wondering, and as the congregation swung on through the verses of the grand old psalm there crept into her heart a new and deeper emotion than she had ever known.

"Listen to the words, Maimie dear," whispered her aunt. And as Maimie listened, the noble words, borne on the mighty swing of St. Paul's, lifted up by six hundred voices – for men, women, and children were singing with all their hearts – awakened echoes from great deeps within her as yet unsounded. The days for such singing are, alas! long gone. The noble rhythm, the stately movement, the continuous curving stream of melody, that once marked the praise service of the old Scottish church, have given place to the light, staccato tinkle of the revival chorus, or the shorn and mutilated skeleton of the ancient psalm tune.

But while the psalm had been moving on in its solemn and stately way, Ranald had been enduring agony at the hands of Peter Ruagh sitting just behind him. Peter, whose huge, clumsy body was a fitting tabernacle for the soul within, labored under the impression that he was a humorist, and indulged a habit of ponderous joking, trying enough to most people, but to one of Ranald's temperament exasperating to a high degree. His theme was Ranald's rescue of Maimie, and the pauses of the singing he filled in with humorous comments that, outside, would have produced only weariness, but in the church, owing to the strange perversity of human nature, sent a snicker along the seat. Unfortunately for him, Ranald's face was so turned that he could not see it, and so he had no hint of the wrath that was steadily boiling up to the point of overflow.

They were nearing the close of the last verse of the psalm, when Hughie, whose eyes never wandered long from Ranald's direction, uttered a sharp "Oh, my!" There was a shuffling confusion under the gallery, and when Maimie and her aunt looked, Peter Ruagh's place was vacant.

By this time the minister was standing up for prayer. His eye, too, caught the movement in the back seat.

"Young men," he said, sternly, "remember you are in God's house. Let me not have to mention your names before the congregation. Let us pray."

As the congregation rose for prayer, Mrs. Murray noticed Peter Ruagh appear from beneath the bookboard and quietly slip out by the back door with his hand to his face and the blood streaming between his fingers; and though Ranald was standing up straight and stiff in his place, Mrs. Murray could read from his rigid look the explanation of Peter's bloody face. She gave her mind to the prayer with a sore heart, for she had learned enough of those wild, hot-headed youths to know that before Peter Ruagh's face would be healed more blood would have to flow.

The prayer proceeded in its leisurely way, indulging here and there in quiet reverie, or in exultant jubilation over the "attributes," embracing in its worldwide sweep "the interests of the kingdom" far and near, and of that part of humanity included therein present and to come, and buttressing its petitions with theological argument, systematic and unassailable. Before the close, however, the minister came to deal with the needs of his own people. Old and young, absent and present, the sick, the weary, the sin-burdened – all were remembered with a warmth of sympathy, with a directness of petition, and with an earnestness of appeal that thrilled and subdued the hearts of all, and made even the boys, who had borne with difficulty the last half-hour of the long prayer, forget their weariness.

The reading of Scripture followed the prayer. In this the minister excelled. His fine voice and his dramatic instinct combined to make this an impressive and beautiful portion of the service. But to-day much of the beauty and impressiveness of the reading was lost by the frequent interruptions caused by the entrance of late comers, of whom, owing to the bad roads, there were a larger number than usual. The minister was evidently annoyed, not so much by the opening and shutting of the door as by the inattention of his hearers, who kept turning round their heads to see who the new arrivals were. At length the minister could bear it no longer.

"My dear people," he said, pausing in the reading, "never mind those coming in. Give you heed to the reading of God's Word, and if you must know who are entering, I will tell you. Yes," he added, deliberately, "give you heed to me, and I will let you know who these late comers are."

With that startling declaration, he proceeded with the reading, but had not gone more than a few verses when "click" went the door-latch. Not a head turned. It was Malcolm Monroe, slow-going and good-natured, with his quiet little wife following him.

The minister paused, looking toward the door, and announced: "My dear people, here comes our friend Malcolm Monroe, and his good wife with him, and a long walk they have had. Come away, Malcolm; come away; we will just wait for you."

Malcolm's face was a picture. Surprise, astonishment, and confusion followed each other across his stolid countenance; and with quicker pace than he was ever known to use in his life before, he made his way to his seat. No sooner had the reading began again when once more the door clicked. True to his promise, the minister paused and cheerfully announced to his people: "This, my friends, is John Campbell, whom you all know as 'Johnnie Sarah,' and we are very glad to see him, for, indeed, he has not been here for some time. Come away, John; come away, man," he added, impatiently, "for we are all waiting for you."

Johnnie Sarah stood paralyzed with amazement and seemed uncertain whether to advance or to turn and flee. The minister's impatient command, however, decided him, and he dropped into the nearest seat with all speed, and gazed about him as if to discover where he was. He had no sooner taken his seat than the door opened again, and some half-dozen people entered. The minister stood looking at them for some moments and then said, in a voice of resignation: "Friends, these are some of our people from the Island, and there are some strangers with them. But if you want to know who they are, you will just have to look at them yourselves, for I must get on with the reading."

Needless to say, not a soul of the congregation, however

consumed with curiosity, dared to look around, and the reading of the chapter went gravely on to the close. To say that Maimie sat in utter astonishment during this extraordinary proceeding would give but a faint idea of her state of mind. Even Mrs. Murray herself, who had become accustomed to her husband's eccentricities, sat in a state of utter bewilderment, not knowing what might happen next; nor did she feel quite safe until the text was announced and the sermon fairly begun.

Important as were the exercises of reading, praise, and prayer, they were only the "opening services," and merely led up to the event of the day, which was the sermon. And it was the event, not only of the day, but of the week. It would form the theme of conversation and afford food for discussion in every gathering of the people until another came to take its place. To-day it lasted a full hour and a half, and was an extraordinary production. Calm, deliberate reasoning, flights of vivid imagination, passionate denunciation, and fervid appeal, marked its course. Its subject was the great doctrine of Justification by Faith, and it contained a complete system of theology arranged with reference to that doctrine. Ancient heresies were attacked and exposed with completeness amounting to annihilation. Modern errors, into which our "friends" of the different denominations had fallen, were deplored and corrected, and all possible misapplications of the doctrine to practical life guarded against. On the positive side the need, the ground, the means, the method, the agent, the results, of Justification, were fully set forth and illustrated. There were no anecdotes and no poetry. The subject was much too massive and tremendous to permit of any such trifling.

As the sermon rolled on its majestic course, the congregation listened with an attentive and discriminating appreciation that testified to their earnestness and intelligence. True, one here and there dropped into a momentary doze, but his slumber was never easy, for he was harassed by the terrible fear of a sudden summons by name from the pulpit to "awake and give heed to the message," which for the next few minutes would have an application so personal and pungent that it would effectually prevent sleep for that and some successive Sabbaths. The only apparent lapse of attention occurred when Donald Ross opened his horn snuff-box, and after tapping solemnly upon its lid, drew forth a huge pinch of snuff and passed it to his neighbor, who, after helping himself in like manner, passed the box on. That the lapse was only apparent was made evident by the air of abstraction with which this operation was carried on, the snuff being held between the thumb and forefinger for some moments, until a suitable resting-place in the sermon was reached.

When the minister had arrived at the middle of the second head, he made the discovery, as was not frequently the case, that the remotest limits of the alloted time had been passed, and announcing that the subject would be concluded on the following Sabbath, he summarily brought the English service to a close, and dismissed the congregation with a brief prayer, two verses of a psalm, and the benediction.

When Maimie realized that the service was really over, she felt as if she had been in church for a week. After the benediction the congregation passed out into the churchyard and disposed themselves in groups about the gate and along the fences discussing the sermon and making brief inquiries as to the "weal and ill" of the members of their families. Mrs. Murray, leaving Hughie and Maimie to wander at will, passed from group to group, welcomed by all with equal respect and affection. Young men and old men, women and girls alike, were glad to get her word. To-day, however, the young men were not at first to be seen, but Mrs. Murray knew them well enough to suspect that they would be found at the back of the church, so she passed slowly around the church, greeting the people as she went, and upon turning the corner she saw a crowd under the big maple, the rendezvous for the younger portion of the congregation before "church went in." In the center of the group stood Ranald and Don, with Murdie, Don's eldest brother, a huge, good-natured man, beside them, and Peter Ruagh, with his cousin Aleck, and others of the clan. Ranald was standing, pale and silent, with his head thrown back, as his manner was when in passion. The talk was mainly between Aleck and Murdie, the others crowding eagerly about and putting in a word as they could. Murdie was reasoning good-humoredly, Aleck replying fiercely.

"It was good enough for him," Mrs. Murray heard Don interject, in a triumphant tone, to Murdie. But Murdie shut him off sternly.

"Whisht, Don, you are not talking just now."

Don was about to reply when he caught sight of Mrs. Murray. "Here's the minister's wife," he said, in a low tone, and at once the group parted in shamefaced confusion. But Murdie kept his face unmoved, and as Mrs. Murray drew slowly near, said, in a quiet voice of easy good-humor, to Aleck, who was standing with a face like that of a detected criminal: "Well, we will see about it to-morrow night, Aleck, at the post-office," and he faced about to meet Mrs. Murray with an easy smile, while Aleck turned away. But Mrs. Murray was not deceived, and she went straight to the point.

"Murdie," she said, quietly, when she had answered his greeting, "will you just come with me a little; I want to ask you about something." And Murdie walked away with her, followed by the winks and nods of the others.

What she said Murdie never told, but he came back to them more determined upon peace than ever. The difficulty lay, not with the good-natured Peter, who was ready enough to settle with Ranald, but with the fiery Aleck, who represented the non-respectable section of the clan McRae, who lived south of the Sixteenth, and had a reputation for wildness. Fighting was their glory, and no one cared to enter upon a feud with any one of them. Murdie had interfered on Ranald's behalf, chiefly because he was Don's friend, but also because he was unwilling that Ranald should be involved in a quarrel with the McRaes, which he knew would be a serious affair for him. But now his strongest reason for desiring peace was that he had pledged himself to the minister's wife to bring it about in some way or other. So he took Peter off by himself, and without much difficulty, persuaded him to act the magnanimous part and drop the quarrel.

With Ranald he had a harder task. That young man was prepared to see his quarrel through at whatever consequences to himself. He knew the McRaes, and knew well their reputation, but that only made it more impossible for him to retreat. But Murdie knew better than to argue with him, so he turned away from him with an indifferent air, saying: "Oh, very well. Peter is willing to let it drop. You can do as you please, only I know the minister's wife expects you to make it up."

"What did she say to you, then?" asked Ranald, fiercely.

"She said a number of things that you don't need to know, but she said this, whatever, 'He will make it up for my sake, I know.'"

Ranald stood a moment silent, then said, suddenly: "I will, too," and walking straight over to Peter, he offered his hand, saying, "I was too quick, Peter, and I am willing to take as much as I gave. You can go on."

But Peter was far too soft-hearted to accept that invitation, and seizing Ranald's hand, said, heartily: "Never mind, Ranald, it was my own fault. We will just say nothing more about it."

"There is the singing, boys," said Murdie. "Come away. Let us go in."

He was all the more anxious to get the boys into the church when he saw Aleck making toward them. He hurried Peter in before him, well pleased with himself and his success as peacemaker, but especially delighted that he could now turn his face toward the minister's pew, without shame. And as he took his place in the back seat, with Peter Ruagh beside him, the glance of pride and gratitude that flashed across the congregation to him from the gray-brown eyes made Murdie feel more than ever pleased at what he had been able to do. But he was somewhat disturbed to notice that neither Ranald nor Don nor Aleck had followed him into the church, and he waited uneasily for their coming.

In the meantime Straight Rory was winding his sinuous way through Coleshill, the Gaelic rhythm of the psalm allowing of quavers and turns impossible in the English.

In the pause following the second verse, Murdie was startled at the sound of angry voices from without. More than Murdie heard that sound. As Murdie glanced toward the pulpit he saw that the minister had risen and was listening intently.

"Behold – the – sparrow – findeth – out –" chanted the precentor.

"You are a liar!" The words, in Aleck's fiery voice outside, fell distinctly upon Murdie's ear, though few in the congregation seemed to have heard. But while Murdie was making up his mind to slip out, the minister was before him. Quickly he stepped down the pulpit stairs, psalm-book in hand, and singing as he went, walked quietly to the back door, and leaving his book on the window-sill, passed out. The singing went calmly on, for the congregation were never surprised at anything their minister did.

The next verse was nearly through, when the door opened, and in came Don, followed by Aleck, looking somewhat disheveled and shaken up, and two or three more. In a few moments the minister came in, took his psalm-book from the window-sill, and striking up with the congregation, "Blest is the man whose strength thou art," marched up to the pulpit again, with only an added flash in his blue eyes and a little more triumphant swing to his coat-tails to indicate that anything had taken place. But Murdie looked in vain for Ranald to appear, and waited, uncertain what to do. He had a wholesome fear of the minister, more especially in his present mood. Instinctively he turned toward the minister's pew, and reading the look of anxious entreaty from the pale face there, he waited till the congregation rose for prayer and then slipped out, and was seen no more in church that day.

On the way home not a word was said about the disturbance. But after the evening worship, when the minister had gone to his study for a smoke, Hughie, who had heard the whole story from Don, told it to his mother and Maimie in his most graphic manner.

"It was not Ranald's fault, mother," he declared. "You know Peter would not let him alone, and Ranald hit him in the nose, and served him right, too. But they made it all up, and they were just going into the church again, when that Aleck McRae pulled Ranald back, and Ranald did not want to fight at all, but he called Ranald a liar, and he could not help it, but just hit him."

"Who hit who?" said Maimie. "You're not making it very clear, Hughie."

"Why, Ranald, of course, hit Aleck, and knocked him over, too," said Hughie, with much satisfaction; "and then Aleck – he is an awful fighter, you know – jumped on Ranald and was pounding him just awful, the great big brute, when out came papa. He stepped up and caught Aleck by the neck and shook him just like a baby, saying, all the time, 'Would ye? I will teach you to fight on the Sabbath day! Here! in with you, every one of you!' and he threw him nearly into the door, and then they all skedaddled into the church, I tell you, Don said. They were pretty badly scart, too, but Don did not know what papa did to Ranald, and he did not know where Ranald went, but he is pretty badly hurted, I am sure. That great big Aleck McRae is old enough to be his father. Wasn't it mean of him, mother?"

Poor Hughie was almost in tears, and his mother, who sat listening too eagerly to correct her little boy's ethics or grammar, was as nearly overcome as he. She wished she knew where Ranald was. He had not appeared at the evening Bible class, and Murdie had reported that he could not find him anywhere.

She put Hughie to bed, and then saw Maimie to her room. But Maimie was very unwilling to go to bed.

"Oh, auntie," she whispered, as her aunt kissed her good night, "I cannot go to sleep!" And then, after a pause, she said, shyly, "Do you think he is badly hurt?"

Then the minister's wife, looking keenly into the girl's face, made light of Ranald's misfortune.

"Oh, he will be all right," she said, "as far as his hurt is concerned. That is the least part of his trouble. You need not worry about that. Good night, my dear." And Maimie, relieved by her aunt's tone, said "good night" with her heart at rest.

Then Mrs. Murray went into the study, determined to find out what had passed between her husband and Ranald. She found him lying on his couch, luxuriating in the satisfaction of a good day's work behind him, and his first pipe nearly done. She at once ventured upon the thing that lay heavy upon her heart. She began by telling all she knew of the trouble from its beginning in the church, and then waited for her husband's story.

For some moments he lay silently smoking.

"Ah, well," he said, at length, knocking out his pipe, "perhaps I was a little severe with the lad. He may not have been so much to blame."

"Oh, papa! What did you do?" said his wife, in an anxious voice.

"Well," said the minister, hesitating, "I found that the young rascal had struck Aleck McRae first, and a very bad blow it was. So I administered a pretty severe rebuke and sent him home."

"Oh, what a shame!" cried his wife, in indignant tears. "It was far more the fault of Peter and Aleck and the rest. Poor Ranald!"

"Now, my dear," said the minister, "you need not fear for Ranald. I do not suppose he cares much. Besides, his face was not fit to be seen, so I sent him home. Well, it –"

"Yes," burst in his wife, "great, brutal fellow, to strike a boy like that!"

"Boy?" said her husband. "Well, he may be, but not many men would dare to face him." Then he added, "I wish I had known – I fear I spoke – perhaps the boy may feel unjustly treated. He is as proud as Lucifer."

"Oh, papa!" said his wife, "what did you say?"

"Nothing but what was true. I just told him that a boy who would break the Lord's Day by fighting, and in the very shadow of the Lord's house, when Christian people were worshiping God, was acting like a savage, and was not fit for the company of decent folk."

To this his wife made no reply, but went out of the study, leaving the minister feeling very uncomfortable indeed. But by the end of the second pipe he began to feel that, after all, Ranald had got no more than was good for him, and that he would be none the worse of it; in which comforting conviction he went to rest, and soon fell into the sleep which is supposed to be the right of the just.

Not so his wife. Wearied though she was with the long day, its excitements and its toils, sleep would not come. Anxious thoughts about the lad she had come to love as if he were her own son or brother kept crowding in upon her. The vision of his fierce, dark, stormy face held her eyes awake and at length drew her from her bed. She went into the study and fell upon her knees. The burden had grown too heavy for her to bear alone. She would share it with Him who knew what it meant to bear the sorrows and the sins of others.

As she rose, she heard Fido bark and whine in the yard below, and going to the window, she saw a man standing at the back door, and Fido fawning upon him. Startled, she was about to waken her husband, when the man turned his face so that the moonlight fell upon it, and she saw Ranald. Hastily she threw on her dressing-gown, put on her warm bedroom slippers and cloak, ran down to the door, and in another moment was standing before him, holding him by the shoulders.

"Ranald!" she cried, breathlessly, "what is it?"

"I am going away," he said, simply. "And I was just passing by – and –" he could not go on.

"Oh, Ranald!" she cried, "I am glad you came this way. Now tell me where you are going."

The boy looked at her as if she had started a new idea in his mind, and then said, "I do not know."

"And what are you going to do, Ranald?"

"Work. There is plenty to do. No fear of that."

"But your father, Ranald?"

The boy was silent for a little, and then said, "He will soon be well, and he will not be needing me, and he said I could go." His voice broke with the remembrance of the parting with his father.

"And why are you going, Ranald?" she said, looking into his eyes.

Again the boy stood silent.

"Why do you go away from your home and your father, and – and – all of us who love you?"

"Indeed, there is no one," he replied, bitterly; "and I am not for decent people. I am not for decent people. I know that well enough. There is no one that will care much."

"No one, Ranald?" she asked, sadly. "I thought –" she paused, looking steadily into his face.

Suddenly the boy turned to her, and putting out both his hands, burst forth, his voice coming in dry sobs: "Oh, yes, yes! I do believe you. I do believe you. And that is why I came this way. I wanted to see your door again before I went. Oh, I will never forget you! Never, never, and I am glad I am seeing you, for now you will know – how much –" The boy was unable to proceed. His sobs were shaking his whole frame, and to his shy Highland Scotch nature, words of love and admiration were not easy. "You will not be sending me back home again?" he pleaded, anticipating her. "Indeed, I cannot stay in this place after to-day."

But the minister's wife kept her eyes steadily upon his face without a word, trying in vain to find her voice, and the right words to say. She had no need of words, for in her face, pale, wet with her flowing tears, and illumined with her gray-brown eyes, Ranald read her heart.

"Oh!" he cried again, "you are wanting me to stay, and I will be ashamed before them all, and the minister, too. I cannot stay. I cannot stay."

"And I cannot let you go, Ranald, my boy," she said, commanding her voice to speech. "I want you to be a brave man. I don't want you to be afraid of them."

"Afraid of them!" said the boy, in scornful surprise. "Not if they were twice as more and twice as beeg."

Mrs. Murray saw her advantage, and followed it up.

"And the minister did not know the whole truth, Ranald, and he was sorry he spoke to you as he did."

"Did he say that?" said Ranald, in surprise. It was to him, as to any one in that community, a terrible thing to fall under the displeasure of the minister and to be disgraced in his eyes.

"Yes, indeed, Ranald, and he would be sorry if you should go away. I am sure he would blame himself."

This was quite a new idea to the boy. That the minister should think himself to be in the wrong was hardly credible.

"And how glad we would be," she continued, earnestly, "to see you prove yourself a man before them all."

Ranald shook his head. "I would rather go away."

"Perhaps, but it's braver to stay, and to do your work like a man." And then, allowing him no time for words, she pictured to him the selfish, cowardly part the man plays who marches bravely enough in the front ranks until the battle begins, but who shrinks back and seeks an easy place when the fight comes on, till his face fell before her in shame. And then she showed him what she would like him to do, and what she would like him to be in patience and in courage, till he stood once more erect and steady.

"Now, Ranald," she said, noting the effect of her words upon him, "what is it to be?"

"I will go back," he said, simply; and turning with a single word of farewell, he sprang over the fence and disappeared in the woods. The minister's wife stood looking the way he went long after he had passed out of sight, and then, lifting her eyes to the radiant sky with its shining lights, "He made the stars also," she whispered, and went up to her bed and laid her down and slept in peace. Her Sabbath day's work was done.

THE HOME-COMING OF THE SHANTYMEN

For some weeks Ranald was not seen by any one belonging to the manse. Hughie reported that he was not at church, nor at Bible class, and although this was not in itself an extraordinary thing, still Mrs. Murray was uneasy, and Hughie felt that church was a great disappointment when Ranald was not there.

In their visits to Macdonald Dubh the minister and his wife never could see Ranald. His Aunt Kirsty could not understand or explain his reluctance to attend the public services, nor his unwillingness to appear in the house on the occasion of the minister's visits. "He is busy with the fences and about the stables preparing for the spring's work," she said; "but, indeed, he is very queer whatever, and I cannot make him out at all." Macdonald Dubh himself said nothing. But the books and magazines brought by the minister's wife were always read. "Indeed, when once he gets down to his book," his aunt complained, "neither his bed nor his dinner will move him."

The minister thought little of the boy's "vagaries," but to his wife came many an anxious thought about Ranald and his doings. She was more disappointed than she cared to confess, even to herself, that the boy seemed to be quite indifferent to the steadily deepening interest in spiritual things that marked the members of her Bible class.

While she was planning how to reach him once more, an event occurred which brought him nearer to her than he had ever been before. As they were sitting one evening at tea, the door unexpectedly opened, and without announcement, in walked Ranald, splashed with hard riding, pale, and dazed. Without a word of reply to the greetings that met him from all at the table, he went straight to the minister's wife, handed her an opened letter, and stood waiting. It was addressed to Ranald himself, and was the first he had ever received in his life. It was from Yankee Jim, and read as follows:

> Dear Ranald – The Boss aint feelin like ritin much and the rest of the boys is all broke up, and so he told me to rite to you and to tell you some purty bad news. I don't know how to go about it, but the fact is, Mack Cameron got drownded yesterday tryin to pull a little fool of a Frenchman out of the river just below the Lachine. We'd just got through the rough water and were lyin nice and quiet, gettin things together again when that ijit Frenchman got tite and got tryin some fool trick or other walking a timber stick and got upsot into the wet. I'd a let him go, you bet, but Mack cudn't stand to see him bobbin up and down so he ripped off and in after him. He got him too, but somehow the varmint gripped him round the neck. They went down but we got em out purty quick and the Frenchman come round all right, but somehow Mack wouldn't, choked appearinly by that tarnel little fool who aint worth one

> of Mack's fingers, and if killin him wud do any good, then he wudn't be livin long. We are all feelin purty bad. We are comin' home on Thursday by Cornwall, eight or ten of us. The rest will go on with the rafts. The Boss says, better have rigs to meet us and Mack. That's all. I haint no good at weepin', never was, wish I cud somehow, it might ease off a feller a little, but tell you what, Ranald, I haint felt so queer since I was a boy lookin at my mother in her coffin. There was nothin mean about Mack. He was good to the heart. He wud do his work slick and never a growl or a groan, and when you wanted a feller to your back, Mack was there. I know there aint no use goin on like this. All I say is, ther's a purty big hole in the world for us to-night. Boss says you'd better tell the minister. He says he's good stuff and he'll know what to do at Mack's home. No more at present. Good-bye. Yours truely,
>
> J. LATHAM.

The minister's wife began reading the letter, wondering not a little at Ranald's manner, but when she came to the words, "Mack Cameron got drownded," she laid the letter down with a little cry. Her husband came quickly to her, took up the letter, and read it to the end.

"I will go at once," he said, and rang the bell. "Tell Lambert to put Black in the buggy immediately, Jessie," he said, when the maid appeared. "Do you think you ought to go, my dear?"

"Yes, yes, I shall be ready in a moment; but, oh, what can we do or say?"

"Perhaps you had better not go. It will be very trying," said the minister.

"Oh, yes, I must go. I must. The poor mother!" Then she turned to Ranald as the minister left the room. "You are going home, Ranald, I suppose," she said.

"No, I was thinking I would go to tell the people. Donald Ross will go, and the Campbells, and Farquhar McNaughton's light wagon would be best – for the – for Mack. And then I will go round by the McGregors."

Ranald had been thinking things out and making his plans.

"But that will be a long round for you," said Mrs. Murray. "Could not we go by the Campbells', and they will send word to Donald Ross?"

"I think it would be better for me to go, to make sure of the teams."

"Very well, then. Good by, Ranald," said the minister's wife, holding out her hand to him.

But still Ranald lingered. "It will be hard on Bella Peter," he said, in a low voice, looking out of the window.

"Bella Peter? Bella McGregor?"

"Yes," said Ranald, embarrassed and hesitating. "She was Mack's – Mack was very fond of her, whatever."

"Oh, Ranald!" she cried, "do you say so? Are you sure of that?"

"Yes, I am sure," said Ranald, simply. "The boys in the shanty would be teasing Mack about it, and one day Mack told me something, and I know quite well."

"I will go to her," said Mrs. Murray.

"That will be very good," said Ranald, much relieved. "And I will be going with you that way."

As Mrs. Murray left the room, Maimie came around to where Ranald was standing and said to him, gently, "You knew him well, didn't you?"

"Yes," replied Ranald, in an indifferent tone, as if unwilling to talk with her about it.

"And you were very fond of him?" went on Maimie.

Ranald caught the tremor in her voice and looked at her. "Yes," he said, with an effort. "He was good to me in the camp. Many's the time he made it easy for me. He was next to Macdonald Bhain with the ax, and, man, he was the grand fighter – that is," he added, adopting the phrase of the Macdonald gang, "when it was a plain necessity." Then, forgetting himself, he began to tell Maimie how Big Mack had borne himself in the great fight a few weeks before. But he had hardly well begun when suddenly he stopped with a groan. "But now he is dead – he is dead. I will never see him no more."

He was realizing for the first time his loss. Maimie came nearer him, and laying her hand timidly on his arm, said, "I am sorry, Ranald"; and Ranald turned once more and looked at her, as if surprised that she should show such feeling.

"Yes," he said, "I believe you are sorry."

Her big blue eyes filled suddenly with tears.

"Do you wonder that I am sorry? Do you think I have no heart at all?" she burst forth, impetuously.

"Indeed, I don't know," said Ranald. "Why should you care? You do not know him."

"But haven't you just told me how splendid he was, and how good he was to you, and how much you thought of him, and –" Maimie checked her rush of words with a sudden blush, and then hurried on to say, "Besides, think of his mother, and all of them."

While Maimie was speaking, Ranald had been scanning her face as if trying to make up his mind about her.

"I am glad you are sorry," he said, slowly, gazing with so searching a look into her eyes that she let them fall.

At this moment Mrs. Murray entered ready for her ride.

"Is the pony come?" she asked.

"Indeed, it is the slouch I am," said Ranald, and he hurried off to the stable, returning in a very short time with the pony saddled.

"You would not care to go with your uncle, Maimie?" said Mrs. Murray, as Lambert drove up Black in the buggy.

"No, auntie, I think not," said Maimie. "I will take care of Hughie and the baby."

"Good by, then, my dear," said Mrs. Murray, kissing her.

"Good by, Ranald," said Maimie, as he turned away to get his colt.

"Good by," he said, awkwardly. He felt like lifting his cap, but hesitated to do anything so extremely unnatural. With the boys in that country such an act of courtesy was regarded as a sign of "pride," if not of weakness.

Their way lay along the concession line for a mile, and then through the woods by the bridle-path to Peter McGregor's clearing. The green grass ran everywhere – along the roadside, round the great stump roots, over the rough pasture-fields, softening and smoothing wherever it went. The woods were flushing purple, with just a tinge of green from the bursting buds. The balsams and spruces still stood dark in the swamps, but the tamaracks were shyly decking themselves in their exquisite robes of spring, and through all the bush the air was filled with soft sounds and scents. In earth and air, in field and forest, life, the new spring life, ran riot. How strangely impertinent death appeared, and how unlovely in such a world of life!

As they left the concession road and were about to strike into the woods, Mrs. Murray checked her pony, and looking upon the loveliness about her, said, softly, "How beautiful it all is!"

There was no response from Ranald, and Mrs. Murray, glancing at his gloomy face, knew that his heart was sore at the thought of the pain they were bearing with them. She hesitated a few moments, and then said, gently: "And I saw a new heaven and a new earth. And there shall be no more death."

But still Ranald made no reply, and they rode on through the bush in silence till they came to the clearing beyond. As they entered the *brûlé*, Ranald checked his colt, and holding up his hand, said, "Listen!"

Through the quiet evening air, sweet and clear as a silver bell, came the long, musical note of the call that brings the cows home for the milking. It was Bella's voice: "Ko – boss, ko – boss, ko – boss!"

Far across the *brûlé* they could see her standing on a big pine stump near the bars, calling to her cows that were slowly making toward her through the fallen timber, pausing here and there to crop an especially rich mouthful, and now and then responding to her call with soft lowings. Gently Bella chid them. "Come, Blossom, come away now; you are very lazy. Come, Lily; what are you waiting for? You slow old poke!" Then again the long, musical note: "Ko – boss, ko – boss, ko – boss!"

Ranald groaned aloud, "Och-hone! It will be her last glad hour," he said; "it is a hard, hard thing."

"Poor child, poor child!" said Mrs. Murray; "the Lord help her. It will be a cruel blow."

"That it is, a cruel blow," said Ranald, bitterly; so bitterly that Mrs. Murray glanced at him in surprise and saw his face set in angry pain.

"The Lord knows best, Ranald," she said, gravely, "and loves best, too."

"It will break her heart, whatever," answered Ranald, shortly.

"He healeth the broken in heart," said Mrs. Murray, softly. Ranald made no reply, but let the colt take her way through the *brûlé* toward the lane into which Bella had now got her cows. How happy the girl was! Joy filled every tone of her voice. And why not? It was the springtime, the time of life and love. Long winter was gone, and soon her brothers would be back from the shanties. "And Mack, too," she whispered to her happy heart.

"And are ye sure the news is true?
    And are ye sure he's weel?
Is this a time to think o' wark?
    Ye jades, fling by your wheel.

"For there's nae luck aboot the hoose,
    There's nae luck ava,
There's little pleesure in the hoose
    When oor gude man's awa."

So she sang, not too loud; for the boys were at the barn and she would never hear the end of it.

"Well, Bella, you are getting your cows home. How are you, my dear?"

Bella turned with a scarlet face to meet the minister's wife, and her blushes only became deeper when she saw Ranald, for she felt quite certain that Ranald would understand the meaning of her song.

"I will go on with the cows," said Ranald, in a hoarse voice, and Mrs. Murray, alighting, gave him her pony to lead.

Peter McGregor was a stern man to his own family, and to all the world, with the single exception of his only daughter, Bella. His six boys he kept in order with a firm hand, and not one of them would venture to take a liberty with him. But Bella had no fear of his grim face and stern ways, and "just twiddled her father round her finger," as her mother said, with a great show of impatience. But, in spite of all her petting from her big brothers and her father, Bella remained quite unspoiled, the light of her home and the joy of her father's heart. It had not escaped the father's jealous eye that Big Mack Cameron found occasion for many a visit to the boys on an evening when the day's work was done, and that from the meetings he found his shortest way home round by the McGregors'. At first the old man was very gruff with him, and was for sending him about his business, but his daughter's happy face, and the light in her eyes, that could mean only one thing, made him pause, and after a long and sleepless night, he surprised his daughter the next morning with a word of gentle greeting and an unusual caress, and thenceforth took Big Mack to his heart. Not that any word or explanation passed between them; it had not come to that as yet; but Big Mack felt the change, and gave him thenceforth the obedience and affection of a son.

The old man was standing in the yard, waiting to help with the milking.

Ranald drove the cows in, and then, tying up the horses, went straight to him.

"I bring bad news, Mr. McGregor," he said, anxious to get done with his sad task. "There has been an accident on the river, and Mack Cameron is drowned."

"What do you say, boy?" said Peter, in a harsh voice.

"He was trying to save a Frenchman, and when they got him out he was dead," said Ranald, hurrying through his tale, for he saw the two figures coming up the lane and drawing nearer.

"Dead!" echoed the old man. "Big Mack! God help me."

"And they will be wanting a team," continued Ranald, "to go to Cornwall to-morrow."

The old man stood for a few moments, looking stupidly at Ranald. Then, lifting his hat from his gray head, he said, brokenly: "My poor girl! Would God I had died for him."

Ranald turned away and stood looking down the lane, shrinking from the sight of the old man's agony. Then, turning back to him, he said: "The minister's wife is coming yonder with Bella."

The old man started, and with a mighty effort commanding himself, said, "Now may God help me!" and went to meet his daughter.

Through the gloom of the falling night Ranald could see the frightened white face and the staring, tearless eyes. They came quite near before Bella caught sight of her father. For a moment she hesitated, till the old man, without a word, beckoned her to him. With a quick little run she was in his arms, where she lay moaning, as if in sore bodily pain. Her father held her close to him, murmuring over her fond Gaelic words, while Ranald and Mrs. Murray went over to the horses and stood waiting there.

"I will go now to Donald Ross," Ranald said, in a low voice, to the minister's wife. He mounted the colt and was riding off, when Peter called him back.

"The boys will take the wagon to-morrow," he said.

"They will meet at the Sixteenth at daylight," replied Ranald; and then to Mrs. Murray he said, "I will come back this way for you. It will soon be dark."

But Bella, hearing him, cried to her: "Oh, you will not go?"

"Not if you need me, Bella," said Mrs. Murray, putting her arms around her. "Ranald will run in and tell them at home." This Ranald promised to do, and rode away on his woeful journey; and before he reached home that night, the news had spread far and wide, from house to house, like a black cloud over a sunny sky.

The home-coming of the men from the shanties had ever been a time of rejoicing in the community. The Macdonald gang were especially welcome, for they always came back with honor and with the rewards of their winter's work. There was always a series of welcoming gatherings in the different homes represented in the gang, and there, in the midst of the admiring company, tales would be told of the deeds done and the trials endured, of the adventures on the river and the wonders of the cities where they had been. All were welcome everywhere, and none more than Big Mack Cameron. Brimming with good nature, and with a remarkable turn for stories, he was the center of every group of young people wherever he went; and at the "bees" for logging or for building or for cradling, Big Mack was held in honor, for he was second in feats of strength only to Macdonald Bhain himself. It was with no common grief that people heard the word that they were bringing him home dead.

At the Sixteenth next morning, before the break of day, Ranald stood in the gloom waiting for the coming of the teams. He had been up most of the night and he was weary in body and sore at heart, but Macdonald Bhain had trusted him, and there must be no mistake. One by one the teams arrived. First to appear was Donald Ross, the elder. For years he had given over the driving of his team to his boys, but to-day he felt that respect to the family demanded his presence on such an errand as this; and besides, he knew well that his son Dannie, Mack's special chum, would expect him to so honor the home-coming of his dead friend. Peter McGregor, fearing to leave his daughter for that long and lonely day, sent his son John in his place. It was with difficulty that Mack's father, Long John Cameron, had been persuaded to remain with the mother and to allow Murdie to go in his stead.

The last to arrive was Farquhar McNaughton, Kirsty's Farquhar, with his fine black team and new light wagon. To him was to be given the honor of bearing the body home. Gravely they talked and planned, and then left all to Ranald to execute.

"You will see to these things, Ranald, my man," said Donald Ross, with the air of one giving solemn charge. "Let all things be done decently and in order."

"I will try," said Ranald, simply. But Farquhar McNaughton looked at him doubtfully.

"It is a peety," he said, "there is not one with more experience. He is but a lad."

But Donald Ross had been much impressed with Ranald's capable manner the night before.

"Never you fear, Farquhar," he replied; "Ranald is not one to fail us."

As Ranald stood watching the wagons rumbling down the road and out of sight, he felt as if years must have passed since he had received the letter that had laid on him the heavy burden of this sad news. That his uncle, Macdonald Bhain, should have sent the word to him brought Ranald a sense of responsibility that awakened the man in him, and he knew he would feel himself a boy no more. And with that new feeling of manhood stirring within him, he went about his work that day, omitting no detail in arrangement for the seemly conduct of the funeral.

Night was falling as the wagons rumbled back again from Cornwall, bringing back the shantymen and their dead companion. Up through the Sixteenth, where a great company of people stood silent and with bared heads, the sad procession moved, past the old church, up through the swamp, and so onward to the home of the dead. None of the Macdonald gang turned aside to their homes till they had given their comrade over into the keeping of his own people. By the time the Cameron's gate was reached the night had grown thick and black, and the drivers were glad enough of the cedar bark torches that Ranald and Don waved in front of the teams to light the way up the lane. In silence Donald Ross, who was leading, drove up his team to the little garden gate and allowed the great Macdonald and Dannie to alight.

At the gate stood Long John Cameron, silent and self-controlled, but with face showing white and haggard in the light of the flaring torches. Behind him, in the shadow, stood the minister. For a few moments they all remained motionless and silent. The time was too great for words, and these men knew when it was good to hold their peace. At length Macdonald Bhain broke the silence, saying in his great deep voice, as he bared his head: "Mr. Cameron, I have brought you back your son, and God is my witness, I would his place were mine this night."

"Bring him in, Mr. Macdonald," replied the father, gravely and steadily. "Bring him in. It is the Lord; let Him do what seemeth Him good."

Then six of the Macdonald men came forward from the darkness, Curly and Yankee leading the way, and lifted the coffin from Farquhar's wagon, and reverently, with heads uncovered, they followed the torches to the door. There they stopped suddenly, for as they reached the threshold, there arose a low, long, heart-smiting cry from within. At the sound of that cry Ranald staggered as if struck by a blow, and let his torch fall to the ground. The bearers waited, looking at each other in fear.

"Whisht, Janet, woman!" said Long John, gravely. "Your son is at the door."

"Ah, indeed, that he is, that he is! My son! My son!"

She stood in the doorway with hands uplifted and with tears streaming down her face. "Come in, Malcolm; come in, my boy. Your mother is waiting for you."

Then they carried him in and laid him in the "room," and retiring to the kitchen, sat down to watch the night.

In half an hour the father came out and found them there.

"You have done what you could, Mr. Macdonald," he said, addressing him for all, "and I will not be unmindful of your kindness. But now you can do no more. Your wife and your people will be waiting you."

"And, please God, in good time they will be seeing us. As for me, I will neither go to my home nor up into my bed, but I will watch by the man who was my faithful friend and companion till he is laid away." And in this mind he and his men remained firm, taking turns at the watching all that night and the next day.

As Macdonald finished speaking, the minister came into the kitchen, bringing with him the mother and the children. The men all rose to their feet, doing respect to the woman and to her grief. When they were seated again, the minister rose and said: "My friends, this is a night for silence and not for words. The voice of the Lord is speaking in our ears. It becomes us to hear, and to submit ourselves to His holy will. Let us pray."

As Ranald listened to the prayer, he could not help thinking how different it was from those he was accustomed to hear from the pulpit. Solemn, simple, and direct, it lifted the hearts of all present up to the throne of God, to the place of strength and of peace. There was no attempt to explain the "mystery of the Providence," but there was a sublime trust that refused to despair even in the presence of impenetrable darkness.

After the minister had gone, Macdonald Bhain took Ranald aside and asked him as to the arrangements for the funeral. When Ranald had explained to him every detail, Macdonald laid his hand on his nephew's shoulder and said, kindly, "It is well done, Ranald. Now you will be going home, and in the morning you will see your aunt, and if she will be wishing to come to the wake to-morrow night, then you will bring her."

Then Ranald went home, feeling well repaid for his long hours of anxiety and toil.

THE WAKE

The wake was an important feature in the social life of the people of Indian Lands. In ancient days, in the land of their forefathers, the wake had been deemed a dire necessity for the safeguarding of the dead, who were supposed to be peculiarly exposed to the malicious attacks of evil spirits. Hence, with many lighted candles, and with much incantation, friends would surround the body through the perilous hours of darkness. It was a weird and weary vigil, and small wonder if it appeared necessary that the courage and endurance of the watchers should be fortified with copious draughts of "mountain dew," with bread and cheese accompaniments. And the completeness of their trust in the efficacy of such supports was too often evidenced by the condition of the watchers toward the dawn of the morning. And, indeed, if the spirits were not too fastidious, and if they had so desired, they could have easily flown away, not only with the "waked," but with the "wakers" as well.

But those days and those notions had long passed away. The wake still remained, but its meaning and purpose had changed. No longer for the guarding of the dead, but for the comfort of the living, the friends gathered to the house of mourning and watched the weary hours. But highland courtesy forbade that the custom of refreshing the watchers should be allowed to die out, and hence, through the night, once and again, the whisky, bread, and cheese were handed around by some close friend of the family, and were then placed upon the table for general use. It was not surprising that, where all were free to come and welcome to stay, and where anything like scantiness in providing or niggardliness in serving would be a matter of family disgrace, the wake often degenerated into a frolic, if not a debauch. In order to check any such tendency, it had been the custom of late years to introduce religious services, begun by the minister himself and continued by the elders.

As the evening fell, a group of elders stood by the back door of Long John Cameron's sorrow-stricken home, talking quietly over the sad event and arranging for the "exercises" of the night. At a little distance from them sat Yankee, with Ranald beside him, both silent and listening somewhat indifferently to the talk of the others. Yankee was not in his element. He was always welcome in the homes of his comrades, for he was ready with his tongue and clever with his fingers, but with the graver and religious side of their lives he had little in common. It was, perhaps, this feeling that drew him toward Macdonald Dubh and Ranald, so that for weeks at a time he would make their house his home. He had "no use for wakes," as he said himself, and had it not been that it was one of the gang that lay dead within, Yankee would have avoided the house until all was over and the elders safely away.

Of the elders, only four were present as yet: Donald Ross, who was ever ready to bring the light of his kindly face to cheer the hearts of the mourners; Straight Rory, who never, by any chance, allowed himself to miss the solemn joy of leading the funeral psalm; Peter McRae, who carried behind his stern old face a heart of genuine sympathy; and Kenny Crubach, to whom attendance at funerals was at once a duty and a horror.

Donald Ross, to whom all the elders accorded, instinctively, the place of leader, was arranging the order of "the exercises."

"Mr. McCuaig," he said to Straight Rory, "you will take charge of the singing. The rest of us will, in turn, give out a psalm and read a portion of Scripture with a few suitable remarks, and lead in prayer. We will not be forgetting, brethren," said old Donald, "that there will be sore hearts here this night."

Straight Rory's answer was a sigh so woeful and so deep that Yankee looked over at him and remarked in an undertone to Ranald, "He ain't so cheerful as he might be. He must feel awful inside."

"It is a sad and terrible day for the Camerons," said Peter McRae.

"Aye, it is sad, indeed," replied Donald Ross. "He was a good son and they will be missing him bad. It is a great loss."

"Yes, the loss is great," said Peter, grimly. "But, after all, that is a small thing."

Straight Rory sighed again even more deeply than before. Donald Ross said nothing.

"What does the old duck mean, anyhow?" said Yankee to Ranald.

The boy made no reply. His heart was sick with horror at Peter's meaning, which he understood only too well.

"Aye," went on Peter, "it is a terrible, mysterious Providence, and a heavy warning to the ungodly and careless."

"He means me, I guess," remarked Yankee to Ranald.

"It will perhaps be not amiss to any of us," said Kenny Crubach, sharply.

"Indeed, that is true," said Donald Ross, in a very humble voice.

"Yes, Mr. Ross," said Peter, ignoring Kenny Crubach, "but at times the voice of Providence cannot be misunderstood, and it will not do for the elders of the church to be speaking soft things when the Lord is speaking in judgment and wrath."

Donald was silent, while Straight Rory assented with a heartrending "Aye, aye," which stirred Yankee's bile again.

"What's he talkin' about? He don't seem to be usin' my language," he said, in a tone of wrathful perplexity. Ranald was too miserable to answer, but Kenny was ready with his word.

"Judgment and wrath," he echoed, quickly. "The man would require to be very skillful whatever in interpreting the ways of Providence, and very bold to put such a meaning into the death of a young man such as Malcolm yonder." The little man's voice was vibrating with feeling.

Then Yankee began to understand. "I'll be gol-blamed to a cinder!" he exclaimed, in a low voice, falling back upon a combination that seemed more suitable to the circumstances. "They ain't sendin' him to hell, are they?" He shut up the knife with which he had been whittling with a sharp snap, and rising to his feet, walked slowly over to the group of elders.

"Far be it from me to judge what is not to be seen," said Peter. "But we are allowed and commanded to discern the state of the heart by the fruits."

"Fruits?" replied Kenny, quickly. "He was a good son and brother and friend; he was honest and clean, and he gave his life for another at the last."

"Exactly so," said Peter. "I am not denying much natural goodness, for indeed he was a fine lad; but I will be looking for the evidence that he was in a state of grace. I have not heard of any, and glad would I be to hear it."

The old man's emotion took the sharpness out of Kenny's speech, but he persisted, stoutly, "Goodness is goodness, Mr. McRae, for all that."

"You will not be holding the Armenian doctrine of works, Mr. Campbell?" said Peter, severely. "You would not be pointing to good works as a ground of salvation?"

Yankee, who had been following the conversation intently, thought he saw meaning in it at last.

"If I might take a hand," he said, diffidently, "I might contribute somethin' to help you out."

Peter regarded him a little impatiently. He had forgotten the concrete, for the moment, in the abstract, and was donning his armor for a battle with Kenny upon the "fundamentals." Hence he was not too well pleased with Yankee's interruption. But Donald Ross gladly welcomed the diversion. The subject was to him extremely painful.

"We will be glad," he said to Yankee, "to hear you, Mr. Latham."

"Well," said Yankee, slowly, "from your remarks I gathered that you wanted information about the doings of –" he jerked his head toward the house behind him. "Now, I want to say," he continued, confidentially, "you've come to the right shop, for I've ate and slept, I've worked and fought, I've lived with him by day and by night, and right through he was the straightest, whitest man I ever seen, and I won't except the boss himself." Yankee paused to consider the effect of this statement, and to allow its full weight to be appreciated; and then he continued: "Yes, sir, you may just bet your – you may be right well sure," correcting himself, "that you're safe in givin'" – here he dropped his voice, and jerked his head toward the house again – "in givin' the highest marks, full value, and no discount. Why," he went on, with an enthusiasm rare in him, "ask any man in the gang, any man on the river, if they ever seen or heard of his doin' a mean or crooked thing, and if you find any feller who says he did, bring him here, and, by" – Yankee remembered himself in time – "and I give you my solemn word that I'll eat him, hat and boots." Yankee brought his bony fist down with a whack into his hand. Then he relapsed into his lazy drawl again: "No, siree, hoss! If it's doin's you're after, don't you be slow in bankin' your little heap on *his* doin's."

Donald Ross grasped Yankee's hand and shook it hard. "I will be thanking you for that word," he said, earnestly.

But Peter felt that the cause of truth demanded that he should speak out. "Mr. Latham," he said, solemnly, "what you have been saying is very true, no doubt, but if a man is not 'born again he cannot see the kingdom of God.' These are the words of the Lord himself."

"Born again!" said Yankee. "How? I don't seem to get you. But I guess the feller that does the right thing all round has got a purty good chance."

"It is not a man's deeds, we are told," said Peter, patiently, "but his heart."

"There you are," said Yankee, warmly, "right again, and that's what I always hold to. It's the heart a man carries round in his inside. Never mind your talk, never mind your actin' up for people to see. Give me the heart that is warm and red, and beats proper time, you bet. Say! you're all right." Yankee gazed admiringly at the perplexed and hopeless Peter.

"I am afraid you are not remembering what the Apostle Paul said, Mr. Latham," said Peter, determined to deal faithfully with Yankee. "'By the deeds of the law shall no flesh be justified.'"

It was now Yankee's turn to gaze helplessly at Peter. "I guess you have dropped me again," he said, slowly.

"Man," said Peter, with a touch of severity, "you will need to be more faithful with the Word of God. The Scriptures plainly declare, Mr. Latham, that it is impossible for a man to be saved in his natural state."

Yankee looked blank at this.

"The prophet says that the plowing and sowing, the very prayers, of the wicked are an abomination to the Lord."

"Why, now you're talkin', but look here." Yankee lowered his tone. "Look here, you wouldn't go for to call" – here again he jerked his head toward the house – "wicked, would you? Fur if you do, why, there ain't any more conversation between you and me."

Yankee was terribly in earnest.

"'There is none righteous, no, not one,'" quoted Peter, with the air of a man who forces himself to an unpleasant duty.

"That's so, I guess," said Yankee, meditatively, "but it depends some on what you mean. I don't set myself up for any copy-book head-line, but as men go – men, say, just like you here – I'd put – I'd put him alongside, wouldn't you? You expect to get through yourself, I judge?"

This was turning the tables somewhat sharply upon Peter, but Yankee's keen, wide-open eyes were upon him, and his intensely earnest manner demanded an answer.

"Indeed, if it will be so, it will not be for any merit of my own, but only because of the mercy of the Lord in Christ Jesus." Peter's tone was sincerely humble.

"Guess you're all right," said Yankee, encouragingly; "and as for – as for – him – don't you worry about that. You may be dead sure about his case."

But Peter only shook his head hopelessly. "You are sorely in need of instruction, Mr. Latham," he said, sadly. "We cannot listen to our hearts in this matter. We must do honor to the justice of God, and the word is clear, 'Ye must be born again.' Nothing else avails." Peter's tone was final.

Then Yankee drew a little nearer to him, as if settling down to work.

"Now look here. You let me talk awhile. I ain't up in your side of the business, but I guess we are tryin' to make the same point. Now supposin' you was in for a hoss race, which I hope ain't no offense, seein' it ain't likely but suppose, and to take first money you had to perdoose a two-fifteen gait. 'Purty good lick,' says you; 'now where will I get the nag?' Then you sets down and thinks, and, says you, 'By gum,' which of course you wouldn't, but supposin' says you, 'a Blue Grass bred is the hoss for that gait'; and you begin to inquire around, but there ain't no Blue Grass bred stock in the country, and that race is creepin' up close. One day, just when you was beginnin' to figure on takin' the dust to the hull field, you sees a colt comin' along the road hittin' up a purty slick gait. 'Hello,' says you, 'that looks likely,' and you begin to negotiate, and you finds out that colt's all right and her time's two-ten. Then you begin to talk about the weather and the crops until you finds out the price, and you offer him half money. Then, when you have fetched him down to the right figure, you pulls out your wad, thinkin' how that colt will make the rest look like a line of fenceposts. 'But hold on,' says you, 'is this here colt Blue Grass bred?' 'Blue Grass! Not much. This here's Grey Eagle stock, North Virginny' says he. 'Don't want her,' says you. 'What's the matter with the colt?' says he. 'Nothin', only she ain't Blue Grass. Got to be Blue Grass.' 'But she's got the gait, ain't she?' 'Yes, the gait's all right, action fine, good-looking, too, nothing wrong, but she ain't Blue Grass bred.' And so you lose your race. Now what kind of a name would you call yourself?"

Peter saw Yankee's point, but he only shook his head more hopelessly than before, and turned to enter the house, followed by Straight Rory, still sighing deeply, and old Donald Ross. But Kenny remained a moment behind the others, and offering his hand to Yankee, said: "You are a right man, and I will be proud to know you better."

Yankee turned a puzzled face to Kenny. "I say," he inquired, in an amazed voice, "do you think he didn't catch on to me?"

Kenny nodded. "Yes, he understood your point."

"But look here," said Yankee, "they don't hold that – that he is –" Yankee paused. The thought was too horrible, and these men were experts, and were supposed to know.

"It's hard to say," said Kenny, diplomatically.

"See here," said Yankee, facing Kenny squarely, "you're a purty level-headed man, and you're up in this business. Do you think with them? No monkeying. Straight talk now." Yankee was in no mood to be trifled with. He was in such deadly earnest that he had forgotten all about Ranald, who was now standing behind him, waiting, with white face and parted lips, for Kenny's answer.

"Whisht!" said Kenny, pointing into the kitchen behind. Yankee looked and saw Bella Peter and her father entering. But Ranald was determined to know Kenny's opinion.

"Mr. Campbell," he whispered, eagerly, and forgetting the respect due to an elder, he grasped Kenny's arm, "do you think with them?"

"That I do not," said Kenny, emphatically, and Yankee, at that word, struck his hand into Kenny's palm with a loud smack.

"I knew blamed well you were not any such dumb fool," he said, softening his speech in deference to Kenny's office and the surrounding circumstances. So saying, he went away to the stable, and when Ranald and his uncle, Macdonald Bhain, followed a little later to put up Peter McGregor's team, they heard Yankee inside, swearing with a fluency and vigor quite unusual with him.

"Whisht, man!" said Macdonald Bhain, sternly. "This is no place or time to be using such language. What is the matter with you, anyway?"

But Macdonald could get no satisfaction out of him, and he said to his nephew, "What is it, Ranald?"

"It is the elders, Peter McRae and Straight Rory," said Ranald, sullenly. "They were saying that – Mack was – that Mack was –"

"Look here, boss," interrupted Yankee, "I ain't well up in Scriptures, and don't know much about these things, and them elders do, and they say – some of them, anyway – are sending Mack to hell. Now, I guess you're just as well up as they are in this business, and I want your solemn opinion." Yankee's face was pale, and his eyes were glaring like a wild beast's. "What I say is," he went on, "if a feller like Mack goes to hell, then there ain't any. At least none to scare me. Where Mack is will be good enough for me. What do you say, boss?"

"Be quiet, man," said Macdonald Bhain, gravely, but kindly. "Do you not know you are near to blasphemy there? But I forgive you for the sore heart you have; and about poor Mack yonder, no one will be able to say for certain. I am a poor sinner, and the only claim I have to God's mercy is the claim of a poor sinner. But I will dare to say that I have hope in the Lord for myself, and I will say that I have a great deal more for Mack."

"I guess that settles it all right, then," said Yankee, drawing a big breath of content and biting off a huge chew from his plug. "But what the blank blank," he went on, savagely, "do these fellers mean, stirring up a man's feelin's like that? Seem to be not a bad sort, either," he added, meditatively.

"Indeed, they are good men," said Macdonald Bhain, "but they will not be knowing Mack as I knew him. He never made any profession at all, but he had the root of the matter in him."

Ranald felt as if he had wakened out of a terrible nightmare, and followed his uncle into the house, with a happier heart than he had known since he had received Yankee's letter.

As they entered the room where the people were gathered, Donald Ross was reading the hundred and third psalm, and the words of love and pity and sympathy were dropping from his kindly lips like healing balm upon the mourning hearts, and as they rose and fell upon the cadences of "Coleshill," the tune Straight Rory always chose for this psalm, the healing sank down into all the sore places, and the peace that passeth understanding began to take possession of them.

Softly and sweetly they sang, the old women swaying with the music:

"For, as the heaven in its height
The earth surmounteth far,
So great to those that do him fear,
His tender mercies are."

When they reached that verse, the mother took up the song and went bravely on through the words of the following verse:

> "As far as east is distant from
> The west, so far hath he
> From us removed, in his love,
> All our iniquity."

As she sang the last words her hand stole over to Bella, who sat beside her quiet but tearless, looking far away. But when the next words rose on the dear old minor strains,

> "Such pity as a father hath
> Unto his children dear,"

Bella's lip began to tremble, and two big tears ran down her pale cheeks, and one could see that the sore pain in her heart had been a little eased.

After Donald Ross had finished his part of the "exercises," he called upon Kenny Crubach, who read briefly, and without comment, the exquisite Scottish paraphrase of Luther's "little gospel":

> "Behold the amazing gift of love
> The Father hath bestowed
> On us, the sinful sons of men,
> To call us sons of God –"

and so on to the end.

All this time Peter McRae, the man of iron, had been sitting with hardening face, his eyes burning in his head like ing coals; and when Donald Ross called upon him for ome words of exhortation and comfort suitable to the occa-ion," without haste and without hesitation the old man rose, and trembling with excitement and emotion, he began abruptly: "An evil spirit has been whispering to me, as to the prophet of old, 'Speak that which is good,' but the Lord hath delivered me from mine enemy, and my answer is, 'As the Lord liveth, what the Lord said unto me, that will I speak'; and it is not easy."

As the old man paused, a visible terror fell upon all the company assembled. The poor mother sat, looking at him with the look of one shrinking from a blow, while Bella Peter's face expressed only startled fear.

"And this is the word of the Lord this night to me," the elder went on, his voice losing its tremor and ringing out strong and clear: "'There is none righteous, no, not one, for all have sinned and come short of the glory of God. He that believeth shall be saved, and he that believeth not shall be damned.' That is my message, and it is laid upon me as a sore burden to hear the voice of the Lord in this solemn Providence, and to warn one and all to flee from the wrath to come."

He paused long, while men could hear their hearts beat. Then, raising his voice, he cried aloud: "Woe is me! Alas! it is a grievous burden. The Lord pity us all, and give grace to this stricken family to kiss the rod that smites."

At this word the old man's voice suddenly broke, and he sat down amid an awful silence. No one could misunderstand his meaning. As the awful horror of it gradually made its way into her mind, Mrs. Cameron threw up her apron over her head and rocked in an agony of sobs, while Long John sat with face white and rigid. Bella Peter, who had been gazing with a fascinated stare upon the old elder's face while he was speaking his terrible words, startled by Mrs. Cameron's sobs, suddenly looked wildly about as if for help, and then, with a wild cry, fled toward the door. But before she had reached it a strong hand caught her and a great voice, deep and tender, commanded her: "Wait, lassie, sit down here a meenute." It was Macdonald Bhain. He stood a short space silent before the people, then, in a voice low, deep, and thrilling, he began: "You have been hearing the word of the Lord through the lips of his servant, and I am not saying but it is the true word; but I believe that the Lord will be speaking by different voices, and although I hev not the gift, yet it is laid upon me to declare what is in my heart, and a sore heart it is, and sore hearts hev we all. But I will be thinking of a fery joyful thing, and that is that 'He came to call, not the righteous, but sinners,' and that in His day many sinners came about Him and not one would He turn away. And I will be remembering a fery great sinner who cried out in his dying hour, 'Lord, remember me,' and not in vain. And I'm thinking that the Lord will be making it easy for men to be saved, and not hard, for He was that anxious about it that He gave up His own life. But it is not given me to argue, only to tell you what I know about the lad who is lying yonder silent. It will be three years since he will be coming on the shanties with me, and from the day that he left his mother's door, till he came back again, never once did he fail me in his duty in the camp, or on the river, or in the town, where it was fery easy to be forgetting. And the boys would be telling me of the times that he would be keeping them out of those places. And it is not soon that Dannie Ross will be forgetting who it was that took him back from the camp when the disease was upon him and all were afraid to go near him, and for seex weeks, by day and by night, watched by him and was not thinking of himself at all. And sure am I that the lessons he would be hearing from his mother and in the Bible class and in the church were not lost on him whatever. For on the river, when the water was quiet and I would be lying in the tent reading, it is often that Mack Cameron would come in and listen to the Word. Aye, he was a good lad" – the great voice shook a little – "he would not be thinking of himself, and at the last, it was for another man he gave his life."

Macdonald stood for a few moments silent, his face working while he struggled with himself. And then all at once he grew calm, and throwing back his head, he looked through the door, and pointing into the darkness, said: "And yonder is the lad, and with him a great company, and his face is smiling, and, oh! it is a good land, a good land!" His voice dropped to a whisper, and he sank into his seat.

"God preserve us!" Kenny Crubach ejaculated; but old Donald Ross rose and said, "Let us call upon the name of the Lord." From his prayer it was quite evident that for him at least all doubts and fears as to poor Mack's state were removed. And even Peter McRae, subdued not so much by any argument of Macdonald Bhain's as by his rapt vision, followed old Donald's prayer with broken words of hope and thanksgiving; and it was Peter who was early at the manse next morning to repeat to the minister the things he had seen and heard the night before. And all next day, where there had been the horror of unnamable fear, hope and peace prevailed.

The service was held under the trees, and while the mother and Bella Peter sat softly weeping, there was no bitterness in their tears, for the sermon breathed of the immortal hope, and the hearts of all were comforted. There was no parade of grief, but after the sermon was over the people filed quietly through the room to take the last look, and then the family, with Bella and her father, were left alone a few moments with their dead, while the Macdonald men kept guard at the door till the time for "the lifting" would come.

After Long John passed out, followed by the family, Macdonald Bhain entered the room, closed the lid down upon the dead face, and gave the command to bear him forth.

So, with solemn dignity, as befitted them, they carried Big Mack from his home to Farquhar McNaughton's light wagon. Along the concession road, past the new church, through the swamp, and on to the old churchyard the long procession slowly moved. There was no unseemly haste, and by the time the last words were spoken, and the mound decently rounded, the long shadows from the woods lay far across the fields. Quietly the people went their ways homeward, back to their life and work, but for many days they carried with them the memory of those funeral scenes. And Ranald, though he came back from Big Mack's grave troubled with questions that refused to be answered, still carried with him a heart healed of the pain that had torn it these last days. He believed it was well with his friend, but about many things he was sorely perplexed, and it was this that brought him again to the minister's wife.

SEED-TIME

The day after Big Mack's funeral, Ranald was busy polishing Lisette's glossy skin, before the stable door. This was his favorite remedy for gloomy thoughts, and Ranald was full of gloomy thoughts to-day. His father, though going about the house, was still weak, and worse than all, was fretting in his weakness. He was oppressed with the terrible fear that he would never again be able to do a man's work, and Ranald knew from the dark look in his father's face that day and night the desire for vengeance was gnawing at his heart, and Ranald also knew something of the bitterness of this desire from the fierce longing that lay deep in his own. Some day, when his fingers would be feeling for LeNoir's throat, he would drink long and fully that sweet draught of vengeance. He knew, too, that it added to the bitterness in his father's heart to know that, in the spring's work that every warm day was bringing nearer, he could take no part; and that was partly the cause of Ranald's gloom. With the slow-moving oxen, he could hardly hope to get the seed in in time, and they needed the crop this year if ever they did, for last year's interest on the mortgage was still unpaid and the next installment was nearly due.

As he was putting the finishing touches upon Lisette's satin skin, Yankee drove up to the yard with his Fox horse and buckboard. His box was strapped on behind, and his blankets, rolled up in a bundle, filled the seat beside him.

"Mornin'," he called to Ranald. "Purty fine shine, that, and purty fine mare, all round," he continued, walking about Lisette and noting admiringly her beautiful proportions.

"Purty fine beast," he said, in a low tone, running his hands down her legs. "Guess you wouldn't care to part with that mare?"

"No," said Ranald, shortly; but as he spoke his heart sank within him.

"Ought to fetch a fairly good figure," continued Yankee, meditatively. "Le's see. She's from La Roque's Lisette, ain't she? Ought to have some speed." He untied Lisette's halter. "Take her down in the yard yonder," he said to Ranald.

Ranald threw the halter over Lisette's neck, sprang on her back, and sent her down the lane at a good smart pace. At the bottom of the lane he wheeled her, and riding low upon her neck, came back to the barn like a whirlwind.

"By jings!" exclaimed Yankee, surprised out of his lazy drawl; "she's got it, you bet your last brick. See here, boy, there's money into that animal. Thought I would like to have her for my buckboard, but I have got an onfortunit conscience that won't let me do up any partner, so I guess I can't make any offer."

Ranald stood beside Lisette, his arm thrown over her beautiful neck, and his hand fondling her gently about the ears. "I will not sell her." His voice was low and fierce, and all the more so because he knew that was just what he would do, and his heart was sick with the pain of the thought.

"I say," said Yankee, suddenly, "cudn't bunk me in your loft, cud you! Can't stand the town. Too close."

The confining limitations of the Twentieth, that metropolitan center of some dozen buildings, including the sawmill and blacksmith shop, were too trying for Yankee's nervous system.

"Yes, indeed," said Ranald, heartily. "We will be very glad to have you, and it will be the very best thing for father."

"S'pose old Fox cud nibble round the *brûlé*," continued Yankee, nodding his head toward his sorrel horse. "Don't think I will do much drivin' machine business. Rather slow." Yankee spent the summer months selling sewing-machines and new patent churns.

"There's plenty of pasture," said Ranald, "and Fox will soon make friends with Lisette. She is very kind, whatever."

"Ain't ever hitched her, have you?" said Yankee.

"No."

"Well, might hitch her up some day. Guess you wudn't hurt the buckboard."

"Not likely," said Ranald, looking at the old, ramshackle affair.

"Used to drive some myself," said Yankee. But to this idea Ranald did not take kindly.

Yankee stood for a few moments looking down the lane and over the fields, and then, turning to Ranald, said, "Guess it's about ready to begin plowin'. Got quite a lot of it to do, too, ain't you?"

"Yes," said Ranald, "I was thinking I would be beginning to-morrow."

"Purty slow business with the oxen. How would it do to hitch up Lisette and old Fox yonder?"

Then Ranald understood the purpose of Yankee's visit.

"I would be very glad," said Ranald, a great load lifting from his heart. "I was afraid of the work with only the oxen." And then, after a pause, he added, "What did you mean about buying Lisette?" He was anxious to have that point settled.

"I said what I meant," answered Yankee. "I thought perhaps you would rather have the money than the colt; but I tell you what, I hain't got money enough to put into that bird, and don't you talk selling to any one till we see her gait hitched up. But I guess a little of the plow won't hurt for a few weeks or so."

Next day Lisette left behind her forever the free, happy days of colthood. At first Ranald was unwilling to trust her to any other hands than his own, but when he saw how skillfully and gently Yankee handled her, soothing her while he harnessed and hitched her up, he recognized that she was safer with Yankee than with himself, and allowed him to have the reins.

They spent the morning driving up and down the lane with Lisette and Fox hitched to the stone-boat. The colt had been kindly treated from her earliest days, and consequently knew nothing of fear. She stepped daintily beside old Fox, fretting and chafing in the harness, but without thought of any violent objection. In the afternoon the colt was put through her morning experience, with the variation that the stone-boat was piled up with a fairly heavy load of earth and stone. And about noon the day following, Lisette was turning her furrow with all the steadiness of a horse twice her age.

Before two weeks were over, Yankee, with the horses, and Ranald, with the oxen, had finished the plowing, and in another ten days the fields lay smooth and black, with the seed harrowed safely in, waiting for the rain.

Yankee's visit had been a godsend, not only to Ranald with his work, but also to Macdonald Dubh. He would talk to the grim, silent man by the hour, after the day's work was done, far into the night, till at length he managed to draw from him the secret of his misery.

"I will never be a man again," he said, bitterly, to Yankee. "And there is the farm all to pay for. I have put it off too long and now it is too late, and it is all because of that – that – brute beast of a Frenchman."

"Mean cuss!" ejaculated Yankee.

"And I am saying," continued Macdonald Dubh, opening his heart still further, "I am saying, it was no fair fight, whatever. I could whip him with one hand. It was when I was pulling out Big Mack, poor fellow, from under the heap, that he took me unawares."

"That's so," assented Yankee. "Blamed lowdown trick."

"And, oh, I will be praying God to give me strength just to meet him! I will ask no more. But," he added, in bitter despair, "there is no use for me to pray. Strength will come to me no more."

"Well," said Yankee, brightly, "needn't worry about that varmint. He ain't worth it, anyhow."

"Aye, he is not worth it, indeed, and that is the man who has brought me to this." That was the bitter part to Macdonald Dubh. A man he despised had beaten him.

"Now look here," said Yankee, "course I ain't much good at this, but if you will just quit worryin', I'll undertake to settle this little account with Mr. LeNware."

"And what good would that be to me?" said Macdonald Dubh. "It is myself that wants to meet him." It was not so much the destruction of LeNoir that he desired as that he should have the destroying of him. While he cherished this feeling in his heart, it was not strange that the minister in his visits found Black Hugh unapproachable, and concluded that he was in a state of settled "hardness of heart." His wife knew better, but even she dared not approach Macdonald Dubh on that subject, which had not been mentioned between them since the morning he had opened his heart to her. The dark, haggard, gloomy face haunted her. She longed to help him to peace. It was this that sent her to his brother, Macdonald Bhain, to whom she told as much of the story as she thought wise.

"I am afraid he will never come to peace with God until he comes to peace with this man," she said, sadly, "and it is a bitter load that he is carrying with him."

"I will talk with him," answered Macdonald Bhain, and at the end of the week he took his way across to his brother's home.

He found him down in the *brûlé* where he spent most of his days toiling hard with his ax, in spite of the earnest entreaties of Ranald. He was butting a big tree that the fire had laid prone, but the ax was falling with the stroke of a weak man.

As he finished his cut, his brother called to him, "That is no work for you, Hugh; that is no work for a man who has been for six weeks in his bed."

"It is work that must be done, however," Black Hugh answered, bitterly.

"Give me the ax," said Macdonald Bhain. He mounted the tree as his brother stepped down, and swung his ax deep into the wood with a mighty blow. Then he remembered, and stopped. He would not add to his brother's bitterness by an exhibition of his mighty, unshaken strength. He stuck the ax into the log, and standing up, looked over the *brûlé*. "It is a fine bit of ground, Hugh, and will raise a good crop of potatoes."

"Aye," said Macdonald Dubh, sadly. "It has lain like this for three years, and ought to have been cleared long ago, if I had been doing my duty."

"Indeed, it will burn all the better for that," said his brother, cheerfully. "And as for the potatoes, there is a bit of my clearing that Ranald might as well use."

But Black Hugh shook his head. "Ranald will use no man's clearing but his own," he said. "I am afraid he has got too much of his father in him for his own good."

Macdonald Bhain glanced at his brother's face with a look of mingled pity and admiration. "Ah," he said, "Hugh, it's a proud man you are. Macdonalds have plenty of that, whatever, and we come by it good enough. Do you remember at home, when our father" – and he went off into a reminiscence of their boyhood days, talking in gentle, kindly, loving tones, till the shadow began to lift from his brother's face, and he, too, began to talk. They spoke of their father, who had always been to them a kind of hero; and of their mother, who had lived, and toiled, and suffered for her family with uncomplaining patience.

"She was a good woman," said Macdonald Bhain, with a note of tenderness in his voice. "And it was the hard load she had to bear, and I would to God she were living now, that I might make up to her something of what she suffered for me."

"And I am thankful to God," said his brother, bitterly, "that she is not here to see me now, for it would but add to the heavy burden I often laid upon her."

"You will not be saying that," said Macdonald Bhain. "But I am saying that the Lord will be honored in you yet."

"Indeed, there is not much for me," said his brother, gloomily, "but the sick-bed and six feet or more of the damp earth."

"Hugh, man," said his brother, hastily, "you must not be talking like that. It is not the speech of a brave man. It is the speech of a man that is beaten in his fight."

"Beaten!" echoed his brother, with a kind of cry. "You have said the word. Beaten it is, and by a man that is no equal of mine. You know that," he said, appealing, almost anxiously, to his brother. "You know that well. You know that I am brought to this" – he held up his gaunt, bony hands – "by a man that is no equal of mine, and I will never be able to look him in the face and say as much to him. But if the Almighty would send him to hell, I would be following him there."

"Whisht, Hugh," said Macdonald Bhain, in a voice of awe. "It is a terrible word you have said, and may the Lord forgive you."

"Forgive me!" echoed his brother, in a kind of frenzy. "Indeed, he will not be doing that. Did not the minister's wife tell me as much?"

"No, no," said his brother. "She would not be saying that."

"Indeed, that is her very word," said Black Hugh.

"She could not say that," said his brother, "for it is not the Word of God."

"Indeed," replied Black Hugh, like a man who had thought it all out, "she would be reading it out of the Book to me that unless I would be forgiving, that – that –" he paused, not being able to find a word, but went on – "then I need not hope to be forgiven my own self."

"Yes, yes. That is true," assented Macdonald Bhain. "But, by the grace of God, you will forgive, and you will be forgiven."

"Forgive!" cried Black Hugh, his face convulsed with passion. "Hear me!" – he raised his hand to heaven. – "If I ever forgive –"

But his brother caught his arm and drew it down swiftly, saying: "Whisht, man. Don't tempt the Almighty." Then he added, "You would not be shutting yourself out from the presence of the Lord and from the presence of those he has taken to himself."

His brother stood silent a few moments, his hard, dark face swept with a storm of emotions. Then he said, brokenly: "It is not for me, I doubt."

But his brother caught him by the arm and said to him, "Hear me, Hugh. It is for you."

They walked on in silence till they were near the house. Ranald and Yankee were driving their teams into the yard.

"That is a fine lad," said Macdonald Bhain, pointing to Ranald.

"Aye," said his brother; "it is a pity he has not a better chance. He is great for his books, but he has no chance whatever, and he will be a bowed man before he has cleared this farm and paid the debt on it."

"Never you fear," said his brother. "Ranald will do well. But, man, what a size he is!"

"He is that," said his father, proudly. "He is as big as his father, and I doubt some day he may be as good a man as his uncle."

"God grant he may be a better!" said Macdonald Bhain, reverently.

"If he be as good," said his brother, kindly, "I will be content; but I will not be here to see it."

"Whisht, man," said his brother, hastily. "You are not to speak such things, nor have them in your mind."

"Ah," said Macdonald Dubh, sadly, "my day is not far off, and that I know right well."

Macdonald Bhain flung his arm hastily round his brother's shoulder. "Do not speak like that, Hugh," he said, his voice breaking suddenly. And then he drew away his arm as if ashamed of his emotion, and said, with kindly dignity, "Please God, you will see many days yet, and see your boy come to honor among men."

But Black Hugh only shook his head in silence.

Before they came to the door, Macdonald Bhain said, with seeming indifference, "You have not been to church since you got up, Hugh. You will be going to-morrow, if it is a fine day?"

"It is too long a walk, I doubt," answered his brother.

"That it is, but Yankee will drive you in his buckboard," said Macdonald Bhain.

"In the buckboard?" said Macdonald Dubh. "And, indeed, I was never in a buckboard in my life."

"It is not too late to begin to-morrow," said his brother, "and it will do you good."

"I doubt that," said Black Hugh, gloomily. "The church will not be doing me much good any more."

"Do not say such a thing; and Yankee will drive you in his buckboard to-morrow."

His brother did not promise, but next day the congregation received a shock of surprise to see Macdonald Dubh walk down the aisle to his place in the church. And through all the days of the spring and summer his place was never empty; and though the shadow never lifted from his face, the minister's wife felt comforted about him, and waited for the day of his deliverance.

THE LOGGING BEE

Macdonald Bhain's visit to his brother was fruitful in another way. After taking counsel with Yankee and Kirsty, he resolved that he would speak to his neighbors and make a "bee," to attack the *brûlé*. He knew better than to consult either his brother or his nephew, feeling sure that their Highland pride would forbid accepting any such favor, and all the more because it seemed to be needed. But without their leave the bee was arranged, and in the beginning of the following week the house of Macdonald Dubh was thrown into a state of unparalleled confusion, and Kirsty went about in a state of dishevelment that gave token that the daily struggle with dirt had reached the acute stage. From top to bottom, inside and outside, everything that could be scrubbed was scrubbed, and then she settled about her baking, but with all caution, lest she should excite her brother's or her nephew's suspicion. It was a good thing that little baking was required, for the teams that brought the men with their axes and logging-chains for the day's work at the *brûlé* brought also their sisters and mothers with baskets of provisions. A logging bee without the sisters and mothers with their baskets would hardly be an unmixed blessing.

The first man to arrive with his team was Peter McGregor's Angus, and with him came his sister Bella. He was shortly afterward followed by other teams in rapid succession – the Rosses, the McKerachers, the Camerons, both Don and Murdie, the Rory McCuaigs, the McRaes two or three families of them, the Frasers, and others – till some fifteen teams and forty men, and boys, who thought themselves quite men, lined up in front of the *brûlé*.

The bee was a great affair, for Macdonald Bhain was held in high regard by the people; and besides this, the misfortune that had befallen his brother, and the circumstances under which it had overtaken him, had aroused in the community a very deep sympathy for him, and people were glad of the opportunity to manifest this sympathy. And more than all, a logging bee was an event that always promised more or less excitement and social festivity.

Yankee was "boss" for the day. This position would naturally have fallen to Macdonald Bhain, but at his brother's bee, Macdonald Bhain shrank from taking the leading place.

The men with the axes went first, chopping up the half-burned logs into lengths suitable for the burning-piles, clearing away the brushwood, and cutting through the big roots of the fire-eaten stumps so that they might more easily be pulled. Then followed the teams with their logging-chains, hauling the logs to the piles, jerking out and drawing off the stumps whose huge roots stuck up high into the air, and drawing great heaps of brush-wood to aid in reducing the heavy logs to ashes. At each log-pile stood a man with a hand-spike to help the driver to get the log into position, a work requiring strength and skill, and above all, a knowledge of the ways of logs which comes only by experience. It was at this work that Macdonald Bhain shone. With his mighty strength he could hold steady one end of a log until the team could haul the other into its place.

The stump-pulling was always attended with more or less interest and excitement. Stumps, as well as logs, have their ways, and it takes a long experience to understand the ways of stumps.

In stump-hauling, young Aleck McGregor was an expert. He rarely failed to detect the weak side of a stump. He knew his team, and what was of far greater importance, his team knew him. They were partly of French-Canadian stock, not as large as Farquhar McNaughton's big, fat blacks, but "as full of spirit as a bottle of whisky," as Aleck himself would say. Their first tentative pulls at the stump were taken with caution, until their driver and themselves had taken the full measure of the strength of the enemy. But when once Aleck had made up his mind that victory was possible, and had given them the call for the final effort, then his team put their bodies and souls into the pull, and never drew back till something came. Their driver was accustomed to boast that never yet had they failed to honor his call.

Farquhar's handsome blacks, on the other hand, were never handled after this fashion. They were slow and sure and steady, like their driver. Their great weight gave them a mighty advantage in a pull, but never, in all the solemn course of their existence, had they thrown themselves into any doubtful trial of strength. In a slow, steady haul they were to be relied upon; but they never could be got to jerk, and a jerk is an important feature in stump-hauling tactics. To-day, however, a new experience was awaiting them. Farquhar was an old man and slow, and Yankee, while he was unwilling to hurry him, was equally unwilling that his team should not do a full day's work. He persuaded Farquhar that his presence was necessary at one of the piles, not with the hand-spike, but simply to superintend the arranging of the mass for burning. "For it ain't every man," Yankee declared, "could build a pile to burn." As for his team, Yankee persuaded the old man that Ranald was unequaled in handling horses; that last winter no driver in the camp was up to him. Reluctantly Farquhar handed his team over to Ranald, and stood for some time watching the result of the new combination.

Ranald was a born horseman. He loved horses and understood them. Slowly he moved the blacks at their work, knowing that horses are sensitive to a new hand and voice, and that he must adapt himself to their ways, if he would bring them at last to his. Before long Farquhar was contented to go off to his pile, satisfied that his team was in good hands, and not sorry to be relieved of the necessity of hurrying his pace through the long, hot day, as would have been necessary in order to keep up with the other drivers.

For each team a strip of the *brûlé* was marked out to clear after the axes. The logs, brush, and stumps had to be removed and dragged to the burning-piles. Aleck, with his active, invincible French-Canadians, Ranald with Farquhar's big, sleek blacks, and Don with his father's team, worked side by side. A contest was inevitable, and before an hour had passed Don and Aleck, while making a great show of deliberation, were striving for the first place, with Aleck easily leading. Like a piece of machinery, Aleck and his team worked together. Quickly and neatly both driver and horses moved about their work with perfect understanding of each other. With hardly a touch of the lines, but almost entirely by word of command, Aleck guided his team. And when he took up the whiffletrees to swing them around to a log or stump, his horses wheeled at once into place. It was beautiful to see them, wheeling, backing, hauling, pulling, without loss of time or temper.

With Don and his team it was all hard work. His horses were willing and quick enough, but they were ill-trained and needed constant tugging at the lines. In vain Don shouted and cracked his whip, hurrying his team to his pile and back again; the horses only grew more and more awkward, while they foamed and fretted and tired themselves out.

Behind came Ranald, still humoring his slow-going team with easy hand and quiet voice. But while he refrained from hurrying his horses, he himself worked hard, and by his good judgment and skill with the chain, and in skidding the logs into his pile, in which his training in the shanty had made him more than a match for any one in the field, many minutes were saved.

When the cowbell sounded for dinner, Aleck's team stepped off for the barn, wet, but fresh and frisky as ever, and in perfect heart. Don's horses appeared fretted and jaded, while Ranald brought in his blacks with their glossy skins white with foam where the harness had chafed, but unfretted, and apparently as ready for work as when they began.

"You have spoiled the shine of your team," said Aleck, looking over Ranald's horses as he brought them up to the trough. "Better turn them out for the afternoon. They can't stand much more of that pace."

Aleck was evidently trying to be good-natured, but he could not hide the sneer in his tone. They had neither of them forgotten the incident at the church door, and both felt that it would not be closed until more had been said about it. But to-day, Ranald was in the place of host, and it behooved him to be courteous, and Aleck was in good humor with himself, for his team had easily led the field; and besides, he was engaged in a kind and neighborly undertaking, and he was too much of a man to spoil it by any private grudge. He would have to wait for his settlement with Ranald.

During the hour and a half allowed for dinner, Ranald took his horses to the well, washed off their legs, removed their harness, and led them to a cool spot behind the barn, and there, while they munched their oats, he gave them a good hard rub-down, so that when he brought them into the field again, his team looked as glossy and felt as fresh as before they began the day's work.

As Ranald appeared on the field with his glossy blacks, Aleck glanced at the horses, and began to feel that, in the contest for first place, it was Ranald he had to fear, with his cool, steady team, rather than Don. Not that any suspicion crossed his mind that Farquhar McNaughton's sleek, slow-going horses could ever hold their own with his, but he made up his mind that Ranald, at least, was worth watching.

"Bring up your gentry," he called to Ranald, "if you are not too fine for common folks. Man, that team of yours," he continued, "should never be put to work like this. Their feet should never be off pavement."

"Never you mind," said Ranald, quietly. "I am coming after you, and perhaps before night the blacks may show you their heels yet."

"There's lots of room," said Aleck, scornfully, and they both set to work with all the skill and strength that lay in themselves and in their teams.

For the first hour or two Ranald was contented to follow, letting his team take their way, but saving every moment he could by his own efforts. So that, without fretting his horses in the least, or without moving them perceptibly out of their ordinary gait, he found himself a little nearer to Aleck than he had been at noon; but the heavy lifting and quick work began to tell upon him. His horses, he knew, would not stand very much hurrying. They were too fat for any extra exertion in such heat, and so Ranald was about to resign himself to defeat, when he observed that in the western sky clouds were coming up. At the same time a cool breeze began to blow, and he took fresh heart. If he could hurry his team a little more, he might catch Aleck yet; so he held his own a little longer, preserving the same steady pace, until the clouds from the west had covered all the sky. Then gradually he began to quicken his horses' movements and to put them on heavier loads. Wherever opportunity offered, instead of a single log, or at most two, he would take three or four for his load; and in ways known only to horsemen, he began to stir up the spirit of his team, and to make them feel something of his own excitement.

To such good purpose did he plan, and so nobly did his team respond to his quiet but persistent pressure, that, ere Aleck was aware, Ranald was up on his flank; and then they each knew that until the supper-bell rang he would have to use to the best advantage every moment of time and every ounce of strength in himself and his team if he was to win first place.

Somehow the report of the contest went over the field, till at length it reached the ears of Farquhar. At once the old man, seized with anxiety for his team, and moved by the fear of what Kirsty might say if the news ever reached her ears, set off across the *brûlé* to remonstrate with Ranald, and if necessary, rescue his team from peril.

But Don saw him coming, and knowing that every moment was precious, and dreading lest the old man would snatch from Ranald the victory which seemed to be at least possible for him, he arrested Farquhar with a call for assistance with a big log, and then engaged him in conversation upon the merits of his splendid team.

"And look," cried he, admiringly, "how Ranald is handling them! Did you ever see the likes of that?"

The old man stood watching for a few moments, doubtfully enough, while Don continued pouring forth the praises of his horses, and the latter, as he noticed Farquhar's eyes glisten with pride, ventured to hint that before the day was done "he would make Aleck McRae and his team look sick. And without a hurt to the blacks, too," he put in, diplomatically, "for Ranald is not the man to hurt a team." And as Farquhar stood and watched Ranald at his work, and noted with surprise how briskly and cleverly the blacks swung into their places, and detected also with his experienced eye that Aleck was beginning to show signs of hurry, he entered into the spirit of the contest, and determined to allow his team to win victory for themselves and their driver if they could.

The ax men had finished their "stent." It wanted still an hour of supper-time, and surely if slowly, Ranald was making toward first place. The other teams were left far behind with their work, and the whole field began to center attention upon the two that were now confessedly engaged in desperate conflict at the front. One by one the ax men drew toward the end of the field, where Ranald and Aleck were fighting out their fight, all pretense of deliberation on the part of the drivers having by this time been dropped. They no longer walked as they hitched their chains about the logs or stumps, but sprang with eager haste to their work. One by one the other teamsters abandoned their teams and moved across the field to join the crowd already gathered about the contestants. Among them came Macdonald Bhain, who had been working at the farthest corner of the *brûlé*. As soon as he arrived upon the scene, and understood what was going on, he cried to Ranald: "That will do now, Ranald; it will be time to quit."

Ranald was about to stop, and indeed had checked his horses, when Aleck, whose blood was up, called out tauntingly, "Aye, it would be better for him and his horses to stop. They need it bad enough."

This was too much for even Farquhar's sluggish blood. "Let them go, Ranald!" he cried. "Let them go, man! Never you fear for the horses, if you take down the spunk o' yon crowing cock."

It was just what Ranald needed to spur him on – a taunt from his foe and leave from Farquhar to push his team.

Before each lay a fallen tree cut into lengths and two or three half-burned stumps. Ranald's tree was much the bigger. A single length would have been an ordinary load for the blacks, but their driver felt that their strength and spirit were both equal to much more than this. He determined to clear away the whole tree at a single load. As soon as he heard Farquhar's voice, he seized hold of the whiffletrees, struck his team a sharp blow with the lines – their first blow that day – swung them round to the top of the tree, ran the chain through its swivel, hooked an end round each of the top lengths, swung them in toward the butt, unhooked his chain, gathered all three lengths into a single load, faced his horses toward the pile, and shouted at them. The blacks, unused to this sort of treatment, were prancing with excitement, and when the word came they threw themselves into their collars with a fierceness that nothing could check, and amid the admiring shouts of the crowd, tore the logs through the black soil and landed them safely at the pile. It was the work of only a few minutes to unhitch the chain, haul the logs, one by one, into place, and dash back with his team at the gallop for the stumps, while Aleck had still another load of logs to draw.

Ranald's first stump came out with little trouble, and was borne at full speed to the pile. The second stump gave him more difficulty, and before it would yield he had to sever two or three of its thickest roots.

Together the teams swung round to their last stump. The excitement in the crowd was intense. Aleck's team was moving swiftly and with the steadiness of clockwork. The blacks were frantic with excitement and hard to control. Ranald's last stump was a pine of medium size, whose roots were partly burned away. It looked like an easy victim. Aleck's was an ugly-looking little elm.

Ranald thought he would try his first pull without the use of the ax. Quickly he backed up his team to the stump, passed the chain round a root on the far side, drew the big hook far up the chain, hitched it so as to give the shortest possible draught, threw the chain over the top of the stump to give it purchase, picked up his lines, and called to his team. With a rush the blacks went at it. The chain slipped up on the root, tightened, bit into the wood, and then the blacks flung back. Ranald swung them round the point and tried them again, but still the stump refused to budge.

All this time he could hear Aleck chopping furiously at his elm-roots, and he knew that unless he had his stump out before his rival had his chain hitched for the pull the victory was lost.

For a moment or two he hesitated, looking round for the ax.

"Try them again, Ranald," cried Farquhar. "Haw them a bit."

Once more Ranald picked up the lines, swung his horses round to the left, held them steady a moment or two, and then with a yell sent them at their pull. Magnificently the blacks responded, furiously tearing up the ground with their feet. A moment or two they hung straining on their chain, refusing to come back, when slowly the stump began to move.

"You have got it," cried Farquhar. "Gee them a point or two."

But already Ranald had seen that this was necessary, and once more backed his team to readjust the chain which had slipped off the top. As he fastened the hook he heard a sharp "Back!" behind him, and he knew that the next moment Aleck's team would be away with their load. With a yell he sprang at his lines, lashed the blacks over the back, and called to them once more. Again his team responded, and with a mighty heave, the stump came slowly out, carrying with it what looked like half a ton of earth. But even as it heaved, he heard Aleck's call and the answering crash, and before he could get his team a-going, the French-Canadians were off for their pile at a gallop, with the lines flying in the air behind them. A moment later he followed, the blacks hauling their stump at a run.

Together he and Aleck reached the pile. It only remained now to unhook the chain. In vain he tugged and hauled. The chain was buried deep beneath the stump and refused to move, and before he could swing his team about and turn the stump over, he heard Aleck's shout of victory.

But as he dropped his chain and was leisurely backing his horses, he heard old Farquhar cry, "Hurry, man! Hurry, for the life of you!"

Without waiting to inquire the reason, Ranald wheeled his team, gave the stump a half turn, released his chain, and drove off from the pile, to find Aleck still busy hooking his chain to his whiffletree.

Aleck had had the same difficulty in freeing his chain as Ranald, but instead of trying to detach it from the stump, he had unhooked the other end, and then, with a mighty backward jerk, had snatched it from the stump. But before he could attach it to his place on the whiffletree again, Ranald stood ready for work.

"A win, lad! A win!" cried old Farquhar, more excited than he had been for years.

"It is no win," said Aleck, hotly.

"No, no, lads," said Macdonald Bhain, before Farquhar could reply. "It is as even a match as could well be. It is fine teams you both have got, and you have handled them well."

But all the same, Ranald's friends were wildly enthusiastic over what they called his victory, and Don could hardly keep his hands off him, for very joy.

Aleck, on the other hand, while claiming the victory because his team was at the pile first, was not so sure of it but that he was ready to fight with any one venturing to dispute his claim. But the men all laughed at him and his rage, until he found it wiser to be good-humored about it.

"Yon lad will be making as good a man as yourself," said Farquhar, enthusiastically, to Macdonald Bhain, as Ranald drove his team to the stable.

"Aye, and a better, pray God," said Macdonald Bhain, fervently, looking after Ranald with loving eyes. There was no child in his home, and his brother's son was as his own.

Meanwhile Don had hurried on, leaving his team with Murdie that he might sing Ranald's praises to "the girls," with whom Ranald was highly popular, although he avoided them, or perhaps because he did so, the ways of women being past understanding.

To Mrs. Murray and Maimie, who with the minister and Hughie, had come over to the supper, he went first with his tale. Graphically he depicted the struggle from its beginning to the last dramatic rush to the pile, dilating upon Ranald's skill and pluck, and upon the wonderful and hitherto unknown virtues of Farquhar's shiny blacks.

"You ought to see them!" cried Don. "You bet they never moved in their lives the way they did today. Tied him!" he continued. "Tied him! Beat him, I say, but Macdonald Bhain says 'Tied him' – Aleck McRae, who thinks himself so mighty smart with his team."

Don forgot in his excitement that the McRaes and their friends were there in numbers.

"So he is," cried Annie Ross, one of Aleck's admirers. "There is not a man in the Indian Lands that can beat Aleck and his team."

"Well," exulted Don, "a boy came pretty near it to-day."

But Annie only stuck out her lip at him in the inimitable female manner, and ran off to add to the mischief that Don had already made between Ranald and his rival.

But now the day's work was over, and the hour for the day's event had come, for supper was the great event to which all things moved at bees. The long tables stood under the maple trees, spread with the richest, rarest, deadliest dainties known to the housewives and maidens of the countryside. About the tables stood in groups the white-aproned girls, tucked and frilled, curled and ribboned into all degrees of bewitching loveliness. The men hurried away with their teams, and then gave themselves to the serious duty of getting ready for supper, using many pails of water in their efforts to remove the black from the burnt wood of the *brûlé*.

At length the women lost all patience with them, and sent Annie Ross, with two or three companions, to call them to supper. With arms intertwined, and with much chattering and giggling, the girls made their way to the group of men, some of whom were engaged in putting the finishing touches to their toilet.

"Supper is ready," cried Annie, "and long past ready. You need not be trying to fix yourselves up so fine. You are just as bad as any girls. Oh!" Her speech ended in a shriek, which was echoed by the others, for Aleck McRae rushed at them, stretching out his black hands toward them. But they were too quick for him, and fled for protection to the safe precincts of the tables.

At length, when the last of the men had made themselves, as they thought, presentable, they began to make their approach to the tables, slowly and shyly for the most part, each waiting for the other. Aleck McRae, however, knew little of shyness, but walked past the different groups of girls, throwing on either hand a smile, a wink, or a word, as he might find suitable.

Suddenly he came upon the group where the minister's wife and her niece were standing. Here, for the moment, his ease forsook him, but Mrs. Murray came to meet him with outstretched hand.

"So you still retain your laurels?" she said, with a frank smile. "I hear it was a great battle."

Aleck shook hands with her rather awkwardly. He was not on the easiest terms with the minister and his wife. He belonged distinctly to the careless set, and rather enjoyed the distinction.

"Oh, it was not much," he said; "the teams were well matched."

"Oh, I should like to have been there. You should have told us beforehand."

"Oh, it was more than I expected myself," he said. "I didn't think it was in Farquhar's team."

He could not bring himself to give any credit to Ranald, and though Mrs. Murray saw this, she refused to notice it. She was none the less anxious to win Aleck's confidence, because she was Ranald's friend.

"Do you know my niece?" she said, turning to Maimie.

Aleck looked into Maimie's face with such open admiration that she felt the blush come up in her cheeks.

"Indeed, she is worth knowing, but I don't think she will care to take such a hand as that," he said, stretching out a hand still grimy in spite of much washing. But Maimie had learned something since coming to her aunt, and she no longer judged men by the fit of their clothes, or the color of their skin, or the length of their hair; and indeed, as she looked at Aleck, with his close-buttoned smock, and overalls with the legs tucked neatly into the tops of his boots, she thought he was the trimmest figure she had seen since coming to the country. She took Aleck's hand and shook it warmly, the full admiration in his handsome black eyes setting her blood tingling with that love of conquest that lies in every woman's heart. So she flung out her flag of war, and smiled back at him her sweetest.

"You have a fine team, I hear," she said, as her aunt moved away to greet some of the other men, who were evidently waiting to get a word with her.

"That I have, you better believe," replied Aleck, proudly.

"It was very clever of Ranald to come so near beating you, wasn't it?" she said, innocently. "He must be a splendid driver."

"He drives pretty well," admitted Aleck. "He did nothing else all last winter in the shanties."

"He is so young, too," went on Maimie. "Just a boy, isn't he?"

Aleck was not sure how to take this. "He does not think so," he answered, shortly. "He thinks he is no end of a man, but he will have to learn something before he is much older."

"But he can drive, you say," continued Maimie, wickedly keeping her finger on the sore spot.

"Oh, pshaw!" replied Aleck, boldly. "You think a lot of him, don't you? And I guess you are a pair."

Maimie tossed her head at this. "We are very good friends, of course," she said, lightly. "He is a very nice boy, and we are all fond of him; but he is just a boy; he is Hughie's great friend."

"A boy, is he?" laughed Aleck. "That may be, but he is very fond of you, whatever, and indeed, I don't wonder at that. Anybody would be," he added, boldly.

"You don't know a bit about it," said Maimie, with cheeks glowing.

"About what?"

"About Ranald and – and – what you said."

"What I said? About being fond of you? Indeed, I know all about that. The boys are all broke up, not to speak of myself."

This was going a little too fast for Maimie. She knew nothing, as yet, of the freedom of country banter. She was new to the warfare, but she was not going to lower her flag or retreat. She changed the subject. "Your team must have been very tired."

"Tired!" exclaimed Aleck, "not a bit. They will go home like birds. Come along with me, and you will see."

Maimie gasped. "I –" she hesitated, glanced past Aleck, blushed, and stammered.

Aleck turned about quickly and saw Ranald staring at Maimie. "Oh," he said, banteringly, "I see. You would not be allowed."

"Allowed!" echoed Maimie. "And why not, pray? Who will hinder me?"

But Aleck only shrugged his shoulders and looked at Ranald, who passed on to his place at the table, black as a thunder-cloud. Maimie was indignant at him. What right had he to stare and look so savage? She would just show him. So she turned once more to Aleck, and with a gay laugh, cried, "Some day I will accept your invitation, so just make ready."

"Any day, or every day, and the more days the better," cried Aleck, as he sat down at the table, where all had now taken their places.

The supper was a great success. With much laughter and chaffing, the girls flitted from place to place, pouring cups of tea and passing the various dishes, urging the men to eat, till, as Don said, they were "full to the neck."

When all had finished, Mr. Murray, who sat at the head of the table, rose in his place and said: "Gentlemen, before we rise from this table, which has been spread so bountifully for us, I wish to return thanks on behalf of Mr. Macdonald to the neighbors and friends who have gathered to-day to assist in this work. Mr. Macdonald asked me to say that he is all the more surprised at this kindness, in that he feels himself to be so unworthy of it. I promised to speak this word for him, but I do not agree with the sentiment. Mr. Macdonald is a man whom we all love, and in whose misfortune we deeply sympathize, and I only hope that this Providence may be greatly blessed to him, and that we will all come to know him better, and to see God's hand in his misfortune."

The minister then, after some further remarks expressive

of the good will of the neighbors for Mr. Macdonald, and in appreciation of the kind spirit that prompted the bee, returned thanks, and the supper was over.

As the men were leaving the table, Aleck watched his opportunity and called to Maimie, when he was sure Ranald could hear, "Well, when will you be ready for that drive?"

And Maimie, who was more indignant at Ranald than ever because he had ignored all her advances at supper, and had received her congratulations upon his victory with nothing more than a grunt, answered Aleck brightly. "Oh, any day that you happen to remember."

"Remember!" cried Aleck; "then that will be every day until our ride comes off."

A few minutes later, as Ranald was hitching up Farquhar's team, Aleck passed by, and in great good humor with himself, chaffingly called out to Ranald in the presence of a number of the men, "That's a fine girl you've got, Ranald. But you better keep your eye on her."

Ranald made no reply. He was fast losing command of himself.

"Pretty skittish to handle, isn't she?" continued Aleck.

"What y're talkin' 'bout? That Lisette mare?" said Yankee, walking round to Ranald's side. "Purty slick beast, that. Guess there ain't anythin' in this country will make her take dust."

Then in a low voice he said to Ranald, hurriedly, "Don't you mind him; don't you mind him. You can't touch him to-day, on your own place. Let me handle him."

"No," said Aleck. "We were talking about another colt of Ranald's."

"What's that?" said Yankee, pretending not to hear. "Yes, you bet," he continued. "Ranald can handle her all right. He knows something about horses, as I guess you have found out, perhaps, by this time. Never saw anything so purty. Didn't know your team had got that move in them, Mr. McNaughton," Yankee went on to Farquhar, who had just come up.

"Indeed, they are none the worse of it," said Farquhar, rubbing his hands over the sleek sides of his horses.

"Worse!" cried Yankee. "They're worth a hundred dollars more from this day on."

"I don't know that. The hundred dollars ought to go upon the driver," said Farquhar, putting his hand kindly upon Ranald's shoulder.

But this Ranald warmly repudiated. "They are a great team," he said to Farquhar. "And they could do better than they did to-day if they were better handled."

"Indeed, it would be difficult to get that," said Farquhar, "for, in my opinion, there is not a man in the country that could handle them as well."

This was too much for Aleck, who, having by this time got his horses hitched, mounted his wagon seat and came round to the door at a gallop.

"Saved you that time, my boy," said Yankee to Ranald. "You would have made a fool of yourself in about two minutes more, I guess."

But Ranald was still too wrathful to be grateful for Yankee's help. "I will be even with him some day," he said, between his teeth.

"I guess you will have to learn two or three things first," said Yankee, slowly.

"What things?"

"Well, how to use your head, first place, and then how to use your hands. He is too heavy for you. He would crumple you up in a couple of minutes."

"Let him, then," said Ranald, recklessly.

"Rather onpleasant. Better wait awhile till you learn what I told you."

"Yankee," said Ranald, after a pause, "will you show me?"

"Why, sartin sure," said Yankee, cheerfully. "You have got to lick him some day, or he won't be happy; and by jings! it will be worth seein', too."

By this time Farquhar had come back from saying good by to Macdonald Dubh and Mr. and Mrs. Murray, who were remaining till the last.

"You will be a man yet," said Farquhar, shaking Ranald's hand. "You have got the patience and the endurance." These were great virtues in Farquhar's opinion.

"Not much patience, I am afraid," said Ranald, "But I am glad you trusted me with your team."

"And any day you want them you can have them," said Farquhar, his reckless mood leading him to forget Kirsty for the moment.

"Thank you, sir," said Ranald, wondering what Kirsty would look like should he ever venture to claim Farquhar's offer.

One by one the teams drove away with their loads, till only the minister and his party were left. Away under the trees Mr. Murray was standing, earnestly talking to Macdonald Dubh. He had found the opportunity he had long waited for and was making the most of it. Mrs. Murray was busy with Kirsty, and Maimie and Hughie came toward the stable where Yankee and Ranald were still standing. As soon as Ranald saw them approaching he said to Yankee, abruptly, "I am going to get the minister's horse," and disappeared into the stable. Nor did he come forth again till he heard his father calling to him: "What is keeping you, Ranald? The minister is waiting for his horse."

"So you won a great victory, Ranald, I hear," said the minister, as Ranald brought Black to the door.

"It was a tie," said Ranald.

"Oh, Ranald!" cried Hughie, "you beat him. Everybody says so. You had your chain hitched up and everything before Aleck."

"I hear it was a great exhibition, not only of skill, but of endurance and patience, Ranald," said the minister. "And these are noble virtues. It is a great thing to be able to endure."

But Ranald made no reply, busying himself with Black's bridle. Mrs. Murray noticed his gloom and guessed its cause.

"We will see you at the Bible class, Ranald," she said, kindly, but still Ranald remained silent.

"Can you not speak, man?" said his father. "Do you not hear the minister's wife talking to you?"

"Yes," said Ranald, "I will be there."

"We will be glad to see you," said Mrs. Murray, offering him her hand. "And you might come in with Hughie for a few minutes afterward," she continued, kindly, for she noted the misery in his face.

"And we will be glad to see you, too, Mr. Macdonald, if it would not be too much for you, and if you do not scorn a woman's teaching."

"Indeed, I would be proud," said Macdonald Dubh, courteously, "as far as that is concerned, for I hear there are better men than me attending."

"I am sure Mrs. Murray will be glad to see you, Mr. Macdonald," said the minister.

"I will be thinking of it," said Macdonald Dubh, cautiously. "And you are both very kind, whatever," he said, losing for a time his habitual gloom.

"Well, then, I will look for you both," said Mrs. Murray, as they were about to drive off, "so do not disappoint me."

"Good by, Ranald," said Maimie, offering Ranald her hand.

"Good by," said Ranald, holding her hand for a moment and looking hard into her eyes, "and I hope you will enjoy your ride, whatever."

Then Maimie understood Ranald's savage manner, and as she thought it over she smiled to herself. She was taking her first sips of that cup, to woman's lips the sweetest, and she found it not unpleasant. She had succeeded in making one man happy and another miserable. But it was when she said to herself, "Poor Ranald!" that she smiled most sweetly.

SHE WILL NOT FORGET

If Mrs. Murray was not surprised to see Macdonald Dubh and Yankee walk in on Sabbath evening and sit down in the back seat, her class were. Indeed the appearance of these two men at the class was considered an event so extraordinary as to give a decided shock to those who regularly attended, and their presence lent to the meeting an unusual interest, and an undertone of excitement. To see Macdonald Dubh, whose attendance at the regular Sabbath services was something unusual, present at a religious meeting which no one would consider it a duty to attend, was enough in itself to excite surprise, but when Yankee came in and sat beside him, the surprise was considerably intensified. For Yankee was considered to be quite outside the pale, and indeed, in a way, incapable of religious impression. No one expected Yankee to be religious. He was not a Presbyterian, knew nothing of the Shorter Catechism, not to speak of the Confession of Faith, and consequently was woefully ignorant of the elements of Christian knowledge that were deemed necessary to any true religious experience.

It was rumored that upon Yankee's first appearance in the country, some few years before, he had, in an unguarded moment, acknowledged that his people had belonged to the Methodists, and that he himself "leaned toward" that peculiar sect. Such a confession was in itself enough to stamp him, in the eyes of the community, as one whose religious history must always be attended with more or less uncertainty. Few of them had ever seen a Methodist in the flesh. There were said to be some at Moose Creek (Mooscrick, as it was called), but they were known only by report. The younger and more untraveled portion of the community thought of them with a certain amount of awe and fear.

It was no wonder, then, that Yankee's appearance in Bible class produced a sensation. It was an evening of sensations, for not only were Macdonald Dubh and Yankee present, but Aleck McRae had driven up a load of people from below the Sixteenth. Ranald regarded his presence with considerable contempt.

"It is not much he cares for the Bible class, whatever," he confided to Don, who was sitting beside him.

But more remarkable and disturbing to Ranald than the presence of Aleck McRae, was that of a young man sitting between Hughie and Maimie in the minister's pew. He was evidently from the city. One could see that from his fine clothes and his white shirt and collar. Ranald looked at him with deepening contempt. "Pride" was written all over him. Not only did he wear fine clothes, and a white shirt and collar, but he wore them without any sign of awkwardness or apology in his manner, and indeed as if he enjoyed them. But the crowning proof of his "pride," Don noted with unutterable scorn.

"Look at him," he said, "splits his head in the middle."

Ranald found himself wondering how the young fop would look sitting in a pool of muddy water. How insufferable the young fellow's manners were! He sat quite close to Maimie, now and then whispering to her, evidently quite ignorant of how to behave in church. And Maimie, who ought to know better, was acting most disgracefully as well, whispering back and smiling right into his face. Ranald was thoroughly ashamed of her. He could not deny that the young fellow was handsome, hatefully so, but he was evidently stuck full of conceit, and as he let his eyes wander over the congregation assembled, with a bold and critical stare, making remarks to Maimie in an undertone which could be heard over the church, Ranald felt his fingers twitching. The young man was older than Ranald, but Ranald would have given a good deal for an opportunity to "take him with one hand."

At this point Ranald's reflections were interrupted by Mrs. Murray rising to open the class.

"Will some one suggest a Psalm?" she asked, her cheek, usually pale, showing a slight color. It was always an ordeal for her to face her class, ever since the men had been allowed to come, and the first moments were full of trial to her. Only her conscience and her fine courage kept her from turning back from this, her path of duty.

At once, from two or three came responses to her invitation, and a Psalm was chosen.

The singing was a distinct feature of the Bible class. There was nothing like it, not only in the other services of the congregation, but in any congregation in the whole county. The young people that formed that Bible class have long since grown into old men and women, but the echoes of that singing still reverberate through the chambers of their hearts when they stand up to sing certain tunes or certain Psalms. Once a week, through the long winter, they used to meet and sing to John "Aleck's" sounding beat for two or three hours. They learned to sing, not only the old psalm tunes but psalm tunes never heard in the congregation before, as also hymns and anthems. The anthems and hymns were, of course, never used in public worship. They were reserved for the sacred concert which John "Aleck" gave once a year. It was in the Bible class that he and his fellow enthusiasts found opportunity to sing their new Psalm tunes, with now and then a hymn. When John "Aleck," a handsome, broad-shouldered, six-footer, stood up and bit his tuning-fork to catch the pitch, the people straightened up in their seats and prepared to follow his lead. And after his great resonant voice had rolled out the first few notes of the tune, they caught him up with a vigor and enthusiasm that carried him along, and inspired him to his mightiest efforts. Wonderful singing it was, full toned, rhythmical and well balanced.

With characteristic courage, the minister's wife had chosen Paul's Epistle to the Romans for the subject of study, and to-night the lesson was the redoubtable ninth chapter, that arsenal for Calvinistic champions. First the verses were repeated by the class in concert, and the members vied with each other in making this a perfect exercise, then the teaching of the chapter was set forth in simple, lucid speech. The last half hour was devoted to the discussion of questions, raised either by the teacher or by any member of the class. To-night the class was slow in asking questions. They were face to face with the tremendous Pauline Doctrine of Sovereignty. It was significant that by Macdonald Dubh, his brother, and the other older and more experienced members of the class, the doctrine was regarded as absolutely inevitable and was accepted without question, while by Yankee and Ranald and all the younger members of the class, it was rejected with fierce resentment. The older men had been taught by the experience of long and bitter years, that above all their strength, however mighty, a power, resistless and often inscrutable, determined their lives. The younger men, their hearts beating with conscious power and freedom, resented this control, or accepting it, refused to assume the responsibility for the outcome of their lives. It was the old, old strife, the insoluble mystery; and the minister's wife, far from making light of it, allowed its full weight to press in upon the members of her class, and wisely left the question as the apostle leaves it, with a statement of the two great truths of Sovereignty and Free Will without attempting the impossible task of harmonizing these into a perfect system. After a half-hour of discussion, she brought the lesson to a close with a very short and very simple presentation of the practical bearing of the great doctrine. And while the mystery remained unsolved, the limpid clearness of her thought, the humble attitude of mind, the sympathy with doubt, and above all, the sweet and tender pathos that filled her voice, sent the class away humbled, subdued, comforted, and willing to wait the day of clearer light. Not that they were done with Pharaoh and his untoward fate; that occupied them for many a day.

The class was closed with prayer and singing. As a kind of treat, the last singing was a hymn and they stood up to sing it. It was Perronet's great hymn sung to old Coronation, and when they came to the refrain, "Crown him Lord of all," the very rafters of the little church rang with the mighty volume of sound. The Bible class always closed with a great outburst of singing, and as a rule, Ranald went out tingling and thrilling through and through. But tonight, so deeply was he exercised with the unhappy doom of the unfortunate king of Egypt, from which, apparently, there was no escape, fixed as it was by the Divine decree, and oppressed with the feeling that the same decree would determine the course of his life, he missed his usual thrill. He was walking off by himself in a perplexed and downcast mood, avoiding every one, even Don, and was nearly past the minister's gate when Hughie, excited and breathless, caught up to him and exclaimed: "Oh, Ranald, was not that splendid? Man, I like to hear John 'Aleck' sing 'Crown him' that way. And I say," he continued, "mother wants you to come in."

Then all at once Ranald remembered the young man who had behaved so disgracefully in church.

"No," he said, firmly, "I must be hurrying home. The cows will be to milk yet."

"Oh, pshaw! you must come," pleaded Hughie. "We will have some singing. I want you to sing bass. Perhaps John 'Aleck' will come in." This was sheer guessing, but it was good bait. But the young man with "his head split in the middle" would be there, and perhaps Maimie would be "going on" with him as she did in the Bible class.

"You will tell your mother I could not come," he said. "Yankee and father are both out, and there will be no one at home."

"Well, I think you are pretty mean," said Hughie, grievously disappointed. "I wanted you to come in, and mother wanted Cousin Harry to see you."

"Cousin Harry?"

"Yes; Maimie's brother came last night, you know, and Maimie is going back with him in two weeks."

"Maimie's brother. Well, well, is that the nice-looking fellow that sat by you?"

"Huh-huh, he is awful nice, and mother wanted –"

"Indeed he looks it, I am sure," Ranald said, with sudden enthusiasm; "I would just like to know him. If I thought Yankee would –"

"Oh, pshaw! Of course Yankee will milk the cows," exclaimed Hughie. "Come on, come on in." And Ranald went to meet one of the great nights of his life.

"Here is Ranald!" called Hughie at the top of his voice, as he entered the room where the family were gathered.

"You don't say so, Hughie?" answered his cousin, coming forward. "You ought to make that fact known. We all want to hear it."

Ranald liked him from the first. He was not a bit "proud" in spite of his fine clothes and his head being "split in the middle."

"You're the chap," he said, stretching out his hand to Ranald, "that snatched Maimie from the fire. Mighty clever thing to do. We have heard a lot about you at our house. Why, every week –"

"Let some one else talk, Harry," interrupted Maimie, with cheeks flaming. "We are going to have some singing now. Here is auntie. Mayn't we use the piano?"

"Why, yes, I suppose so," said Mrs. Murray. "I was glad to see your father there to-night," she said to Ranald.

"And Yankee, mother."

"Hush, Hughie; you must call people by their right names. Now let us have some singing. I hear Ranald is singing bass these days."

"And bully good bass, too," cried Hughie. "John 'Aleck' says that it's the finest bass in the whole singing school."

"Well, Hughie," said his mother, quietly, "I don't think it is necessary to shout even such pleasant information as that. Now go to your singing, and I shall listen."

She lay back in the big chair, looking so pale and weary that Harry hardly believed it was the same woman that had just been keeping a hundred and fifty people keenly alert for an hour and a half, and leading them with such intellectual and emotional power.

"That class is too hard for you, auntie," he said. "If I were your husband I would not let you keep it on."

"But you see my husband is not here. He is twelve miles away."

"Then I would lock you up, or take you with me."

"Oh!" cried Hughie, "I would much rather teach the Bible class than listen to another sermon."

"Something in that," said his cousin, "especially if I were the preacher, eh?" at which they all laughed.

It was a happy hour for Ranald. He had been too shy to join the singing school, and had never heard any part singing till he began to attend the Bible class. There he made the delightful discovery that, without any instruction, he could join in the bass, and had made, also, the further discovery that his voice, which he had thought rough and coarse, and for a year past, worse than ever, could reach to extraordinary depths. One Sabbath evening, it chanced that John "Aleck," who always had an ear open for a good voice, heard him rolling out his deep bass, and seizing him on the spot, had made him promise to join the singing school. There he discovered a talent and developed a taste for singing that delighted his leader's heart, and opened out to himself a new world. The piano, too, was a new and rare treat to Ranald. In all the country there was no other, and even in the manse it was seldom heard, for Mrs. Murray found little time, amid the multitude of household and congregational duties, to keep up her piano practice. That part of her life, with others of like kind, she had been forced to lose.

But since Maimie's coming, the piano had been in daily use, and even on the Sabbath days, though not without danger to the sensibilities of the neighbors, she had used it to accompany the hymns with which the day always closed.

"Let us have the parts," cried Hughie. "Maimie and I will take the air, and Ranald will take the bass. Cousin Harry, can you sing?"

"Oh, I'll hum."

"Nonsense," said Maimie, "he sings tenor splendidly."

"Oh, that's fine!" cried Hughie, with delight. He himself was full of music. "Come on, Ranald, you stand up behind Maimie, you will need to see the notes; and I will sit here," planting himself beside his mother.

So Hughie arranged it all, and for an hour the singing went on, the favorite hymns of each being sung in turn. For the most part, Mrs. Murray sat silent, but now and then she would join with the others, singing alto when she did so, by Hughie's special direction. Her voice was not strong, but it was true, mellow, and full of music. Hughie loved to hear her sing alto, and more especially because he liked to join in with her, which he was too shy to do alone, even in his home, and which he would never think of doing in the Bible class, or in the presence of any of the boys who might, for this reason, think him "proud." When they came to Hughie's turn, he chose the hymn by Bliss, recently published, "Whosoever will," the words seem to strike him tonight.

"Mother," he said, after singing it through, "does that mean everybody that likes?"

"Yes, my dear, any one that wishes."

"Pharaoh, mother?"

"Yes, Pharaoh, too."

"But, mother, you said he could not possibly."

"Only because he did not want to."

"But he could not, even if he did want to."

"I hope I did not say that," said his mother, smiling at the eager and earnest young face.

"No, auntie," said Harry, taking up Hughie's cause, "not exactly, but something very like it. You said that Pharaoh could not possibly have acted in any other way than he did."

"Yes, I said that."

"Not even if he wanted to?" asked Hughie.

"Oh, I did not say that."

"The Lord hardened Pharaoh's heart," quoted Ranald, who knew his Bible better than Harry.

"Yes, that is it," said Harry, "and so that made it impossible for Pharaoh to do anything else. He could not help following after those people."

"Why not?" said Mrs. Murray. "What made him follow? Now just think, what made him follow after those people?"

"Why, he wanted to get them back," said Hughie.

"Quite true," said his mother. "So you see, he did exactly as he wanted to."

"Then you mean the Lord had nothing to do with it?" asked Ranald.

"No, I could not say that."

"Then," said Harry, "Pharaoh could not help himself. Now, could he?"

"He did what he wished to do," said his aunt.

"Yes," said Ranald, quickly, "but could he help wishing to do what he did?"

"If he had been a different man, more humble minded, and more willing to be taught, he would not have wished to do what he did."

"Mother," said Hughie, changing his ground a little, and lowering his voice, "do you think Pharaoh is lost, and all his soldiers, and – and all the people who were bad?"

Mrs. Murray looked at him in silence for a few moments, then said, very sadly, "I can't answer that question, Hughie. I do not know."

"But, mother," persisted Hughie, "are not wicked people lost?"

"Yes, Hughie," replied his mother, "all those who do not repent of their sins and cry to God for mercy."

"Oh, mother," cried Hughie, "forever?"

His mother did not reply.

"Will He never let them out, mother?" continued Hughie, in piteous appeal.

"Listen to me, Hughie," said his mother, very gently. "We know very little about this. Would you be very sorry, even for very bad men?"

"Oh, mother," cried Hughie, his tender little heart moved with a great compassion, "think of a whole year, all summer long, and all winter long. I think I would let anybody out."

"Then, Hughie, dear," said his mother, "remember that God is much kinder than you are, and has a heart far more tender, and while He will be just and must punish sin, He will do nothing unjust or unkind, you may be quite sure of that. Do not forget how He gave up His own dear son for us."

Poor Hughie could bear it no longer. He put his head in his mother's lap and sobbed out, "Oh, mother, I hope he will let them out."

As he uttered this pitiful little cry, his cousin Harry got up from his chair, and moved across to the window, while Maimie openly wiped her eyes, but Ranald sat with his face set hard, and his eyes gleaming, waiting eagerly for Mrs. Murray's answer.

The mother stroked Hughie's head softly, and while her tears fell on the brown curls, said to him, "You would not be afraid to trust your mother, Hughie, and our Father in heaven loves us all much more than I love you."

And with that Hughie was content.

"Now let us sing one more hymn," said his mother. "It's my choice." And she chose one of the new hymns which they had just learned in the singing school, and of which Hughie was very fond, the children's hymn, "Come to the Saviour." While they were singing they heard Mr. Murray drive into the yard.

"There's papa," said Mrs. Murray. "He will be tired and hungry," and she hurried out to meet her husband, followed by Harry and Hughie, leaving Ranald and Maimie in the room together. Ranald had never been alone with her before, nor indeed had he ever spent five minutes of his life alone with any girl before now. But he did not feel awkward or shy; he was thinking now, as he had been thinking now and then through the whole evening, of only one thing, that Maimie was going away. That would make a great difference to him, so great that he was conscious of a heart-sinking at the mere thought of it. During the last weeks, his life had come to move about a center, and that center was Maimie; and now that she was going away, there would be nothing left. Nothing, that is, that really mattered. But the question he was revolving in his mind was, would she forget all about him. He knew he would never forget her, that was, of course, impossible, for so many things would remind him of her. He would never see the sunlight falling through the trees as it fell that night of the sugaring-off, without thinking of her. He would never see the shadows in the evening, or hear the wind in the leaves, without thinking of her. The church and the minister's pew, the manse and all belonging to it would remind him of Maimie. He would recall how she looked at different times and places, the turn of her head, the way her hair fell on her neck, her laugh, the little toss of her chin, and the curve in her lips. He would remember everything about her. Would she remember him, or would she forget him? That was the question burning in his heart; and that question he must have settled, and this was the time.

But though these thoughts and emotions were rushing through his brain and blood, he felt strangely quiet and self-controlled as he walked over to her where she stood beside the piano, and looking into her eyes with an intensity of gaze she could not meet, said, in a low, quick voice: "You are going away?"

"Yes," she replied, so startled that the easy smile with which she had greeted him faded out of her face. "In two weeks I shall be gone."

"Gone!" echoed Ranald. "Yes, you will be gone. Will you forget me?" His tone was almost stern.

"Why, no," she said, in a surprised voice. "Of course not. Did not you save my life? You will be far more likely to forget me."

"No," he said, simply, as if that possibility need not be considered. "I will never forget you. I will always be thinking of you. Will you think of me?" he persisted.

"Why, certainly. Wouldn't I be a very ungrateful girl if I did not?"

"Ungrateful!" exclaimed Ranald, impatiently. "What I did was nothing. Forget that. Do you not understand me? I will be thinking of you every day, in the morning and at night, and I never thought of any one else before for a day. Will you be thinking of me?"

There was a movement in the kitchen, and they could hear the minister talking to Harry; and some one was moving toward the door.

"Tell me, Maimie, quick," said Ranald, and though his voice was intense and stern, there was appeal in it as well.

She took a step nearer him, and looking up into his face, said, in a whisper, "Yes, Ranald, I will always remember you, and think of you."

Swiftly, almost fiercely, he threw his arms about her, and kissed her lips, then he stood back looking at her.

"I could not help it," he said, boldly. "You made me."

"Made you?" exclaimed Maimie, her face hot with blushes.

"Yes, you made me. I could not help it," he repeated. "And I do not care if you are angry. I am glad I did it."

"Glad?" echoed Maimie again, not knowing what to say.

"Yes, glad," he said, exultantly. "Are you?"

She made no reply. The door opened behind them. She sank down upon the piano-stool and let her hands fall upon the keys.

"Are you?" he demanded, ignoring the interruption.

With her head low down, while she struck the chords of the hymn they had just sung, she said, hesitatingly, "I am not sorry."

"Sorry for what?" said Harry.

"Oh, nothing," said Maimie, lightly.

"Nobody is, if he has got any sense."

Then Mrs. Murray came in. "Won't you stay for supper, Ranald? You must be hungry."

"No, thank you," said Ranald. "I must go now."

He shook hands with an ease and freedom that the minister had never seen in him, and went out.

"That young man is coming on," said the minister. "I never saw any one change and develop as he has in the last few months. Let me see. He is only eighteen, isn't he, and he might be twenty-one." The minister spoke as if he were not too well pleased with this precocity in Ranald.

But little did Ranald care. That young man was striding homeward through the night, his head striking the stars. His path lay through the woods, and when he came to the "sugar camp" road, he stood still, and let the memories of the night when he had snatched Maimie from the fire troop through his mind. Suddenly he thought of Aleck McRae, and laughed aloud.

"Poor Aleck," he said. Aleck seemed so harmless to him now. And then he stood silent, motionless, looking straight toward the stars, but seeing them not. He was remembering Maimie's face when she said, "Yes, Ranald, I will always remember you and think of you"; and then the thought of what followed, sent the blood jumping through his veins.

"She will not forget," he said aloud, and went on his way. It was his happy night, the happiest of his life thus far, and he would always be happy. What difference could anything make?

THE REVIVAL

Those last days of Maimie's visit sped by on winged feet. To Ranald they were brimming with happiness, every one of them. It was the slack time of the year, between seeding and harvest, and there was nothing much to keep him at home. And so, with Harry, his devoted companion, Ranald roamed the woods, hitching up Lisette in Yankee's buckboard, put her through her paces, and would now and then get up such bursts of speed as took Harry's breath away; and more than all, there was the chance of a word with Maimie. He had lost much of his awkwardness. He went about with an air of mastery, and why not? He had entered upon his kingdom. The minister noticed and wondered; his wife noticed and smiled sometimes, but oftener sighed, wisely keeping silence, for she knew that in times like this the best words were those unspoken.

The happiest day of all for Ranald was the last, when, after a long tramp with Harry through the woods, he drove him back to the manse, coming up from the gate to the door like a whirlwind.

As Lisette stood pawing and tossing her beautiful head, Mrs. Murray, who stood with Maimie watching them drive up, cried out, admiringly: "What a beauty she is!"

"Isn't she!" cried Harry, enthusiastically. "And such a flyer! Get in, auntie, and see."

"Do," said Ranald; "I would be very glad. Just to the church hill and back."

"Go, auntie," pleaded Harry. "She is wonderful."

"You go, Maimie," said her aunt, to whom every offered pleasure simply furnished an opportunity of thought for others.

"Nonsense!" cried Harry, impatiently. "You might gratify yourself a little for once in your life. Besides," he added, with true brotherly blindness, "it's you Ranald wants. At least he talks enough about you."

"Yes, auntie, do go! It will be lovely," chimed in Maimie, with suspicious heartiness.

So, with many protestations, Mrs. Murray took her place beside Ranald and was whirled off like the wind. She returned in a very few minutes, her hair blown loose till the little curls hung about her glowing face and her eyes shining with excitement.

"Oh, she is perfectly splendid!" she exclaimed. "And so gentle. You must go, Maimie, if only to the gate." And Maimie went, but not to turn at even the church hill.

For a mile down the concession road Ranald let Lisette jog at an easy pace while he told Maimie some of his aims and hopes. He did not mean to be a farmer nor a lumberman. He was going to the city, and there make his fortune. He did not say it in words, but his tone, his manner, everything about him, proclaimed his confidence that some day he would be a great man. And Maimie believed him, not because it seemed reasonable, or because there seemed to be any ground for his confidence, but just because Ranald said it. His superb self-confidence wrought in her assurance.

"And then," he said, proudly, "I am going to see you."

"Oh, I hope you will not wait till then," she answered.

"I do not know," he said. "I cannot tell, but it does not matter much. I will be always seeing you."

"But I will want to see you," said Maimie.

"Yes," said Ranald, "I know you will," as if that were a thing to be expected. "But you will be coming back to your aunt here." But of this Maimie could not be sure.

"Oh, yes, you will come," he said, confidently; "I am sure you will come. Harry is coming, and you will come, too." And having settled this point, he turned Lisette and from that out gave his attention to his driving. The colt seemed to realize the necessity of making a display of her best speed, and without any urging, she went along the concession road, increasing her speed at every stride till she wheeled in at the gate. Then Ranald shook the lines over her back and called to her. Magnificently Lisette responded, and swept up to the door with such splendid dash that the whole household greeted her with waving applause. As the colt came to a stand, Maimie stepped out from the buckboard, and turning toward Ranald, said in a low, hurried voice: "O, Ranald, that was splendid, and I am so happy; and you will be sure to come?"

"I will come," said Ranald, looking down into the blue eyes with a look so long and steady and so full of passionate feeling that Maimie knew he would keep his word.

Then farewells were said, and Ranald turned away, Harry and Mrs. Murray watching him from the door till he disappeared over the church hill.

"Well, that's the finest chap I ever saw," said Harry, with emphasis. "And what a body he has! He would make a great half-back."

"Poor Ranald! I hope he will make a great and good man," said his aunt, with a ring of sadness in her voice.

"Why poor, auntie?"

"I'm sure I do not know," she said, with a very uncertain smile playing about her mouth. Then she went upstairs and found Maimie sitting at the window overlooking the church hill, and once more she knew how golden is silence. So she set to work to pack Maimie's trunk for her.

"It will be a very early start, Maimie," she said, "and so we will get everything ready to-night."

"Yes, auntie," said Maimie, going to her and putting her arms about her. "How happy I have been, and how good you have been to me!"

"And how glad I have been to have you!" said her aunt.

"Oh, I will never forget you! You have taught me so much that I never knew before. I see everything so differently. It seems easy to be good here, and, oh! I wish you were not so far away from me, auntie. I am afraid – afraid –"

The tears could no longer be denied. She put her head in her aunt's lap and sobbed out her heart's overflow. For an hour they sat by the open trunk, forgetting all about the packing, while her aunt talked to Maimie as no one had ever talked to her before; and often, through the long years of suffering that followed, the words of that evening came to Maimie to lighten and to comfort an hour of fear and sorrow. Mrs. Murray was of those to whom it is given to speak words that will not die with time, but will live, for that they fall from lips touched with the fire of God.

Before they had finished their talk Harry came in, and

then Mrs. Murray told them about their mother, of her beauty and her brightness and her goodness, but mostly of her goodness.

"She was a dear, dear girl," said their aunt, "and her goodness was of the kind that makes one think of a fresh spring morning, so bright, so sweet, and pure. And she was beautiful, too. You will be like her, Maimie," and, after a pause, she added, softly, "And, most of all, she loved her Saviour, and that was the secret of both her beauty and her goodness."

"Auntie," said Harry, suddenly, "don't you think you could come to us for a visit? It would do father – I mean it would be such a great thing for father, and for me, too, for us all."

Mrs. Murray thought of her home and all its ties, and then said, smiling: "I am afraid, Harry, that could hardly be. Besides, my dear boy, there is One who can always be with you, and no one can take His place."

"All the same, I wish you could come," said Harry. "When I am here I feel like doing something with my life, but at home I only think of having fun."

"But, Harry," said his aunt, "life is a very sacred and very precious thing, and at all costs, you must make it worthy of Him who gave it to you."

Next morning, when Harry was saying "Farewell" to his aunt, she put her arms round him, and said: "Your mother would have wished you to be a noble man, and you must not disappoint her."

"I will try, auntie," he said, and could say no more.

For the next few weeks the minister and his wife were both busy and anxious. For more than eight years they had labored with their people without much sign of result. Week after week the minister poured into his sermons the strength of his heart and mind, and then gave them to his people with all the fervor of his nature. Week after week his wife, in her women's meetings and in her Bible class, lavished freely upon them the splendid riches of her intellectual and spiritual powers, and together in the homes of the people they wrought and taught. At times it seemed to the minister that they were spending their strength for naught, and at such times he bitterly grudged, not his own toils, but those of his wife. None knew better than he how well fitted she was, both by the native endowments of her mind and by the graces of her character, to fill the highest sphere, and he sometimes grew impatient that she should spend herself without stint and reap no adequate reward.

These were his thoughts as he lay on his couch, on the evening of the last Sabbath in the old church, after a day's work more than usually exhausting. The new church was to be opened the following week. For months it had been the burden of their prayers that at the dedication of their church, which had been built and paid for at the cost of much thought and toil, there should be some "signal mark of the divine acceptance." No wonder the minister was more than usually depressed to-night.

"There is not much sign of movement among the dry bones," he said to his wife. "They are as dry and as dead as ever."

His wife was silent for some time, for she, too, had her moments of doubt and fear, but she said: "I think there is some sign. The people were certainly much impressed this morning, and the Bible class was very large, and they were very attentive."

"So they are every day," said the minister, rather bitterly. "But what does it amount to? There is not a sign of one of these young people 'coming forward.' Just think, only one young man a member of the church, and he hasn't got much spunk in him. And many of the older men remain as hard as the nether millstone."

"I really think," said his wife, "that a number of the young people would 'come forward' if some one would make a beginning. They are all very shy."

"So you always say," said her husband, with a touch of impatience; "but there is no shyness in other things, in their frolics and their fightings. I am sure this last outrageous business is enough to break one's heart."

"What do you mean?" said his wife.

"Oh, I suppose you will hear soon enough, so I need not try to keep it from you. It was Long John Cameron told me. It is strange that Hughie has not heard. Indeed, perhaps he has, but since his beloved Ranald is involved, he is keeping it quiet."

"What is it?" said his wife, anxiously.

"Oh, nothing less than a regular pitched battle between the McGregors and the McRaes of the Sixteenth, and all on Ranald's account, too, I believe."

Mrs. Murray sat in silent and bitter disappointment. She had expected much from Ranald. Her husband went on with his tale.

"It seems there was an old quarrel between young Aleck McRae and Ranald, over what I cannot find out; and young Angus McGregor, who will do anything for a Macdonald, must needs take Ranald's part, with the result that that hot-headed young fire-eater Aleck McRae must challenge the whole clan McGregor. So it was arranged, on Sunday morning, too, mind you, two weeks ago, after the service, that six of the best of each side should meet and settle the business. Of course Ranald was bound to be into it, and begged and pleaded with the McGregors that he should be one of the six; and I hear it was by Yankee's advice that his request was granted. That godless fellow, it seems, has been giving Ranald daily lessons with the boxing-gloves, and to some purpose, too, as the fight proved. It seems that young Aleck McRae, who is a terrible fighter, and must be forty pounds heavier than Ranald, was, by Ranald's especial desire and by Yankee's arrangement, pitted against the boy, and by the time the fight was over, Ranald, although beaten and bruised to a 'bloody pulp,' as Long John said, had Aleck thoroughly whipped. And nobody knows what would have happened, so fierce was the young villain, had not Peter McGregor and Macdonald Bhain appeared upon the scene. It appears Aleck had been saying something about Maimie, Long John did not know what it was; but Ranald was determined to finish Aleck up there and then. It must have been a disgusting and terrible sight; but Macdonald Bhain apparently settled them in a hurry; and what is more, made them all shake hands and promise to drop the quarrel thenceforth. I fancy Ranald's handling of young Aleck McRae did more to bring about the settlement than anything else. What a lot of savages they are!" continued the minister. "It really does not seem much use to preach to them."

"We must not say that, my dear," said his wife, but her tone was none too hopeful. "I must confess I am disappointed in Ranald. Well," she continued, "we can only wait and trust."

From Hughie, who had had the story from Don, and who had been pledged to say nothing of it, she learned more about the fight.

"It was Aleck's fault, mother," he said, anxious to screen his hero. "He said something about Maimie, that Don wouldn't tell me, at the blacksmith shop in the Sixteenth, and

Ranald struck him and knocked him flat, and he could not get up for a long time. Yankee has been showing him how. I am going to learn, mother," interjected Hughie. "And then Angus McGregor took Ranald's part, and it was all arranged after church, and Ranald was bound to be in it, and said he would stop the whole thing if not allowed. Don said he was just terrible. It was an awful fight. Angus McGregor fought Peter McRae, Aleck's brother, you know and –"

"Never mind, Hughie," said his mother. "I don't want to hear of it. It is too disgusting. Was Ranald much hurt?"

"Oh, he was hurt awful bad, and he was going to be licked, too. He wouldn't keep cool enough, and he wouldn't use his legs."

"Use his legs?" said his mother; "what do you mean?"

"That's what Don says, and Yankee made him. Yankee kept calling to him, 'Now get away, get away from him! Use your legs! Get away from him!' and whenever Ranald began to do as he was told, then he got the better of Aleck, and he gave Aleck a terrible hammering, and Don said if Macdonald Bhain had not stopped them Aleck McRae would not have been able to walk home. He said Ranald was awful. He said he never saw him like he was that day. Wasn't it fine, mother?"

"Fine, Hughie!" said his mother. "It is anything but fine. It is simply disgusting to see men act like beasts. It is very, very sad. I am very much disappointed in Ranald."

"But, mother, Ranald couldn't help it. And anyway, I am glad he gave that Aleck McRae a good thrashing. Yankee said he would never be right until he got it."

"You must not repeat what Yankee says," said his mother. "I am afraid his influence is not of the best for any of those boys."

"Oh, mother, he didn't set them on," said Hughie, who wanted to be fair to Yankee. "It was when he could not help it that he told Ranald how to do. I am glad he did, too."

"I am very, very sorry about it," said his mother, sadly. It was a greater disappointment to her than she cared to acknowledge either to her husband or to herself.

But the commotion caused in the community by the fight was soon swallowed up in the interest aroused by the opening of the new church, an event for which they had made long and elaborate preparation. The big bazaar, for which the women had been sewing for a year or more, was held on Wednesday, and turned out to be a great success, sufficient money being realized to pay for the church furnishing, which they had undertaken to provide.

The day following was the first of the "Communion Season." In a Highland congregation the Communion Seasons are the great occasions of the year. For weeks before, the congregation is kept in mind of the approaching event, and on the Thursday of the communion week the season opens with a solemn fast day.

The annual Fast Day, still a national institution in Scotland, although it has lost much of its solemnity and sacredness in some places, was originally associated with the Lord's Supper, and was observed with great strictness in the matter of eating and drinking; and in Indian Lands, as in all congregations of that part of the country, the custom of celebrating the Fast Day was kept up. It was a day of great solemnity in the homes of the people of a godly sort. There was no cooking of meals till after "the services," and, indeed, some of them tasted neither meat nor drink the whole day long. To the younger people of the congregation it was a day of gloom and terror, a kind of day of doom. Even to those advanced in godliness it brought searchings of heart, minute and diligent, with agonies of penitence and remorse. It was a day, in short, in which conscience was invited to take command of the memory and the imagination to the scourging of the soul for the soul's good. The sermon for the day was supposed to stimulate and to aid conscience in this work.

For the communion service Mr. Murray always made it a point to have the assistance of the best preachers he could procure, and on this occasion, when the church opening was combined with the sacrament, by a special effort two preachers had been procured – a famous divine from Huron County, that stronghold of Calvinism, and a college professor who had been recently appointed, but who had already gained a reputation as a doctrinal preacher, and who was, as Peter McRae reported, "grand on the Attributes and terrible fine on the Law." To him was assigned the honor of preaching the Fast Day sermon, and of declaring the church "open."

The new church was very different from the old. Instead of the high crow's nest, with the wonderful sounding-board over it, the pulpit was simply a raised platform partly inclosed, with the desk in front. There was no precentor's box, over the loss of which Straight Rory did not grieve unduly, inasmuch as the singing was to be led, in the English at least, by John "Aleck." Henceforth the elders would sit with their families. The elders' seat was gone; Peter McRae's wrath at this being somewhat appeased by his securing for himself one of the short side seats at the right of the pulpit, from which he could command a view of both the minister and the congregation – a position with obvious advantages. The minister's pew was at the very back of the church.

It was a great assemblage that gathered in the new church to hear the professor discourse, as doubtless he would, it being the Fast Day, upon some theme of judgment. With a great swing of triumph in his voice, Mr. Murray rose and announced the Hundredth Psalm. An electric thrill went through the congregation as, with a wave of his hand, he said: "Let us rise and sing. Now, John, Old Hundred."

Never did John "Aleck" and the congregation of Indian Lands sing as they did that morning. It was the first time that the congregation, as a whole, had followed the lead of that great ringing voice, and they followed with a joyous, triumphant shout, as of men come to victory.

"For why? The Lord our God is good,"

rolled out the majestic notes of Old Hundred.

"What's the matter, mother?" whispered Hughie, who was standing up in the seat that he might look on his mother's book.

"Nothing, darling," said his mother, her face radiant through her tears. After long months of toil and waiting, they were actually singing praise to God in the new church.

When the professor arose, it was an eager, responsive congregation that waited for his word. The people were fully prepared for a sermon that would shake them to their souls' depths. The younger portion shivered and shrank from the ordeal; the older and more experienced shivered and waited with not unpleasing anticipations; it did them good, that remorseless examination of their hearts' secret depravities. To some it was a kind of satisfaction offered to conscience, after which they could more easily come to peace. With others it was an honest, heroic effort to know themselves and to right themselves with their God.

The text was disappointing. "Above all these things, put on charity, which is the bond of perfectness," read the professor from that exquisite and touching passage which begins at the twelfth verse of the fifteenth chapter of Colossians. "Love, the bond of perfectness," was his theme, and in simple, calm, lucid speech he dilated upon the beauty, the excellence, and the supremacy of this Christian grace. It was the most Godlike of all the virtues, for God was love; and more than zeal, more than knowledge, more than faith, it was "the mark" of the new birth.

Peter McRae was evidently keenly disappointed, and his whole bearing expressed stern disapproval. And as the professor proceeded, extolling and illustrating the supreme grace of love, Peter's hard face grew harder than ever, and his eyes began to emit blue sparks of fire. This was no day for the preaching of smooth things. The people were there to consider and to lament their Original and Actual sin; and they expected and required to hear of the judgments of the Lord, and to be summoned to flee from the wrath to come.

Donald Ross sat with his kindly old face in a glow of delight, but with a look of perplexity on it which his furtive glances in Peter's direction did not help to lessen. The sermon was delighting and touching him, but he was not quite sure whether this was a good sign in him or no. He set himself now and then to find fault with the sermon, but the preacher was so humble, so respectful, and above all, so earnest, that Donald Ross could not bring himself to criticise.

The application came under the third head. As a rule, the application to a Fast Day sermon was delivered in terrifying tones of thunder or in an awful whisper. But to-day the preacher, without raising his voice, began to force into his hearers' hearts the message of the day.

"This is a day for self-examination," he said, and his clear, quiet tones fell into the ears of the people with penetrating power. "And self-examination is a wise and profitable exercise. It is an exercise of the soul designed to yield a discovery of sin in the heart and life, and to induce penitence and contrition and so secure pardon and peace. But too often, my friends," and here his voice became a shade softer, "it results in a self-righteous and sinful self-complaisance. What is required is a simple honesty of mind and spiritual illumination, and the latter cannot be without the former. There are those who are ever searching for 'the marks' of a genuinely godly state of heart, and they have the idea that these marks are obscure and difficult for plain people to discover. Make no mistake, my brethren, they are as easily seen as are the apples on a tree. The fruits of the spirit are as discernible to any one honest enough and fearless enough to look; and the first and supreme of all is that which we have been considering this morning. The question for you and for me, my brethren, is simply this: Are our lives full of the grace of love? Do not shrink from the question. Do not deceive yourselves with any substitutes; there are many offering zeal, the gift of prayer or of speech, yea, the gift of faith itself. None of these will atone for the lack of love. Let each ask himself, Am I a loving man?"

With quiet persistence he pursued them into all their relations in life – husbands and wives, fathers and sons, neighbor and neighbor. He would not let them escape. Relentlessly he forced them to review their habits of speech and action, their attitude toward each other as church members, and their attitude toward "those without." Behind all refuges and through all subterfuges he made his message follow them, searching their deepest hearts. And then, with his face illumined as with divine fire, he made his final appeal, while he reminded them of the Infinite love that had stooped to save, and that had wrought itself out in the agonies of the cross. And while he spoke his last words, all over the church the women were weeping, and strong men were sitting trembling and pale.

After a short prayer, the professor sat down. Then the minister rose, and for some little time stood facing his people in silence, the gleam in his eyes showing that his fervent Highland nature was on fire.

"My people," he began, and his magnificent voice pealed forth like a solemn bell, "this is the message of the Lord. Let none dare refuse to hear. It is a message to your minister, it is a message to you. You are anxious for 'the marks.' Search you for this mark." He paused while the people sat looking at him in fixed and breathless silence. Then, suddenly, he broke forth into a loud cry: "Where are your children at this solemn time of privilege? Fathers, where are your sons? Why were they not with you at the Table? Are you men of love? Are you men of love, or by lack of love are you shutting the door of the Kingdom against your sons with their fightings and their quarrelings?" Then, raising his hands high, he lifted his voice in a kind of wailing chant: "Woe unto you! Woe unto you! Your house is left unto you desolate, and the voice of love is crying over you. Ye would not! Ye would not! O, Lamb of God, have mercy upon us! O, Christ, with the pierced hands, save us!" Again he paused, looking upward, while the people waited with uplifted white faces.

"Behold," he cried, in a soul-thrilling voice, "I see heaven open, and Jesus standing at the right hand of God, and I hear a voice, 'Turn ye, turn ye. Why will ye die?' Lord Jesus, they will not turn." Again he paused. "Listen. Depart from me, ye cursed, into everlasting fire. Depart ye! Nay, Lord Jesus! not so! Have mercy upon us!" His voice broke in its passionate cry. The effect was overwhelming. The people swayed as trees before a mighty wind, and a voice cried aloud from the congregation: "God be merciful to me, a sinner!"

It was Macdonald Dubh. At that loud cry, women began to sob, and some of the people rose from their seats.

"Be still," commanded the minister. "Rend your hearts and not your garments. Let us pray." And as he prayed, the cries and sobs subsided and a great calm fell upon all. After prayer, the minister, instead of giving out a closing psalm, solemnly charged the people to go to their homes and to consider that the Lord had come very near them, and adjured them not to grieve the Holy Spirit of God. Then he dismissed them with the benediction.

The people went out of the church, subdued and astonished, speaking, if at all, in low tones of what they had seen and heard.

Immediately after pronouncing the benediction, the minister came down to find Macdonald Dubh, but he was nowhere to be seen. Toward evening Mrs. Murray rode over to his house but found that he had not returned from the morning service.

"He will be at his brother's," said Kirsty, "and Ranald will drive over for him."

Immediately Ranald hitched up Lisette and drove over to his uncle's, but as he was returning he sent in word to the manse, his face being not yet presentable, that his father was nowhere to be found. It was Macdonald Bhain that found him at last in the woods, prone upon his face, and in an agony.

"Hugh, man," he cried, "what ails you?" But there were only low groans for answer.

"Rise up, man, rise up and come away."

Then from the prostrate figure he caught the words, "Depart from me! Depart from me! That is the word of the Lord."

"That is not the word," said Macdonald Bhain, "for any living man, but for the dead. But come, rise, man; the neighbors will be here in a meenute." At that Black Hugh rose.

"Let me away," he said. "Let me not see them. I am a lost man."

And so his brother brought him home, shaken in spirit and exhausted in body with his long fast and his overpowering emotion. All night through his brother watched with him alone, for Macdonald Dubh would have no one else to see him, till, from utter exhaustion, toward the dawning of the day, he fell asleep.

In the early morning the minister and his wife drove over to see him, and leaving his wife with Kirsty, the minister passed at once into Macdonald Dubh's room. But, in spite of all his reasoning, in spite of all his readings and his prayers, the gloom remained unbroken except by occasional paroxysms of fear and remorse.

"There is no forgiveness! There is no forgiveness!" was the burden of his cry.

In vain the minister proclaimed to him the mercy of God. At length he was forced to leave him to attend the "Question Meeting" which was to be held in the church that day. But he left his wife behind him.

Without a word, Mrs. Murray proceeded to make the poor man comfortable. She prepared a dainty breakfast and carried it in to him, and then she sat beside him while he fell into a deep sleep.

It was afternoon when Macdonald Dubh awoke and greeted her with his wonted grave courtesy.

"You are better, Mr. Macdonald," she said, brightly. "And now I will make you a fresh cup of tea"; and though he protested, she hurried out, and in a few moments brought him some tea and toast. Then, while he lay in gloomy silence, she read to him, as she did once before from his Gaelic psalm book, without a word of comment. And then she began to tell him of all the hopes she had cherished in connection with the opening of the new church, and how that day she had felt at last the blessing had come.

"And, O, Mr. Macdonald," she said, "I was glad to hear you cry, for then I knew that the Spirit of God was among us."

"Glad!" said Macdonald Dubh, faintly.

"Yes, glad. For a cry like that never comes but when the Spirit of God moves in the heart of a man."

"Indeed, I will be thinking that He has cast me off forever," he said, wondering at this new phase of the subject.

"Then you must thank Him, Mr. Macdonald, that He has not so done; and the sure proof to you is that He has brought you to cry for mercy. That is a glad cry, in the ears of the Saviour. It is the cry of the sheep in the wilderness, that discovers him to the shepherd." And then, without argument, she took him into her confidence and poured out to him all her hopes and fears for the young people of the congregation, and especially for Ranald, till Macdonald Dubh partly forgot his own fears in hers. And then, just before it was time for Kirsty to arrive from the "Question Meeting," she took her Gaelic Bible and opened at the Lord's Prayer, as she had done once before.

"It is a terrible thing to be unforgiven, Mr. Macdonald," she said, "by man or by God. And God is unwilling that any of us should feel that pain, and that is why he is so free with his offer of pardon to all who come with sorrow to him. They come with sorrow to him now, but they will come to him some day with great joy." And then she spoke a little of the great company of the forgiven before the throne, and at the very last, a few words about the gentle little woman that had passed out from Macdonald Dubh's sight so many years before. Then, falling on her knees, she began in the Gaelic,

"Our Father which art in Heaven."

Earnestly and brokenly Macdonald Dubh followed, whispering the petitions after her. When they came to

"Forgive us our debts, as we forgive our debtors,"

Macdonald Dubh broke forth: "Oh, it is a little thing, whatever! It is little I have to forgive." And then, in a clear, firm voice, he repeated the words after her to the close of the prayer.

Then Mrs. Murray rose, and taking him by the hand to bid him good by, she said, slowly: "'For if ye forgive men their trespasses, your heavenly Father will also forgive you your trespasses.' You have forgiven, Mr. Macdonald."

"Indeed, it is nothing," he said, earnestly.

"Then," replied Mrs. Murray, "the Lord will not break his promise to you." And with that she went away.

On Saturday morning the session met before the service for the day. In the midst of their deliberations the door opened and Macdonald Bhain and his brother, Macdonald Dubh, walked in and stood silent before the elders. Mr. Murray rose astonished, and coming forward, said to Macdonald Bhain: "What is it, Mr. Macdonald? You wish to see me?"

"I am here," he said, "for my own sake and for my brother's. We wish to make confession of our sins, in that we have not been men of love, and to seek the forgiveness of God."

The minister stood and gazed at him in amazed silence for some moments, and then, giving his hand to Macdonald Dubh, he said, in a voice husky with emotion: "Come away, my brother. The Lord has a welcome for you."

And there were no questions that day asked in the session before Macdonald Dubh received his token.

AND THE GLORY

The first communion in the new church was marked by very great solemnity. There were few new members, but among the older men who had hitherto kept "back from the table" there was a manifest anxiety, and among the younger people a very great seriousness. The "coming forward" of Macdonald Dubh was an event so remarkable as to make a great impression not only upon all the Macdonald men who had been associated with him so many years in the lumbering, but also upon the whole congregation, to whom his record and reputation were well known. His change of attitude to the church and all its interests, as well as his change of disposition and temperament, were so striking as to leave in no one's mind any doubt as to the genuineness of his "change of heart," and every week made this more apparent. A solemn sense of responsibility and an intensity of earnestness seemed to possess him, while his humility and gentleness were touching to see.

On the evening of Monday, the day of thanksgiving in the Sacrament Week, a great congregation assembled for the closing meeting of the Communion Season. During the progress of the meeting, Mr. Murray and the ministers assisting him became aware that they were in the presence of some remarkable and mysterious phenomenon. The people listened to the Word with an intensity, response, and eagerness that gave token of a state of mind and heart wholly unusual. Here and there, while the psalms were being sung or prayers being offered, women and men would break down in audible weeping; and in the preaching the speaker was conscious of a power possessing him that he could not explain.

At length the last psalm was given out, and the congregation, contrary to their usual custom, by the minister's direction, rose to sing. As John "Aleck" led the people in that great volume of praise, the ministers held a hasty consultation in the pulpit. The professor had never seen anything so marvelous; Mr. Murray was reminded of the days of W. C. Burns. The question was, What was to be done? Should the meetings be continued, or should they close to-night? They had a great fear of religious excitement. They had seen something of the dreadful reaction following a state of exalted religious feeling. It was the beginning of harvest, too. Would it be advisable to call the people from their hard work in the fields to nightly meetings?

At length, as the congregation were nearing the close of the psalm, the professor spoke. "Brethren," he said, "this is not our work. Let us leave it to the Lord to decide. Put the question to the people and abide by their decision."

After the psalm was sung, the minister motioned the congregation to their seats, and without comment or suggestion, put before them the question that had been discussed in the pulpit. Was it their desire that the meetings should be continued or not? A deep, solemn silence lay upon the crowded church, and for some time no one moved. Then the congregation were startled to see Macdonald Dubh rise slowly from his place in the middle of the church.

"Mr. Murray," he said, in a voice that vibrated strangely, "you will pardon me for letting my voice be heard in this place. It is the voice of a great sinner."

"Speak, Mr. Macdonald," said the minister, "and I thank God for the sound of your voice in His house."

"It is not for me to make any speeches here. I will only make bold to give my word that the meetings be continued. It may be that the Lord, who has done such great things for me, will do great things for others also." And with that he sat down.

"I will take that for a motion," said the minister. "Will any one second it?"

Kenny Crubach at once rose and said: "We are always slow at following the Lord. Let us go forward."

The minister waited for some moments after Kenny had spoken, and then said, in a voice grave and with a feeling of responsibility in it: "You have heard these brethren, my people. I wait for the expression of your desire."

Like one man the great congregation rose to their feet. It was a scene profoundly impressive, and with these serious-minded, sober people, one that indicated overwhelming emotion.

And thus the great revival began.

For eighteen months, night after night, every night in the week except Saturday, the people gathered in such numbers as to fill the new church to the door. Throughout all the busy harvest season, in spite of the autumn rains that filled the swamps and made the roads almost impassable, in the face of the driving snows of winter, through the melting ice of the spring, and again through the following summer and autumn, the great revival held on. No fictitious means were employed to stir the emotions of the people or to kindle excitement among them. There were neither special sermons nor revival hymns. The old doctrines were proclaimed, but proclaimed with a fullness and power unknown at other times. The old psalms were sung, but sung perhaps as they had never been before. For when John "Aleck's" mighty voice rolled forth in its full power, and when his band of trained singers followed, lifting onward with them the great congregation – for every man, woman, and child sang with full heart and open throat – the effect was something altogether wonderful and worth hearing. Each night there was a sermon by the minister, who, for six months, till his health broke down, had sole charge of the work. Then the sermon was followed by short addresses or prayers by the elders, and after that the minister would take the men, and his wife the women, for closer and more personal dealing.

As the revival deepened it became the custom for others than the elders to take part, by reading a psalm or other Scripture, without comment, or by prayer. There was a shrinking from anything like a violent display of emotion, and from any unveiling of the sacred secrets of the heart, but Scripture reading or quoting was supposed to express the thoughts, the hopes, the fears, the gratitude, the devotion, that made the religious experience of the speaker. This was as far as they considered it safe or seemly to go.

One of the first, outside the ranks of the elders, to take part in this way was Macdonald Dubh; then Long John Cameron followed; then Peter McGregor and others of the men of maturer years. A distinct stage in the revival was reached when young Aleck McRae rose to read his Scripture. He was quickly followed by Don, young Findlayson, and others of that age, and from that time onward the old line that had so clearly distinguished age from youth in respect to religious duty and privilege, was obliterated forever. It had been a strange, if not very doubtful, phenomenon to see a young man "coming forward," or in any way giving indication of religious feeling. But this would never be again.

It was no small anxiety and grief to Mrs. Murray that Ranald, though he regularly attended the meetings, seemed to remain unmoved by the tide of religious feeling that was everywhere surging through the hearts of the people. The minister advised letting him alone, but Mrs. Murray was anxiously waiting for the time when Ranald would come to her. That time came, but not until long months of weary waiting on her part, and of painful struggle on his, had passed.

From the very first of the great movement his father threw himself into it with all the earnest intensity of his nature, but at the same time with a humility that gave token that the memory of the wild days of his youth and early manhood were never far away from him. He was eager to serve in the work, and was a constant source of wonder to all who had known him in his youth and early manhood. At all the different meetings he was present. Nothing could keep him away. "Night cometh," he said to his brother, who was remonstrating with him. His day's work was drawing to its close.

But Ranald would not let himself see the failing of his father's health, and when, in the harvest, the slightest work in the fields would send his father panting to the shade, Ranald would say, "It is the hot weather, father. When the cool days come you will be better. And why should you be bothering yourself with the work, anyway? Surely Yankee and I can look after that." And indeed they seemed to be quite fit to take off the harvest.

Day by day Ranald swung his cradle after Yankee with all a man's steadiness till all the grain was cut; and by the time the harvest was over, Ranald had developed a strength of muscle and a skill in the harvest work that made him equal of almost any man in the country. He was all the more eager to have the harvest work done in time, that his father might not fret over his own inability to help. For Ranald could not bear to see the look of disappointment that sometimes showed itself in his father's face when weakness drove him from the field, and it was this that made him throw himself into the work as he did. He was careful also to consult with his father in regard to all the details of the management of the farm, and to tell him all that he was planning to do as well as all that was done. His father had always been a kind of hero to Ranald, who admired him for his prowess with the gun and the ax, as well as for his great strength and courage. But ever since calamity had befallen him, the boy's heart had gone out to his father in a new tenderness, and the last months had drawn the two very close together. It was a dark day for Ranald when he was forced to face the fact that his father was growing daily weaker. It was his uncle, Macdonald Bhain, who finally made him see it.

"Your father is failing, Ranald," he said one day toward the close of harvest.

"It is the hot weather," said Ranald. "He will be better in the fall."

"Ranald, my boy," said his uncle, gravely, "your father will fade with the leaf, and the first snow will lie upon him."

And then Ranald fairly faced the fact that before long he would be alone in the world. Without any exchange of words, he and his father came to understand each other, and they both knew that they were spending their last days on earth together.

On the son's side, they were days of deepening sorrow; but with the father, every day seemed to bring him a greater peace of mind and a clearer shining of the light that never fades. To his son, Macdonald Dubh never spoke of the death that he felt to be drawing nearer, but he often spoke to him of the life he would like his son to live. His only other confidant in these matters was the minister's wife. To her Macdonald Dubh opened up his heart, and to her, more than to any one else, he owed his growing peace and light; and it was touching to see the devotion and the tenderness that he showed to her as often as she came to see him. With his brother, Macdonald Bhain, he made all the arrangements necessary for the disposal of the farm and the payment of the mortgage.

Ranald had no desire to be a farmer, and indeed, when the mortgage was paid there would not be much left.

"He will be my son," said Macdonald Bhain to his brother; "and my home will be his while I live."

So in every way there was quiet preparation for Macdonald Dubh's going, and when at last the day came, there was no haste or fear.

It was in the afternoon of a bright September day, as the sun was nearing the tops of the pine-trees in the west. His brother was supporting him in his strong arms, while Ranald knelt by the bedside. Near him sat the minister's wife, and at a little distance Kirsty.

"Lift me up, Tonal," said the dying man; "I will be wanting to see the sun again, and then I will be going. I will be going to the land where they will not need the light of the sun. Tonal, bhodaich, it is the good brother you have been to me, and many's the good day we have had together."

"Och, Hugh, man. Are you going from me?" said Macdonald Bhain, with great sorrow in his voice.

"Aye, Tonal, for a little." Then he looked for a few moments at Kirsty, who was standing at the foot of the bed.

"Come near me, Kirsty," he said; and Kirsty came to the bedside.

"You have always been kind to me and mine, and you were kind to *her* as well, and the reward will come to you." Then he turned to Mrs. Murray, and said, with a great light of joy in his eyes: "It is you that came to me as the angel of God with a word of salvation, and forever more I will be blessing you." And then he added, in a voice full of tenderness, "I will be telling her about you." He took Mrs. Murray's hand and tremblingly lifted it to his lips.

"It has been a great joy to me," said Mrs. Murray, with difficulty steadying her voice, "to see you come to your Saviour, Mr. Macdonald."

"Aye, I know it well," he said; and then he added, in a voice that sank almost to a whisper, "Now you will be reading the prayer." And Mrs. Murray, opening her Gaelic Bible, repeated in her clear, soft voice, the words of the Lord's Prayer. Through all the petitions he followed her, until he came to the words, "Forgive us our debts." There he paused.

"Ranald, my man," he said, raising his hand with difficulty and laying it upon the boy's head, "you will listen to me now. Some day you will find the man that brought me to this, and you will say to him that your father forgave him freely, and wished him all the blessing of God. You will promise me this, Ranald?" said Macdonald Dubh.

"Yes, father," said Ranald, lifting his head, and looking into his father's face.

"And, Ranald, you, too, will be forgiving him?" But to this there was no reply. Ranald's head was buried in the bed.

"Ah," said Macdonald Dubh, with difficulty, "you are

your father's son; but you will not be laying this bitterness upon me now. You will be forgiving him, Ranald?"

"Oh, father!" cried Ranald, with a breaking voice, "how can I forgive him? How can I forgive the man who has taken you away from me?"

"It is no man," replied his father, "but the Lord himself; the Lord who has forgiven your father much. I am waiting to hear you, Ranald."

Then, with a great sob, Ranald broke forth: "Oh, father, I will forgive him," and immediately became quiet, and so continued to the end.

After some moments of silence, Macdonald Dubh looked once more toward the minister's wife, and a radiant smile spread over his face.

"You will be finishing," he said.

Her face was wet with tears, and for a few moments she could not speak. But it was no time to fail in duty, so, commanding her tears, with a clear, unwavering voice she went on to the end of the prayer –

"For thine is the kingdom and the power and the glory, forever and ever. Amen."

"Glory!" said Macdonald Dubh after her. "Aye, the Glory. Ranald, my boy, where are you? You will be following me, lad, to the Glory. *She* will be asking me about you. You will be following me, lad?"

The anxious note in his voice struck Ranald to the heart.

"Oh, father, it is what I want," he replied, brokenly. "I will try."

"Aye," said Macdonald Dubh, "and you will come. I will be telling *her*. Now lay me down, Tonal; I will be going."

Macdonald Bhain laid him quietly back on his pillow, and for a moment he lay with his eyes closed.

Once more he opened his eyes, and with a troubled look upon his face, and in a voice of doubt and fear, he cried: "It is a sinful man, O Lord, a sinful man."

His eyes wandered till they fell on Mrs. Murray's face, and then the trouble and fear passed out of them, and in a gentler voice he said: "Forgive us our debts." Then, feeling with his hand till it rested on his son's head, Macdonald Dubh passed away, at peace with men and with God.

There was little sadness and no bitter grief at Macdonald Dubh's funeral. The tone all through was one of triumph, for they all knew his life, and how sore the fight had been, and how he had won his victory. His humility and his gentleness during the last few weeks of his life had removed all the distance that had separated him from the people, and had drawn their hearts toward him; and now in his final triumph they could not find it in their hearts to mourn.

But to Ranald the sadness was more than the triumph. Through the wild, ungoverned years of his boyhood his father had been more than a father to him. He had been a friend, sharing a common lot, and without much show of tenderness, understanding and sympathizing with him, and now that his father had gone from him, a great loneliness fell upon the lad.

The farm and its belongings were sold. Kirsty brought with her the big box of blankets and linen that had belonged to Ranald's mother. Ranald took his mother's Gaelic Bible, his father's gun and ax, and with the great deerhound, Bugle, and his colt, Lisette, left the home of his childhood behind him, and with his Aunt Kirsty, went to live with his uncle.

Throughout the autumn months he was busy helping his uncle with the plowing, the potatoes, and the fall work. Soon the air began to nip, and the night's frost to last throughout the shortening day, and then Macdonald Bhain began to prepare wood for the winter, and to make all things snug about the house and barn; and when the first fall of snow fell softly, he took down his broadax, and then Ranald knew that the gang would soon be off again for the shanties. That night his uncle talked long with him about his future.

"I have no son, Ranald," he said, as they sat talking; "and for your father's sake and for your own, it is my desire that you should become a son to me, and there is no one but yourself to whom the farm would go. And glad will I be if you will stay with me. But, stay or not, all that I have will be yours, if it please the Lord to spare you."

"I would want nothing better," said Ranald, "than to stay with you and work with you, but I do not draw toward the farm."

"And what else would you do, Ranald?"

"Indeed, I know not," said Ranald, "but something else than farming. But meantime I should like to go to the shanties with you this winter."

And so, when the Macdonald gang went to the woods that winter, Ranald, taking his father's ax, went with them. And so clever did the boy prove himself that by the time they brought down their raft in the spring there was not a man in all the gang that Macdonald Bhain would sooner have at his back in a tight place than his nephew Ranald. And, indeed, those months in the woods made a man out of the long, lanky boy, so that, on the first Sabbath after the shantymen came home, not many in the church that day would have recognized the dark-faced, stalwart youth had it not been that he sat in the pew beside Macdonald Bhain. It was with no small difficulty that the minister's wife could keep her little boy quiet in the back seat, so full of pride and joy was he at the appearance of his hero; but after the service was over, Hughie could be no longer restrained. Pushing his way eagerly through the crowd, he seized upon Ranald and dragged him to his mother.

"Here he is, mother!" he exclaimed, to Ranald's great confusion, and to the amusement of all about him. "Isn't he splendid?"

And as Ranald greeted Mrs. Murray with quiet, grave courtesy, she felt that his winter in the woods and on the river had forever put behind him his boyhood, and that henceforth he would take his place among the men. And looking at his strong, composed, grave face, she felt that that place ought not to be an unworthy one.

LeNOIR'S NEW MASTER

The shantymen came back home to find the revival still going on. Not a home but had felt its mighty power, and not a man, woman, or even child but had come more or less under its influence. Indeed, so universal was that power that Yankee was heard to say, "The boys wouldn't go in swimmin' without their New Testaments" – not but that Yankee was in very fullest sympathy with the movement. He was regular in his attendance upon the meetings all through spring and summer, but his whole previous history made it difficult for him to fully appreciate the intensity and depth of the religious feeling that was everywhere throbbing through the community.

"Don't see what the excitement's for," he said to Macdonald Bhain one night after meeting. "Seems to me the Almighty just wants a feller to do the right thing by his neighbor and not be too independent, but go 'long kind o' humble like and keep clean. Somethin' wrong with me, perhaps, but I don't seem to be able to work up no excitement about it. I'd like to, but somehow it ain't in me."

When Macdonald Bhain reported this difficulty of Yankee's to Mrs. Murray, she only said: "'What doth the Lord require of thee, but to do justly, and to love mercy, and to walk humbly with thy God?'" And with this Macdonald Bhain was content, and when he told Yankee, the latter came as near to excitement as he ever allowed himself. He chewed vigorously for a few moments, then, slapping his thigh, he exclaimed: "By jings! That's great. She's all right, ain't she? We ain't all built the same way, but I'm blamed if I don't like her model."

But the shantymen noticed that the revival had swept into the church, during the winter months, a great company of the young people of the congregation; and of these, a band of some ten or twelve young men, with Don among them, were attending daily a special class carried on in the vestry of the church for those who desired to enter training for the ministry.

Mrs. Murray urged Ranald to join this class, for, even though he had no intention of becoming a minister, still the study would be good for him, and would help him in his after career. She remembered how Ranald had told her that he had no intention of being a farmer or lumberman. And Ranald gladly listened to her, and threw himself into his study, using his spare hours to such good purpose throughout the summer that he easily kept pace with the class in English, and distanced them in his favorite subject, mathematics.

But all these months Mrs. Murray felt that Ranald was carrying with him a load of unrest, and she waited for the time when he would come to her. His uncle, Macdonald Bhain, too, shared her anxiety in regard to Ranald.

"He is the fine, steady lad," he said one night, walking home with her from the church; "and a good winter's work has he put behind him. He is that queeck, there is not a man like him on the drive; but he is not the same boy that he was. He will not be telling me anything, but when the boys will be sporting, he is not with them. He will be reading his book, or he will be sitting by himself alone. He is like his father in the courage of him. There is no kind of water he will not face, and no man on the river would put fear on him. And the strength of him! His arms are like steel. But," returning to his anxiety, "there is something wrong with him. He is not at peace with himself, and I wish you could get speech with him."

"I would like it, too," replied Mrs. Murray. "Perhaps he will come to me. At any rate, I must wait for that."

At last, when the summer was over, and the harvest all gathered in, the days were once more shortening for the fall, Ranald drove Lisette one day to the manse, and went straight to the minister's wife and opened up his mind to her.

"I cannot keep my promise to my father, Mrs. Murray," he said, going at once to the heart of his trouble. "I cannot keep the anger out of my heart. I cannot forgive the man that killed my father. I will be waking at night with the very joy of feeling my fingers on his throat, and I feel myself longing for the day when I will meet him face to face and nothing between us. But," he added, "I promised my father, and I must keep my word, and that is what I cannot do, for the feeling of forgiveness is not here," smiting his breast. "I can keep my hands off him, but the feeling I cannot help."

For a long time Mrs. Murray let him go on without seeking to check the hot flow of his words and without a word of reproof. Then, when he had talked himself to silence, she took her Bible and read to him of the servant who, though forgiven, took his fellow-servant by the throat, refusing to forgive. And then she turned over the leaves and read once more: "'God commendeth his love toward us, in that, while we were yet sinners, Christ died for us.'"

She closed the book and sat silent, waiting for Ranald to speak.

"I know," he said, deliberately; "I have read that often through the winter, but it does not help the feeling I have. I think it only makes it worse. There is some one holding my arm, and I want to strike."

"And do you forget," said Mrs. Murray, and her voice was almost stern, "and do you forget how, for you, God gave His Son to die?"

Ranald shook his head. "I am far from forgetting that."

"And are you forgetting the great mercy of God to your father?"

"No, no," said Ranald; "I often think of that. But when I think of that man, something stirs within me and I cannot see, for the daze before my eyes, and I know that some day I will be at him. I cannot help my feeling."

"Ranald," said Mrs. Murray, "have you ever thought how he will need God's mercy like yourself? And have you never thought that perhaps he has never had the way of God's mercy put before him? To you the Lord has given much, to him little. It is a terrible thing to be ungrateful for the mercy of God; and it is a shameful thing. It is unworthy of any true man. How can any one take the fullness of God's mercy and his patience every day, and hold an ungrateful heart?"

She did not spare him, and as Ranald sat and listened, his life and character began to appear to him small and mean and unworthy.

"The Lord means you to be a noble man, Ranald – a man with the heart and purpose to do some good in the world, to be a blessing to his fellows; and it is a poor thing to be so filled up with selfishness as to have no thought of the honor of God or of the good of men. Louis LeNoir has done you a great wrong, but what is that wrong compared with the wrong you have done to Him who loved you to His own death?"

Then she gave him her last word: "When you see Louis LeNoir, think of God's mercy, and remember you are to do him good and not evil."

And with that word in his heart, Ranald went away, ashamed and humbled, but not forgiving. The time for that had not yet come. But before he left for the shanties, he saw Mrs. Murray again to say good by. He met her with a shamed face, fearing that she must feel nothing but contempt for him.

"You will think ill of me," he said, and in spite of his self-control his voice shook. "I could not bear that."

"No, I could never think ill of you, Ranald, but I would be grieved to think that you should fail of becoming a noble man, strong and brave; strong enough to forgive and brave enough to serve."

Once more Ranald went to the woods, with earnest thoughts in his mind, hoping he should not meet LeNoir, and fighting out his battle to victory; and by the time the drive had reached the big water next spring, that battle was almost over. The days in the silent woods and the nights spent with his uncle in the camp, and afterward in his cabin on the raft, did their work with Ranald.

The timber cut that year was the largest that had ever been known on the Upper Ottawa. There was great crowding of rafts on the drive, and for weeks the chutes were full, and when the rafts were all brought together at Quebec, not only were the shores lined and Timber Cove packed, but the broad river was full from Quebec to Levis, except for the steamboat way which must be kept open.

For the firm of Raymond & St. Clair this meant enormous increase of business, and it was no small annoyance that at this crisis they should have detected their Quebec agent in fraud, and should have been forced to dismiss him. The situation was so critical that Mr. St. Clair himself, with Harry as his clerk, found it necessary to spend a month in Quebec. He took with him Maimie and her great friend Kate Raymond, the daughter of his partner, and established himself in the Hotel Cheval Blanc.

On the whole, Maimie was not sorry to visit the ancient capital of Canada, though she would have chosen another time. It was rather disappointing to leave her own city in the West, just at the beginning of the spring gayeties. It was her first season, and the winter had been distinguished by a series of social triumphs. She was the toast of all the clubs and the belle of all the balls. She had developed a rare and fascinating beauty, and had acquired an air so *distingué* that even her aunt, Miss St. Clair, was completely satisfied. It was a little hard for her to leave the scene of her triumphs and to abandon the approaching gayeties.

But Quebec had its compensations, and then there were the De Lacys, one of the oldest English families of Quebec. The St. Clairs had known them for many years. Their blood was unquestionably blue, they were wealthy, and besides, the only son and representative of the family was now lieutenant, attached to the garrison at the Citadel. Lieutenant De Lacy suggested possibilities to Maimie. Quebec might be endurable for a month.

"What a lovely view, and how picturesque!"

Maimie was standing at the window looking down upon the river with its fleet of rafts. Beside her stood Kate, and at another window Harry.

"What a lot of timber!" said Harry. "And the town is just full of lumbermen. A fellow said there must be six thousand of them, so there will be lots of fun."

"Fun!" exclaimed Kate.

"Fun! rather. These fellows have been up in the woods for some five or six months, and when they get to town where there is whisky and – and – that sort of thing, they just get wild. They say it is awful."

"Just horrible!" said Maimie, in a disgusted tone.

"But splendid," said Kate; "that is, if they don't hurt any one."

"Hurt anybody!" exclaimed Harry. "Oh, not at all; they are always extremely careful not to hurt any one. They are as gentle as lambs. I say, let us go down to the river and look at the rafts. De Lacy was coming up, but it is too late now for him. Besides, we might run across Maimie's man from Glengarry."

"Maimie's man from Glengarry!" exclaimed Kate. "Has she a man there, too?"

"Nonsense, Kate!" said Maimie, blushing. "He is talking about Ranald, you know. One of Aunt Murray's young men, up in Glengarry. You have heard me speak of him often."

"Oh, the boy that pulled you out of the fire," said Kate.

"Yes," cried Harry, striking an attitude, "and the boy that for love of her entered the lists, and in a fistic tournament upheld her fair name, and –"

"Oh, Harry, do have some sense!" said Maimie, impatiently. "Hush, here comes some one; Lieutenant De Lacy, I suppose."

It was the lieutenant, handsome, tall, well made, with a high-bred if somewhat dissipated face, an air of *blasé* indifference a little overdone, and an accent which he had brought back with him from Oxford, and which he was anxious not to lose. Indeed, the bare thought of the possibility of his dropping into the flat, semi-nasal of his native land filled the lieutenant with unspeakable horror.

"We were just going down to the river," said Maimie, after the introductions were over, "but I suppose it is all old to you, and you would not care to go?"

"Aw, charmed, I'm sure." (The lieutenant pronounced it "shuah.") "But it is rathaw, don't you know, not exactly clean."

"He is thinking of his boots," said Harry, scornfully, looking down at the lieutenant's shining patent leathers.

"Really," said the lieutenant, mildly, "awfully dirty street, though."

"But we want to see the shantymen," said Kate, frankly.

"Oh, the men! Very proper, but not so very discriminating, you know."

"I love the shantymen," exclaimed Kate, enthusiastically. "Maimie told me all about them."

"By Jove! I'll join to-morrow," exclaimed the lieutenant with gentle excitement.

"They would not have you," answered Kate. "Besides, you would have to eat pork and onions and things."

The lieutenant shuddered, gazing reproachfully at Kate.

"Onions!" he gasped; "and you love them?"

"Let us go along, then," said Harry. "We will have a look at them, anyway."

"From the windward side, I hope," said the lieutenant, gently.

"I am going right on the raft," declared Kate, stoutly, "if we can only find Ranald."

"Meaning who, exactly?" questioned De Lacy.

"A lumberman whom Maimie adores."

"How happy!" said De Lacy.

"Nonsense, Lieutenant De Lacy," said Maimie, impatiently and a little haughtily; "he is a friend of my aunt's up in the county of Glengarry."

"No nonsense about it," said Harry, indignant that his sister should seem indifferent to Ranald. "He is a great friend of us all; and you will see – she will fly into his arms."

"Heaven forbid!" ejaculated the lieutenant, much shocked.

"Harry, how can you be so – ?" said Maimie, much annoyed. "What will the lieutenant think of me?"

"Ah, if I only might tell!" said the lieutenant, looking at her with languishing eyes. But already Kate was downstairs and on her way to the street.

As they neared the lower town, the narrow streets became more and more crowded with men in the shantymen's picturesque dress, and they had some difficulty in making their way through the jolly, jostling crowds. As they were nearing the river, they saw coming along the narrow sidewalk a burly French-Canadian, dressed in the gayest holiday garb of the shantymen – red shirt and sash, corduroys tucked into red top-boots, a little round soft hat set upon the back of his black curls, a gorgeous silk handkerchief around his neck, and a big gold watch-chain with seals at his belt. He had a bold, handsome face, and swaggered along the sidewalk, claiming it all with an assurance fortified by whisky enough to make him utterly regardless of any but his own rights.

"Hello!" he shouted, as he swaggered along. "Make way, I'm de boss bully on de reever Hottawa." It was his day of glory, and it evidently pleased him much that the people stood aside to let him pass. Then he broke into song: –

"En roulant ma boule roulant,
En roulant me boule."

"This, I suppose, is one of your beloved shantymen," said the lieutenant, turning to Kate, who was walking with Harry behind.

"Isn't he lovely!" exclaimed Kate.

"Oh," cried Maimie, in terror, "let us get into a shop!"

"Quite unnecessary, I assure you," said the lieutenant, indifferently; "I have not the least idea that he will molest you."

The lumberman by this time had swaggered up to the party, expecting them to make way, but instead, De Lacy stiffened his shoulder, caught the Frenchman in the chest, and rolled him off into the street. Surprised and enraged, the Frenchman turned to demolish the man who had dared to insult the "boss bully on de reever Hottawa."

"Vous n'avez pas remarqué la demoiselle," said the lieutenant, in a tone of politeness.

The lumberman, who had swaggered up ready to strike, glanced at Maimie, took off his hat, and made a ceremonious bow.

"Eh bien! Non! Pardon, Mams'elle."

"Bon jour," said Lieutenant De Lacy, with a military salute, and moved on, leaving the lumberman staring after them as if he had seen a vision.

"Beauty and the Beast," murmured the lieutenant. "Thought I was in for it, sure. Really wonderful, don't you know!"

"Do you think we had better go on?" said Maimie, turning to Kate and Harry.

"Why not? Why, certainly!" they exclaimed.

"These horrid men," replied Maimie.

"Dear creatures!" said the lieutenant, glancing at Kate with a mildly pathetic look. "Sweet, but not always fragrant."

"Oh, they won't hurt us. Let us go on."

"Certainly, go on," echoed Harry, impatiently.

"Safe enough, Miss St. Clair, but," pulling out his perfumed handkerchief, "rather trying."

"Oh, get on, De Lacy," cried Harry, and so they moved on.

The office of Raymond & St. Clair stood near the wharves. Harry paused at the door, not quite sure whether to go in or not. It was easy to discover work in that office.

"You might ask if Ranald has come," said Kate. "Maimie is too shy."

Harry returned in a few moments, quite excited.

"The Macdonald gang are in, and the Big Macdonald was here not half an hour ago, and Ranald is down at the raft beyond the last wharf. I know the place."

"Oh, do let us go on!" cried Kate, to whom Harry had been extolling Ranald on the way down. "You really ought to inspect your timber, Harry, shouldn't you?"

"Most certainly, and right away. No saying what might happen."

"Awful slush," said the lieutenant, glancing at Maimie's face. "Do you think the timber wouldn't keep for a week?"

"Oh, rubbish! A week!" cried Harry. "He is thinking of his boots again."

To be quite fair to the lieutenant, it was Maimie's doubtful face, rather than his shiny boots, that made him hesitate. She was evidently nervous and embarrassed. The gay, easy manner which was her habit was gone.

"I think perhaps we had better go, since we are here," she said, doubtfully.

"Exactly; it is what I most desired," said the lieutenant, gallantly.

Scores of rafts lay moored along the wharves and shore, and hundreds of lumbermen were to be seen everywhere, not only on the timber and wharves, but crowding the streets and the doors of the little saloons.

For half an hour they walked along, watching the men at work with the timber on the river. Some were loading the vessels lying at anchor, some were shifting the loose timber about. When they reached the end of the last wharf, they saw a strapping young lumberman, in a shanty costume that showed signs of the woods, running some loose sticks of timber round the end of the raft. With great skill he was handling his pike, walking the big sticks and running lightly over the timber too small to carry him, balancing himself on a single stick while he moved the timber to the bit of open water behind the raft, and all with a grace and dexterity that excited Kate's admiration to the highest degree.

"Rather clever, that," said the lieutenant, lazily. "Hello! close call, that; ha! bravo!" It was not often the lieutenant allowed himself the luxury of excitement, but the lumberman running his timber slipped his pike pole and found himself balancing on the edge of open water. With a mighty spring he cleared the open space, touched a piece of small timber that sank under him, and at the next spring landed safe on the raft. Maimie's scream sounded with the lieutenant's "bravo." At the cry the young fellow looked up. It was Ranald.

"Hello, there!" cried Harry; and with an answering shout, Ranald, using his pike as a jumping-pole, cleared the open space, ran lightly over the floating sticks, and with another spring reached the shore. Without a moment's hesitation he dropped his pole and came almost running toward them, his face radiant with delight.

"Maimie!" he exclaimed, holding out his hand, wet and none too clean.

"How do you do?" said Maimie. She had noticed the look of surprise and mild disgust on the lieutenant's face, and she was embarrassed. Ranald was certainly not lovely to look at. His shirt was open at the neck, torn, and dirty. His trousers and boots were much the worse of their struggle with the bush.

"This is Mr. Macdonald, Lieutenant De Lacy," Maimie hurried to say. The lieutenant offered a limp hand.

"Chawmed, I'm suah," he murmured.

"What?" said Ranald.

"Lovely weather," murmured the lieutenant again, looking at his fingers that Ranald had just let go.

"Well, old chap," said Harry, grasping Ranald's hand and throwing his arm about his shoulder, "I am awfully glad to find you. We have been hunting you for half an hour. But hold up, here you are. Let me introduce you to Miss Kate Raymond, the best girl anywhere."

Kate came forward with a frank smile. "I am very glad to meet you," she said. "I have heard so much about you, and I am going to call you Ranald, as they all do."

"How lovely!" sighed De Lacy.

Her greeting warmed Ranald's heart that somehow had been chilled in the meeting. Something was wrong. Was it this fop of a soldier, or had Maimie changed? Ranald glanced at her face. No, she was the same, only more beautiful than he had dreamed.

But while she was shaking hands with him, there flashed across his mind the memory of the first time he had seen her, and the look of amusement upon her face then, that had given him such deadly offense. There was no amusement now, but there was embarrassment and something else. Ranald could not define it, but it chilled his heart, and at once he began to feel how badly dressed he was. The torn shirt, the ragged trousers, and the old, unshapely boots that he had never given a thought to before, now seemed to burn into his flesh. Unconsciously he backed away and turned to go.

"Where are you off to?" cried Harry; "do you think we are going to let you go now? We had hard enough work finding you. Come up to the office and see the governor. He wants to see you badly."

Ranald glanced at the lieutenant, immaculate except where the slush had speckled his shiny boots, and then at his own ragged attire. "I think I will not go up now," he said.

"Well, come up soon," said Maimie, evidently relieved.

"No!" said Kate, impetuously, "come right along now." As she spoke she ranged herself beside him.

For a moment or two Ranald hesitated, shot a searching glance at Maimie's face, and then, with a reckless laugh, said, "I will go now," and set off forthwith, Kate proudly marching at one side, and Harry on the other, leaving Maimie and the lieutenant to follow after.

And a good thing it was for Ranald that he did go that day with Harry to his "governor's" office. They found the office in a "swither," as Harry said, over the revelations of fraud that were coming to light every day – book-keeper, clerk, and timber-checker having all been in conspiracy to defraud the company.

"Where have you been, Harry?" said his father in an annoyed tone as his son entered the office. "You don't seem to realize how much there is to do just now."

"Looking up Ranald, father," said Harry, cheerfully.

"Ah, the young man from Glengarry?" said Mr. St. Clair, rising. "I am glad to know you, and to thank you in person for your prompt courage in saving my daughter."

"Lucky dog!" groaned the lieutenant, in an undertone to Maimie.

Mr. St. Clair spoke to Ranald of his father and his uncle in words of highest appreciation, and as Ranald listened, the reckless and hard look which had been gathering ever since his meeting with Maimie passed away, and his face became earnest and touched with a tender pride.

"I hear about you frequently from my sister, Mr. Macdonald – or shall I say Ranald?" said Mr. St. Clair, kindly. "She apparently thinks something of you."

"I am proud to think so," replied Ranald, his face lighting up as he spoke; "but every one loves her. She is a wonderful woman, and good."

"Yes," said Mr. St. Clair, "that's it; wonderful and good."

Then Maimie drew nearer. "How is auntie?" she said. "What a shame not to have asked before!"

"She was very well last fall," said Ranald, looking keenly into Maimie's face; "but she is working too hard at the meetings."

"Meetings!" exclaimed Harry.

"Aye, for a year and more she has been at them every night till late."

"At meetings for a year! What meetings?" cried Harry, astonished.

"Oh, Harry, you know about the great revival going on quite well," said Maimie.

"Oh, yes. I forgot. What a shame! What is the use of her killing herself that way?"

"There is much use," said Ranald, gravely. "They are making bad men good, and the whole countryside is new, and she is the heart of it all."

"I have no doubt about that," said Mr. St. Clair. "She will be the head and heart and hands and feet."

"You're just right, governor," said Harry, warmly. "There is no woman living like Aunt Murray."

There was silence for a few moments. Then Mr. St. Clair said suddenly: "We are in an awful fix here. Not a man to be found that we can depend upon for book-keeper, clerk, or checker."

Harry coughed slightly.

"Oh, of course, Harry is an excellent book-keeper," Harry bowed low; "while he is at it," added Mr. St. Clair.

"Very neat one," murmured the lieutenant.

"Now, father, do not spoil a fine compliment in that way," cried Harry.

"But now the checker is gone," said Mr. St. Clair, "and that is extremely awkward."

"I say," cried Harry, "what will you give me for a checker right now?"

Mr. St. Clair looked at him and then at the lieutenant.

"Pardon me, Mr. St. Clair." said that gentleman, holding up his hand. "I used to check a little at Rugby, but –"

"Not you, by a long hand," interrupted Harry, disdainfully.

"This awfully charming brother of yours, so very frank, don't you know!" said the lieutenant, softly, to Maimie, while they all laughed.

"But here is your man, governor," said Harry, laying his hand on Ranald.

"Ranald!" exclaimed Mr. St. Clair. "Why, the very man! You understand timber, and you are honest."

"I will answer for both with my head," said Harry.

"What do you say, Ranald?" said Mr. St. Clair. "Will you take a day to think it over?"

"No," said Ranald; "I will be your checker." And so Ranald became part of the firm of Raymond & St. Clair.

"Come along, Ranald," said Harry. "We will take the girls home, and then come back to the office."

"Yes, do come," said Kate, heartily. Maimie said nothing.

"No," said Ranald; "I will go back to the raft first, and then come to the office. Shall I begin tonight?" he said to Mr. St. Clair.

"To-morrow morning will do, Ranald," said Mr. St. Clair. "Come up to the hotel and see us to-night." But Ranald said nothing. Then Maimie went up to him.

"Good by, just now," she said, smiling into his face. "You will come and see us to-night, perhaps?"

Ranald looked at her, while the blood mounted slowly into his dark cheek, and said: "Yes, I will come."

"What's the matter with you, Maimie?" said Harry, indignantly, when they had got outside. "You would think Ranald was a stranger, the way you treat him."

"And he is just splendid! I wish he had pulled *me* out of the fire," cried Kate.

"You might try the river," said the lieutenant. "I fancy he would go in. Looks that sort."

"Go in?" cried Harry, "he would go anywhere." The lieutenant made no reply. He evidently considered that it was hardly worth the effort to interest himself in the young lumberman, but before he was many hours older he found reason to change his mind.

After taking the young ladies to their hotel there was still an hour till the lieutenant's dinner, so, having resolved to cultivate the St. Clair family, he proposed accompanying Harry back to the office.

As they approached the lower portion of the town they heard wild shouts, and sauntering down a side street, they came upon their French-Canadian friend of the afternoon. He was standing with his back against a wall trying to beat off three or four men, who were savagely striking and kicking at him, and crying the while: "Gatineau! Gatineau!"

It was the Gatineau against the Ottawa.

"Our friend seems to have found the object of his search," said the lieutenant, as he stood across the street looking at the mêlée.

"I say, he's a good one, isn't he?" cried Harry, admiring the Ottawa's dauntless courage and his fighting skill.

"His eagerness for war will probably be gratified in a few minutes, by the look of things," replied the lieutenant.

The Gatineaus were crowding around, and had evidently made up their minds to bring the Ottawa champion to the dust. That they were numbers to one mattered not at all. There was little chivalry in a shantymen's fight.

"Ha! Rather a good one, that," exclaimed the lieutenant, mildly interested. "He put that chap out somewhat neatly." He lit a cigar and stood coolly watching the fight.

"Where are the Ottawas – the fellow's friends?" said Harry, much excited.

"I rather think they camp on another street further down."

The Ottawa champion was being sorely pressed, and it looked as if in a moment or two more he would be down.

"What a shame!" cried Harry.

"Well," said the lieutenant, languidly, "it's beastly dirty, but the chap's done rather well, so here goes."

Smoking his cigar, and followed by Harry, he pushed across the street to the crowd, and got right up to the fighters.

"Here, you fellows," he called out, in a high, clear voice, "what the deuce do you mean, kicking up such a row? Come now, stop, and get out of here."

The astonished crowd stopped fighting and fell back a little. The calm, clear voice of command and her majesty's uniform awed them.

"Mon camarade!" said the lieutenant, removing his cigar and saluting, "rather warm, eh?"

"You bet! Ver' warm tam," was the reply.

"Better get away, mon ami. The odds are rather against you," said the lieutenant. "Your friends are some distance down the next street. You better go along." So saying, he stepped out toward the crowd of Gatineaus who were consulting and yelling.

"Excuse me, gentlemen," he said, politely, waving his little cane. Those immediately in front gave back, allowed the lieutenant, followed by the Ottawa man and Harry, to pass, and immediately closed in behind. They might have escaped had it not been that the Ottawa man found it impossible to refrain from hurling taunts at them and inviting them to battle. They had gone not more than two blocks when there was a rush from behind, and before they could defend themselves they were each in the midst of a crowd, fighting for their lives. The principal attack was, of course, made upon the Ottawa man, but the crowd was quite determined to prevent the lieutenant and Harry from getting near him. In vain they struggled to break through the yelling mass of Gatineaus, who now had become numerous enough to fill the street from wall to wall, and among whom could be seen some few of the

Ottawa men trying to force their way toward their champion. By degrees both Harry and De Lacy fought their way to the wall, and toward each other.

"Looks as if our man had met his Waterloo," said the lieutenant, waiting for his particular man to come again.

"What a lot of beasts they are!" said Harry, disgustedly, beating off his enemy.

"Hello! Here they come again. We shall have to try another shot, I suppose," said the lieutenant, as the crowd, which had for a few moments surged down the street, now came crushing back, with the Ottawa leader, and some half-dozen of his followers in the center.

"Well, here goes," said De Lacy, leaving the wall and plunging into the crowd, followed by Harry. As they reached the center a voice called out: "À bas les Anglais!"

And immediately the cry, a familiar enough one in those days, was taken up on all sides. The crowd stiffened, and the attack upon the center became more determined than ever. The little company formed a circle, and standing back to back, held their ground for a time.

"Make for the wall. Keep together," cried De Lacy, pushing out toward the side, and followed by his company. But, one by one, the Ottawas were being dragged down and trampled beneath the "corked" boots of their foes, till only two of them, with their leader, beside Harry and De Lacy, were left.

At length the wall was gained. There they faced about and for a time held their lives safe. But every moment fresh men rushed in upon them, yelling their cries, "Gatineau! Gatineau! À bas les Anglais!"

The Ottawa leader was panting hard, and he could not much longer hold his own. His two companions were equally badly off. Harry was pale and bleeding, but still in good heart.

The lieutenant was unmarked as yet, and coolly smoking his cigar, but he knew well that unless help arrived their case was hopeless.

"We can't run," he remarked, calmly, "but a dignified and speedy retreat is in order if it can be executed. There is a shop a little distance down here. Let us make for it."

But as soon as they moved two more of the Ottawas were dragged down and trampled on.

"It begins to look interesting," said the lieutenant to Harry. "Sorry you are into this, old chap. It was rather my fault. It is so beastly dirty, don't you know."

"Oh, fault be hanged!" cried Harry. "It's nobody's fault, but it looks rather serious. Get back, you brute!" So saying, he caught a burly Frenchman under the chin with a straight left-hander and hurled him back upon the crowd.

"Ah, rather pretty," said the lieutenant, mildly. "It is not often you can just catch them that way." They were still a few yards from the shop door, but every step of their advance had to be fought.

"I very much fear we can't make it," said the lieutenant, quietly to Harry. "We had better back up against the wall here and fight it out."

But as he spoke they heard a sound of shouting down the street a little way, which the Ottawa leader at once recognized, and raising his voice he cried: "Hottawa! Hottawa! Hottawa à moi!"

Swiftly, fiercely, came the band of men, some twenty of them, cleaving their way through the crowd like a wedge. At their head, and taller than the others, fought two men, whose arms worked with the systematic precision of piston-rods, and before whom men fell on either hand as if struck with sledge-hammers.

"Hottawa à moi!" cried the Ottawa champion again, and the relieving party faced in his direction.

"I say," said the lieutenant, "that first man is uncommonly like your Glengarry friend."

"What, Ranald?" cried Harry. "Then we are all right. I swear it is," he said, after a few moments, and then, remembering the story of the great fight on the Nation, which he had heard from Hughie and Maimie, he raised the Macdonald war-cry: "Glengarry! Glengarry!"

Ranald paused and looked about him.

"Here, Ranald!" yelled Harry, waving his white handkerchief. Then Ranald caught sight of him.

"Glengarry!" he cried, and sprang far into the crowd in Harry's direction.

"Glengarry! Glengarry forever!" echoed Yankee – for he it was – plunging after his leader.

Swift and sharp like the thrust of a lance, the Glengarry men pierced the crowd, which gave back on either side, and soon reached the group at the wall.

"How in the world did *you* get here?" cried Ranald to Harry; then, looking about him, cried: "Where is LeNware? I heard he was being killed by the Gatineaus, and I got a few of our men and came along."

"LeNware? That is our Canadian friend, I suppose," said the lieutenant. "He was here a while ago. By Jove! There he is."

Surrounded by a crowd of the Gatineaus, LeNoir, for he was the leader of the Ottawas, was being battered about and like to be killed.

"Glengarry!" cried Ranald, and like a lion he leaped upon them, followed by Yankee and the others. Right and left he hurled the crowd aside, and seizing LeNoir, brought him out to his own men.

"Who are you?" gasped LeNoir. "Why, no, it ees not possible. Yes, it is Yankee for sure! And de Macdonald gang, but –" turning to Ranald – "who are *you*?" he said again.

"Never mind," said Ranald, shortly, "let us get away now, quick! Go on, Yankee."

At once, with Yankee leading, the Glengarry men marched off the field of battle bearing with them the rescued party. There was no time to lose. The enemy far outnumbered them, and would soon return to the attack.

"But how did you know we were in trouble, Ranald?" said Harry as he marched along.

"I didn't know anything about you," said Ranald. "Some one came and said that the bully of the Ottawa was being killed, so I came along."

"And just in time, by Jove!" said the lieutenant, aroused from his languor for once. "It was a deucedly lucky thing, and well done, too, 'pon my soul."

That night, as Ranald and his uncle were in their cabin on the raft talking over the incidents of the day, and Ranald's plans for the summer, a man stood suddenly in the doorway.

"I am Louis LeNoir," he said, "and I have some word to say to de young Macdonald. I am sore here," he said, striking his breast. "I cannot spik your languige. I cannot tell." He stopped short, and the tears came streaming down his face. "I cannot tell," he repeated, his breast heaving with mighty sobs. "I would be glad to die – to mak' over – to not mak' – I cannot say de word – what I do to your fadder. I would give my life," he said, throwing out both his hands. "I would give my life. I cannot say more."

Ranald stood looking at him for a few moments in silence when he finished; then he said slowly and distinctly, "My father told me to say that he forgave you everything, and that he prayed the mercy of God for you, and," added Ranald, more slowly, "I – forgive – you – too."

The Frenchman listened in wonder, greatly moved, but he could only reiterate his words: "I cannot spik what I feel here."

"Sit down, Mr. LeNoir," said Macdonald Bhain, gravely, pointing to a bench, "and I will be telling you something."

LeNoir sat down and waited.

"Do you see that young man there?" said Macdonald Bhain, pointing to Ranald. "He is the strongest man in my gang, and indeed, I will not be putting him below myself." Here Ranald protested. "And he has learned to use his hands as I cannot. And of all the men I have ever seen since I went to the woods, there is not one I could put against him. He could kill you, Mr. LeNoir."

The Frenchman nodded his head and said: "Das so. Das pretty sure."

"Yes, that is very sure," said Macdonald Bhain. "And he made a vow to kill you," went on Macdonald Bhain, "and to-night he saved your life. Do you know why?"

"No, not me."

"Then I will be telling you. It is the grace of God."

LeNoir stared at him, and then Macdonald Bhain went on to tell him how his brother had suffered and struggled long, and how the minister's wife had come to him with the message of the forgiveness of the great God. And then he read from Ranald's English Bible the story of the unforgiving debtor, explaining it in grave and simple speech.

"That was why," he concluded. "It was because he was forgiven, and on his dying bed he sent you the word of forgiveness. And that, too, is the very reason, I believe, why the lad here went to your help this day."

"I promised the minister's wife I would do you good and not ill, when it came to me," said Ranald. "But I was not feeling at all like forgiving you. I was afraid to meet you."

"Afraid?" said LeNoir, wondering that any of that gang should confess to fear.

"Yes, afraid of what I would do. But now, to-night, it is gone," said Ranald, simply, "I can't tell you how."

"Das mos' surprise!" exclaimed LeNoir. "Ne comprenne pas. I never see lak dat, me!"

"Yes, it is wonderful," said Macdonald Bhain. "It is very wonderful. It is the grace of God," he said again.

"You mak' de good frien' wit me?" asked LeNoir, rising and putting his hand out to Macdonald Bhain. Macdonald Bhain rose from his place and stepped toward the Frenchman, and took his hand.

"Yes, I will be friends with you," he said, gravely, "and I will seek God's mercy for you."

Then LeNoir turned to Ranald, and said: "Will you be frien' of me? Is it too moche?"

"Yes," said Ranald, slowly, "I will be your friend, too. It is a little thing," he added, unconsciously quoting his father's words. Then LeNoir turned around to Macdonald Bhain, and striking an attitude, exclaimed: "See! You be my boss, I be your man – what you call – slave. I work for noting, me. Das sure."

Macdonald Bhain shook his head.

"You could not belong to us," he said, and explained to him the terms upon which the Macdonald men were engaged. LeNoir had never heard of such terms.

"You not drink whisky?"

"Not too much," said Macdonald Bhain.

"How many glass? One, two, tree?"

"I do not know," said Macdonald Bhain. "It depends upon the man. He must not take more than is good for him."

"Bon!" said LeNoir, "das good. One glass he mak' me feel good. Two das nice he mak' me feel ver fonny. Three glass yes das mak' me de frien' of hevery bodie. Four das mak' me feel big; I walk de big walk; I am de bes' man all de place. Das good place for stop, eh?"

"No," said Macdonald Bhain, gravely, "you need to stop before that."

"Ver' good. Ver' good me stop him me. You tak' me on for your man?"

Macdonald Bhain hesitated. LeNoir came nearer him and lowering his voice said: "I'm ver' bad man me. I lak to know how you do dat – what you say – forgive. You show me how."

"Come to me next spring," said Macdonald Bhain.

"Bon!" said LeNoir. "I be dere on de Nation camp."

And so he was. And when Mrs. Murray heard of it from Macdonald Bhain that summer, she knew that Ranald had kept his word and had done LeNoir good and not evil.

HE IS NOT OF MY KIND

The story of the riot in which Ranald played so important a part filled the town and stirred society to its innermost circles – those circles, namely, in which the De Lacys lived and moved. The whole town began talking of the Glengarry men, and especially of their young leader who had, with such singular ability and pluck, rescued the Ottawas with Harry and Lieutenant De Lacy, from their perilous position.

The girls had the story from Harry's lips, and in his telling of it, Ranald's courage and skill certainly lost nothing; but to Maimie, while it was pleasant enough for her to hear of Ranald's prowess, and while she enjoyed the reflected glory that came to her as his friend, the whole incident became altogether hateful and distressing. She found herself suddenly famous in her social world; every one was talking of her, but to her horror, was connecting Ranald's name with hers in a most significant way. It was too awful, and if her Aunt Frances should hear of it, the consequences would be quite too terrible for her to imagine. She must stop the talk at once. Of course she meant to be kind to Ranald; he had done her great service, and he was her Aunt Murray's friend, and besides, she liked him; how much she hardly cared to say to herself. She had liked him in Glengarry. There was no doubt of that, but that was two years ago, and in Glengarry everything was different! There every one was just as good as another, and these people were all her Aunt Murray's friends. Here the relations were changed. She could not help feeling that however nice he might be, and however much she might like him, Ranald was not of her world.

"Well, tell him so; let him see that," said Kate, with whom Maimie was discussing her difficulty.

"Yes, and then he would fly off and I – we would never see him again," said Maimie. "He's as proud as – any one!"

"Strange, too," said Kate, "when he has no money to speak of!"

"You know I don't mean that, and I don't think it's very nice of you. You have no sympathy with me!"

"In what way?"

"Well, in this very unpleasant affair; every one is talking about Ranald and me, as if I – as if we had some understanding."

"And have you not? I thought –" Kate hesitated to remind Maimie of certain confidences she had received two years ago after her friend had returned from Glengarry.

"Oh, absurd – just a girl and boy affair," said Maimie, impatiently.

"Then there's nothing at all," said Kate, with a suspicion of eagerness in her voice.

"No, of course not – that is, nothing really serious."

"Serious? You mean you don't care for him at all?" Kate looked straight at her friend.

"O, you are so awfully direct. I don't know. I do care; he's nice in many ways, and he's – I know he likes me and – I would hate to wound him, but then you know he's not just one of us. You know what I mean!"

"Not exactly," said Kate, quietly. "Do you mean he is not educated?"

"Oh, no, I don't mean education altogether. How very tiresome you are! He has no culture, and manners, and that sort of thing."

"I think he has very fine manners. He is a little quaint, but you can't call him rude."

"Oh, no, he's never rude; rather abrupt, but oh, dear, don't you know? What would Aunt Frank say to him?"

Kate's lip curled a little. "I'm very sure I can't say, but I can imagine how she would look."

"Well, that's it –"

"But," went on Kate, "I can imagine, too, how Ranald would look back at her if he caught her meaning."

"Well, perhaps," said Maimie, with a little laugh, "and that's just it. Oh, I wish he were –"

"A lieutenant?" suggested Kate.

"Well, yes, I do," said Maimie, desperately.

"And if he were, you would marry him," said Kate, a shade of contempt in her tone that Maimie failed to notice.

"Yes, I would."

Kate remained silent.

"There now, you think I am horrid, I know," said Maimie. "I suppose you would marry him if he were a mere nobody!"

"If I loved him," said Kate, with slow deliberation, and a slight tremor in her voice, "I'd marry him if he were – a shantyman!"

"I believe you would," said Maimie, with a touch of regret in her voice; "but then, you've no Aunt Frank!"

"Thank Providence," replied Kate, under her breath.

"And I'm sure I don't want to offend her. Just listen to this." Maimie pulled out a letter, and turning over the pages, found the place and began to read: "'I am so glad to hear that you are enjoying your stay in Quebec' – um-um-um – 'fine old city' – um-um-um – 'gates and streets,' 'old days' – um-um-um – 'noble citadel,' 'glorious view' – um-um-um-um – 'finest in the world' – No, that isn't it – O, yes, here it is: 'The De Lacys are a very highly connected English family and very old friends of my friends, the Lord Archers, with whom I visited in England, you know. The mother is a dear old lady – so stately and so very particular – with old-fashioned ideas of breeding and manners, and of course, very wealthy. Her house in Quebec is said to be the finest in the Province, and there are some English estates, I believe, in their line. Lieutenant De Lacy is her only son, and from what you say, he seems to be a very charming young man. He will occupy a very high place some day. I suppose Kate will' – um-um-um – 'Oh yes, and if Mrs. De Lacy wishes you to visit her you might accept' – um-um-um – 'and tell Kate that I should be delighted if she could accompany me on a little jaunt through the Eastern States. I have asked permission of her father, but she wrote you herself about that, didn't she?' – um-um-um – And then listen to this! 'How very odd you should have come across the young man from Glengarry again – Mac Lennon, is it? Mac-something-or-other! Your Aunt Murray seems to consider him a very steady and worthy young man. I hope he may not degenerate in his present circumstances and calling, as so many of his class do. I am glad your father was able to do something for him. These people ought to be encouraged.' Now you see!" Maimie's tone was quite triumphant.

"Yes!" said Kate. "I do see! These people should be encouraged to make our timber for us that we may live in ease and luxury, and even to save us from fire and from bloodthirsty mobs, as occasions may offer, but as for friendships and that sort of thing –"

"Oh, Kate," burst in Maimie, almost in tears, "you are so very unkind. You know quite well what I mean."

"Yes, I know quite well; you would not invite Ranald, for instance, to dine at your house, to meet your Aunt Frank and the Evanses and the Langfords and the Maitlands," said Kate, spacing her words with deliberate indignation.

"Well, I would not, if you put it in that way," said Maimie, petulantly, "and you wouldn't either!"

"I would ask him to meet every Maitland of them if I could," said Kate, "and it wouldn't hurt them either."

"Oh, you are so peculiar," said Maimie, with a sigh of pity.

"Am I," said Kate; "ask Harry," she continued, as that young man came into the room.

"No, you needn't mind," said Maimie; "I know well he will just side with you. He always does."

"How very amiable of me," said Harry; "but what's the particular issue?"

"Ranald," said Kate.

"Then I agree at once. Besides, he is coming to supper next Sunday evening!"

"Oh, Harry," exclaimed Maimie, in dismay, "on Sunday evening?"

"He can't get off any other night; works all night, I believe, and would work all Sunday, too, if his principles didn't mercifully interfere. He will be boss of the concern before summer is over."

"Oh, Harry," said Maimie, in distress, "and I asked Lieutenant De Lacy and his friend, Mr. Sims, for Sunday evening –"

"Sims," cried Harry; "little cad!"

"I'm sure he's very nice," said Maimie, "and his family –"

"Oh, hold up; don't get on to your ancestor worship," cried Harry, impatiently. "Anyway Ranald's coming up Sunday evening."

"Well, it will be very awkward," said Maimie.

"I don't see why," said Kate.

"Oh," cried Harry, scornfully, "he will have on his red flannel shirt and a silk handkerchief, and his trousers will be in his boots; that's what Maimie is thinking of!"

"You are very rude, Harry," said Maimie. "You know quite well that Ranald will not enjoy himself with the others. He has nothing in common with them."

"Oh, I wouldn't worry about that, Maimie," said Kate; "I will talk to Ranald." But Maimie was not quite sure how she should like that.

"You are just your Aunt Frank over again," said Harry, in a disgusted tone; "clothes and people!"

Maimie was almost in tears.

"I think you are both very unkind. You know Ranald won't enjoy it. He will be quite miserable, and – they'll just laugh at him!"

"Well, they'd better laugh at him when he isn't observing," said Harry.

"Do you think Ranald would really mind?" interposed Kate, addressing Harry. "Do you think he will feel shy and awkward? Perhaps we'd better have him another evening."

"No," said Harry, decidedly; "he is coming, and he's coming on Sunday evening. He can't get off any other night, and besides, I'd have to lie to him, and he has an unpleasant way of finding you out when you are doing it, and once he does find out why he is not asked for Sunday evening, then you may say good by to him for good and all."

"Oh, no fear of that," said Maimie, confidently; "Ranald has good sense, and I know he will come again."

"Well," cried Harry, "if you are not going to treat him as you would treat De Lacy and that idiotic Sims, I won't bring him!" And with that he flung out of the room.

But Harry changed his mind, for next Sunday evening as the young ladies with De Lacy and his friend were about to sit down to supper in their private parlor, Harry walked in with Ranald, and announced in triumph: "The man from Glengarry!" Maimie looked at him in dismay, and indeed she well might, for Ranald was dressed in his most gorgeous shanty array, with red flannel shirt and silk handkerchief, and trousers tucked into his boots. Sims gazed at him as if he were an apparition. It was Kate who first broke the silence.

"We are delighted to see you," she cried, going forward to Ranald with hands outstretched; "you are become quite a hero in this town."

"Quite, I assure you," said the lieutenant, in a languid voice, but shaking Ranald heartily by the hand.

Then Maimie came forward and greeted him with ceremonious politeness and introduced him to Mr. Sims, who continued to gaze at the shantyman's attire with amused astonishment.

The supper was not a success; Ranald sat silent and solemn, eating little and smiling not at all, although Mr. Sims executed his very best jokes. Maimie was nervous and visibly distressed, and at the earliest possible moment broke up the supper party and engaged in conversation with the lieutenant and his witty friend, leaving Harry and Kate to entertain

Ranald. But in spite of all they could do a solemn silence would now and then overtake the company, till at length Maimie grew desperate, and turning to Ranald said: "What are you thinking of? You are looking very serious."

"He is 'thinking of home and mother,'" quoted Mr. Sims, in a thin, piping voice, following his quotation with a silly giggle.

Kate flushed indignantly. "I am quite sure his thoughts will bear telling," she said.

"I am sure they would," said Maimie, not knowing what to say. "What were they, Ran – Mr. Macdonald?"

"I was thinking of you," said Ranald, gravely, looking straight at her.

"How lovely," murmured the lieutenant.

"And of your aunt, Mrs. Murray, and of what they would be doing this night –"

"And what would that be?" said Kate, coming to the relief of her friend. But Ranald was silent.

"I know," cried Harry. "Let's see, it is ten o'clock; they will all be sitting in the manse dining-room before the big fire; or, no, they will be in the parlor where the piano is, and John 'Aleck' will be there, and they will be singing"; and he went on to describe his last Sabbath evening, two years ago, in the Glengarry manse. As he began to picture his aunt and her work, his enthusiasm carried him away, and made him eloquent.

"I tell you," he concluded "she's a rare woman, and she has a hundred men there ready to die for her, eh, Ranald?"

"Yes," said Ranald, and his deep voice vibrated with intense feeling. "They would just die for her, and why not? She is a great woman and a good." His dark face was transformed, and his eyes glowed with an inner light.

In the silence that followed Kate went to the harmonium and began to play softly. Ranald stood up as to go, but suddenly changed his mind, and went over and stood beside her.

"You sing, don't you?" said Kate, as she played softly.

"You ought to just hear him," said Harry.

"Oh, what does he sing?"

"I only sing the psalm tunes in church," said Ranald, "and a few hymns."

"Ye gods!" ejaculated the lieutenant to Maimie, "psalms and hymns; and how the fellow knocked those Frenchmen about!"

"Sing something, Kate, won't you?" said Maimie, and Kate, without a word began the beautiful air from Mendelssohn's St. Paul: –

"But the Lord is mindful of His own,"

singing it with a power of expression marvellous in so young a girl. Then, without further request, she glided into the lovely *aria*, "O Rest in the Lord." It was all new and wonderful to Ranald. He did not dream that such majesty and sweetness could be expressed in music. He sat silent with eyes looking far away, and face alight with the joy that filled his soul.

"Oh, thanks, very much," murmured the lieutenant, when Kate had finished. "Lovely thing that *aria*, don't you know?"

"Very nice," echoed Mr. Sims, "and so beautifully done, too."

Ranald looked from one to the other in indignant surprise, and then turning away from them to Kate, said, in a tone almost of command: "Sing it again."

"I'll sing something else," she said. "Did you ever hear –"

"No, I never heard anything at all like that," interrupted Ranald. "Sing some more like the last."

The deep feeling showing in his face and in his tone touched Kate.

"How would this do?" she replied. "It is a little high for me, but I'll try."

She played a few introductory chords, and then began that sweetest bit of the greatest of all the oratorios "He shall Feed His Flock." And from that passed into the soul-moving "He Was Despised" from the same noble work. The music suited the range and quality of her voice perfectly, and she sang with her heart thrilling in response to the passionate feeling in the dark eyes fixed upon her face. She had never sung to any one who listened as Ranald now listened to her. She forgot the others. She was singing for him, and he was compelling her to her best. She was conscious of a subtle sense of mastery overpowering her, and with a strange delight she yielded herself to that commanding influence; but as she sang she began to realize that he was thinking not of her, but of her song, and soon she, too, was thinking of it. She knew that his eyes were filled with the vision of "The Man of Sorrows" of whom she sang, and before she was aware, the pathos of that lonely and despised life, set forth in the noble words of the ancient prophet, was pouring forth in the great Master's music.

When the song was ended, no one spoke for a time, and even Mr. Sims was silent. Then the lieutenant came over to the harmonium, and leaning toward Kate, said, in an earnest voice, unusual with him, "Thank you Miss Raymond. That was truly great."

"Great indeed"; said Harry, with enthusiasm. "I never heard you sing like that before, Kate."

But Ranald sat silent, finding no words in which to express the thoughts and feelings her singing had aroused in him.

There is that in noble music that forbids unreality, rebukes frivolity into silence, subdues ignoble passions, soothes the heart's sorrow, and summons to the soul high and holy thoughts. It was difficult to begin the conversation; the trivial themes of the earlier part of the evening seemed foreign to the mood that had fallen upon the company. At length Mr. Sims ventured to remark, with a giggle: "It's awfully fine, don't you know, but a trifle funereal. Makes one think of graves and that sort of thing. Very nice, of course," he added, apologetically, to Kate. Ranald turned and regarded the little man for some moments in silence, and then, with unutterable scorn, exclaimed: "Nice! man, it's wonderful, wonderful to me whatever! Makes me think of all the great things I ever saw."

"What things?" Kate ventured to say.

For a few moments Ranald paused, and then replied: "It makes me think of the big pine trees waving and wailing over me at night, and the big river rolling down with the moonlight on it – and – other things."

"What other things, Ranald," persisted Kate.

But Ranald shook his head and sat silent for some time. Then he rose abruptly.

"I will be going now," he said.

"You will come again soon, Ranald," said Maimie, coming toward him with a look on her face that reminded him of the days in the Glengarry manse. She had forgotten all about his red shirt and silk handkerchief. As Ranald caught that look a great joy leaped into his eyes for a moment, then faded into a gaze of perplexity.

"Yes, do come," added Kate.

"Will you sing again?" he asked, bluntly.

"Yes, indeed," she replied with a slight blush, "if you want me to."

"I will come. When? To-morrow night?"

"Yes, certainly, to-morrow night," said Kate, blushing deeply now, for she noticed the slight smile on Harry's face, and the glance that passed between Mr. Sims and the lieutenant. Then Ranald said good night.

"I have never had such pleasure in my life," he said, holding her hand a moment, and looking into her eyes that sparkled with a happy light. "That is," he added, with a swift glance at Maimie, "from music or things like that."

Kate caught the glance, and the happy light faded from her eyes.

"Good night," said Ranald, offering his hand to Maimie. "I am glad I came now. It makes me think of the last night at the manse, although I am always thinking of it," he added, simply, with a touch of sadness in his voice. Maimie's face grew hot with blushes.

"Yes," she answered, hurriedly. "Dear Aunt Murray!"

He stood a moment or two as if about to speak, while Maimie waited in an agony of fear, not knowing what to expect in this extraordinary young man. Then he turned abruptly away, and with a good night to De Lacy and a nod to Mr. Sims, strode from the room.

"Great Cæsar's ghost!" exclaimed the lieutenant; "pardon me, but has anything happened? That young man now and then gives me a sense of tragedy. What *has* taken place?" he panted, weakly.

"Nonsense," laughed Maimie, "your nervous system is rather delicate."

"Ah, thanks, no doubt that's it. Miss Kate, how do you feel?"

"I," said Kate, waking suddenly, "thank you, quite happy."

"Happy," sighed De Lacy. "Ah, fortunate young man!"

"Great chap, that," cried Harry, coming back from seeing Ranald to the door.

"Very," said De Lacy, so emphatically that every one laughed.

"Some one really ought to dress him, though," suggested Mr. Sims, with a slight sneer.

"Why?" said Kate, quietly, facing him.

"Oh, well, you know, Miss Raymond," stammered Mr. Sims, "that sort of attire, you know, is hardly the thing for the drawing-room, you know."

"He is a shantyman," said Maimie, apologetically, "and they all dress like that. I don't suppose that he has any other clothes with him."

"Oh, of course," assented Mr. Sims, retreating before this double attack.

"Besides," continued Kate, "it is good taste to dress in the garb of your profession, isn't it, Lieutenant De Lacy?"

"Oh, come now, Miss Kate, that's all right," said the lieutenant, "but you must draw the line somewhere, you know. Those colors now you must confess are a little startling."

"You didn't mind the colors when he saved you the other day from that awful mob!"

"One for you, De Lacy," cried Harry.

"Quite right," answered the lieutenant, "but don't mistake me. I distinguish between a fellow and his clothes."

"For my part," said Kate, "I don't care how a man is dressed; if I like him, I like him should he appear in a blanket and feathers."

"Don't speak of it," gasped the lieutenant.

"Do let's talk of something else," said Maimie, impatiently.

"Delighted, I am sure," said De Lacy; "and that reminds me that madam was thinking of a picnic down the river this week – just a small company, you know. The man would drive her down and take the hamper and things, and we would go down by boat. Awful pull back, though," he added, regretfully, "but if it should give any pleasure – delighted, you know," bowing gallantly to the ladies.

"Delightful!" cried Maimie.

"And Ranald pulls splendidly," said Kate.

Maimie looked at her, wondering how she knew that. "I don't think Ranald can get away every day. I'm sure he can't; can he, Harry?" she said.

"No," said Harry, "no more can I, worse luck! The governor is sticking awfully close to work just now."

"And, of course, you can't be spared," said Kate, mockingly. "But couldn't you both come later? We could wait tea for you."

"Might," said Harry. "I shall make my best endeavor for your sake," bowing toward Kate, "but I am doubtful about Ranald. Perhaps we'd better not –"

"Why, certainly, old chap," said the lieutenant, "what's the matter?"

"Well, the fact is," blurted out Harry, desperately, "I don't want to drag in Ranald. I like him awfully, but you may feel as if he were not quite one of us. You know what I mean; your mother doesn't know him."

Harry felt extremely awkward knowing that he came perilously near to suspecting the lieutenant of the most despicable snobbery.

"Why, certainly," repeated the lieutenant. "That's all right. Bring your Glengarry man along if any one wants him."

"I do," said Kate, decidedly.

"Kismet," replied the lieutenant. "It is decreed. The young man must come, for I suspect he is very much 'one of us.'" But of this the lieutenant was not quite so certain by the time the day of the picnic had arrived.

ONE GAME AT A TIME

The Glengarry men were on the Montreal boat leaving for home. Macdonald Bhain's farewell to his nephew was full of sadness, for he knew that henceforth their ways would lie apart, and full of solemn warnings against the dangers of the city where Ranald was now to be.

"It is a wicked place, and the pitfalls are many, and they are not in the places where the eyes will be looking for them. Ye are taking the way that will be leading you from us all, and I will not be keeping you back, nor will I be laying any vows upon you. You will be a true man, and you will keep the fear of God before your eyes, and you will remember that a Macdonald never fails the man that trusts him." And long after the great man was gone his last words kept tugging at Ranald's heart: "Ranald, lad, remember us up yonder in the Indian Lands," he said, holding his hand with a grip that squeezed the bones together; "we will be always thinking of you, and more than all, at the Bible class and the meetings she will be asking for you and wondering how you are doing, and by night and by day the door will be on the latch for your coming; for, laddie, laddie, you are a son to me and more!" The break in the big Macdonald's voice took away from Ranald all power of speech, and without a word of reply, he had to let his uncle go.

Yankee's good by was characteristic. "Well, guess I'll git along. Wish you were comin' back with us, but you've struck your gait, I guess, and you're goin' to make quite a dust. Keep your wind till the last quarter; that's where the money's lost. I ain't 'fraid of you; you're green, but they can't break you. Keep your left eye on the suckers. There ain't no danger from the feller that rips and rares and gits up on his hind legs, but the feller that sidles raound and sorter chums it up to you and wants to pay fer your drinks, by jings, kick him. And say," Yankee's voice here grew low and impressive, "git some close. These here are all right for the woods, but with them people close counts an awful lot. It's the man inside that wins, but the close is outside. Git 'em and git 'em good; none of your second-hand Jew outfits. It'll cost, of course, but – (here Yankee closed up to Ranald) but here's a wad; ain't no pertickaler use to me."

Then Ranald smote him in the chest and knocked him back against a lumber pile.

"I know you," he cried; "you would be giving me the coat off your back. If I would be taking money from any man I'd take it from you, but let me tell you I will have no money that I do not earn"; then, seeing Yankee's disappointed face, he added, "but indeed, I owe you for your help to me – and – mi – mine, when help was needed sore, more than I can ever pay back." Then, as they shook hands, Ranald spoke again, and his voice was none too steady. "And I have been thinking that I would like you to have Lisette, for it may be a long time before I will be back again, and I know you will be good to her; and if ever I need your help in this way, I promise I will come to you."

Yankee chewed his quid of tobacco hard and spat twice before he could reply. Then he answered slowly: "Now look-ye-here, I'll take that little mare and look after her, but the mare's yours and if – and if – which I don't think will happen – if you don't come back soon, why – I will send you her equivalent in cash; but I'd ruther see – I'd ruther see you come back for it!"

It was with a very lonely heart that Ranald watched out of sight the steamboat that carried to their homes in the Indian Lands the company of men who had been his comrades for the long months in the woods and on the river, and all the more that he was dimly realizing that this widening blue strip of flowing river was separating him forever from the life he so passionately loved. As his eyes followed them he thought of the home-coming that he would have shared; their meetings at the church door, the grave handshakings from the older folk, the saucy "horos" from the half-grown boys, the shy blushing glances from the maidens, and last and dearest of all, the glad, proud welcome in the sweet, serious face with the gray-brown eyes. It was with the memory of that face in his heart that he turned to meet what might be coming to him, with the resolve that he would play the man.

"Hello, old chap, who's dead?" It was Harry's gay voice. "You look like a tomb." He put his arm through Ranald's and walked with him up the street.

"Where are you going now?" he asked, as Ranald walked along in silence.

"To get some clothes."

"Thank the great powers!" ejaculated Harry to himself.

"What?"

"And where are you going to get them?"

"I do not know – some store, I suppose." Ranald had the vaguest notions not only of where he should go, but of the clothes in which he ought to array himself, but he was not going to acknowledge this to his friend.

"You can't get any clothes fit to wear in this town," said Harry, in high contempt. Ranald's heart sank. "But come along, we will find something."

As they passed in front of the little French shops, with windows filled inside and out with ready-made garments, Ranald paused to investigate.

"Oh! pshaw," cried Harry, "don't know what you'll get here. We'll find something better than this cheap stuff," and Ranald, glad enough of guidance, though uncertain as to where it might lead him, followed meekly.

"What sort of a suit do you want?" said Harry.

"I don't know," said Ranald, doubtfully. It had never occurred to him that there could be any great difference in suits. There had never been any choosing of suits with him.

"Like yours, I suppose," he continued, glancing at Harry's attire, but adding, cautiously, "if they do not cost too much."

"About forty dollars," said Harry, lightly; then, noticing the dismayed look on Ranald's face, he added quickly, "but you don't need to spend that much, you know. I say, you let me manage this thing." And fortunate it was for Ranald that he had his friend's assistance in this all-important business, but it took all Harry's judgment, skill, and delicacy of handling to pilot his friend through the devious ways of outfitters, for Ranald's ignorance of all that pertained to a gentleman's wardrobe was equaled only by the sensitive pride on the one hand that made him shrink from appearing poor and mean, and by his Scotch caution on the other that forbade undue extravagance. It was a hard hour and a half for them both, but when all was over, Ranald's gratitude more than repaid Harry for his pains.

"Come up to-night," said Harry, as they stood at the door of the Hotel du Nord, where Ranald had taken up his quarters.

"No," said Ranald, abruptly, unconsciously glancing down at his rough dress.

"Then I'll come down here," said Harry, noting the glance.

"I will be very glad," replied Ranald, his face lighting up, for he was more afraid than he cared to show of the lonely hours of that night. It would be the first night in his life away from his own kin and friends. But he was not so glad when, after tea, as he stood at the door of the hotel, he saw sauntering toward him not only Harry, but also Lieutenant De Lacy and his friend Mr. Sims.

"These fellows would come along," cried Harry; "I told them you didn't want them."

"Showed how little he knew," said the lieutenant. "I told him you would be delighted."

"Will you come in?" said Ranald, rather grudgingly, "though there is nothing much inside."

"What a bear," said Mr. Sims to Harry, disgustedly, in a low voice.

"Nothing much!" said the lieutenant, "a good deal I should say from what one can hear."

"Oh, that is nothing," replied Ranald; "the boys are having some games."

The bar-room was filled with men in shanty dress, some sitting with chairs tipped back against the wall, smoking the black French "twist" tobacco; others drinking at the bar; and others still at the tables that stood in one corner of the room playing cards with loud exclamations and oaths of delight or disgust, according to their fortune. The lieutenant pushed his way through the crowd, followed by the others.

"A jolly lot, by Jove!" he exclaimed, looking with mild

interest on the scene, "and with the offer of some sport, too," he added, glancing at the card-players in the corner, where men were losing their winter's wages.

"What will you take?" said Ranald, prompted by his Highland sense of courtesy, "and would you have it in the next room?"

"Anywhere," said the lieutenant, with alacrity; "a little brandy and soda for me; nothing else in these places is worth drinking."

Ranald gave the order, and with some degree of pride, noticed the obsequious manner of the bar-tender toward him and his distinguished guests. They passed into an inner and smaller room, lit by two or three smoky lamps in brackets on the walls. In this room, sitting at one of the tables, were two Frenchmen playing *écarté*. As the lieutenant entered, one of them glanced up and uttered an exclamation of recognition.

"Ah, it is our warlike friend," cried De Lacy, recognizing him in return; "you play this game also," he continued in French.

"Not moche," said LeNoir, for it was he, with a grand salute. "Will the capitaine join, and his friends?"

Ranald shook his head and refused.

"Come along," said the lieutenant, eagerly, to Ranald. The game was his passion. "Mr. Sims, you will; Harry, what do you say?"

"I will look on with Ranald."

"Oh, come in Macdonald," said the lieutenant, "the more the better, and we'll make it poker. You know the game?" he said, turning to LeNoir; "and your friend – I have not the pleasure –"

"Mr. Rouleau," said Ranald and LeNoir together, presenting the young Frenchman who spoke and looked like a gentleman.

"Do you play the game?" said the lieutenant.

"A verie leetle, but I can learn him."

"That's right," cried the lieutenant, approvingly.

"What do you say, Ranald," said Harry, who also loved the game.

"No," said Ranald, shortly, "I never play for money."

"Make it pennies," said Mr. Sims, with a slight laugh.

"Go on, De Lacy," said Harry, angry at Mr. Sims's tone. "You've got four – that'll do!"

"Oh, very well," said De Lacy, his easy, languid air returning to him. "What shall it be – quarter chips with a dollar limit? Brandy and soda, Mr. LeNoir? And you, Mr. Rouleau? Two more glasses, garçon," and the game began.

From the outset Rouleau steadily won till his chips were piled high in front of him.

"You play the game well," said the lieutenant. "Shall we raise the limit?"

"As you lak," said Rouleau, with a polite bow.

"Let's make it five dollars," suggested Mr. Sims, to which all agreed.

But still the game was Rouleau's, who grew more and more excited with every win. The lieutenant played coolly, and with seeming indifference, in which he was imitated by Mr. Sims, the loss of a few dollars being a matter of small moment to either.

"It would make it more interesting if we made it a dollar to play," at length said Mr. Sims. The suggestion was accepted, and the game went on. At once the luck began to turn, and in a half hour's play Rouleau's winnings disappeared and passed over to the lieutenant's hand. In spite of his bad luck, however, Rouleau continued to bet eagerly and recklessly, until Ranald, who hated to see the young lumberman losing his season's wages, suggested that the game come to an end.

"The night is early," said the lieutenant, "but if you have had enough," he said, bowing to LeNoir and Rouleau –

"*Non!*" exclaimed Rouleau, "the fortune will to me *encore*. We mak it de two-dollar to play. Dat will brak de luck."

"I think you ought to stop it," said Harry.

But the demon of play had taken full possession of both Rouleau and the lieutenant and they were not to be denied. Rouleau took from his pocket a roll of bills and counted them.

"Fifty dollars," he cried. "*Bon!* I play him, me!"

The others deposited a like sum before them, and the game proceeded. The deal was De Lacy's. After a few moment's consideration, Mr. Sims and LeNoir each drew three cards. In a tone of triumph which he could not altogether suppress, Rouleau exclaimed, "Dees are good enough for me." The lieutenant drew one card, and the betting began.

Twice Rouleau, when it came to his turn, bet the limit, the others contenting themselves by "raising" one dollar. On the third round LeNoir, remarking, "Das leetle too queek for me," dropped out.

Once more Rouleau raised the bet to the limit, when Mr. Sims refused, and left the game to him and the lieutenant. There was no mistaking the eager triumph in the Frenchman's pale face. He began to bet more cautiously, his only fear being that his opponent would "call" too soon. Dollar by dollar the bet was raised till at last Rouleau joyously gathered his last chips, raised the bet once more by the limit, exclaiming, as he did so, "Alas! dere ees no more!"

He had played his season's wages that night, but now he would receive all.

De Lacy, whose coolness was undisturbed, though his face showed signs of his many brandy-and-sodas, covered the bet.

"*Holà!*" exclaimed Rouleau in triumph. "Eet ees to me!" He threw down his cards and reached for the pile.

"Excuse me," said the lieutenant, quietly looking at Rouleau's cards. "Ah, a straight flush, queen high." Coolly he laid his cards on the table. "Thought you might have had the ace," he said, languidly, leaning back in his chair. He, too, held a straight flush, but with the king.

Rouleau gazed thunderstruck.

"*Mort Dieu!*" he exclaimed, excitedly. "The deal was from you."

"Mine," said De Lacy, quietly, looking up at the excited Frenchman.

"Ah," cried Rouleau, beside himself. "It is – what you call? One cheat! cheat!"

The lieutenant sat up straight in his chair.

"Do you mean that I cheated you?" he said, with slow emphasis. "Beware what you say."

"*Oui!*" cried the Frenchman; "*sacr-r-re* – so I mean!"

Before the words had well left his lips, and before any one could interfere De Lacy shot out his arm, lifted the Frenchman clear off his feet, and hurled him to the floor.

"Stop! you coward!" Ranald stood before the lieutenant with eyes blazing and breath coming quick.

"Coward?" said De Lacy, slowly.

"You hit a man unprepared."

"You are prepared, I suppose," replied De Lacy, deliberately.

"Yes! Yes!" cried Ranald, eagerly, the glad light of battle coming into his eyes.

"Good," said De Lacy, slowly putting back his chair, and proceeding to remove his coat.

"Glengarry!" cried LeNoir, raising the battle-cry he had cause to remember so well; and flinging off his coat upon the floor, he patted Ranald on the back, yelling, "Go in, bully boy!"

"Shut the door, LeNoir," said Ranald, quickly, "and keep it shut."

"De Lacy," cried Harry, "this must not go on! Ranald, think what you are doing!"

"You didn't notice his remark, apparently, St. Clair," said the lieutenant, calmly.

"Never mind," cried Harry, "he was excited, and anyway the thing must end here."

"There is only one way. Does he retract?" said De Lacy, quietly.

"Ranald," Harry cried, beseechingly, "you know he is no coward; you did not mean that."

By this time Ranald had himself in hand.

"No," he said, regretfully, forcing himself to speak the truth. "I know he is no coward; I have seen him where no coward would be, but," he added, "he struck a man unguarded, and that was a coward's blow."

"Macdonald," said De Lacy deliberately, "you are right. True, he called me a cheat, but I should have given him time. Still," he added, rolling up his sleeves, "I hope you will not deprive yourself or me of the privilege of settling this little business."

"I will be glad," said Ranald, his eyes once more lighting up. "Very glad indeed, if you wish."

"Nonsense," cried Harry, passionately, "I tell you I will not have it. He has given you ample apology, De Lacy; and you, Ranald, I thought a Macdonald never fought except for sufficient cause!" Harry remembered the fighting rule of the Macdonald gang.

"That is true," said Ranald, gravely, "but it was a cruel blow," pointing to Rouleau, who, supported by LeNoir, was sitting on a chair, his face badly cut and bleeding, "and that, too, after taking from him the wages of six months in the bush!"

"I suppose you admit the game was fair," said the lieutenant, moving nearer to Ranald, the threat in his tone evident to all.

"The game was fair," said Ranald, facing De Lacy, "but I will say the lad was no fair match for you!"

"He chose to risk his money, which you were not willing to do." De Lacy felt that he was being put in an unpleasant light and was determined to anger Ranald beyond control. Ranald caught the sneer.

"If I did not play," he cried, hotly, "it was for no fear of you or any of you. It was no man's game whatever," he continued, contemptuously.

"Now, De Lacy," cried Harry, again, "let this stop. The man who fights will first fight me!"

"Perhaps Mr. Macdonald would show us how the game should be played," said Mr. Sims, coming as near to a sneer as he dared.

"It would not be hard to show you this game," said Ranald, ignoring Mr. Sims, and looking the lieutenant in the eyes, "or perhaps the other!"

"Good!" cried Harry, gladly seizing the opportunity of averting a fight. "The game! Take your places, gentlemen!"

The lieutenant hesitated for a moment, as if uncertain what to do. Then, with a slight laugh, he said, "Very well, one thing at a time, the other can wait."

"Come on!" cried Harry, "who goes in? LeNoir, you?"

LeNoir looked at Ranald.

"What you say?"

"No," said Ranald, shortly, "this is my game!" With that he turned aside from the table and spoke a few words in a low tone to LeNoir, who assisted Rouleau from the room, and after some minutes' absence, returned with a little linen bag. Ranald took the bag and began to count out some money upon the table before him.

"I will play to one hundred dollars," he said.

The lieutenant and Mr. Sims each laid the same amount before them upon the table.

"I have not so much on me," said Harry, "but perhaps my I. O. U. will do."

"What shall we say," said Mr. Sims, "a dollar to play and five dollars limit?"

"Say five and twenty-five," said De Lacy, who was commanding himself with a great effort.

"Is that too high?" said Harry, looking toward Ranald.

"No," said Ranald, "the higher the better."

It was soon evident that Ranald knew the game. He had learned it during the long winter nights in the Shanty from Yankee, who was a master at it, and he played it warily and with iron nerve. He seemed to know as by instinct when to retreat and when to pursue; and he played with the single purpose of bleeding the lieutenant dry. Often did he refuse to take toll of Harry or Mr. Sims when opportunity offered, but never once did he allow the lieutenant to escape.

"You flatter me," said the lieutenant, sarcastically, as Ranald's purpose became increasingly clear.

"I will have from you all you have won," replied Ranald, in a tone of such settled resolve that it seemed as if nothing could prevent the accomplishment of his purpose. In vain the lieutenant sought to brace his nerves with his brandy-and-sodas. He played now recklessly and again with over-caution, while Ranald, taking advantage of every slip and every sign of weakness, followed him with relentless determination.

With such stakes the game was soon over. It was not long before the lieutenant was stripped of his hundred, while Harry and Mr. Sims had each lost smaller amounts.

"You will try another hundred?" said the lieutenant, burning to get revenge.

Without a word Ranald laid down his hundred; the others did likewise, and once more the game proceeded. There was no change in Ranald's play. Thorough knowledge of the game, absolute self-command, an instinctive reading of his opponent's mind, and unswerving purpose soon brought about the only result possible. The lieutenant's second hundred with a part of Harry's and Mr. Sims's passed into Ranald's possession.

Again De Lacy challenged to play.

"No," said Ranald, "I have done." He put back into his linen bag his one hundred dollars, counted out two hundred, and gave it to LeNoir, saying: "That is Rouleau's," and threw the rest upon the table. "I want no man's money," he said, "that I do not earn."

The lieutenant sprang to his feet.

"Hold!" he cried, "you forget, there is something else!"

"No," said Ranald, as Harry and Mr. Sims put themselves in De Lacy's way, "there is nothing else to-night; another day, and any day you wish, you can have the other game," and with that he passed out of the room.

HER CLINGING ARMS

The ancient capital of Canada – the old gray queen of the mighty St. Lawrence – is a city of many charms and of much stately beauty. Its narrow, climbing streets, with their quaint shops and curious gables, its old market, with chaffering *habitant* farmers and their wives, are full of living interest. Its noble rock, crowned with the ancient citadel, and its sweeping tidal river, lend it a dignity and majestic beauty that no other city knows; and everywhere about its citadel and walls, and venerable, sacred buildings, there still linger the romance and chivalry of heroic days long gone. But there are times when neither the interests of the living present nor the charms of the romantic past can avail, and so a shadow lay upon Maimie's beautiful face as she sat in the parlor of the Hotel de Cheval Blanc, looking out upon the mighty streets and the huddled roofs of the lower town. She held in her hand an open note.

"It is just awfully stupid," she grumbled, "and I think pretty mean of him!"

"Of whom, may I ask?" said Kate, pausing in her singing, "or is there any need? What says the gallant lieutenant?"

Maimie tossed her the note.

"The picnic is postponed. Well, of course the rain told us that; and he is unavoidably prevented from calling, and entreats your sympathy and commiseration. Well, that's a very nice note, I am sure."

"Where has he been these three days! He might have known it would be stupid, and Harry gives one no satisfaction." Maimie was undeniably cross. "And Ranald, too," she went on, "where has he been? Not even your music could bring him!" with a little spice of spite. "I think men are just horrid, anyway."

"Especially when they will keep away," said Kate.

"Well, what are they good for if not to entertain us? I wish we could do without them! But I do think Ranald might have come."

"Well," said Kate, emphatically, "I can't see why you should expect him."

"Why not?"

"I think you ought to know."

"I, how should I know?" Maimie's innocent blue eyes were wide open with surprise.

"Nonsense," cried Kate, with impatience rare in her, "don't be absurd, Maimie; I am not a child."

"What do *you* mean?"

"You needn't tell me you don't know why Ranald comes. Do you want him to come?"

"Why, of course I do; how silly you are."

"Well," said Kate, deliberately, "I would rather be silly than cruel and unkind."

"Why, Kate, how dreadful of you!" exclaimed Maimie; "'cruel and unkind!'"

"Yes," said Kate; "you are not treating Ranald well. You

should not encourage him to – to – care for you when you do not mean to – to – go on with it."

"Oh, what nonsense; Ranald is not a baby; he will not take any hurt."

"Oh, Maimie," said Kate, and her voice was low and earnest, "Ranald is not like other men. He does not understand things. He loves you and he will love you more every day if you let him. Why don't you let him go?"

"Let him go!" cried Maimie, "who's keeping him?" But as she spoke the flush in her cheek and the warm light in her eye told more clearly than words that she did not mean to let him go just then.

"You are," said Kate, "and you are making him love you."

"Why, how silly you are," cried Maimie; "of course he likes me, but –"

"No, Maimie," said Kate, with sad earnestness, "he loves you; you can see it in the way he looks at you; in his voice when he speaks and – oh, you shouldn't let him unless you mean to – to – go on. Send him right away!" There were tears in Kate's dark eyes.

"Why, Katie," cried Maimie, looking at her curiously, "what difference does it make to you? And besides, how can I send him away? I just treat him as I do Mr. De Lacy."

"De Lacy!" cried Kate, indignantly. "De Lacy can look after himself, but Ranald is different. He is so serious and – and so honest, and he means just what he says, and you are so nice to him, and you look at him in such a way!"

"Why, Kate, do you mean that I try to –" Maimie was righteously indignant.

"You perhaps don't know," continued Kate, "but you can't help being fascinating to men; you know you are, and Ranald believes you so, and – and you ought to be quite straightforward with him!" Poor Kate could no longer command her voice.

"There, now," said Maimie, caressing her friend, not unpleased with Kate's description of her; "I'm going to be good. I will just be horrid to both of them, and they'll go away! But, oh, dear, things are all wrong! Poor Ranald," she said to herself, "I wonder if he will come to the picnic on Saturday?"

Kate looked at her friend a moment and wiped away her tears.

"Indeed I hope he will not," she said, indignantly, "for I know you mean to just lead him on. I have a mind to tell him."

"Tell him what?" said Maimie, smiling.

"Just what you mean to do."

"I wish you would tell me that."

"Now I tell you, Maimie," said Kate, "if you go on with Ranald so any longer I will just tell him you are playing with him."

"Do," said Maimie, scornfully, "and be careful to make clear to him at the same time that you are speaking solely in his interest!"

Kate's face flushed red at the insinuation, and then grew pale. She stood for some time looking in silence at her friend, and then with a proud flash of her dark eyes, she swept from the room without a word, nor did Maimie see her again that afternoon, though she stood outside her door entreating with tears to be forgiven. Poor Kate! Maimie's shaft had gone too near a vital spot, and the wound amazed and terrified her. Was it for Ranald's sake alone she cared? Yes, surely it was. Then why this sharp new pain under the hand pressing hard upon her heart?

Oh, what did that mean? She put her face in her pillow to hide the red that she knew was flaming in her cheeks, and for a few moments gave herself up to the joy that was flooding her whole heart and soul and all her tingling veins. Oh, how happy she was, for long she had heard of the Glengarry lad from Maimie and more from Harry till there had grown up in her heart a warm, admiring interest. And now she had come to know him for herself! How little after all had they told her of him. What a man he was! How strong and how fearless! How true-hearted and how his eyes could fill with love! She started up. Love? Love? Ah, where was her joy! How chill the day had grown and how hateful the sunlight on the river. She drew down the blind and threw herself once more upon the bed, shivering and sick with pain – the bitterest that heart can know. Once more she started up.

"She is not worthy of him!" she exclaimed, aloud; "her heart is not deep enough; she does not, cannot love him, and oh, if some one would only let him know!"

She would tell him herself. No! No! Maimie's sharp arrow was quivering still in her heart. Once more she threw herself upon the bed. How could she bear this that had stricken her? She would go home. She would go to her mother to-morrow. Go away forever from – ah – could she? No, anything but that! She could not go away.

Over the broad river the warm sunlight lay with kindly glow, and the world was full of the soft, sweet air of spring, and the songs of mating birds; but the hours passed, and over the river the shadows began to creep, and the whole world grew dark, and the songs of the birds were hushed to silence. Then, from her room, Kate came down with face serene, and but for the eyes that somehow made one think of tears, without a sign of the storm that had swept her soul. She did not go home. She was too brave for that. She would stay and fight her battle to the end.

That was a dreary week for Ranald. He was lonely and heartsick for the woods and for his home and friends, but chiefly was he oppressed with the sense of having played the fool in his quarrel with De Lacy, whom he was beginning to admire and like. He surely might have avoided that; and yet whenever he thought of the game that had swept away from Rouleau all his winter's earnings, and of the cruel blow that had followed, he felt his muscles stiffen and his teeth set tight in rage. No, he would do it all again, nor would he retreat one single step from the position he had taken, but would see his quarrel through to the end. But worst of all he had not seen Maimie all the week. His experience with Harry in the ordering of his suit had taught him the importance of clothes, and he now understood as he could not before, Maimie's manner to him. "That would be it," he said to himself, "and no wonder. What would she do with a great, coarse tyke like me!" Then, in spite of all his loyalty, he could not help contrasting with Maimie's uncertain and doubtful treatment of him, the warm, frank friendliness of Kate. "*She* did not mind my clothes," he thought, with a glow of gratitude, but sharply checking himself, he added, "but why should she care?" It rather pleased him to think that Maimie cared enough to feel embarrassed at his rough dress. So he kept away from the Hotel de Cheval Blanc till his new suit should be ready. It was not because of his dress, however, that he steadily refused Harry's invitation to the picnic.

"No. I will not go," he said, with blunt decision, after listening to Harry's pleading. "It is Lieutenant De Lacy's picnic, and I will have nothing to do with him, and indeed he will not be wanting me!"

"Oh, he's forgotten all about that little affair," cried Harry.

"Has he? Indeed then if he is a man he has not!"

"I guess he hasn't remembered much of anything for the last week," said Harry, with a slight laugh.

"Why not?"

"Oh, pshaw, he's been on a big tear. He only sobered up yesterday."

"Huh!" grunted Ranald, contemptuously. He had little respect for a man who did not know when he had had enough. "What about his job?" he asked.

"His job? Oh, I see. His job doesn't worry him much. He's absent on sick-leave. But he's all fit again and I know he will be disappointed if you do not come to-morrow."

"I will not go," said Ranald, with final decision, "and you can tell him so, and you can tell him why."

And Harry did tell him with considerable fullness and emphasis not only of Ranald's decision, but also Ranald's opinion of him, for he felt that it would do that lordly young man no harm to know that a man whom he was inclined to patronize held him in contempt and for cause. The lieutenant listened for a time to all Harry had to say with apparent indifference, then suddenly interrupting him, he said: "Oh, I say, old chap, I wouldn't rub it in if I were you. I have a more or less vague remembrance of having rather indulged in heroics. One can't keep his head with poker and unlimited brandy-and-sodas; they don't go together. It's a thing I almost never do; never in a big game, but the thing got interesting before I knew. But I say, that Glengarry chap plays a mighty good game. Must get him on again. Feels hot, eh? I will make that all right, and what's the French chap's name – Boileau, Rondeau, eh? Rouleau. Yes, and where could one see him?"

"I can find out from LeNoir, who will be somewhere near Ranald. You can't get him away from him."

"Well, do," said the lieutenant, lazily. "Bring LeNoir to see me. I owe that Rouleau chap an apology. Beastly business! And I'll fix it up with Macdonald. He has the right of it, by Jove! Rather lucky, I fancy, he didn't yield to my solicitations for a try at the other game – from what I remember of the street riot, eh? Would not mind having a go with him with the gloves, though. I will see him to-morrow morning. Keep your mind at rest."

Next morning when LeNoir came to his work he was full of the lieutenant's praises to Ranald.

"Das fine feller le Capitaine, eh? Das de Grand Seigneur for sure! He's mak eet all right wit Rouleau! He's pay de cash money and he's mak eet de good posish for him, an' set him up the champagne, too, by gar!"

"Huh," grunted Ranald. "Run that crib around the boom there LeNoir; break it up and keep your gang moving to-day!"

"*Bon!*" said LeNoir, with alacrity. "I give 'em de big move, me!"

But however unwilling Ranald was to listen to LeNoir singing the lieutenant's praises, when he met Harry at noon in the office he was even more enthusiastic than LeNoir in his admiration of De Lacy.

"I never saw the likes of him," he said. "He could bring the birds out of the trees with that tongue of his. Indeed, I could not have done what he did whatever. Man, but he is a gentleman!"

"And are you going this evening?"

"That I am," said Ranald. "What else could I do? I could not help myself; he made me feel that mean that I was ready to do anything."

"All right," said Harry, delighted, "I will take my canoe around for you after six."

"And," continued Ranald, with a little hesitation, "he told me he would be wearing a jersey and duck trousers, and I think that was very fine of him."

"Why, of course," said Harry, quite mystified, "what else would he wear?"

Ranald looked at him curiously for a moment, and said: "A swallow-tail, perhaps, or a blanket, maybe," and he turned away leaving Harry more mystified than ever.

Soon after six, Harry paddled around in his canoe, and gave the stern to Ranald. What a joy it was to him to be in a canoe stern again; to feel the rush of the water under his knees; to have her glide swiftly on her soundless way down the full-bosomed, sunbathed river; to see her put her nose into the little waves and gently, smoothly push them asunder with never a splash or swerve; to send her along straight and true as an arrow in its flight, and then flip! flip to swing her off a floating log or around an awkward boat lumbering with clumsy oars. That was to be alive again. Oh, the joy of it! Of all things that move to the will of man there is none like the canoe. It alone has the sweet, smooth glide, the swift, silent dart answering the paddle sweep; the quick swerve in response to the return of the wrist. Ranald felt as if he could have gladly paddled on right out to the open sea; but sweeping around a bend a long, clear call hailed them, and there, far down at the bottom of a little bay, at the foot of the big, scarred, and wrinkled rock the smoke and glimmer of the camp-fire could be seen. A flip of the stern paddle, and the canoe pointed for the waving figure, and under the rhythmic sweep of the paddles, sped like an arrow down the waters, sloping to the shore. There, on a great rock, stood Kate, directing their course.

"Here's a good landing," she cried. Right at the rock dashed the canoe at full speed. A moment more and her dainty nose would be battered out of all shape on the cruel rock, but a strong back stroke, a turn of the wrist, flip, and she lay floating quietly beside the rock.

"Splendid!" cried Kate.

"Well done, by Jove!" exclaimed the lieutenant, who was himself an expert with the paddle.

"I suppose you have no idea how fine you look," cried Kate.

"And I am quite sure," answered Harry, "you have no suspicion of what a beautiful picture you all make." And a beautiful picture it was: the great rocky cliff in the background, tricked out in its new spring green of moss and shrub and tree; the grassy plot at its foot where a little stream gurgled out from the rock; the blazing camp-fire with the little group about it; and in front the sunlit river. How happy they all were! And how ready to please and to be pleased. Even little Mr. Sims had his charm. And at the making of the tea, which Kate had taken in charge with Ranald superintending, what fun there was with burning of fingers and upsetting of kettles! And then, the talk and the laughter at the lieutenant's brilliant jokes, and the chaffing of the "lumbermen" over their voracious appetites! It was an hour of never-to-be-forgotten pleasure. They were all children again, and with children's hearts were happy in childhood's simple joys. And why not? There are no joys purer than those of the open air; of grass and trees flooded with the warm light and sweet scents of the soft springtime. Too soon it all came to an end, and then they set off to convoy the stately old lady to her carriage at the top of the cliff. Far in front went Kate, disdaining the assistance of Harry and Mr. Sims, who escorted her. Near at hand the lieutenant was in attendance upon Maimie, who seemed to need his constant assistance; for the way was rough, and there were so many jutting points of rock for wonderful views, and often the very prettiest plants were just out of reach. Last of all came Madame De Lacy, climbing the steep path with difficulty and holding fast to Ranald's arm. With charming grace she discoursed of the brave days of old in which her ancestors had played a worthy part. An interesting tale it was, but in spite of all her charm of speech, and grace of manner, Ranald could not keep his mind from following his heart and eyes that noted every step and move of the beautiful girl, flitting in and out among the trees before them. And well it was that his eyes were following so close; for, as she was reaching for a dainty spray of golden birch, holding by the lieutenant's hand, the treacherous moss slipped from under Maimie's feet, and with a piercing shriek she went rolling down the sloping mountain-side, dragging her escort with her. Like a flash of light Ranald dropped madame's arm, and, seizing the top of a tall birch that grew up from the lower ledge, with a trick learned as a boy in the Glengarry woods, he swung himself clear over the edge, and dropping lightly on the mossy bank below, threw himself in front of the rolling bodies, and seizing them held fast. In another moment leaving the lieutenant to shift for himself, Ranald was on his knees beside Maimie, who lay upon the moss, white and still. "Some water, for God's sake!" he cried, hoarsely, to De Lacy, who stood dazed beside him, and then, before the lieutenant could move, Ranald lifted Maimie in his arms, as if she had been an infant, and bore her down to the river's edge, and laid her on the grassy bank. Then, taking up a double handful of water, he dashed it in her face. With a little sigh she opened her eyes, and letting them rest upon his face, said, gently, "Oh, Ranald, I am so glad you – I am so sorry I have been so bad to you." She could say no more, but from her closed eyes two great tears made their way down her pale cheeks.

"Oh, Maimie, Maimie," said Ranald, in a broken voice, "tell me you are not hurt."

Again she opened her eyes and said, "No, I am not hurt, but you will take me home; you will not leave me!" Her fingers closed upon his hand.

With a quick, strong clasp, he replied: "I will not leave you."

In a few minutes she was able to sit up, and soon they were all about her, exclaiming and lamenting.

"What a silly girl I am," she said, with a little tremulous laugh, "and what a fright I must have given you all!"

"Don't rise, my dear," said Madame De Lacy, "until you feel quite strong."

"Oh, I am quite right," said Maimie, confidently; "I am sure I am not hurt in the least."

"Oh, I am so thankful!" cried Kate.

"It is the Lord's mercy," said Ranald, in a voice of deep emotion.

"Are you quite sure you are not hurt?" said Harry, anxiously.

"Yes, I really think I am all right, but what a fright I must look!"

"Thank God!" said Harry fervently; "I guess you're improving," at which they all laughed.

"Now I think we must get home," said Madame De Lacy. "Do you think you can walk, Maimie?"

"Oh, yes," cried Maimie, and taking Ranald's hand, she tried to stand up, but immediately sank back with a groan.

"Oh, it is my foot," she said, "I am afraid it is hurt."

"Let me see!" cried Harry. "I don't think it is broken," he

said, after feeling it carefully, "but I have no doubt it is a very bad sprain. You can't walk for certain."

"Then we shall have to carry her," said Madame De Lacy, and she turned to her son.

"I fear I can offer no assistance," said the lieutenant, pointing to his arm which was hanging limp at his side.

"Why, Albert, are you hurt? What is the matter? You are hurt!" cried his mother, anxiously.

"Not much, but I fear my arm is useless. You might feel it," he said to Ranald.

Carefully Ranald passed his hand down the arm.

"Say nothing," whispered the lieutenant to him. "It's broken. Tie it up some way." Without a word Ranald stripped the bark of a birch tree, and making a case, laid the arm in it and bound it firmly with his silk handkerchief.

"We ought to have a sling," he said, turning to Kate.

"Here," said Madame De Lacy, untying a lace scarf from her neck, "take this."

Kate took the scarf, and while Ranald held the arm in place she deftly made it into a sling.

"There," said the lieutenant, "that feels quite comfortable. Now let's go."

"Come, Maimie, I'll carry you up the hill," said Harry.

"No," said Ranald, decidedly, "she will go in the canoe. That will be easier."

"Quite right," said the lieutenant. "Sims, perhaps you will give my mother your arm, and if Miss Kate will be kind enough to escort me, we can all four go in the carriage; but first we shall see the rest of the party safely off."

"Come, then, Maimie," said Harry, approaching his sister; "let me carry you."

But Maimie glanced up at Ranald, who without a word, lifted her in his arms.

"Put your arm about his neck, Maimie," cried Harry, "you will go more comfortably that way. Ranald won't mind," he added, with a laugh.

At the touch of her clinging arms the blood mounted slowly into Ranald's neck and face, showing red through the dark tan of his skin.

"How strong you are," said Maimie, softly, "and how easily you carry me. But you would soon tire of me," she added with a little laugh.

"I would not tire forever," said Ranald, as he laid her gently down in the canoe.

"I shall send the carriage to the wharf for you," said Madame De Lacy, "and you will come right home to me, and you, too, Miss Raymond."

Ranald took his place in the stern with Maimie reclining in the canoe so as to face him.

"You are sure you are comfortable," he said, with anxious solicitude in his tone.

"Quite," she replied, with a cosy little snuggle down among the cushions placed around her.

"Then let her go," cried Ranald, dipping in his paddle.

"Good by," cried Kate, waving her hand at them from the rock. "We'll meet you at the wharf. Take good care of your invalid, Ranald."

With hardly a glance at her Ranald replied: "You may be sure of that," and with a long, swinging stroke shot the canoe out into the river. For a moment or two Kate stood looking after them, and then, with a weary look in her face, turned, and with the lieutenant, followed Madame De Lacy and Mr. Sims.

"You are tired," said the lieutenant, looking into her face.

"Yes," she replied, with a little sigh, "I think I am tired."

The paddle home was all too short to Ranald, but whether it took minutes or hours he could not have told. As in a dream he swung his paddle and guided his canoe. He saw only the beautiful face and the warm light in the bright eyes before him. He woke to see Kate on the wharf before them, and for a moment he wondered how she came there. Once more, as he bore her from the canoe to the carriage, he felt Maimie's arms clinging about his neck and heard her whisper, "You will not leave me, Ranald," and again he replied, "No, I will not leave you."

Swiftly the De Lacy carriage bore them through the crooked, climbing streets of the city and out along the country road, then up a stately avenue of beeches, and drew up before the stone steps, of a noble old château. Once more Ranald lifted Maimie in his arms and carried her up the broad steps, and through the great oak-paneled hall into Madame De Lacy's own cosy sitting-room, and there he laid her safely in a snug nest of cushions prepared for her. There was nothing more to do, but to say good by and come away, but it was Harry that first brought this to Ranald's mind.

"Good by, Ranald," said Maimie, smiling up into his face. "I cannot thank you for all you have done to-day, but I am sure Madame De Lacy will let you come to see me sometimes."

"I shall be always glad to see you," said the little lady, with gentle, old-fashioned courtesy, "for we both owe much to you this day."

"Thank you," said Ranald, quietly, "I will come," and passed out of the room, followed by Harry and Kate.

At the great hall door, Kate stood and watched them drive away, waving her hand in farewell.

"Good by," cried Harry, "don't forget us in your stately palace," but Ranald made no reply. He had no thought for her. But still she stood and watched the carriage till the beeches hid it from her view, and then, with her hand pressed against her side, she turned slowly into the hall.

As the carriage rolled down the stately avenue, Ranald sat absorbed in deepest thought, heeding not his companion's talk.

"What's the matter with you, Ranald? What are you thinking of?" at last cried Harry, impatiently.

"What?" answered Ranald, in strange confusion, "I cannot tell you." Unconsciously as he spoke he put up his hand to his neck, for he was still feeling the pressure of those clinging arms, and all the way back the sounds of the rolling wheels and noisy, rattling streets wrought themselves into one sweet refrain, "You will not leave me, Ranald," and often in his heart he answered, "No, I will not," with such a look on his face as men wear when pledging life and honor.

I WILL REMEMBER

The *Albert* was by all odds the exclusive club in the capital city of upper Canada, for men were loath to drop the old name. Its members belonged to the best families, and moved in the highest circles, and the *entré* was guarded by a committee of exceeding vigilance. They had a very real appreciation of the rights and privileges of their order, and they cherished for all who assayed to enter the most lofty ideal. Not wealth alone could purchase entrance within those sacred precincts unless, indeed, it were of sufficient magnitude and distributed with judicious and unvulgar generosity. A tinge of blue in the common red blood of humanity commanded the most favorable consideration, but when there was neither cerulean tinge of blood nor gilding of station the candidate for membership in the *Albert* was deemed unutterable in his presumption, and rejection absolute and final was inevitable. A single black ball shut him out. So it came as a surprise to most outsiders, though not to Ranald himself, when that young gentleman's name appeared in the list of accepted members in the *Albert*. He had been put up by both Raymond and St. Clair, but not even the powerful influence of these sponsors would have availed with the members had it not come to be known that young Macdonald was a friend of Captain De Lacy's of Quebec, don't you know! and a sport, begad, of the first water; for the *Alberts* favored athletics, and loved a true sport almost as much as they loved a lord. They never regretted their generous concession in this instance, for during the three years of his membership, it was the Glengarry Macdonald that had brought glory to their club more than any half dozen of their other champions. In their finals with the *Montrealers* two years ago, it was he, the prince of all Canadian half-backs, as every one acknowledged, who had snatched victory from the exultant enemy in the last quarter of an hour. Then, too, they had never ceased to be grateful for the way in which he had delivered the name of their club from the reproach cast upon it by the challenge long flaunted before their aristocratic noses by the cads of the Athletic, when he knocked out in a bout with the gloves, the chosen representative of that ill-favored club – a professional, too, by Jove, as it leaked out later.

True, there were those who thought him too particular, and undoubtedly he had peculiar ideas. He never drank, never played for money, and he never had occasion to use words in the presence of men that would be impossible before their mothers and sisters; and there was a quaint, old-time chivalry about him that made him a friend of the weak and helpless, and the champion of women, not only of those whose sheltered lives had kept them fair and pure, but of those others as well, sad-eyed and soul-stained, the cruel sport of lustful men. For his open scorn of their callous lust some hated him, but all with true men's hearts loved him.

The club-rooms were filling up; the various games were in full swing.

"Hello, little Merrill!" Young Merrill looked up from his billiards.

"Glengarry, by all the gods!" throwing down his cue, and rushing at Ranald. "Where in this lonely universe have you been these many months, and how are you, old chap?" Merrill was excited.

"All right, Merrill?" inquired the deep voice.

"Right, so help me –" exclaimed Merrill, solemnly, lifting up his hand. "He's inquiring after my morals," he explained to the men who were crowding about; "and I don't give a blank blank who knows it," continued little Merrill, warmly, "my present magnificent manhood," smiting himself on the breast, "I owe to that same dear old solemnity there," pointing to Ranald.

"Shut up, Merrill, or I'll spank you," said Ranald.

"You will, eh?" cried Merrill, looking at him. "Look at him vaunting his beastly fitness over the frail and weak. I say, men, did you ever behold such condition! See that clear eye, that velvety skin, that – Oh, I say! pax! pax! peccavi!"

"There," said Ranald, putting him down from the billiard-table, "perhaps you will learn when to be seen."

"Brute," murmured little Merrill, rubbing the sore place; "but ain't he fit?" he added, delightedly. And fit he looked. Four years of hard work and clean living had done for him everything that it lies in years to do. They had made of the lank, raw, shanty lad a man, and such a man as a sculptor would have loved to behold. Straight as a column he stood two inches over six feet, but of such proportions that seeing him alone, one would never have guessed his height. His head and neck rose above his square shoulders with perfect symmetry and poise. His dark face, tanned now to a bronze, with features clear-cut and strong, was lit by a pair of dark brown eyes, honest, fearless, and glowing with a slumbering fire that men would hesitate to stir to flame. The lines of his mouth told of self-control, and the cut of his chin proclaimed a will of iron, and altogether, he bore himself with an air of such quiet strength and cool self-confidence that men never feared to follow where he led. Yet there was a reserve about him that set him a little apart from men, and a kind of shyness that saved him from any suspicion of self-assertion. In vain he tried to escape from the crowd that gathered about him, and more especially from the foot-ball men, who utterly adored him.

"You can't do anything for a fellow that doesn't drink," complained Starry Hamilton, the big captain of the foot-ball team.

"Drink! a nice captain you are, Starry," said Ranald, "and Thanksgiving so near."

"We haven't quite shut down yet," explained the captain.

"Then I suppose a cigar is permitted," replied Ranald, ordering the steward to bring his best. In a few minutes he called for his mail, and excusing himself, slipped into one of the private rooms. The manager of the Raymond & St. Clair Company and prominent clubman, much sought after in social circles, he was bound to find letters of importance awaiting him, but hastily shuffling the bundle, he selected three, and put the rest in his pocket.

"So she's back," he said to himself, lifting up one in a square envelope, addressed in large, angular writing. He turned it over in his hand, feasting his eyes upon it, as a boy holds a peach, prolonging the blissful anticipation. Then he opened it slowly and read:

> My Dear Ranald: All the way home I was hoping that on my return, fresh from the "stately homes of England,"

and from association with lords and dukes and things, you would be here to receive your share of the luster and aroma my presence would shed (that's a little mixed, I fear); but with a most horrible indifference to your privileges you are away at the earth's end, no one knows where. Father said you were to be home to-day, so though you don't in the least deserve it, I am writing you a note of forgiveness; and will you be sure to come to my special party to-morrow night? I put it off till to-morrow solely on your account, and in spite of Aunt Frank, and let me tell you that though I have seen such heaps of nice men, and all properly dear and devoted, still I want to see you, so you must come. Everything else will keep.

Yours,
MAIMIE.

Over and over again he read the letter, till the fire in his eyes began to gleam and his face became radiant with a tender glow.

"'Yours, Maimie,' eh? I wonder now what she means" he mused. "Seven years and for my life I don't know yet, but to-morrow night – yes, to-morrow night, I will know!" He placed the letter in its envelope and put it carefully in his inside pocket. "Now for Kate, dear old girl, no better anywhere." He opened his letter and read:

DEAR RANALD: What a lot of people will be delighted to see you back! First, dear old Dr. Marshall, who is in despair over the Institute, of which he declares only a melancholy ruin will be left if you do not speedily return. Indeed, it is pretty bad. The boys are quite terrible, and even my "angels" are becoming infected. Your special pet, Coley, after reducing poor Mr. Locke to the verge of nervous prostration, has "quit," and though I have sought him in his haunts, and used my very choicest blandishments, he remains obdurate. To my remonstrances, he finally deigned to reply: "Naw, they ain't none of 'em any good no more; them ducks is too pious for me." I don't know whether you will consider that a compliment or not. So the Institute and all its people will welcome you with acclaims of delight and sighs of relief. And some one else whom you adore, and who adores you, will rejoice to see you. I have begged her from Maimie for a few precious days. But that's a secret, and last of all and least of all, there is

Your friend,

KATE.

P.S. – Of course you will be at the party to-morrow night. Maimie looks lovelier than ever, and she will be so glad to see you.

K.

"What a trump she is," murmured Ranald; "unselfish, honest to the core, and steady as a rock. 'Some one else whom you adore.' Who can that be? By Jove, is it possible? I will go right up to-night."

His last letter was from Mr. St. Clair, who was the chief executive of the firm. He glanced over it hurriedly, then with a curious blending of surprise, perplexity, and dismay on his face, he read it again with careful deliberation:

My Dear Ranald: Welcome home! We shall all be delighted to see you. Your letter from North Bay, which reached me two days ago, contained information that places us in rather an awkward position. Last May, just after you left for the north, Colonel Thorp, of the British-American Coal and Lumber Company, operating in British Columbia and Michigan, called to see me, and made an offer of $75,000 for our Bass River limits. Of course you know we are rather anxious to unload, and at first I regarded his offer with favor. Soon afterwards I received your first report, sent apparently on your way up. I thereupon refused Colonel Thorp's offer. Then evidently upon the strength of your report, which I showed him, Colonel Thorp, who by the way is a very fine fellow, but a very shrewd business man, raised his offer to an even hundred thousand. This offer I feel inclined to accept. To tell you the truth, we have more standing timber than we can handle, and as you know, we are really badly crippled for ready money. It is a little unfortunate that your last report should be so much less favorable in regard to the east half of the limits. However, I don't suppose there is any need of mentioning that to Colonel Thorp, especially as his company are getting a good bargain as it is, and one which of themselves, they could not possibly secure from the government. I write you this note in case you should run across Colonel Thorp in town to-morrow, and inadvertently say something that might complicate matters. I have no doubt that we shall be able to close the deal in a few days.

Now I want to say again how delighted we all are to have you back. We never realized how much we were dependent upon you. Mr. Raymond and I have been talking matters over, and we have agreed that some changes ought to be made, which I venture to say will not be altogether disagreeable to you. I shall see you first thing in the morning about the matter of the limits.

Maimie has got home, and is, I believe, expecting you at her party to-morrow night. Indeed, I understand she was determined that it should not come off until you had returned, which shows she shares the opinion of the firm concerning you.

I am yours sincerely,
EUGENE ST. CLAIR.

Ranald sat staring at the letter for a long time. He saw with perfect clearness Mr. St. Clair's meaning, and a sense of keen humiliation possessed him as he realized what it was that he was expected to do. But it took some time for the full significance of the situation to dawn upon him. None knew better than he how important it was to the firm that this sale should be effected. The truth was if the money market should become at all close the firm would undoubtedly find themselves in serious difficulty. Ruin to the company meant not only the blasting of his own prospects, but misery to her whom he loved better than life; and after all, what he was asked to do was nothing more than might be done any day in the world of business. Every buyer is supposed to know the value of the thing he buys, and certainly Colonel Thorp should not commit his company to a deal involving such a large sum of money without thoroughly informing himself in regard to the value of the limits in question, and when he, as an employé of the Raymond and St. Clair Lumber Company, gave in his report, surely his responsibility ceased. He was not asked to present any incorrect report; he could easily make it convenient to be absent until the deal was closed. Furthermore, the chances were that the British-American Coal and Lumber Company would still have good value for their money, for the west half of the limits was exceptionally good; and besides, what right had he to besmirch the honor of his employer, and to set his judgment above that of a man of much greater experience? Ranald understood also Mr. St. Clair's reference to the changes in the firm, and it gave him no small satisfaction to think that in four years he had risen from the position of lumber checker to that of manager, with an offer of a partnership; nor could he mistake the suggestion in Mr. St. Clair's closing words. Every interest he had in life would be furthered by the consummation of the deal, and would be imperiled by his refusing to adopt Mr. St. Clair's suggestion. Still, argue as he might, Ranald never had any doubt as to what, as a man of honor, he ought to do. Colonel Thorp was entitled to the information that he and Mr. St. Clair alone possessed. Between his interests and his conscience the conflict raged.

"I wish I knew what I ought to do," he groaned, all the time battling against the conviction that the information he possessed should by rights be given to Colonel Thorp. Finally, in despair of coming to a decision, he seized his hat, saying, "I will go and see Kate," and slipping out of a side door, he set off for the Raymond home. "I will just look up Coley on the way," he said to himself, and diving down an alley, he entered a low saloon with a billiard hall attached. There, as he had expected, acting as marker, he found Coley.

Mike Cole, or Coley, as his devoted followers called him, was king of St. Joseph's ward. Everywhere in the ward his word ran as law. About two years ago Coley had deigned to favor the Institute with a visit, his gang following him. They were welcomed with demonstrations of joy, and regaled with cakes and tea, all of which Coley accepted with lordly condescension.

After consideration, Coley decided that the night classes might afford a not unpleasant alternative on cold nights, to alley-ways and saloons, and he allowed the gang to join. Thenceforth the successful conduct of the classes depended upon the ability of the superintendent to anticipate Coley's varying moods and inclinations, for that young man claimed and exercised the privilege of introducing features agreeable to the gang, though not necessarily upon the regular curriculum of study. Some time after Ranald's appearance in the Institute as an assistant, it happened one night that a sudden illness of the superintendent laid upon his shoulders the responsibility of government. The same night it also happened that Coley saw fit to introduce the enlivening but quite impromptu feature of a song and dance. To this Ranald objected, and was invited to put the gang out if he was man enough. After the ladies had withdrawn beyond the reach of missiles, Ranald adopted the unusual tactics of preventing exit by locking the doors, and then immediately became involved in a discussion with Coley and his followers. It cost the Institute something for furniture and windows, but thenceforth in Ranald's time there was peace. Coley ruled as before, but his sphere of influence was limited, and the day arrived when it became the ambition of Coley's life to bring the ward and its denizens into subjection to his own over-lord, whom he was prepared to follow to the death. But like any other work worth doing, this took days and weeks and months.

"Hello, Coley!" said Ranald, as his eyes fell upon his sometime ally and slave. "If you are not too busy I would like you to go along with me."

Coley looked around as if seeking escape.

"Come along," said Ranald, quietly, and Coley, knowing that anything but obedience was impossible, dropped his marking and followed Ranald out of the saloon.

"Well, Coley, I have had a great summer," began Ranald, "and I wish very much you could have been with me. It would have built you up and made a man of you. Just feel that," and he held out his arm, which Coley felt with admiring reverence. "That's what the canoe did," and then he proceeded to give a graphic account of his varied adventures by land and water during the last six months. As they neared Mr. Raymond's house, Ranald turned to Coley and said: "Now I want you to cut back to the Institute and tell Mr. Locke, if he is there, that I would like him to call around at my office to-morrow. And furthermore, Coley, there's no need of your going back into that saloon. I was a little ashamed to see one of my friends in a place like that. Now, good night, and be a man, and a clean man."

Coley stood with his head hung in abject self-abasement, and then ventured to say, "I couldn't stand them ducks nohow!"

"Who do you mean?" said Ranald.

"Oh, them fellers that runs the Institute now, and so I cut."

"Now look here, Coley," said Ranald, "I wouldn't go throwing stones at better men than yourself, and especially at men who are trying to do something to help other people and are not so beastly mean as to think only of their own pleasure. I didn't expect that of you, Coley. Now quit it and start again," and Ranald turned away.

Coley stood looking after him for a few moments in silence, and then said to himself, in a voice full of emphasis: "Well, there's just one of his kind and there ain't any other." Then he set out at a run for the Institute.

It was Kate herself who came to answer Ranald's ring.

"I knew it was you," she cried, with her hand eagerly outstretched and her face alight with joy. "Come in, we are all waiting for you, and prepare to be surprised." When they came to the drawing-room she flung open the door and with great ceremony announced "The man from Glengarry, as Harry would say."

"Hello, old chap!" cried Harry, springing to his feet, but Ranald ignored him. He greeted Kate's mother warmly for she had shown him a mother's kindness ever since he had come to the city, and they were great friends, and then he turned to Mrs. Murray, who was standing waiting for him, and gave her both his hands.

"I knew from Kate's letter," he said, "that it would be you, and I cannot tell you how glad I am." His voice grew a little unsteady and he could say no more. Mrs. Murray stood holding his hands and looking into his face.

"It cannot be possible," she said, "that this is Ranald Macdonald! How changed you are!" She pushed him a little back from her. "Let me look at you; why, I must say it, you are really handsome!"

"Now, auntie," cried Harry, reprovingly, "don't flatter him. He is utterly ruined now by every one, including both Kate and her mother."

"But really, Harry," continued Mrs. Murray, in a voice of delighted surprise, "it is certainly wonderful; and I am so glad! And I have been hearing about your work with the boys at the Institute, and I cannot tell you the joy it gave me."

"Oh, it is not much that I have done," said Ranald, deprecatingly.

"Indeed, it is a noble work and worthy of any man," said Mrs. Murray, earnestly, "and I thank God for you."

"Then," said Ranald, firmly, "I owe it all to yourself, for it is you that set me on this way."

"Listen to them admiring each other! It is quite shameless," said Harry.

Then they began talking about Glengarry, of the old familiar places, of the woods and the fields, of the boys and girls now growing into men and women, and of the old people, some of whom were passed away. Before long they were talking of the church and all the varied interests centering in it, but soon they went back to the theme that Glengarry people everywhere are never long together without discussing – the great revival. Harry had heard a good deal about it before, but to Kate and her mother the story was mostly new, and they listened with eager interest as Mrs. Murray and Ranald recalled those great days. With eyes shining, and in tones of humble, grateful wonder they reminded each other of the various incidents, the terrors, the struggles, the joyful surprises, the mysterious powers with which they were so familiar during those eighteen months. Then Mrs. Murray told of the permanent results; how over three counties the influence of the movement was still felt, and how whole congregations had been built up under its wonderful power.

"And did you hear," she said to Ranald, "that Donald Stewart was ordained last May?"

"No," replied Ranald; "that makes seven, doesn't it?"

"Seven what?" said Kate.

"Seven men preaching the Gospel to-day out of our own congregation," replied Mrs. Murray.

"But, auntie," cried Harry, "I have always thought that all that must have been awfully hard work."

"It was," said Ranald, emphatically; and he went on to sketch Mrs. Murray's round of duties in her various classes and meetings connected with the congregation.

"Besides what she has to do in the manse!" exclaimed Harry; "but it's a mere trifle, of course, to look after her troop of boys."

"How can you do it?" said Kate, gazing at her in admiring wonder.

"It isn't so terrible as Harry thinks. That's my work, you see," said Mrs. Murray; "what else would I do? And when it goes well it is worth while."

"But, auntie, don't you feel sometimes like getting away and having a little fun? Own up, now."

"Fun?" laughed Mrs. Murray.

"Well, not fun exactly, but a good time with things you enjoy so much, music, literature, and that sort of thing. Do you remember, Kate, the first time you met auntie, when we took her to *Hamlet*?"

Kate nodded.

"She wasn't quite sure about it, but I declare till I die I will never forget the wonder and the delight in her face. I tell you I wept that night, but not at the play. And how she criticised the actors; even Booth himself didn't escape," continued Harry; "and so I say it's a beastly shame that you should spend your whole life in the backwoods there and have so little of the other sort of thing. Why you are made for it!"

"Harry," answered Mrs. Murray, in surprise, "that was my work, given me to do. Could I refuse it? And besides after all, fun, as you say, passes; music stops; books get done with; but those other things, the things that Ranald and I have seen, will go on long after my poor body is laid away."

"But still you must get tired," persisted Harry.

"Yes, I get tired," she replied, quietly. At the little touch of weariness in the voice, Kate, who was looking at the beautiful face, so spiritual, and getting, oh, so frail, felt a sudden rush of tears in her eyes. But there was no self-pity in that heroic soul. "Yes, I get tired," she repeated, "but, Harry, what does that matter? We do our work and then we will rest. But oh, Harry, my boy, when I come to your city and see all there is to do, I wish I were a girl again, and I wonder at people thinking life is just for fun."

Harry, like other young men, hated to be lectured, but from his aunt he never took anything amiss. He admired her for her brilliant qualities, and loved her with a love near to worship.

"I say, auntie," he said, with a little uncertain laugh, "it's like going to church to hear you, only it's a deal more pleasant."

"But, Harry, am I not right?" she replied, earnestly. "Do you think that you will get the best out of your life by just having fun? Oh, do you know when I went with Kate to the Institute the other night and saw those boys my heart ached. I thought of my own boys, and –" The voice ceased in a pathetic little catch, the sensitive lips trembled, the beautiful gray-brown eyes filled with sudden tears. For a few moments there was silence; then, with a wavering smile, and a gentle, apologetic air, she said: "But I must not make Harry think he is in church."

"Dear Aunt Murray," cried Harry, "do lecture me. I'd enjoy it, and you can't make it too strong. You are just an angel." He left his seat, and going over to her chair, knelt down and put his arms about her.

"Don't you all wish she was your aunt?" he said, kissing her.

"She *is* mine," cried Kate, smiling at her through shining tears.

"She's more," said Ranald, and his voice was husky with emotion.

But with the bright, joyous little laugh Ranald knew so well, she smoothed back Harry's hair, and kissing him on the forehead, said: "I am sure you will do good work some day. But I shall be quite spoiled here; I must really get home."

As Ranald left the Raymond house he knew well what he should say to Mr. St. Clair next morning. He wondered at himself that he had ever been in doubt. He had been for an hour in another world where the atmosphere was pure and the light clear. Never till that night had he realized the full value of that life of patient self-sacrifice, so unconscious of its heroism. He understood then, as never before, the mysterious influence of that gentle, sweet-faced lady over every one who came to know her, from the simple, uncultured girls of the Indian Lands to the young men about town of Harry's type. Hers was the power of one who sees with open eyes the unseen, and who loves to the forgetting of self those for whom the Infinite love poured Itself out in death.

"Going home, Harry?" inquired Ranald.

"Yes, right home; don't want to go anywhere else to-night. I say, old chap, you're a better and cleaner man than I am, but it ain't your fault. That woman ought to make a saint out of any man."

"Man, you would say so if you knew her," said Ranald, with a touch of impatience; "but then no one does know her. They certainly don't down in the Indian Lands, for they don't know what she's given up."

"That's the beauty of it," replied Harry; "she doesn't feel it that way. Given up? not she! She thinks she's got everything that's good!"

"Well," said Ranald, thoughtfully, after a pause, "she knows, and she's right."

When they came to Harry's door Ranald lingered just a moment. "Come in a minute," said Harry.

"I don't know; I'm coming in to-morrow."

"Oh, come along just now. Aunt Frank is in bed, but Maimie will be up," said Harry, dragging him along to the door.

"No, I think not to-night." While they were talking the door opened and Maimie appeared.

"Ranald," she cried, in an eager voice, "I knew you would be at Kate's, and I was pretty sure you would come home with Harry. Aren't you coming in?"

"Where's Aunt Frank?" asked Harry.

"She's upstairs," said Maimie.

"Thank the Lord, eh?" added Harry, pushing in past her.

"Go away in and talk to her," said Maimie.

Then turning to Ranald and looking into his devouring eyes, she said, "Well? You might say you're glad to see me." She stood where the full light of the doorway revealed the perfect beauty of her face and figure.

"Glad to see you! There is no need of saying that," replied Ranald, still gazing at her.

"How beautiful you are, Maimie," he added, bluntly.

"Thank you, and you are really quite passable."

"And I *am* glad to see you."

"That's why you won't come in."

"I am coming to-morrow night."

"Everybody will be here to-morrow night."

"Yes, that's certainly a drawback."

"And I shall be very busy looking after my guests. Still," she added, noticing the disappointment in his face, "it's quite possible –"

"Exactly," his face lighting up again.

"Have you seen father's study?" asked Maimie, innocently.

"No," replied Ranald, wonderingly. "Is it so beautiful?"

"No, but it's upstairs, and – quiet."

"Well?" said Ranald.

"And perhaps you might like to see it to-morrow night."

"How stupid I am. Will you show it to me?"

"I will be busy, but perhaps Harry –"

"Will you?" said Ranald, coming close to her, with the old imperative in his voice.

Maimie drew back a little.

"Do you know what you make me think of?" she asked, lowering her voice.

"Yes, I do. I have thought of it every night since."

"You were very rude, I remember."

"You didn't think so then," said Ranald, boldly.

"I ought to have been very angry," replied Maimie, severely.

"But you weren't, you know you weren't; and do you remember what you said?"

"What I said? How awful of you; don't you dare! How can I remember?"

"Yes, you do remember, and then do you remember what *I* said?"

"What *you* said indeed! Such assurance!"

"I have kept my word," said Ranald, "and I am coming to-morrow night. Oh, Maimie, it has been a long, long time." He came close to her and caught her hand, the slumbering fire in his eyes blazing now in flame.

"Don't, don't, I'm sure there's Aunt Frank. No, no," she pleaded, in terror, "not to-night, Ranald!"

"Then will you show me the study to-morrow night?"

"Oh, you are very mean. Let me go!"

"Will you?" he demanded, still holding her hand.

"Yes, yes, you ought to be ashamed of yourself. My hand is quite sore. There, now, good night. No, I won't shake hands! Well, then, if you must have it, good night."

FORGET THAT I LOVED YOU

"The night for dreaming, but the morn for seeing." And so Ranald found it; for with the cold, calm light of the morning, he found himself facing his battle with small sense of victory in his blood. He knew he had to deal that morning with the crisis of his life. Upon the issue his whole future would turn, but his heart without haste or pause preserved its even beat. The hour of indecision had passed. He saw his way and he meant to walk it. What was beyond the turn was hid from his eyes, but with that he need not concern himself now. Meantime he would clear away some of this accumulated correspondence lying on his desk. In the midst of his work Harry came in and laid a bundle of bills before him.

"Here you are, old chap," he said, quietly. "That's the last of it."

Ranald counted the money.

"You are sure you can spare all this? There is no hurry, you know."

"No," said Harry, "I can't spare it, but it's safer with you than with me, and besides, it's yours. And I owe you more than money." He drew a deep breath to steady himself, and then went on: "And I want to say, Ranald, that I have bet my last stake."

Ranald pushed back his chair and rose to his feet.

"Now that's the best thing I've heard for some time," he said, offering Harry his hand; "and that's the last of that business."

He sat down, drew in his chair, and turning over his papers with a nervousness that he rarely showed, he continued: "And, Harry, I want you to do something for me. Before you go home this afternoon, will you come in here? I may want to send a note to Maimie by you."

"But –" began Harry.

"Wait a moment. I want to prevent all possibility of mistake. There may be a reply, and Harry, old chap, I'd rather not answer any questions."

Harry gazed at him a moment in perplexity. "All right, Ranald," he said, quietly, "you can trust me. I haven't the ghost of an idea what's up, but I know you're square."

"Thanks, old fellow," said Ranald, "I will never give you reason to change your opinion. Now get out; I'm awfully busy."

For some minutes after Harry had left the room Ranald sat gazing before him into space.

"Poor chap, he's got his fight, too, but I begin to think he'll win," he said to himself, and once more returned to his work. He had hardly begun his writing when the inner door of his office opened and Mr. St. Clair came in. His welcome was kindly and cordial, and Ranald's heart, which had been under strong discipline all morning, leaped up in warm response.

"You had a pleasant trip, I hope?" inquired Mr. St. Clair.

"Fine most of the way. Through May and June the flies

were bad, but not so bad as usual, they said, and one gets used to them."

"Good sport?"

"Never saw anything like it. What a country that is!" cried Ranald, his enthusiasm carrying him away. "Fishing of all kinds and superb. In those little lonely lakes you get the finest black and white bass, beauties and so gamy. In the bigger waters, maskalonge and, of course, any amount of pike and pickerel. Then we were always running up against deer, moose and red, and everywhere we got the scent of bear. Could have loaded a boat with furs in a week."

"We must go up some day," replied Mr. St. Clair. "Wish I could get away this fall, but the fact is we are in shallow water, Ranald, and we can't take any chances."

Ranald knew well how serious the situation was. "But," continued Mr. St. Clair, "this offer of the British-American Lumber and Coal Company is most fortunate, and will be the saving of us. With one hundred thousand set free we are certain to pull through this season, and indeed, the financial stringency will rather help than hinder our operations. Really it is most fortunate. Indeed," he added, with a slight laugh, "as my sister-in-law would say, quite providential!"

"I have no doubt of that," said Ranald, gravely; "but, Mr. St. Clair –"

"Yes, no doubt, no doubt," said Mr. St. Clair, hastening to recover the tone, which by his unfortunate reference to Mrs. Murray, he had lost. The thought of her was not in perfect harmony with purely commercial considerations. "The fact is," he continued, "that before this offer came I was really beginning to despair. I can tell you that now."

Ranald felt his heart tighten.

"One does not mind for one's self, but when family interests are involved – but that's all over now, thank God!"

Ranald tried to speak, but his mind refused to suggest words. His silence, however, was enough for Mr. St. Clair, who, with nervous haste once more changed the theme. "In my note to you last night – you got it, I suppose – I referred to some changes in the firm."

Ranald felt that he was being crowded against the ropes. He must get to freer fighting ground. "I think before you go on to that, Mr. St. Clair," he began, "I ought to –"

"Excuse me, I was about to say," interrupted Mr. St. Clair, hastily, "Mr. Raymond and I have felt that we must strengthen our executive. As you know, he has left this department almost entirely to me, and he now realizes what I have long felt, that the burden has grown too heavy for one to carry. Naturally we think of you, and I may say we are more than glad, though it is a very unusual thing in the business world, that we can, with the fullest confidence, offer you a partnership." Mr. St. Clair paused to allow the full weight of this announcement to sink into his manager's mind.

Then Ranald pulled himself together. He must break free or the fight would be lost before he had struck a blow.

"I need not say," he began once more, "how greatly gratified I am by this offer, and I feel sure you will believe that I am deeply grateful." Ranald's voice was low and even, but unknown to himself there was in it a tone of stern resolve that struck Mr. St. Clair's ear. He knew his manager. That tone meant war. Hastily he changed his front.

"Yes, yes, we are quite sure of that," he said, with increasing nervousness, "but we are thinking of our own interests as well as yours. Indeed, I feel sure" – here his voice became even more kindly and confidential – "that in advancing your position and prospects we are – I am only doing what will bring myself the greatest satisfaction in the end, for you know, Ranald, I – we do not regard you as a stranger." Ranald winced and grew pale. "We – my family – have always felt toward you as – well, in fact, as if you were one of us."

Mr. St. Clair had delivered his last and deadliest blow and it found Ranald's heart, but with pain blanching his cheek Ranald stood up determined to end the fight. It was by no means easy for him to strike. Before him he saw not this man with his ingenious and specious pleading – it would not have been a difficult matter to have brushed him aside – but he was looking into the blue eyes of the woman he had for seven years loved more than he loved his life, and he knew that when his blow fell it would fall upon the face that, only a few hours ago, had smiled upon him, and upon the lips that had whispered to him, "I will remember, Ranald." Yet he was none the less resolved. With face set and bloodless, and eyes of gleaming fire, he faced the man that represented what was at once dearest in life and what was most loathsome in conduct.

"Give me a moment, Mr. St. Clair," he said, with a note of authority in his tone. "You have made me an offer of a position such as I could hardly hope to expect for years to come, but I value it chiefly because it means you have absolute confidence in me; you believe in my ability and in my integrity. I am determined that you will never have cause to change your opinion of me. You are about to complete a deal involving a very large sum of money. I have a report here," tapping his desk, "which you have not yet seen."

"It really doesn't matter!" interjected Mr. St. Clair; "you see, my dear fellow –"

"It matters to me. It is a report which not only you ought to have, but which, in justice, the buyer of the Bass River

Limits ought to see. That report, Mr. St. Clair, ought to be given to Colonel Thorp."

"This is sheer folly," exclaimed Mr. St. Clair, impatiently.

"It is the only honorable course."

"Do you mean to insult me, sir?"

"There is only one other thing I would rather not do," said Ranald, in a grave voice, "and that is refuse Colonel Thorp the information he is entitled to from us."

"Sir!" exclaimed Mr. St. Clair, "this is outrageous, and I demand an apology or your resignation!"

"Colonel Thorp," announced a clerk, opening the door.

"Tell Colonel Thorp I cannot – ah, Colonel Thorp, I am glad to see you. Will you step this way?" opening the door leading to his own office.

The colonel, a tall, raw-boned, typical "Uncle Sam," even to the chin whisker and quid of tobacco, had an eye like an eagle. He shot a keen glance at Mr. St. Clair and then at Ranald.

"Yes," he said, helping himself to a chair, "this here's all right. This is your manager, eh?"

"Mr. Macdonald," said Mr. St. Clair, introducing him.

"How do you do? Heard about you some," said the colonel, shaking hands with him. "Quite a knocker, I believe. Well, you rather look like it. Used to do some myself. Been up north, so the boss says. Good country, eh?"

"Fine sporting country, Colonel," interrupted St. Clair. "The game, Mr. Macdonald says, come right into your tent and bed to be shot."

"Do, eh?" The colonel's eagle eye lighted up. "Now, what sort of game?"

"Almost every kind, Colonel," replied Ranald.

"Don't say! Used to do a little myself. Moose?"

"Yes, I saw a number of moose and any amount of other deer and, of course, plenty of bear."

"Don't say! How'd you come to leave them? Couldn't have done it myself, by the great Sam! Open timber?"

"Well," replied Ranald, slowly, "on the east of the Bass River –"

"All that north country, Colonel," said Mr. St. Clair, "is pretty much the same, I imagine; a little of all kinds."

"Much water, streams, and such?"

"Yes, on the west side of the Bass there is plenty of water, a number of small streams and lakes, but –"

"Oh, all through that north country, Colonel, you are safe in having a canoe in your outfit," said Mr. St. Clair, again interrupting Ranald.

"Lots of water, eh? Just like Maine, ha, ha!" The colonel's quiet chuckle was good to hear.

"Reminds me" – here he put his hand into his inside pocket and pulled out a flask, "excuse the glass," he said, offering it to Mr. St. Clair, who took a slight sip and handed it back.

"Have a little refreshment," said the colonel, offering it to Ranald.

"I never take it, thank you."

"Don't? Say, by the great Sam, how'd you get through all that wet country? Wall, it will not hurt you to leave it alone," solemnly winking at St. Clair, and taking a long pull himself. "Good for the breath," he continued, putting the flask in his pocket. "Now, about those limits of mine, the boss here has been telling you about our deal?"

"A little," said Ranald.

"We've hardly had time to look into anything yet," said Mr. St. Clair; "but if you will step into my office, Colonel, I have the papers and maps there." Mr. St. Clair's tone was anxious. Once more the colonel shot a glance at him.

"You have been on the spot, I judge," he said to Ranald, rising and following Mr. St. Clair.

"Yes, over it all."

"Wall, come along, you're the map we want, eh? Maps are chiefly for purposes of deception, I have found, ha, ha! and there ain't none of 'em right," and he held the door for Ranald to enter.

Mr. St. Clair was evidently annoyed. Unfolding a map he laid it out on the table. "This is the place, I believe," he said, putting his finger down upon the map.

"Ain't surveyed, I judge," said the colonel to Ranald.

"No, only in part; the old Salter lines are there, but I had to go away beyond these."

"Warn't 'fraid of gettin' lost, eh? Ha, ha! Wall show us your route."

Ranald put his finger on the map, and said: "I struck the Bass River about here, and using that as a base, first explored the whole west side, for, I should say, about ten miles back from the river."

"Don't say! How'd you grub? Game mostly?"

"Well, we carried some pork and Hudson Bay hard tack and tea, and of course, we could get all the fish and game we wanted."

"Lots of game, eh? Small and big?" The colonel was evidently much interested in this part of Ranald's story. "By the great Sam, must go up there!"

"It would do you all the good in the world, Colonel," said Mr. St. Clair, heartily. "You must really go up with your men and help them lay out the ground, you know."

"That's so! Now if you were lumbering in there, how'd you get the timber out?"

"Down the Bass River to Lake Nipissing," said Ranald, pointing out the route.

"Yes, but how'd you get it to the Bass? These limits, I understand, lie on both sides of the Bass, don't they?"

"Yes."

"And the Bass cuts through it the short way?"

"Yes."

"Wall, does that mean six or eight or ten miles of a haul?"

"On the west side," replied Ranald, "no. There are a number of small streams and lakes which you could utilize."

"And on the east side?"

"You see, Colonel," broke in Mr. St. Clair, "that whole country is one net-work of water-ways. Notice the map here; and there are always a number of lakes not marked."

"That is quite true," said Ranald, "as a rule; but on the east side –"

"Oh, of course," said Mr. St. Clair, hastily, "you will find great differences in different parts of the country."

Mr. St. Clair folded up the map and threw it on the table.

"Let's see," said the colonel, taking up the map again. "Now how about the camps, Mr. Macdonald, where do you locate them?"

"I have a rough draught here in which the bases for camps are indicated," said Ranald, ignoring the imploring and angry looks of his chief.

"Let's have a look at 'em," said the colonel.

"Oh, you haven't shown me this," said Mr. St. Clair, taking the draught from Ranald.

"No, sir, you have not seen my final report."

"No, not yet, of course. We have hardly had time yet, Colonel, but Mr. Macdonald will make a copy of this for you and send it in a day or two," replied Mr. St. Clair, folding up the sketch, nervously, and placing it on his desk. The colonel quietly picked up the sketch and opened it out.

"You have got that last report of yours, I suppose," he said, with a swift glance at Mr. St. Clair. That gentleman's face was pallid and damp; his whole fortune hung on Ranald's reply. It was to him a moment of agony.

Ranald glanced at his face, and paused. Then drawing his lips a little tighter, he said: "Colonel Thorp, my final report has not yet been handed in. Mr. St. Clair has not seen it. In my judgment –" here Mr. St. Clair leaned his hand hard upon his desk – "you are getting full value for your money, but I would suggest that you go yourself or send your inspector to explore the limits carefully before you complete the deal."

Colonel Thorp, who had been carefully scanning the sketch in his hand, suddenly turned and looked Ranald steadily in the eye. "These marks on the west side mean camps?"

"Yes."

"There are very few on the east side?"

"There are very few; the east side is inferior to the west."

"Much?"

"Yes, much inferior."

"But in your opinion the limit is worth the figure?"

"I would undertake to make money out of it; it is good value."

The colonel chewed hard for a minute, then turning to Mr. St. Clair, he said: "Wall, Mr. St. Clair, I'll give you one hundred thousand for your limit; but by the great Sam, I'd give twice the sum for your manager, if he's for sale! He's a man!" The emphasis on the he was ever so slight, but it was enough. Mr. St. Clair bowed, and sinking down into his chair, busied himself with his papers.

"Wall," said the colonel, "that's settled; and that reminds me," he added, pulling out his flask, "good luck to the Bass River Limits!"

He handed the flask to Mr. St. Clair, who eagerly seized it and took a long drink.

"Goes good sometimes," said the colonel, innocently. "Wall, here's lookin' at you," he continued, bowing toward Ranald; "and by the great Sam, you suit me well! If you ever feel like a change of air, indicate the same to Colonel Thorp."

"Ah, Colonel," said Mr. St. Clair, who had recovered his easy, pleasant manner, "we can sell limits but not men."

"No, by the great Sammy," replied the colonel, using the more emphatic form of his oath, "ner buy 'em! Wall," he added, "when you have the papers ready, let me know. Good day!"

"Very good, Colonel, good by, good by!"

The colonel did not notice Mr. St. Clair's offered hand, but nodding to Ranald, sauntered out of the office, leaving the two men alone. For a few moments Mr. St. Clair turned over his papers in silence. His face was flushed and smiling.

"Well, that is a most happy deliverance, Ranald," he said, rubbing his hands. "But what is the matter? You are not well."

White to the lips, Ranald stood looking at his chief with a resolved face.

"Mr. St. Clair, I wish to offer you my resignation as manager."

"Nonsense, Ranald, we will say no more about that. I was a little hasty. I hope the change I spoke of will go into immediate effect."

"I must beg to decline." The words came slowly, sternly from Ranald's white lips.

"And why, pray?"

"I have little doubt you can discover the reason, Mr. St. Clair. A few moments ago, for honorable dealing, you would have dismissed me. It is impossible that I should remain in your employ."

"Mr. Macdonald, are you serious in this? Do you know what you are doing? Do you know what you are saying?" Mr. St. Clair rose and faced his manager.

"Only too well," said Ranald, with lips that began to quiver, "and all the more because of what I must say further. Mr. St. Clair, I love your daughter. I have loved her for seven years. It is my one desire in life to gain her for my wife."

Mr. St. Clair gazed at him in utter astonishment.

"And in the same breath," he said at length, "you insult me and ask my permission."

"It is vain to ask your permission, I fear, but it is right that you should know my desire and my purpose."

"Your purpose?"

"My unalterable purpose."

"You take my daughter out of my house in – in spite of my teeth?" Mr. St. Clair could hardly find words.

"She will come with me," said Ranald, a little proudly.

"And may I ask how you know? Have you spoken to my daughter?"

"I have not spoken to her openly." The blood rose in his dark face. "But I believe she loves me."

"Well, Mr. Macdonald, your confidence is only paralleled by your prodigious insolence."

"I hope not," said Ranald, lowering his head from its proud pose. "I have no desire to be insolent."

Once more Mr. St. Clair looked at him in silence. Then slowly and with quiet emphasis, he said: "Mr. Macdonald, you are a determined man, but as God lives, this purpose of yours you will never carry out. I know my daughter, I think, better than you know her, and I tell you," here a slight smile of confidence played for a moment on his face, "she will never be your wife."

Ranald bowed his head.

"It shall be as she wills," he said, in a grave, almost sad, voice. "She shall decide," and he passed into his office.

All day long Ranald toiled at his desk, leaving himself no time for thought. In the late afternoon Harry came in on his way home.

"Thanks, old chap," said Ranald, looking up from his work; "sha'n't be able to come to-night, I am sorry to say."

"Not come?" cried Harry.

"No, it is impossible."

"What rot, and Maimie has waited ten days for you. Come along!"

"It is quite impossible, Harry," said Ranald, "and I want you to take this note to Maimie. The note will explain to her."

"But, Ranald, this is –"

"And, Harry, I want to tell you that this is my last day here."

Harry gazed at him speechless.

"Mr. St. Clair and I have had a difference that can never be made right, and to-night I leave the office for good."

"Leave the office for good? Going to leave us? What the deuce can the office do without you? And what does it all mean? Come, Ranald, don't be such a confounded sphynx! Why do you talk such rubbish?"

"It is true," said Ranald, "though I can hardly realize it myself; it is absolutely and finally settled; and I say, old man, don't make it harder for me. You don't know what it means to me to leave this place, and – you, and – all!" In spite of his splendid nerve Ranald's voice shook a little. Harry gazed at him in amazement.

"I will give your note to Maimie," he said, "but you will be back here if I know myself. I'll see father about this."

"Now, Harry," said Ranald, rising and putting his hand on his shoulder, "you are not going to mix up in this at all; and for my sake, old chap, don't make any row at home. Promise me," said Ranald again holding him fast.

"Well, I promise," said Harry, reluctantly, "but I'll be hanged if I understand it at all; and I tell you this, that if you don't come back here, neither shall I."

"Now you are talking rot, Harry," said Ranald, and sat down again to his desk. Harry went out in a state of dazed astonishment. Alone Ranald sat in his office writing steadily except that now and then he paused to let a smile flutter across his stern, set face, as a gleam of sunshine over a rugged rock on a cloudy day. He was listening to his heart, whose every beat kept singing the refrain, "I love her, I love her; she will come to me!"

At that very moment Maimie was showing her Aunt Murray her London dresses and finery, and recounting her triumphs in that land of social glory.

"How lovely, how wonderfully lovely they are," said Mrs. Murray, touching the beautiful fabrics with fond fingers; "and I am sure they will suit you well, my dear. Have you worn most of them?"

"No, not all. This one I wore the evening I went with the Lord Archers to the Heathcote's ball. Lord Heathcote, you know, is an uncle of Captain De Lacy."

"Was Captain De Lacy there?" inquired Mrs. Murray.

"Yes, indeed," cried Maimie, "and we had a lovely time!" Either the memory of that evening brought the warm blushes to her face, or it may be the thought of what she was about to tell her aunt; "and Captain De Lacy is coming to-morrow."

"Coming to-morrow?"

"Yes, he has written to Aunt Frank, and to papa as well."

Mrs. Murray sat silent, apparently not knowing what to say, and Maimie stood with the dress in her hands waiting for her aunt to speak. At length Mrs. Murray said: "You knew Captain De Lacy before, I think."

"Oh, I have known him for a long time, and he's just splendid, auntie, and he's coming to –" Maimie paused, but her face told her secret.

"Do you mean he is going to speak to your father about you, Maimie?" Maimie nodded. "And are you glad?"

"He's very handsome, auntie, and very nice, and he's awfully well connected, and that sort of thing, and when Lord Heathcote dies he has a good chance of the estates and the title."

"Do you love him, Maimie?" asked her aunt, quietly.

Maimie dropped the dress, and sitting down upon a low stool, turned her face from her aunt, and looked out of the window.

"Oh, I suppose so, auntie," she said. "He's very nice and gentlemanly and I like to be with him –"

"But, Maimie, dear, are you not sure that you love him?"

"Oh, I don't know," said Maimie, petulantly. "Are you not pleased, auntie?"

"Well, I confess I am surprised. I do not know Captain De Lacy, and besides I thought it was – I thought you –" Mrs. Murray paused, while Maimie's face grew hot with fiery blushes, but before she could reply they heard Harry's step on the stairs, and in a moment he burst into the room.

"Ranald isn't coming!" he exclaimed. "Here's a note for you, Maimie. But what the – but what he means," said Harry, checking himself, "I can't make out."

"Not coming?" cried Maimie, the flush fading from her face. "What can he mean?" She opened the note, and as she read the blood rushed quickly into her face again, and as quickly fled, leaving her pale and trembling.

"Well, what does he say?" inquired Harry, bluntly.

"He says it is impossible for him to come to-night," said Maimie, putting the note into her bosom.

"Huh!" grunted Harry, and flung out of the room.

Immediately Maimie pulled out the note.

"Oh, auntie," she cried, "I am so miserable; Ranald is not coming and he says – there read it." She hurriedly thrust the note into Mrs. Murray's hands, and Mrs. Murray, opening it, read:

> My Dear Maimie: It is impossible for me to go to you tonight. Your father and I have had a difference so serious that I can never enter his house again, but I am writing now to tell you what I meant to tell you to-night. I love you, Maimie. I love you with all my heart and soul. I have loved you since the night I pulled you from the fire.

"Maimie," said Mrs. Murray, handing her back the note, "I do not think you ought to give me this. That is too sacred for any eyes but your own."

"Oh, I know, auntie, but what can I do? I am so sorry for Ranald! What shall I do, auntie?"

"My dear child, in this neither I nor any one can advise you. You must be true to yourself."

"Oh, I wish I knew what to do!" cried Maimie. "He wants me to tell him –" Maimie paused, her face once more covered with blushes, "and I do not know what to say!"

"What does your heart say, Maimie?" said Mrs. Murray, quietly.

"Oh, auntie, I am so miserable!"

"But, Maimie," continued her aunt, "in this matter, as I said before, you must be true to yourself. Do you love Ranald?"

"Oh, auntie, I cannot tell," cried Maimie, putting her face in her hands.

"If Ranald were De Lacy would you love him?"

"Oh yes, yes, how happy I would be!"

Then Mrs. Murray rose. "Maimie, dear," she said, and her voice was very gentle but very firm, "let me speak to you for your dear mother's sake. Do not deceive yourself. Do not give your life for anything but love. Ranald is a noble man and he will be a great man some day, and I love him as my own son, but I would not have you give yourself to him unless you truly loved him." She did not mention De Lacy's name nor utter a word in comparison of the two, but listening to her voice, Maimie knew only too well whither her love had gone.

"Oh, auntie," she cried, "I cannot bear it!"

"Yes, Maimie dear, you can bear to do the right, for there is One in whose strength we can do all things."

Before Maimie could reply her Aunt Frances came in.

"It is dinner-time," she announced, "and your father has just come in, Maimie, and we must have dinner over at once."

Maimie rose, and going to the glass, smoothed back her hair. Her Aunt Frances glanced at her face and then at Mrs. Murray, and as if fearing Maimie's reply, went on hurriedly,

"You must look your very best to-night, and even better to-morrow," she said, smiling, significantly. She came and put her hands on Maimie's shoulders, and kissing her, said: "Have you told your Aunt Murray who is coming to-morrow? I am sure I'm very thankful, my dear, you will be very happy. It is an excellent match. Half the girls in town will be wild with envy. He has written a very manly letter to your father, and I am sure he is a noble fellow, and he has excellent prospects. But we must hurry down to dinner," she said, turning to Mrs. Murray, who with a look of sadness on her pale face, left the room without a word.

"Ranald is not coming," said Maimie, when her Aunt Murray had gone.

"Indeed, from what your father says," cried Aunt Frank, indignantly, "I do not very well see how he could. He has been most impertinent."

"You are not to say that, Aunt Frank," cried Maimie. "Ranald could not be impertinent, and I will not hear it." Her tone was so haughty and fierce that Aunt Frank thought it wiser to pursue this subject no further.

"Well," she said, as she turned to leave the room, "I'm very glad he has the grace to keep away tonight. He has always struck me as a young man of some presumption."

When the door closed upon her Maimie tore the note from her bosom and pressed it again and again to her lips: "Oh, Ranald, Ranald," she cried, "I love you! I love you! Oh, why can it not be? Oh, I cannot – I cannot give him up!" She threw herself upon her knees and laid her face in the bed. In a few minutes there came a tap at the door, and her Aunt Frances's voice was heard, "Maimie, your father has gone down; we must not delay." The tone was incisive and matter-of-fact. It said to Maimie, "Now let's have no nonsense. Be a sensible woman of the world." Maimie rose from her knees. Hastily removing all traces of tears from her face, and glancing in the glass, she touched the little ringlets into place and went down to dinner.

It was a depressing meal. Mr. St. Clair was irritable; Harry perplexed and sullen; Maimie nervously talkative. Mrs. Murray was heroically holding herself in command, but the look of pain in her eyes and the pathetic tremor on her lips belied the brave smiles and cheerful words with which she seconded Aunt Frank.

After dinner the company separated, for there were still preparations to make for the evening. As Mrs. Murray was going to her room, she met Harry in the hall with his hat on.

"Where are you going, Harry?"

"Anywhere," he growled, fiercely, "to get out of this damnable hypocrisy! Pardon me, Aunt Murray, I can't help it, it *is* damnable, and a whole lot of them are in it!"

Then Mrs. Murray came, and laying her hand on his arm, said: "Don't go, Harry; don't leave me; I want someone; come upstairs."

Harry stood looking at the sweet face, trying to smile so bravely in spite of the tremulous lips.

"You are a dear, brave little woman," he said, hanging up his hat, "and I'll be hanged if I don't stay by you. Come along upstairs." He stooped, and lifting her in his arms in spite of her laughing protests, carried her upstairs to her room. When they came down to the party they both looked braver and stronger.

The party was a great success. The appointments were perfect; the music the best that could be had, and Maimie more beautiful than ever. In some mysterious way, known only to Aunt Frank, the rumor of Maimie's approaching engagement got about among the guests and produced an undertone of excitement to the evening's gayety. Maimie was too excited to be quite natural, but she had never appeared more brilliant and happy, and surely she had every cause. She had achieved a dizzy summit of social success that made her at once the subject of her friends' congratulations and her rivals' secret envy, and which was the more delightful it would be hard to say. Truly, she was a fortunate girl, but still the night was long, and she was tired of it all before it was over. The room seemed empty, and often her heart gave a leap as her eyes fell upon some form that appeared more handsome and striking than others near, but only to sink again in disappointment when a second glance told her that it was only some ordinary man. Kate, too, kept aloof in a very unpleasant way, and Harry, devoting himself to Kate, had not done his duty. But in spite of everything the party had been a great success, and when it was over Maimie went straight to bed to sleep. She knew that Ranald would be awaiting the answer to his note, but she could not bring herself to face what she knew would be an ordeal that might murder sleep for her, and sleep she must have, for she must be her best to-morrow. It would have been better for all involved had she written her answer that night; otherwise Ranald would not have been standing at her door in the early afternoon asking to see her. It was Aunt Frances who came down to the drawing-room. As Ranald stood up and bowed, she adjusted her *pince-nez* upon her aristocratic nose, viewed him.

"You are wishing to see Miss St. Clair," she said, in her very chilliest tone.

"I asked to see Maimie," said Ranald, looking at her with cool, steady eyes.

"I must say, Mr. Macdonald, that after your conduct to my brother yesterday, I am surprised you should have the assurance to enter his house."

"I would prefer not discussing office matters with you," said Ranald, politely, and with a suspicion of a smile. "I have come to see Maimie."

"That, I am glad to say, is impossible, for she is at present out with Captain De Lacy who has just arrived from the East to – see – to – in short, on a very special errand."

For a moment Ranald stood without reply.

"She is out, you say?" he answered at length.

"She is out with Captain De Lacy." He caught the touch of triumph in her voice.

"Will she be back soon?" inquired Ranald, looking baffled.

"Of course one cannot tell in such a case," answered Miss St. Clair, "but I should think not." Miss St. Clair was enjoying herself. It did her good to see this insolent, square-jawed young man standing helpless before her.

"It is important that I should see her," said Ranald, after a few moments' thought. "I shall wait." Had Miss St. Clair known him better she would have noticed with some concern the slow fires kindling in his eyes. As it was she became indignant.

"That, Mr. Macdonald, you shall not; and allow me to say frankly that your boldness – your insolence – I may say, is beyond all bounds."

"Insolence, and when?" Ranald was very quiet.

"You come to the house of your employer, whom you have insulted, and demand to see his daughter."

"I have a right to see her."

"Right? What right have you, pray?"

Then Ranald stood up and looked Miss St. Clair full in the face with eyes fairly alight.

"Miss St. Clair, have you ever known what it is to love with all your soul and heart?" Miss St. Clair gasped. "Because if not, you will not understand me; if you have you will know why I must see Maimie. It is seven years now since I began to love her. I remember the spot in the woods; I see the big tree there behind her and the rising ground stretching away to the right. I see the place where I pulled her out of the fire. Every morning since that time I have waked with the thought of her; every night my eyes have closed with a vision of her before me. It is for her I have lived and worked. I tell you she is mine! I love her! I love her, and she loves me. I know it." His words came low, fierce, and swift.

Miss St. Clair stood breathless. What a man he looked and how handsome he was!

With but a moment's pause Ranald went on, but his voice took a gentler tone. "Miss St. Clair, do you understand me? Yes, I know you do." The blood came flowing suddenly to her thin cheeks. "You say she is out with Captain De Lacy, and you mean me to think that she is to give herself to him. He loves her; I know, but I say she is mine! Her eyes have told me that. She is mine, I tell you, and no man living will take her from me." The fire that always slumbered in his eyes was now blazing in full fury. The great passion of his life was raging through his soul, vibrating in his voice, and glowing in his dark face. Miss St. Clair sat silent, and then motioned him to a seat.

"Mr. Macdonald," she said, with grave courtesy, "you are too late, I fear. I did not realize – Maimie will never be yours. I know my niece." At the sad earnestness of her voice, Ranald's face began to grow pale.

"I will wait for her," he said, quietly.

"I beg you will not."

"I will wait," he repeated, with lips tight pressed.

"It is vain, Mr. Macdonald, I assure you. Spare yourself and her. I know what – I could have –" Her voice grew husky.

"I will wait," once more replied Ranald, the lines of his face growing tense.

Miss St. Clair rose and gave him her hand. "I will send a friend to you, and I beg you to excuse me," Ranald bowed gravely, "and to forgive me," and she left the room. Ranald heard her pass through the hall and up the stairs and then a door closed behind her. Before he had time to gather his thoughts together he heard a voice outside that made his heart stand still. Then the front door opened quickly and Maimie and De Lacy stood in the hall. She was gayly talking. Ranald rose and stood with his back to the door. Before him was a large mirror which reflected the hall through the open door. He stood waiting for them to enter.

"Hang up your hat, Captain De Lacy, then go in and find a chair while I run upstairs," cried Maimie, gayly. "You must learn your way about here now."

"No," said De Lacy, in a low, distinct voice. "I can wait no longer, Maimie."

She looked at him a moment as if in fear.

"Come," he said, holding out his hands to her. "There was no chance in the park, and I can wait no longer." Slowly she came near. "My darling, my sweetheart," he said, in a low voice full of intense passion. Then, while she lay in his arms, he kissed her on the lips twice. Ranald stood gazing in the mirror as if fascinated. As their lips met a low groan burst from him. He faced about, and with a single step, stood in the doorway. Shriek after shriek echoed through the house as Maimie sprang from De Lacy's arms and shrank back to the wall.

"Great heavens," cried De Lacy, "why it's Macdonald! What the deuce do you mean coming in on people like that?"

"What is it, Maimie," cried her Aunt Frank, hurrying down stairs.

Then she saw Ranald standing in the doorway, with face bloodless, ghastly, livid. Quickly she went up to him, and said, in a voice trembling and not ungentle: "Oh, why did you wait, Mr. Macdonald; go away now, go away."

Ranald turned and looked at her with a curious uncomprehending gaze, and then said, "Yes, I will go away." He took a step toward Maimie, his eyes like lurid flames. She shrank from him, while De Lacy stepped in his path. With a sweep of his arm he brushed De Lacy aside, hurling him crashing against the wall, and stood before the shrinking girl.

"Good by, Maimie; forget that I loved you once."

The words came slowly from his pallid lips. For some moments he stood with his burning eyes fastened upon her face. Then he turned slowly from her and groped blindly for his hat. Miss St. Clair hurried toward him, found his hat, and putting it in his hand, said, in a broken voice, while tears poured down her cheeks: "Here it is; good by, good by."

He looked at her a moment as if in surprise, and then, with a smile of rare sweetness on his white lips, he said, "I thank you," and passed out, going feebly like a man who has got a death wound.

A GOOD TRUE FRIEND

It was springtime and the parks and avenues were in all the dainty splendor of their new leaves. The afternoon May sun was flooding the city with gold and silver light, and all the air was tremulous with the singing of birds. A good day it was to live if one could only live in the sunny air within sight of the green leaves and within sound of the singing birds. A day for life and love it was; at least so Kate thought as she drew up her prancing team at the St. Clair house where Harry stood waiting for her.

"*Dear* Kate," he cried, "how stunning you are! I love you!"

"Come, Harry, jump up! Breton is getting excited."

"Stony-hearted wretch," grumbled Harry. "Did you hear me tell you I love you?"

"Nonsense, Harry, jump in; I'll report to Lily Langford."

"Don't tell," pleaded Harry, "and do keep Breton on all fours. This isn't a circus. You terrify me."

"We have only time to make the train, hurry up!" cried Kate. "Steady, my boys."

"Some day, Kate, those 'boys' of yours will be your death or the death of some of your friends," said Harry, as he sprang in and took his place beside Kate. "That Breton ought to be shot. It really affects my heart to drive with you."

"You haven't any, Harry, you know that right well, so don't be alarmed."

"Quite true," said Harry, sentimentally, "not since that night, don't you remember, Kate, when you –"

"Now, Harry, I only remind you that I always tell my girl friends everything you say. It is this wedding that's got into your blood."

"I suppose so," murmured Harry, pensively; "wish it would get into yours. Now seriously, Kate, at your years you ought –"

"Harry," said Kate, indignantly, "I really don't need you at the station. I can meet your aunt quite well without you. Shall I set you down here, or drive you to the office?"

"Oh, not to the office, I entreat! I entreat! Anything but that! Surely I may be allowed this day! I shall be careful of your sensitive points, but I do hope this wedding of Maimie's will give you serious thoughts."

Kate was silent, giving her attention doubtless to her team. Then, with seeming irrelevance, she said: "Didn't I see Colonel Thorp yesterday in town?"

"Yes, the old heathen! I haven't forgiven him for taking off Ranald as he did."

"He didn't take off Ranald. Ranald was going off anyway."

"How do you know?" said Harry.

"I know," replied Kate, with a little color in her cheek. "He told me himself."

"Well, old Thorp was mighty glad to get him; I can tell you that. The old sinner!"

"He's just a dear!" cried Kate. "Yes, he was glad to get Ranald. What a splendid position he gave him."

"Oh, yes, I know, he adores you like all the rest, and so you think him a dear."

But this Kate ignored for the team were speeding along at an alarming pace. With amazing skill and dash she threaded her way through the crowded streets with almost no checking of her speed.

"Do be careful," cried Harry, as the wheels of their carriage skimmed the noses of the car-horses. "I am quite sure my aunt will not be able to recognize me."

"And why not?"

"Because I shall be gray-haired by the time I reach the station."

"There's the train I do believe," cried Kate, flourishing her whip over her horses' backs. "We must not be late."

"If we ever get there alive," said Harry.

"Here we are sure enough."

"Shall I go to the train?"

"No, indeed," cried Kate. "Do you think I am going to allow any one to meet *my* Aunt Murray but myself? I shall go; you hold the horses."

"I am afraid, really," cried Harry, pretending terror.

"Oh, I fancy you will do," cried Kate, smiling sweetly, as she ran off to meet the incoming train. In a few moments she returned with Mrs. Murray and carrying a large, black valise.

"Hello, auntie dear," cried Harry. "You see I can't leave these brutes of Kate's, but believe me it does me good to see you. What a blessing a wedding is to bring you to us. I suppose you won't come again until it is Kate's or mine."

"That would be sure to bring me," cried Mrs. Murray, smiling her bright smile, "provided you married the right persons."

"Why, auntie," said Harry, dismally, "Kate is so unreasonable. She won't take even me. You see she's so tremendously impressed with herself, and all the fellows spoil her."

By this time Kate had the reins and Harry had climbed into the back seat.

"Dear old auntie," he said, kissing his aunt, "I am really delighted to see you. But to return to Kate. Look at her! Doesn't she look like a Roman princess?"

"Now, Harry, do be sensible, or I shall certainly drive you at once to the office," said Kate, severely.

"Oh, the heartlessness of her. She knows well enough that Colonel Thorp is there, and she would shamelessly exult over his abject devotion. She respects neither innocent youth nor gray hairs, as witness myself and Colonel Thorp."

"Isn't he a silly boy, auntie?" said Kate, "and he is not much improving with age."

"But what's this about Colonel Thorp?" said Mrs. Murray. "Sometimes Ranald writes of him, in high terms, too."

"Well, you ought to hear Thorp abuse Ranald. Says he's ruining the company with his various philanthropic schemes," said Harry, "but you can never tell what he means exactly. He's a wily old customer."

"Don't believe him, auntie," said Kate, with a sagacious smile. "Colonel Thorp thinks that the whole future of his company and of the Province depends solely upon Ranald. It is quite ridiculous to hear him, while all the time he is abusing him for his freaks."

"It must be a great country out there, though," said Harry, "and what a row they are making over Confederation."

"What do you mean, Harry?" said Mrs. Murray. "We hear so little in the country."

"Well, I don't know exactly, but those fellows in British

Columbia are making all sorts of threats that unless this railway is built forthwith they will back out of the Dominion, and some of them talk of annexation with the United States. Don't I wish I was there! What a lucky fellow Ranald is. Thorp says he's a big gun already. No end of a swell. Of course, as manager of a big concern like the British-American Coal and Lumber Company, he is a man of some importance."

"I don't think he is taking much to do with public questions," said Kate, "though he did make a speech at New Westminster not long ago. He has been up in those terrible woods almost ever since he went."

"Hello, how do you know?" said Harry, looking at her suspiciously; "I get a fragment of a note from Ranald now and then, but he is altogether too busy to remember humble people."

"I hear regularly from Coley. You remember Coley, don't you?" said Kate, turning to Mrs. Murray.

"Oh, yes, that's the lad in whom Ranald was so interested in the Institute."

"Yes," replied Kate; "Coley begged and prayed to go with Ranald, and so he went."

"She omits to state," said Harry, "that she also 'begged and prayed' and further that she outfitted the young rascal, though I've reason to thank Providence for removing him to another sphere."

"How does it affect you?" said Mrs. Murray.

"Why, haven't you heard, Aunt Murray, of the tremendous heights to which I have attained? I suppose she didn't tell you of her dinner party. That was after you had left last fall. It was a great bit of generalship. Some of Ranald's foot-ball friends, Little Merrill, Starry Hamilton, that's the captain, you know, and myself among them, were asked to a farewell supper by this young lady, and when the men had well drunk – fed, I mean – and were properly dissolved in tears over the prospect of Ranald's departure, at a critical moment the Institute was introduced as a side issue. It was dear to Ranald's heart. A most effective picture was drawn of the Institute deserted and falling into ruins, so to speak, with Kate heroically struggling to prevent utter collapse. Could this be allowed? No! a thousand times no! Some one would be found surely! Who would it be! At this juncture Kate, who had been maintaining a powerful silence, smiled upon Little Merrill, who being distinctly inflammable, and for some mysterious reason devoted to Ranald, and for an even more mysterious reason devoted to Kate, swore he'd follow if some one would lead. What could I do? My well-known abilities naturally singled me out for leadership, so to prevent any such calamity, I immediately proposed that if Starry Hamilton, the great foot-ball chief, would command this enterprise I would follow. Before the evening was over the Institute was thoroughly manned."

"It is nearly half true, aunt," said Kate.

"And by our united efforts," continued Harry, "the Institute has survived the loss of Ranald."

"I cannot tell you how overjoyed I am, Harry, that both of my boys are taking hold of such good work, you here and Ranald in British Columbia. He must have a very hard time of it, but he speaks very gratefully of Colonel Thorp, who, he says, often opposes but finally agrees with his proposals."

Harry laughed aloud. "Agrees, does he? And do you know why? I remember seeing him one day, and he was in a state of wild fury at Ranald's notions. I won't quote his exact words. The next day I found him in a state of bland approval. Then I learn incidentally that in the meantime Kate has been giving him tea and music."

"Don't listen to his mean insinuations, auntie," said Kate, blushing a little.

Mrs. Murray turned and looked curiously into her face and smiled, and then Kate blushed all the more.

"I think that may explain some things that have been mysterious to me," she said.

"Oh, what, auntie?" cried Harry; "I am most anxious to know."

"Never mind," said Mrs. Murray, "I will explain to Kate."

"That won't help me any. She is a most secretive person, twiddles us all round her fingers and never lets us know anything until it's done. It is most exasperating. Oh, I say, Kate," added Harry, suddenly, "would you mind dropping me at the florist's here?"

"Why? Oh, I see," said Kate, drawing in her team. "How do you do, Lily? Harry is anxious to select some flowers," she said, bowing to a very pretty girl on the sidewalk.

"Kate, do stop it," besought Harry, in a low voice, as he leaped out of the carriage. "Good by, auntie, I'll see you this evening. Don't believe all Kate tells you," he added, as they drove away.

"Are you too tired for a turn in the park," said Kate, "or shall we drive home?"

A drive is always pleasant. Besides, one can talk about some things with more freedom in a carriage than face to face in one's room. The horses require attention at critical moments, and there are always points of interest when it is important that conversation should be deflected from the subject in hand, so since Mrs. Murray was willing, Kate turned into the park. For an hour they drove along its shady, winding roads while Mrs. Murray talked of many things, but mostly of Ranald, and of the tales that the Glengarry people had of him.

For wherever there was lumbering to be done, sooner or later there Glengarry men were to be found, and Ranald had found them in the British Columbia forests. And to their people at home their letters spoke of Ranald and his doings at first doubtfully, soon more confidently, but always with pride. To Macdonald Bhain a rare letter came from Ranald now and then, which he would carry to Mrs. Murray with a difficult pretense of modesty. For with Macdonald Bhain, Ranald was a great man.

"But he is not quite sure of him," said Mrs. Murray. "He thinks it is a very queer way of lumbering, and the wages he considers excessive."

"Does he say that?" asked Kate. "That's just what Colonel Thorp says his company are saying. But he stands up for Ranald even when he can't see that his way is the best. The colonel is not very sure about Ranald's schemes for the men, his reading-room, library, and that sort of thing. But I'm sure he will succeed." But Kate's tone belied her confident words.

Mrs. Murray noticed the anxiety in Kate's voice. "At least we are sure," she said, gently, "that he will do right, and after all that is success."

"I know that right well," replied Kate; "but it is hard for him out there with no one to help him or to encourage him."

Again Mrs. Murray looked at Kate, curiously.

"It must be a terrible place," Kate went on, "especially for one like Ranald, for he has no mind to let things go. He will do a thing as it ought to be done, or not at all." Soon after this Kate gave her mind to her horses, and in a short time headed them for home.

"What a delightful drive we have had," said Mrs. Murray, gratefully, as Kate took her upstairs to her room.

"I hope I have not worried you with my dismal forebodings," she said, with a little laugh.

"No, dear," said Mrs. Murray, drawing her face down to the pillow where Kate had made her lay her head. "I think I understand," she added, in a whisper.

Then Kate laid her face beside that of her friend and whispered, "Oh, auntie, it is so hard for him"; but Mrs. Murray stroked her head softly and said: "There is no fear, Kate; all will be well with him."

Immediately after dinner Kate carried Mrs. Murray with her to her own room, and after establishing her in all possible comfort, she began to read extracts from Coley's letters.

"Here is the first, auntie; they are more picturesque than elegant, but if you knew Coley, you wouldn't mind; you'd be glad to get any letter from him." So saying Kate turned her back to the window, a position with the double advantage of allowing the light to fall upon the paper and the shadow to rest upon her face, and so proceeded to read:

> "DEAR MISS KATE: We got here – ("That is to New Westminster.") last night, and it is a queer town. The streets run every way, the houses are all built of wood, and almost none of them are painted. The streets are full of all sorts of people. I saw lots of Chinamen and Indians. It makes a feller feel kind o' queer as if he was in some foreign country. The hotel where we stopped was a pretty good lookin' place. Of course nothin' like the hotel we stopped at in San Francisco. It was pretty fine inside, but after supper when the crowd began to come in to the bar you never saw such a gang in your life! They knew how to sling their money, I can tell you.

And then they begun to yell and cut up. I tell you it would make the Ward seem like a Sunday school. The Boss, that's what they call him here, I guess didn't like it much, and I don't think you would, either. Next morning we went to look at the mills. They are just sheds with slab roofs. I don't think much of them myself, though I don't know much about mills. The Boss went round askin' questions and I don't think he liked the look of them much either. I know he kept his lips shut pretty tight as we used to see him do sometimes in the Institute. I am awful glad he brought me along. He says I have got to write to you at least once a month, and I've got to take care of my writin' too and get the spellin' right. When I think of the fellers back in the alleys pitchin' pennies I tell you I'd ruther die than go back. Here a feller feels he's alive. I wish I'd paid more attention to my writin' in the night school, but I guess I was pretty much of a fool them days, and you were awful good to me. The Boss says that a man must always pay his way, and when I told him I wanted to pay for them clothes you gave me he looked kind o' funny, but he said "that's right," so I want you to tell me what they cost and I will pay you first thing, for I'm goin' to be a man out in this country. We're goin' up the river next week and see the gangs workin' up there in the bush. It's kind o' lonesome here goin' along the street and lookin' people in the faces to see if you can see one you know. Lots of times I thought I did see some one I knew but it wasn't. Good by, I'll write you soon again.

Yours truly,
MICHAEL COLE.

"The second letter," Kate went on, "is written from the camp, Twentymile Camp, he calls it. He tells how they went up the river in the steamer, taking with them some new hands for their camp, and how these men came on board half drunk, and how all the way up to Yale they were drinking and fighting. It must have been horrible. After that they went on smaller boats and then by wagons. On the roads it must have been terrible. Coley seems much impressed with the big trees. He says:

> "These big trees are pretty hard to write about without sayin' words the Boss don't allow. It makes you think of bein' in St. Michaels, it's so quiet and solemn-like, and I never felt so small in all my life. The Boss and me walked the last part of the way, and got to camp late and pretty tired, and the men we brought in with us was all pretty mad, but the Boss never paid no attention to 'em but went whistlin' about as if everything was lovely. We had some pork and beans for supper, then went to sleep in a bunk nailed up against the side of the shanty. It was as hard as a board, but I tell you it felt pretty good. Next day I went wanderin' 'round with the foreman and the Boss. I tell you I was afraid to get very far away from 'em, for I'd be sure to get lost; the bush is that thick that you can't see your own length ahead of you. That night, when the Boss and me and the foreman was in the shanty they call the office, after supper, we heard a most awful row. 'What's that?' says the Boss. 'O, that's nothin',' says the foreman; 'the boys is havin' a little fun, I guess.' He didn't say anything, but went on talkin', but in a little while the row got worse, and we heard poundin' and smashin'. 'Do you allow that sort of thing?' says

the Boss. 'Well,' he says, 'Guess the boys got some whiskey last night. I generally let 'em alone.' 'Well,' says the Boss, quiet-like, 'I think you'd better go in and stop it.' 'Not if I know myself,' says the foreman, 'I ain't ordered my funeral yet.' 'Well, we'll go in and see, anyway,' says the Boss. I tell you I was kind o' scared, but I thought I might as well go along. When we got into the sleepin' shanty there was a couple of fellers with hand-spikes breakin' up the benches and knockin' things around most terrible. 'Say, boys,' yelled the foreman, and then he began to swear most awful. They didn't seem to pay much attention, but kept on knockin' around and swearin'. 'Come, now,' says the foreman, kind o' coaxin' like, 'this ain't no way to act. Get down and behave yourselves.' But still they didn't pay no attention. Then the Boss walked up to the biggest one, and when he got quite close to 'em they all got still lookin' on. 'I'll take that hand-spike,' says the Boss. 'Help yourself,' says the man swingin' it up. I don't know what happened, it was done so quick, but before you could count three that feller was on his knees bleedin' like a pig and the hand-spike was out of the door, and the Boss walks up to the other feller and says, 'Put that hand-spike outside.' He begun to swear. 'Put it out,' says the Boss, quiet-like, and the feller backs up and throws his hand-spike out. And the Boss up and speaks and says, 'Look here, men, I don't want to interfere with nobody, and won't while he behaves himself, but there ain't goin' to be any row like that in this camp.' Say, you ought to have seen 'em! They sat like the gang used to in the night school, and then he turned and walked out and we all follered him. I guess they ain't used to that sort of

> thing in this camp. I heard the men talkin' next day pretty big of what they was goin' to do, but I don't think they'll do much. They don't look that kind. Anyway, if there's goin' to be a fight, I'd feel safer with the Boss than with the whole lot of 'em."

"The letter after this," went on Kate, "tells of what happened the Sunday following."

> "We'd gone out in the afternoon, Boss and me, for a walk, and when we got back the camp was just howlin' drunk, and the foreman was worst of all. They kind o' quieted down for a little when we come in and let us get into the office, but pretty soon they began actin' up funny again and swearin' most awful. Then I see the Boss shut up his lips hard, and I says to myself 'Look out for blood.' Then he starts over for the bunk shanty. I was mighty scared, and follered him close. Just as we shoved open the door a bottle come singin' through the air and smashed to a thousand bits on the beam above. 'Is that the kind of cowards you are?' says the Boss, quite cool. He didn't speak loud, but I tell you everybody heard him and got dead still. 'No, Boss,' says one feller, 'not all.' 'The man that threw that bottle,' says the Boss, 'is a coward, and the meanest kind. He's afraid to step out here for five minutes.' Nobody moved. 'Step up, ye baste,' says an Irishman, 'or it's mesilf will kick ye out of the camp.' And out the feller comes. It was the same duck that the Boss scared out of the door the first night. 'Sthand up till 'im Billie,' says the Irishman; 'we'll see fair play. Sthand up to the gintleman.' 'Billie,' says the Boss, and his eyes was blazin' like candles; 'yer goin' to

leave this camp to-morrow mornin'. You can take your choice; will you get onto your knees now or later?' With that Billie whipped out a knife and rushes at him; but the Boss grabs his wrist and gives it a twist, and the knife fell onto the floor. The Boss holds him like a baby, and picks up the knife and throws it into the fire. 'Now.' says he, 'get onto your knees. Quick!' And the feller drops on his knees, and bellered like a calf.

"'Let's pray,' says some one, and the crowd howls. 'Give us yer hand, Boss,' says the Irishman. 'Yer the top o' this gang.' The Irishman shoves out his clipper, and the Boss takes it in an easy kind of a way. My you o't to seen that Irishman squirm. 'Howly Mither!' he yells, and dances round. 'what do ye think yer got?' and he goes off lookin' at his fingers, and the Boss stands lookin' at 'em, and says, 'You'r a nice lot of fellers, you don't deserve it; but I'm goin' to treat you fair. I know you feel Sunday pretty slow, and I'll try to make it better for you; but I want you to know that I won't have any more row in this camp, and I won't have any man here that can't behave himself. To-morrow morning, *you*,' pointin' at the foreman, 'and you, Billie, and *you*,' pointin' at another chap, 'leave the camp,' and they did too, though they begged and prayed to let 'em stay, and by next Sunday we had a lot of papers and books, with pictures in 'em, and a bang-up dinner, and everything went nice. I am likin' it fine. I'm time-keeper, and look after the store; but I drive the team too every chance I get, and I'd ruther do that a long way. But many a night I tell you when the Boss and me is alone we talk about you and the Institute fellers, and the Boss –"

"Well, that's all," said Kate, "but isn't it terrible? Aren't they dreadful?"

"Poor fellows," said Mrs. Murray; "it's a very hard life for them."

"But isn't it awful, auntie? They might kill him," said Kate.

"Yes, dear," said Mrs. Murray, in a soothing voice, "but it sounds worse to us perhaps than it is."

Mrs. Murray had not lived in the Indian Lands for nothing.

"Oh, if anything should happen to him?" said Kate, with sudden agitation.

"We must just trust him to the great Keeper," said Mrs. Murray, quietly, "in Whose keeping all are safe whether there or here."

Then going to her valise, she took out a letter and handed it to Kate, saying: "That's his last to me. You can look at it, Kate."

Kate took the letter and put it in her desk. "I think, perhaps, we had better go down now," she said; "I expect Colonel Thorp has come. I think you will like him. He seems a little rough, but he is a gentleman, and has a true heart," and they went downstairs.

It is the mark of a gentleman to know his kind. He has an instinct for what is fine and offers ready homage to what is worthy. Any one observing Colonel Thorp's manner of receiving Mrs. Murray would have known him at once for a gentleman, for when that little lady came into the drawing-room, dressed in her decent silk gown, with soft white lace at her throat, bearing herself with sweet dignity, and stepping with dainty grace on her toes, after the manner of the fine ladies of the old school, and not after the flat-footed, heel-first modern style, the colonel abandoned his usual careless manner and rose and stood rigidly at attention.

"Auntie, this is my friend, Colonel Thorp," said Kate.

"Proud to know you madam," said the colonel, with his finest military bow.

"And I am glad to meet Colonel Thorp; I have heard so much of him through my friends," and she smiled at him with such genuine kindliness that the gallant colonel lost his heart at once.

"Your friends have been doing me proud," he said, bowing to her and then to Kate.

"Oh, you needn't look at me," said Kate; "you don't imagine I have been saying nice things about you? She has other friends that think much of you."

"Yes," said Mrs. Murray, "Ranald has often spoken of you, Colonel Thorp, and of your kindness," said Mrs. Murray.

The colonel looked doubtful. "Well, I don't know that he thinks much of me. I have had to be pretty hard on him."

"Why?" asked Mrs. Murray.

"Well, I reckon you know him pretty well," began the colonel.

"Well, she ought to," said Kate, "she brought him up, and his many virtues he owes mostly to my dear aunt's training."

"Oh, Kate, you must not say that," said Mrs. Murray, gravely.

"Then," said the colonel, "you ought to be proud of him. You produced a rare article in the commercial world, and that is a man of honor. He is not for sale, and I want to say that I feel safe about the company's money out there, as I was settin' on it; but he needs watching," added the colonel, "he needs watching."

"What do you mean?" said Mrs. Murray, whose pale face

had flushed with pleasure and pride at the colonel's praise of Ranald.

"Too much philanthropy," said the colonel, bluntly; "the British-American Coal and Lumber Company ain't a benevolent society exactly."

"I am glad you spoke of that, Colonel Thorp; I want to ask you about some things that I don't understand. I know that the company are criticising some of Ranald's methods, but don't know why exactly."

"Now, Colonel," cried Kate, "stand to your guns."

"Well," said the colonel, "I am going to execute a masterly retreat, as they used to say when a fellow ran away. I am going to get behind my company. They claim, you see, that Ranald ain't a paying concern."

"But how?" said Mrs. Murray.

Then the colonel enumerated the features of Ranald's management most severely criticised by the company. He paid the biggest wages going; the cost of supplies for the camps was greater, and the company's stores did not show as large profits as formerly; "and of course," said the colonel, "the first aim of any company is to pay dividends, and the manager that can't do that has to go."

Then Mrs. Murray proceeded to deal with the company's contentions, going at once with swift intuition to the heart of the matter. "You were speaking of honor a moment ago, Colonel. There is such a thing in business?"

"Certainly, that's why I put that young man where he is."

"That means that the company expect him to deal fairly by them."

"That's about it."

"And being a man of honor, I suppose he will also deal fairly by the men and by himself."

"I guess so," said the colonel.

"I don't pretend to understand the questions fully, but from Ranald's letters I have gathered that he did not consider that justice was being done either to the men or to the company. For instance, in the matter of stores – I may be wrong in this, you will correct me, Colonel – I understand it was the custom to charge the men in the camps for the articles they needed prices three or four times what was fair."

"Well," said the colonel, "I guess things *were* a little high, but that's the way every company does."

"And then I understand that the men were so poorly housed and fed and so poorly paid that only those of the inferior class could be secured."

"Well, I guess they weren't very high-class," said the colonel, "that's right enough."

"But, Colonel, if you secure a better class of men, and you treat them in a fair and honorable way with some regard to their comfort you ought to get better results in work, shouldn't you?"

"Well, that's so," said the colonel; "there never was such an amount of timber got out with the same number of men since the company started work, but yet the thing don't pay, and that's the trouble. The concern must pay or go under."

"Yes, that's quite true, Colonel," said Mrs. Murray; "but why doesn't your concern pay?"

"Well, you see, there's no market; trade is dull and we can't sell to advantage."

"But surely that is not your manager's fault," said Mrs. Murray, "and surely it would be an unjust thing to hold him responsible for that."

"But the company don't look at things in that light," said the colonel. "You see they figure it this way, stores ain't bringing in the returns they used to, the camps cost a little more, wages are a little higher, there ain't nothing coming in, and they say, Well, that chap out there means well with his reading-rooms for the mill hands, his library in the camp, and that sort of thing, but he ain't sharp enough!"

"Sharp enough! that's a hard word, Colonel," said Mrs. Murray, earnestly, "and it may be a cruel word, but if Ranald were ever so sharp he really couldn't remove the real cause of the trouble. You say he has produced larger results than ever before, and if the market were normal there would be larger returns. Then, it seems to me, Colonel, that if Ranald suffers he is suffering, not because he has been unfaithful or incompetent, but because the market is bad, and that I am certain you would not consider fair."

"You must not be too hard on us," said the colonel. "So far as I am concerned, I think you are right, but it is a hard thing to make business men look at these things in anything but a business way."

"But it should not be hard, Colonel," said Mrs. Murray, with sad earnestness, "to make even business men see that when honor is the price of dividends the cost is too great," and without giving the colonel an opportunity of replying, she went on with eager enthusiasm to show how the laws of the kingdom of heaven might be applied to the great problems of labor. "And it would pay, Colonel," she cried, "it would pay in money, but far more it would pay in what cannot be bought for money – in the lives and souls of men, for unjust and uncharitable dealing injures more the man who is guilty of it than the man who suffers from it in the first instance."

"Madam," answered the colonel, gravely, "I feel you are right, and I should be glad to have you address the meeting of our share-holders, called for next month, to discuss the question of our western business."

"Do you mean Ranald's position?" asked Kate.

"Well, I rather think that will come up."

"Then," said Mrs. Murray, unconsciously claiming the colonel's allegiance, "I feel sure there will be one advocate at least for fair and honorable dealing at that meeting." And the colonel was far too gallant to refuse to acknowledge the claim, but simply said: "You may trust me, madam; I shall do my best."

"I only wish papa were here," said Kate. "He is a shareholder, isn't he? And wish he could hear you, auntie, but he and mamma won't be home for two weeks."

"Oh, Kate," cried Mrs. Murray, "you make me ashamed, and I fear I have been talking too much."

At this point Harry came in. "I just came over to send you to bed," he said, kissing his aunt, and greeting the others. "You are all to look your most beautiful to-morrow."

"Well," said the colonel, slowly, "that won't be hard for the rest of you, and it don't matter much for me, and I hope we ain't going to lose our music."

"No, indeed!" cried Kate, sitting down at the piano, while the colonel leaned back in his easy chair and gave himself up to an hour's unmingled delight.

"You have given more pleasure than you know to a wayfaring man," he said, as he bade her good night.

"Come again, when you are in town, you are always welcome, Colonel Thorp," she said.

"You may count me here every time," said the colonel. Then turning to Mrs. Murray, with a low bow, he said, "you have given me some ideas madam, that I hope may not be quite unfruitful, and as for that young man of yours, well – I – guess – you ain't – hurt his cause any. We'll put up a fight, anyway."

"I am glad to have met you, Colonel Thorp," said Mrs. Murray, "and I am quite sure you will stand up for what is right," and with another bow the colonel took his leave.

"Now, Harry, you must go, too," said Kate; "you can see your aunt again after to-morrow, and I must get my beauty sleep, besides I don't want to stand up with a man gaunt and hollow-eyed for lack of sleep," and she bundled him off in spite of his remonstrances. But eager as Kate was for her beauty sleep, the light burned late in her room; and long after she had seen Mrs. Murray snugly tucked in for the night, she sat with Ranald's open letter in her hand, reading it till she almost knew it by heart. It told, among other things, of his differences with the company in regard to stores, wages, and supplies, and of his efforts to establish a reading-room at the mills, and a library at the camps; but there was a sentence at the close of the letter that Kate read over and over again with the light of a great love in her eyes and with a cry of pain in her heart. "The magazines and papers that Kate sends are a great boon. Dear Kate, what a girl she is! I know none like her; and what a friend she has been to me ever since the day she stood up for me at Quebec. You remember I told you about that. What a guy I must have been, but she never showed a sign of shame. I often think of that now, how different she was from another! I see it now as I could not then – a man is a fool once in his life, but I have got my lesson and still have a good true friend." Often she read and long she pondered the last words. It was so easy to read too much into them. "A good, true friend." She looked at the words till the tears came. Then she stood up and looked at herself in the glass.

"Now, young woman," she said, severely, "be sensible and don't dream dreams until you are asleep, and to sleep you must go forthwith." But sleep was slow to come, and strange to say, it was the thought of the little woman in the next room that quieted her heart and sent her to sleep, and next day she was looking her best. And when the ceremony was over, and the guests were assembled at the wedding breakfast, there were not a few who agreed with Harry when, in his speech, he threw down his gage as champion for the peerless bridesmaid, whom for the hour – alas, too short – he was privileged to call his "lady fair." For while Kate had not the beauty of form and face and the fascination of manner that turned men's heads and made Maimie the envy of all her set, there was in her a wholesomeness, a fearless sincerity, a noble dignity, and that indescribable charm of a true heart that made men trust her and love her as only good women are loved. At last the brilliant affair was all over, the rice and old boots were thrown, the farewell words spoken, and tears shed, and then the aunts came back to the empty and disordered house.

"Well, I am glad for Maimie," said Aunt Frank; "it is a good match."

"Dear Maimie," replied Aunt Murray, with a gentle sigh, "I hope she will be happy."

"After all it is much better," said Aunt Frank.

"Yes, it is much better," replied Mrs. Murray; and then she added, "How lovely Kate looked! What a noble girl she is," but she did not explain even to herself, much less to Aunt Frank, the nexus of her thoughts.

THE WEST

The meeting of the share-holders of the British-American Lumber and Coal Company was, on the whole, a stormy one, for the very best of reasons – the failure of the company to pay dividends. The annual report which the president presented showed clearly that there was a slight increase in expenditure and a considerable falling off in sales, and it needed but a little mathematical ability to reach the conclusion that in a comparatively short time the company would be bankrupt. The share-holders were thoroughly disgusted with the British Columbia end of the business, and were on the lookout for a victim. Naturally their choice fell upon the manager. The concern failed to pay. It was the manager's business to make it pay and the failure must be laid to his charge. Their confidence in their manager was all the more shaken by the reports that had reached them of his peculiar fads – his reading-room, library, etc. These were sufficient evidence of his lack of business ability. He was undoubtedly a worthy young man, but there was every ground to believe that he was something of a visionary, and men with great hesitation intrust hard cash to the management of an idealist. It was, perhaps, unfortunate for Mr. St. Clair that he should be appealed to upon this point, for his reluctance to express an opinion as to the ability of the manager, and his admission that possibly the young man might properly be termed a visionary, brought Colonel Thorp sharply to his feet.

"Mr. St. Clair," said the colonel, in a cool, cutting voice, "will not hesitate to bear testimony to the fact that our manager is a man whose integrity cannot be tampered with. If I mistake not, Mr. St. Clair has had evidence of this."

Mr. St. Clair hastened to bear the very strongest testimony to the manager's integrity.

"And Mr. St. Clair, I have no doubt," went on the colonel, "will be equally ready to bear testimony to the conspicuous ability our manager displayed while he was in the service of the Raymond and St. Clair Lumber Company."

Mr. St. Clair promptly corroborated the colonel's statement.

"We are sure of two things, therefore," continued the colonel, "that our manager is a man of integrity, and that he has displayed conspicuous business ability in his former positions."

At this point the colonel was interrupted, and his attention was called to the fact that the reports showed an increase of expenditure for supplies and for wages, and on the other hand a falling off in the revenue from the stores. But the colonel passed over these points as insignificant. "It is clear," he proceeded, "that the cause of failure does not lie in the management, but in the state of the market. The political situation in that country is very doubtful, and this has an exceedingly depressing effect upon business."

"Then," interrupted a share-holder, "it is time the company should withdraw from that country and confine itself to a district where the market is sure and the future more stable."

"What about these fads, Colonel?" asked another share-holder; "these reading-rooms, libraries, etc? Do you think we pay a man to establish that sort of thing? To my mind they simply put a lot of nonsense into the heads of the working-men and are the chief cause of dissatisfaction." Upon this point the colonel did not feel competent to reply; consequently the feeling of the meeting became decidedly hostile to the present manager, and a resolution was offered demanding his resignation. It was also agreed that the board of directors should consider the advisability of withdrawing altogether from British Columbia, inasmuch as the future of that country seemed to be very uncertain. Thereupon Colonel Thorp rose and begged leave to withdraw his name from the directorate of the company. He thought it was unwise to abandon a country where they had spent large sums of money, without a thorough investigation of the situation, and he further desired to enter his protest against the injustice of making their manager suffer for a failure for which he had in no way been shown to be responsible. But the share-holders refused to even consider Colonel Thorp's request, and both the president and secretary exhausted their eloquence in eulogizing his value to the company. As a compromise it was finally decided to continue operations in British Columbia for another season. Colonel Thorp declared that the reforms and reorganization schemes inaugurated by Ranald would result in great reductions in the cost of production, and that Ranald should be given opportunity to demonstrate the success or failure of his plans; and further, the political situation doubtless would be more settled. The wisdom of this decision was manifested later.

The spirit of unrest and dissatisfaction appeared again at the next annual meeting, for while conditions were improving, dividends were not yet forthcoming. Once again Colonel Thorp successfully championed Ranald's cause, this time insisting that a further test of two seasons be made, prophesying that not only would the present deficit disappear, but that their patience and confidence would be amply rewarded.

Yielding to pressure, and desiring to acquaint himself with actual conditions from personal observation, Colonel Thorp concluded to visit British Columbia the autumn preceding the annual meeting which was to succeed Ranald's period of probation.

Therefore it was that Colonel Thorp found himself on the coast steamship *Oregon* approaching the city of Victoria. He had not enjoyed his voyage, and was, consequently, in no mood to receive the note which was handed him by a brisk young man at the landing.

"Who's this from, Pat," said the colonel, taking the note.

"Mike, if you please, Michael Cole, if you don't mind; and the note is from the boss, Mr. Macdonald, who has gone up the country, and can't be here to welcome you."

"Gone up the country!" roared the colonel; "what the blank, blank, does he mean by going up the country at this particular time?"

But Mr. Michael Cole was quite undisturbed by the colonel's wrath. "You might find the reason in the note," he said, coolly, and the colonel, glaring at him, opened the note and read:

> "My Dear Colonel Thorp: I am greatly disappointed in not being able to meet you. The truth is I only received your letter this week. Our mails are none too prompt, and so I have been unable to re-arrange my plans. I find it necessary to run up the river for a couple

of weeks. In the meantime, thinking that possibly you might like to see something of our country, I have arranged that you should join the party of the Lieutenant Governor on their trip to the interior, and which will take only about four weeks' time. The party are going to visit the most interesting districts of our country, including both the famous mining district of Cariboo and the beautiful valley of the Okanagan. Mr. Cole, my clerk, will introduce you to Mr. Blair, our member of Parliament for Westminster, who will present you to the rest of the party. Mr. Blair, I need not say, is one of the brightest business men in the West. I shall meet you at Yale on your return. If it in absolutely impossible for you to take this trip, and necessary that I should return at once, Mr. Cole will see that a special messenger is sent to me, but I would strongly urge that you go, if possible.

"With kind regards."

"Look here, young man," yelled the colonel, "do you think I've come all this way to go gallivanting around the country with any blank, blank royal party?"

"I don't know, Colonel," said young Cole, brightly; "but I tell you I'd like mighty well to go in your place."

"And where in the nation *is* your boss, and what's he after, anyway?"

"He's away up the river looking after business, and pretty big business, too," said Coley, not at all overawed by the colonel's wrath.

"Well, I hope he knows himself," said the colonel.

"Oh, don't make any mistake about that, Colonel," said young Cole; "he always knows where he's going and what he wants, and he gets it." But the colonel made no reply, nor did he deign to notice Mr. Michael Cole again until they had arrived at the New Westminster landing.

"The boss didn't know," said Coley, approaching the colonel with some degree of care, "whether you would like to go to the hotel or to his rooms; you can take your choice. The hotel is not of the best, and he thought perhaps you could put up with his rooms."

"All right," said the colonel; "I guess they'll suit me."

The colonel made no mistake in deciding for Ranald's quarters. They consisted of two rooms that formed one corner of a long wooden, single-story building in the shape of an L. One of these rooms Ranald made his dining-room and bedroom, the other was his office. The rest of the building was divided into three sections, and constituted a drawing-room, reading-room, and bunk-room for the men. The walls of these rooms were decorated not inartistically with a few colored prints and with cuts from illustrated papers, many and divers. The furniture throughout was home-made, with the single exception of a cabinet organ which stood in one corner of the reading-room. On the windows of the dining-room and bunk-room were green roller blinds, but those of the reading-room were draped with curtains of flowered muslin. Indeed the reading-room was distinguished from the others by a more artistic and elaborate decoration, and by a greater variety of furniture. The room was evidently the pride of the company's heart. In Ranald's private room the same simplicity in furniture and decoration was apparent, but when the colonel was ushered into the bedroom his eye fell at once upon two photographs, beautifully framed, hung on each side of the mirror.

"Hello, guess I ought to know this," he said, looking at one of them.

Coley beamed. "You do, eh? Well, then, she's worth knowin' and there's only one of her kind."

"Don't know about that, young man," said the colonel, looking at the other photograph; "here's one that ought to go in her class."

"Perhaps," said Coley, doubtfully, "the boss thinks so, I guess, from the way he looks at it."

"Young man, what sort of a fellow's your boss?" said the colonel, suddenly facing Coley.

"What sort?" Coley thought a moment. "Well, 'twould need a good eddication to tell, but there's only one in his class, I tell you."

"Then he owes it to this little woman," pointing to one of the photographs, "and she," pointing to the other, "said so."

"Then you may bet it's true."

"I don't bet on a sure thing," said the colonel, his annoyance vanishing in a slow smile, his first since reaching the province.

"Dinner'll be ready in half an hour, sir," said Coley, swearing allegiance in his heart to the man that agreed with him in regard to the photograph that stood with Coley for all that was highest in humanity.

"John," he said, sharply, to the Chinese cook, "got good dinner, eh?"

"Pitty good," said John, indifferently.

"Now, look here, John, him big man." John was not much impressed. "Awful big man, I tell you, big soldier." John preserved a stolid countenance.

"John," said the exasperated Coley, "I'll kick you across this room and back if you don't listen to me. Want big dinner, heap good, eh?"

"Huh-huh, belly good," replied John, with a slight show of interest.

"I say, John, what you got for dinner, eh?" asked Coley, changing his tactics.

"Ham, eggs, lice," answered the Mongolian, imperturbably.

"Gee whiz!" said Coley, "goin' to feed the boss' uncle on ham and eggs?"

"What?" said John, with sudden interest, "Uncle boss, eh?"

"Yes," said the unblushing Coley.

"Huh! Coley heap fool! Get chicken, quick! meat shop, small, eh?" The Chinaman was at last aroused. Pots, pans, and other utensils were in immediate requisition, a roaring fire set a-going, and in three-quarters of an hour the colonel sat down to a dinner of soup, fish, and fowl, with various *entrées* and side dishes that would have done credit to a New York *chef*. Thus potent was the name of the boss with his cook.

John's excellent dinner did much to soothe and mollify his guest; but the colonel was sensitive to impressions other than the purely gastronomic, for throughout the course of the dinner, his eyes wandered to the photographs on the wall, and in fancy he was once more in the presence of the two women, to whom he felt pledged in Ranald's behalf. "It's a one-horse looking country, though," he said to himself, "and no place for a man with any snap. Best thing would be to pull out, I guess, and take him along." And it was in this mind that he received the Honorable Archibald Blair, M. P. P., for New Westminster, president of the British Columbia Canning Company, recently organized, and a director in half a dozen other business concerns.

"Colonel Thorp, this is Mr. Blair, of the British Columbia Canning Company," said Coley, with a curious suggestion of Ranald in his manner.

"Glad to welcome a friend of Mr. Macdonald's," said Mr. Blair, a little man of about thirty, with a shrewd eye and a kindly frank manner.

"Well, I guess I can say the same," said Colonel Thorp, shaking hands. "I judge his friends are of the right sort."

"You'll find plenty in this country glad to class themselves in that list," laughed Mr. Blair; "I wouldn't undertake to guarantee them all, but those he lists that way, you can pretty well bank on. He's a young man for reading men."

"Yes?" said the colonel, interrogatively; "he's very young."

"Young, for that matter so are we all, especially on this side the water here. It's a young man's country."

"Pretty young, I judge," said the colonel, dryly. "Lots of room to grow."

"Yes, thank Providence!" said Mr. Blair, enthusiastically; "but there's lots of life and lots to feed it. But I'm not going to talk, Colonel. It is always wasted breath on an Easterner. I'll let the country talk. You are coming with us, of course."

"Hardly think so; my time is rather limited, and, well, to tell the truth, I'm from across the line and don't cater much to your royalties."

"Royalties!" exclaimed Mr. Blair. "Oh, you mean our governor. Well, that's good rather, must tell the governor that." Mr. Blair laughed long and loud. "You'll forget all that when you are out with us an hour. No, we think it well to hedge our government with dignity, but on this trip we shall leave the gold lace and red tape behind."

"How long do you propose to be gone?"

"About four weeks. But I make you a promise. If after the first week you want to return from any point, I shall send you back with all speed. But you won't want to, I guarantee you that. Why, my dear sir, think of the route," and Mr. Blair went off into a rapturous description of the marvels of the young province, its scenery, its resources, its climate, its sport, playing upon each string as he marked the effect upon his listener. By the time Mr. Blair's visit was over, the colonel had made up his mind that he would see something of this wonderful country.

Next day Coley took him over the company's mills, and was not a little disappointed to see that the colonel was not impressed by their size or equipment. In Coley's eyes they were phenomenal, and he was inclined to resent the colonel's lofty manner. The foreman, Mr. Urquhart, a shrewd Scotchman, who had seen the mills of the Ottawa River and those in Michigan as well, understood his visitor's attitude better; and besides, it suited his Scotch nature to refuse any approach to open admiration for anything out of the old land. His ordinary commendation was, "It's no that bad"; and his superlative was expressed in the daring concession, "Aye, it'll maybe dae, it micht be waur." So he followed the colonel about with disparaging comments that drove Coley to the verge of madness. When they came to the engine room, which was Urquhart's pride, the climax was reached.

"It's a wee bit o' a place, an' no fit for the wark," said Urquhart, ushering the colonel into a snug little engine-room, where every bit of brass shone with dazzling brightness, and every part of the engine moved in smooth, sweet harmony.

"Slick little engine," said the colonel, with discriminating admiration.

"It's no that bad the noo, but ye sud hae seen it afore Jem, there, took a hand o' it – a wheezin' rattlin' pechin thing that ye micht expect tae flee in bits for the noise in the wame o't. But Jemmie sorted it till it's nae despicable for its size. But it's no fit for the wark. Jemmie, lad, just gie't its fill an' we'll pit the saw until a log," said Urquhart, as they went up into the sawing-room where, in a few minutes, the colonel had an exhibition of the saw sticking fast in a log for lack of power.

"Man, yon's a lad that kens his trade. He's frae Gleska. He earns his money's warth."

"How did you come to get him?" said the colonel, moved to interest by Urquhart's unwonted praise.

"Indeed, just the way we've got all our best men. It's the boss picked him oot o' the gutter, and there he is earnin' his twa and a half a day."

"The boss did that, eh?" said the colonel, with one of his swift glances at the speaker.

"Aye, that he did, and he's only one o' many."

"He's good at that sort of business, I guess."

"Aye, he kens men as ye can see frae his gang."

"Doesn't seem to be able to make the company's business pay," ventured the colonel.

"D'ye think ye cud find one that cud?" pointing to the halting saw. "An that's the machine that turned oot thae piles yonder. Gie him a chance, though, an' when the stuff is deesposed of ye'll get y're profit." Urquhart knew what he was about, and the colonel went back with Coley to his rooms convinced of two facts, that the company had a plant that might easily be improved, but a manager that, in the estimation of those who wrought with him, was easily first in his class. Ranald could have adopted no better plan for the enhancing of his reputation than by allowing Colonel Thorp to go in and out among the workmen and his friends. More and more the colonel became impressed with his manager's genius for the picking of his men and binding them to his interests, and as this impression deepened he became the more resolved that it was a waste of good material to retain a man in a country offering such a limited scope for his abilities.

But after four weeks spent in exploring the interior, from Quesnelle to Okanagan, and in the following in and out the water-ways of the coast line, the colonel met Ranald at Yale with only a problem to be solved, and he lost no time in putting it to his manager.

"How in thunder can I get those narrow-gauge, hide-bound Easterners to launch out into business in this country?"

"I can't help you there, Colonel. I've tried and failed."

"By the great Sam, so you have!" said the colonel, with a sudden conviction of his own limitations in the past. "No use tryin' to tell 'em of this," swinging his long arm toward the great sweep of the Fraser Valley, clothed with a mighty forest. "It's only a question of holdin' on for a few years, the thing's dead sure."

"I have been through a good part of it," said Ranald, quietly, "and I am convinced that here we have the pick of Canada, and I venture to say of the American Continent. Timber, hundreds of square miles of it, fish – I've seen that river so packed with salmon that I couldn't shove my canoe through –"

"Hold on, now," said the colonel, "give me time."

"Simple, sober truth of my own proving," replied Ranald. "And you saw a fringe of the mines up in the Cariboo. The Kootenai is full of gold and silver, and in the Okanagan you can grow food and fruits for millions of people. I know what I am saying."

"Tell you what," said the colonel, "you make me think you're speakin' the truth anyhow." Then, with a sudden inspiration, he exclaimed: "By the great Sammy, I've got an idea!"

and then, as he saw Ranald waiting, added, "But I guess I'll let it soak till we get down to the mill."

"Do you think you could spare me, Colonel?" asked Ranald, in a dubious voice; "I really ought to run through a bit of timber here."

"No, by the great Sam, I can't! I want you to come right along," replied the colonel, with emphasis.

"What is he saying, Colonel?" asked Mr. Blair.

"Wants to run off and leave me to paddle my way home alone. Not much! I tell you what, we have some important business to do before I go East. You hear me?"

"And besides, Macdonald, I want you for that big meeting of ours next week. You simply must be there."

"You flatter me, Mr. Blair."

"Not a bit; you know there are a lot of hot-heads talking separation and that sort of thing, and I want some level-headed fellow who is in with the working men to be there."

And as it turned out it was a good thing for Mr. Blair and for the cause he represented that Ranald was present at the great mass-meeting held in New Westminster the next week. For the people were exasperated beyond all endurance at the delay of the Dominion in making good the solemn promises given at the time of Confederation, and were in a mood to listen to the proposals freely made that the useless bond should be severed. "Railway or separation," was the cry, and resolutions embodying this sentiment were actually proposed and discussed. It was Ranald's speech, every one said, that turned the tide. His calm logic made clear the folly of even considering separation; his knowledge of, and his unbounded faith in, the resources of the province, and more than all, his impassioned picturing of the future of the great Dominion reaching from ocean to ocean, knit together by ties of common interest, and a common loyalty that would become more vividly real when the provinces had been brought more closely together by the promised railway. They might have to wait a little longer, but it was worth while waiting, and there was no future in any other policy. It was his first speech at a great meeting, and as Mr. Blair shook him warmly by the hand, the crowd burst into enthusiastic cries, "Macdonald! Macdonald!" and in one of the pauses a single voice was heard, "Glengarry forever!" Then again the crowd broke forth, "Glengarry! Glengarry!" for all who knew Ranald personally had heard of the gang that were once the pride of the Ottawa. At that old cry Ranald's face flushed deep red, and he had no words to answer his friends' warm congratulations.

"Send him East," cried a voice.

"Yes, yes, that's it. Send him to Ottawa to John A. It's the same clan!"

Swiftly Mr. Blair made up his mind. "Gentlemen, that is a good suggestion. I make it a motion." It was seconded in a dozen places, and carried by a standing vote. Then Ranald rose again and modestly protested that he was not the man to go. He was quite unknown in the province.

"We know you!" the same voice called out, followed by a roar of approval.

"And, besides," went on Ranald, "it is impossible for me to get away; I'm a working man and not my own master."

Then the colonel, who was sitting on the platform, rose and begged to be heard. "Mr. Chairman and gentlemen, I ain't a Canadian –"

"Never mind! You can't help that," sang out a man from the back, with a roar of laughter following.

"But if I weren't an American, I don't know anything that

I'd rather be." (Great applause.) "Four weeks ago I wouldn't have taken your province as a gift. Now I only wish Uncle Sam could persuade you to sell." (Cries of "He hasn't got money enough. Don't fool yourself.") "But I want to say that this young man of mine," pointing to Ranald, "has given you good talk, and if you want him to go East, why, I'll let him off for a spell." (Loud cheers for the colonel and for Macdonald.)

A week later a great meeting in Victoria endorsed the New Westminster resolutions with the added demand that the railway should be continued to Esquinalt according to the original agreement. Another delegate was appointed to represent the wishes of the islanders, and before Ranald had fully realized what had happened he found himself a famous man, and on the way to the East with the jubilant colonel.

"What was the great idea, Colonel, that struck you at Yale?" inquired Ranald, as they were fairly steaming out of the Esquinalt harbor.

"This is it, my boy!" exclaimed the colonel, slapping him on the back. "This here trip East. Now we've got 'em over the ropes, by the great and everlasting Sammy!" the form of oath indicating a climax in the colonel's emotion.

"Got who?" inquired Ranald, mystified.

"Them gol-blamed, cross-road hayseeds down East." And with this the colonel became discreetly silent. He knew too well the sensitive pride of the man with whom he had to deal, and he was chiefly anxious now that Ranald should know as little as possible of the real object of his going to British Columbia.

"We've got to make the British-American Coal and Lumber Company know the time of day. It's gittin'-up time out in this country. They were talkin' a little of drawin' out."

Ranald gasped. "Some of them only," the colonel hastened to add, "but I want you to talk like you did the other night, and I'll tell my little tale, and if that don't fetch 'em then I'm a Turk."

"Well, Colonel, here's my word," said Ranald, deliberately, "if the company wish to withdraw they may do so, but my future is bound up with that of the West, and I have no fear that it will fail me. I stake my all upon the West."

GLENGARRY FOREVER

The colonel was an experienced traveler, and believed in making himself comfortable. Ranald looked on with some amusement, and a little wonder, while the colonel arranged his things about the stateroom.

"May as well make things comfortable while we can," said the colonel, "we have the better part of three days before us on this boat, and if it gets rough, it is better to have things neat. Now you go ahead," he added, "and get your things out."

"I think you are right, Colonel. I am not much used to travel, but I shall take your advice on this."

"Well, I have traveled considerable these last twenty years," replied the colonel. "I say, would you mind leaving those out?"

"What?"

"Those photos. They're the two you had up by the glass in your room, aren't they?" Ranald flushed a little.

"Of course it ain't for every one to see, and I would not ask you, but those two ain't like any other two that I have seen, and I have seen a good many in forty years." Ranald said nothing, but set the photographs on a little bracket on the wall.

"There, that makes this room feel better," said the colonel. "That there is the finest, sweetest, truest girl that walks this sphere," he said, pointing at Kate's photograph, "and the other, I guess you know all about her."

"Yes, I know about her," said Ranald, looking at the photograph; "it is to her I owe everything I have that is any good. And Colonel," he added, with an unusual burst of confidence, "when my life was broken off short, that woman put me in the way of getting hold of it again."

"Well, they both think a pile of you," was the colonel's reply.

"Yes, I think they do," said Ranald. "They are not the kind to forget a man when he is out of sight, and it is worth traveling two thousand miles to see them again."

"Ain't it queer, now, how the world is run?" said the colonel. "There's two women, now, the very best; one has been buried all her life in a little hole in the woods, and the other is giving herself to a fellow that ain't fit to carry her boots."

"What!" said Ranald, sharply, "Kate?"

"Yes, they say she is going to throw herself away on young St. Clair. He is all right, I suppose, but he ain't fit for her." Ranald suddenly stooped over his valise and began pulling out his things.

"I didn't hear of that," he said.

"I did," said the colonel; "you see he is always there, and acting as if he owned her. He stuck to her for a long time, and I guess she got tired holding out."

"Harry is a very decent fellow," said Ranald, rising up from his unpacking; "I say, this boat's close. Let us go up on deck."

"Wait," said the colonel, "I want to talk over our plans, and we can talk better here."

"No," said Ranald; "I want some fresh air. Let us go up." And without further words, he hurried up the gangway. It was some time before Colonel Thorp found him in the bow of the boat, and immediately began to talk over their plans.

"You spoke of going to Toronto first thing," he said to Ranald.

"Yes," said Ranald; "but I think I ought to go to Ottawa at once, and then I shall see my people in Glengarry for a few days. Then I will be ready for the meeting at Bay City any time after the second week."

"But you have not put Toronto in there," said the colonel; "you are not going to disappoint that little girl? She would take it pretty hard. Mind you, she wants to see you."

"Oh, of course I shall run in for a day."

"Well," said the colonel, "I want to give you plenty of time. I will arrange that meeting for a month from to-day."

"No, no," said Ranald, impatiently; "I must get back to the West. Two weeks will do me."

"Well, we will make it three," said the colonel. He could not understand Ranald's sudden eagerness to set out for the West again. He had spoken with such enthusiastic delight of his visit to Toronto, and now he was only going to run in for a day or so. And if Ranald himself were asked, he would have found it difficult to explain his sudden lack of interest, not only in Toronto, but in everything that lay in the East. He was conscious of a deep, dull ache in his heart, and he could not quite explain it.

After the colonel had gone down for the night, Ranald walked the deck alone and resolutely faced himself. His first frank look within revealed to him the fact that his pain had come upon him with the colonel's information that Kate had given herself to Harry. It was right that he should be disappointed. Harry, though a decent enough fellow, did not begin to be worthy of her; and indeed no one that he knew was worthy of her. But why should he feel so sorely about it? For years Harry had been her devoted slave. He would give her the love of an honest man, and would surround her with all the comforts and luxuries that wealth could bring. She would be very happy. He had no right to grieve about it. And yet he did grieve. The whole sky over the landscape of his life had suddenly become cold and gray. During these years Kate had grown to be much to him. She had in many ways helped him in his work. The thought of her and her approval had brought him inspiration and strength in many an hour of weakness and loneliness. She had been so loyal and so true from the very first, and it was a bitter thing to feel that another had come between them. Over and over again he accused himself of sheer madness. Why should she not love Harry? That need not make her any less his friend. But in spite of his arguments, he found himself weary of the East and eager to turn away from it. He must hurry on at once to Ottawa, and with all speed get done his business there.

At Chicago he left the colonel with a promise to meet him in three weeks at the headquarters of the British-American Coal and Lumber Company at Bay City. He wired to Ottawa, asking an appointment with the government, and after three days' hard travel found himself in the capital of the Dominion. The premier, Sir John A. MacDonald, with the ready courtesy characteristic of him, immediately arranged for a hearing of the delegation from British Columbia. Ranald was surprised at the indifference with which he approached this meeting. He seemed to have lost capacity for keen feeling of any kind. Sir John A. MacDonald and his cabinet received the delegation with great kindness, and in every possible way strove to make them feel that the government was genuinely interested in the western province, and were anxious to do all that could be done in their interest. In the conference that ensued, the delegate for Victoria took a more prominent part, being an older man, and representing the larger and more important constituency. But when Sir John began to ask questions, the Victoria delegate was soon beyond his depth. The premier showed such an exactness of knowledge and comprehensiveness of grasp that before long Ranald was appealed to for information in regard to the resources of the country, and especially the causes and extent of the present discontent.

"The causes of discontent are very easy to see," said Ranald; "all British Columbians feel hurt at the failure of the Dominion government to keep its solemn obligations."

"Is there nothing else now, Mr. Macdonald?"

"There may be," said Ranald, "some lingering impatience with the government by different officials, and there is a certain amount of annexation sentiment."

"Ah," said Sir John, "I think we have our finger upon it now."

"Do not over-estimate that," said Ranald; "I believe that there are only a very few with annexation sentiments, and all these are of American birth. The great body of the people are simply indignant at, and disappointed with, the Dominion government."

"And would you say there is no other cause of discontent, Mr. Macdonald?" said Sir John, with a keen look at Ranald.

"There is another cause, I believe," said Ranald, "and that is the party depression, but that depression is due to the uncertainty in regard to the political future of the province. When once we hear that the railroad is being built, political interest will revive."

"May I ask where you were born?" said Sir John.

"In Glengarry," said Ranald, with a touch of pride in his voice.

"Ah, I am afraid your people are not great admirers of my government, and perhaps you, Mr. Macdonald, share in the opinion of your county."

"I have no opinion in regard to Dominion politics. I am for British Columbia."

"Well, Mr. Macdonald," said Sir John, rising, "that is right, and you ought to have your road."

"Do I understand you to say that the government will begin to build the road at once?" said Ranald.

"Ah," smiled Sir John, "I see you want something definite."

"I have come two thousand miles to get it. The people that sent me will be content with nothing else. It is a serious time with us, and I believe with the whole of the Dominion."

"Mr. Macdonald," said Sir John, becoming suddenly grave, "believe me, it is a more serious time than you know, but you trust me in this matter."

"Will the road be begun this year?" said Ranald.

"All I can say to-day, Mr. Macdonald," said Sir John, earnestly, "is this, that if I can bring it about, the building of the road will be started at once."

"Then, Sir John," said Ranald, "you may depend that British Columbia will be grateful to you," and the interview was over.

Outside the room, he found Captain De Lacy awaiting him.

"By Jove, Macdonald, I have been waiting here three-quarters of an hour. Come along. Maimie has an afternoon right on, and you are our lion." Ranald would have refused, but De Lacy would not accept any apology, and carried him off.

Maimie's rooms were crowded with all the great social and political people of the city. With an air of triumph, De Lacy piloted Ranald through the crowd and presented him to Maimie. Ranald was surprised to find himself shaking hands with the woman he had once loved, with unquickened pulse and nerves cool and steady. Here Maimie, who was looking more beautiful than ever, and who was dressed in a gown of exquisite richness, received Ranald with a warmth that was almost enthusiastic.

"How famous you have become, Mr. Macdonald," she said, offering him her hand; "we are all proud to say that we know you."

"You flatter me," said Ranald, bowing over her hand.

"No, indeed. Every one is talking of the young man from the West. And how handsome you are, Ranald," she said, in a low voice, leaning toward him, and flashing at him one of her old-time glances.

"I am not used to that," he said, "and I can only reply as we used to in school, 'You, too.'"

"Oh, now you flatter me," cried Maimie, gayly; "but let me introduce you to my dear friend, Lady Mary Rivers. Lady Mary, this is Mr. Macdonald from British Columbia, you know."

"Oh, yes," said Lady Mary, with a look of intelligence in her beautiful dark eyes, "I have heard a great deal about you. Let me see, you opposed separation; saved the Dominion, in short."

"Did I, really?" said Ranald, "and never knew it."

"You see, he is not only famous but modest," said Maimie; "but that is an old characteristic of his. I knew Mr. Macdonald a very long time ago."

"Very," said Ranald.

"When we were quite young."

"Very young," replied Ranald, with great emphasis.

"And doubtless very happy," said Lady Mary.

"Happy," said Ranald, "yes, so happy that I can hardly bear to think of those days."

"Why so?" inquired Lady Mary.

"Because they are gone."

"But all days go and have to be parted with."

"Oh, yes, Lady Mary. That is true and so many things die with them, as, for instance, our youthful beliefs and enthusiasms. I used to believe in every one, Lady Mary."

"And now in no one?"

"God forbid! I discriminate."

"Now, Lady Mary," replied Maimie, "I want my lion to be led about and exhibited, and I give him over to you."

For some time Ranald stood near, chatting to two or three people to whom Lady Mary had introduced him, but listening eagerly all the while to Maimie talking to the men who were crowded about her. How brilliantly she talked, finding it quite within her powers to keep several men busy at the same time; and as Ranald listened to her gay, frivolous talk, more and more he became conscious of an unpleasantness in her tone. It was thin, shallow, and heartless.

"Can it be possible," he said to himself, "that once she had the power to make my heart quicken its beat?"

"Tell me about the West," Lady Mary was saying, when Ranald came to himself.

"If I begin about the West," he replied; "I must have both time and space to deliver myself."

"Come, then. We shall find a corner," said Lady Mary, and for half an hour did Ranald discourse to her of the West, and so eloquently that Lady Mary quite forgot that he was a lion and that she had been intrusted with the duty of exhibiting him. By and by Maimie found them.

"Now, Lady Mary, you are very selfish, for so many people are wanting to see our hero, and here is the premier wanting to see you."

"Ah, Lady Mary," said Sir John, "you have captured the man from Glengarry, I see."

"I hope so, indeed," said Lady Mary; "but why from Glengarry? He is from the West, is he not?"

"Once from Glengarry, now from the West, and I hope he will often come from the West, and he will, no doubt, if those people know what is good for them." And Sir John, skillfully drawing Ranald aside, led him to talk of the political situation in British Columbia, now and then putting a question that revealed a knowledge so full and accurate that Ranald exclaimed, suddenly, "Why, Sir John, you know more about the country than I do!"

"Not at all, not at all," replied Sir John; and then, lowering his voice to a confidential tone, he added, "You are the first man from that country that knows what I want to know." And once more he plied Ranald with questions, listening eagerly and intelligently to the answers so enthusiastically given.

"We want to make this Dominion a great empire," said Sir John, as he said good by to Ranald, "and we are going to do it, but you and men like you in the West must do your part."

Ranald was much impressed by the premier's grave earnestness.

"I will try, Sir John," he said, "and I shall go back feeling thankful that you are going to show us the way."

"Going so soon?" said Maimie, when he came to say good by. "Why I have seen nothing of you, and I have not had a moment to offer you my congratulations," she said, with a significant smile. Ranald bowed his thanks.

"And Kate, dear girl," went on Maimie, "she never comes to see me now, but I am glad she will be so happy."

Ranald looked at her steadily for a moment or two, and then said, quietly, "I am sure I hope so, and Harry is a very lucky chap."

"Oh, isn't he," cried Maimie, "and he is just daft about her. Must you go? I am so sorry. I wanted to talk about old times, the dear old days." The look in Maimie's eyes said much more than her words.

"Yes," said Ranald, with an easy, frank smile; "they were dear days, indeed; I often think of them. And now I must really go. Say good by to De Lacy for me."

He came away from her with an inexplicable feeling of exultation. He had gone with some slight trepidation in his heart, to meet her, and it was no small relief to him to discover that she had lost all power over him.

"What sort of man could I have been, I wonder?" he asked himself; "and it was only three years ago."

Near the door Lady Mary stopped him. "Going so early, and without saying good by?" she said, reproachfully.

"I must leave town to-night," he replied, "but I am glad to say good by to you."

"I think you ought to stay. I am sure his excellency wants to see you."

"I am sure you are good to think so, but I am also quite sure that he has never given a thought to my insignificant self."

"Indeed he has. Now, can't you stay a few days? I want to see more – we all want to hear more about the West."

"You will never know the West by hearing of it," said Ranald, offering his hand.

"Good by," she said, "I am coming."

"Good," he said, "I shall look for you."

As Ranald approached his hotel, he saw a man that seemed oddly familiar, lounging against the door and as he drew near, he discovered to his astonishment and joy that it was Yankee.

"Why, Yankee!" he exclaimed, rushing at him, "how in the world did you come to be here, and what brought you?"

"Well, I came for you, I guess. Heard you were going to be here and were comin' home afterwards, so I thought it would be quicker for you to drive straight across than to go round by Cornwall, so I hitched up Lisette and came right along."

"Lisette! You don't mean to tell me? How is the old girl? Yankee, you have done a fine thing. Now we will start right away."

"All right," said Yankee.

"How long will it take us to get home?"

"'Bout two days easy goin', I guess. Of course if you want, I guess we can do it in a day and a half. She will do all you tell her."

"Well, we will take two days," said Ranald.

"I guess we had better take a pretty early start," said Yankee.

"Can't we get off to-night?" inquired Ranald, eagerly. "We could get out ten miles or so."

"Yes," replied Yankee. "There's a good place to stop, about ten miles out. I think we had better go along the river road, and then take down through the Russell Hills to the Nation Crossing."

In half an hour they were off on their two days' trip to the Indian Lands. And two glorious days they were. The open air with the suggestion of the coming fall, the great forests with their varying hues of green and brown, yellow and bright red, and all bathed in the smoky purple light of the September sun, these all combined to bring to Ranald's heart the rest and comfort and peace that he so sorely needed. And when he drove into his uncle's yard in the late afternoon of the second day he felt himself more content to live the life appointed him; and if anything more were needed to strengthen him in this resolution, and to fit him for the fight lying before him, his brief visit to his home brought it to him. It did him good to look into the face of the great Macdonald Bhain once more, and to hear his deep, steady voice welcome him home. It was the face and the voice of a man who had passed through many a sore battle, and not without honor to himself. And it was good, too, to receive the welcome greetings of his old friends and to feel their pride in him and their high expectation of him. More than ever, he resolved that he would be a man worthy of his race.

His visit to the manse brought him mingled feelings of delight and perplexity and pain. The minister's welcome was kind, but there was a tinge of self-complacent pride in it. Ranald was one of "his lads," and he evidently took credit to himself for the young man's success. Hughie regarded him with reserved approval. He was now a man and teaching school, and before committing himself to his old-time devotion, he had to adjust his mind to the new conditions. But before the evening was half done Ranald had won him once more. His tales of the West, and of how it was making and marring men, of the nation that was being built up, and his picture of the future that he saw for the great Dominion, unconsciously revealed the strong manhood and the high ideals in the speaker, and Hughie found himself slipping into the old attitude of devotion to his friend.

But it struck Ranald to the heart to see the marks of many a long day's work upon the face of the woman who had done more for him than all the rest of the world. Her flock of little children had laid upon her a load of care and toil, which added to the burden she was already trying to carry, was proving more than her delicate frame could bear. There were lines upon her face that only weariness often repeated cuts deep; but there were other lines there, and these were lines of heart pain, and as Ranald watched her closely, with his heart running over with love and pity and indignation for her, he caught her frequent glances toward her first born that spoke of anxiety and fear.

"Can it be the young rascal is bringing her anything but perfect satisfaction and joy in return for the sacrifice of her splendid life?" he said to himself. But no word fell from her to show him the secret of her pain, it was Hughie's own lips that revealed him, and as the lad talked of his present and his future, his impatience of control, his lack of sympathy to all higher ideals, his determination to please himself to the forgetting of all else, his seeming unconsciousness of the debt he owed to his mother, all these became easily apparent. With difficulty Ranald restrained his indignation. He let him talk for some time and then opened out upon him. He read him no long lecture, but his words came forth with such fiery heat that they burned their way clear through all the faults and flimsy selfishness of the younger man till they reached the true heart of him. His last words Hughie never forgot.

"Do you know, Hughie," he said, and the fire in his eyes seemed to burn into Hughie's, "do you know what sort of woman you have for a mother? And do you know that if you should live to be a hundred years, and devoted every day of your life to the doing of her pleasure, you could not repay the debt you owe her? Be a man, Hughie. Thank God for her, and for the opportunity of loving and caring for her."

The night of his first visit to the manse Ranald had no opportunity for any further talk with the minister's wife, but he came away with the resolve that before his week's visit was over, he would see her alone. On his return home, however, he found waiting him a telegram from Colonel Thorp, mailed from Alexandria, announcing an early date for the meeting of share-holders at Bay City, so that he found it necessary to leave immediately after the next day, which was the Sabbath. It was no small disappointment to him that he was to have no opportunity of opening his heart to his friend. But as he sat in his uncle's seat at the side of the pulpit, from which he could catch sight of the minister's pew, and watched the look of peace and quiet courage grow upon her face till all the lines of pain and care were quite smoothed out, he felt his heart fill up with a sense of shame for all his weakness, and his soul knit itself into the resolve that if he should have to walk his way, bearing his cross alone, he would seek the same high spirit of faith and patience and courage that he saw shining in her gray-brown eyes.

After the service he walked home with the minister's wife, seeking opportunity for a few last words with her. He had meant to tell her something of his heart's sorrow and disappointment, for he guessed that knowing and loving Kate as she did, she would understand its depth and bitterness. But when he told her of his early departure, and of the fear that for many years he could not return, his heart was smitten with a great pity for her. The look of disappointment and almost of dismay he could not understand until, with difficulty, she told him how she had hoped that he was to spend some weeks at home and that Hughie might be much with him.

"I wish he could know you better, Ranald. There is no one about here to whom he can look up, and some of his companions are not of the best." The look of beseeching pain in her eyes was almost more than Ranald could bear.

"I would give my life to help you," he said, in a voice hoarse and husky.

"I know," she said, simply; "you have been a great joy to me, Ranald, and it will always comfort me to think of you, and of your work, and I like to remember, too, how you helped Harry. He told me much about you, and I am so glad, especially as he is now to be married."

"Yes, yes," replied Ranald, hurriedly; "that will be a great thing for him." Then, after a pause, he added: "Mrs. Murray, the West is a hard country for young men who are not – not very firmly anchored, but if at any time you think I could help Hughie and you feel like sending him to me, I will gladly do for him all that one man can do for another. And all that I can do will be a very poor return for what you have done for me."

"It's little I have done, Ranald," she said, "and that little has been repaid a thousand-fold, for there is no greater joy than that of seeing my boys grow into good and great men and that joy you have brought me." Then she said good by, holding his hand long, as if hating to let him go.

"I will remember your promise, Ranald," she said, "for it may be that some day I shall need you." And when the chance came to Ranald before many years had gone, he proved himself not unworthy of her trust.

At the meeting of share-holders of the British-American Coal and Lumber Company, held in Bay City, the feeling uppermost in the minds of those present was one of wrath and indignation at Colonel Thorp, for he still clung to the idea that it would be unwise to wind up the British Columbia end of the business. The colonel's speech in reply was a triumph of diplomacy. He began by giving a detailed and graphic account of his trip through the province, lighting up the narrative with incidents of adventure, both tragic and comic, to such good purpose that before he had finished his hearers had forgotten all their anger. Then he told of what he had seen of Ranald's work, emphasizing the largeness of the results he had obtained with his very imperfect equipment. He spoke of the high place their manager held in the esteem of the community as witness his visit to Ottawa as representative, and lastly he touched upon his work for the men by means of the libraries and reading-room. Here he was interrupted by an impatient exclamation on the part of one of the share-holders. The colonel paused, and fastening his eye upon the impatient share-holder, he said, in tones cool and deliberate: "A gentleman says, 'Nonsense!' I confess that before my visit to the West I should have said the same, but I want to say right here and now, that I have come to the opinion that it pays to look after your men – soul, mind, and body. You'll cut more lumber, get better contracts, and increase your dividends. There ain't no manner of doubt about that. Now," concluded the colonel, "you may still want to close up that business, but before you do so, I want you to hear Mr. Macdonald."

After some hesitation, Ranald was allowed to speak for a few minutes. He began by expressing his amazement that there should be any thought on the part of the company of withdrawing from the province at the very time when other firms were seeking to find entrance. He acknowledged that the result for the last years did not warrant any great confidence in the future of their business, but a brighter day had dawned, the railroad was coming, and he had in his pocket three contracts that it would require the company's whole force for six months to fulfill, and these contracts would be concluded the day the first rail was laid.

"And when will that be?" interrupted a share-holder, scornfully.

"I have every assurance," said Ranald, quietly, "from the premier himself, that the building of the railroad will be started this fall."

"Did Sir John A. MacDonald give you a definite promise?" asked the man, in surprise.

"Not exactly a promise," said Ranald.

A chorus of scornful "Ohs" greeted this admission.

"But the premier assured me that all his influence would be thrown in favor of immediate construction."

"For my part," replied the share-holder, "I place not the slightest confidence in any such promise as that."

"And I," said Ranald, calmly, "have every confidence that work on the line will be started this fall." And then he went on to speak of the future that he saw stretching out before the province and the whole Dominion. The feeling of opposition in the air roused him like a call to battle, and the thought that he was pleading for the West that he had grown to love, stimulated him like a draught of strong wine. In the midst of his speech the secretary, who till that moment had not been present, came into the room with the evening paper in his hand. He gave it to the president, pointing out a paragraph. At once the president, interrupting Ranald in his speech, rose and said, "Gentlemen, there is an item of news here that I think you will all agree bears somewhat directly upon this business." He then read Sir John A. MacDonald's famous telegram to the British Columbia government, promising that the Canadian Pacific Railway should be begun that fall. After the cheers had died away, Ranald rose again, and said, "Mr. President and gentlemen, there is no need that I should say anything more. I simply wish to add that I return to British Columbia next week, but whether as manager for this company or not that is a matter of perfect indifference to me." And saying this, he left the room, followed by Colonel Thorp.

"You're all right, pardner," said the colonel, shaking him vigorously by the hand, "and if they don't feel like playing up to your lead, then, by the great and everlasting Sammy, we will make a new deal and play it alone!"

"All right, Colonel," said Ranald; "I almost think I'd rather play it without them and you can tell them so."

"Where are you going now?" said the colonel.

"I've got to go to Toronto for a day," said Ranald; "the boys are foolish enough to get up a kind of dinner at the *Albert*, and besides," he added, resolutely, "I want to see Kate."

"Right you are," said the colonel; "anything else would be meaner than snakes."

But when Ranald reached Toronto, he found disappointment awaiting him. The *Alberts* were ready to give him an enthusiastic reception, but to his dismay both Harry and Kate were absent. Harry was in Quebec and Kate was with her mother visiting friends at the Northern Lake, so Ranald was forced to content himself with a letter of farewell and congratulation upon her approaching marriage. In spite of his disappointment, Ranald could not help acknowledging a feeling of relief. It would have been no small ordeal to him to have met Kate, to have told her how she had helped him during his three years' absence, without letting her suspect how much she had become to him, and how sore was his disappointment that she could never be more than friend to him, and indeed, not even that. But his letter was full of warm, frank, brotherly congratulation and good will.

The dinner at the *Albert* was in every way worthy of the club and of the occasion, but Ranald was glad to get it over. He was eager to get away from the city associated in his mind with so much that was painful.

At length the last speech was made, and the last song was sung, and the men in a body marched to the station carrying their hero with them. As they stood waiting for the train to pull out, a coachman in livery approached little Merrill.

"A lady wishes to see Mr. Macdonald, sir," he said, touching his hat.

"Well, she's got to be quick about it," said Merrill. "Here, Glengarry," he called to Ranald, "a lady is waiting outside to see you, but I say, old chap, you will have to make it short, I guess it will be sweet enough."

"Where is she?" said Ranald to the coachman.

"In here, sir," conducting him to the ladies' waiting-room, and taking his place at the door outside. Ranald hurried into the room, and there stood Kate.

"Dear Kate!" he cried, running toward her with both hands outstretched, "this is more than kind of you, and just like your good heart."

"I only heard last night, Ranald," she said, "from Maimie, that you were to be here to-day, and I could not let you go." She stood up looking so brave and proud, but in spite of her, her lips quivered.

"I have waited to see you so long," she said, "and now you are going away again."

"Don't speak like that, Kate," said Ranald, "don't say those things. I want to tell you how you have helped me these three lonely years, but I can't, and you will never know, and now I am going back. I hardly dared to see you, but I wish you everything that is good. I haven't seen Harry either, but you will wish him joy for me. He is a very lucky fellow."

By this time Ranald had regained control of himself and was speaking in a tone of frank and brotherly affection. Kate looked at him with a slightly puzzled air.

"I've seen Maimie," Ranald went on, "and she told me all about it, and I am – yes, I am very glad." Still Kate looked a little puzzled, but the minutes were precious, and she had much to say.

"Oh, Ranald!" she cried, "I have so much to say to you. You have become a great man, and you are good. I am so proud when I hear of you," and lowering her voice almost to a whisper, "I pray for you every day."

As Ranald stood gazing at the beautiful face, and noticed the quivering lips and the dark eyes shining with tears she was too brave to let fall, he felt that he was fast losing his grip of himself.

"Oh, Kate," he cried, in a low, tense voice, "I must go. You have been more to me than you will ever know. May you both be happy."

"Both?" echoed Kate, faintly.

"Yes," cried Ranald, hurriedly, "Harry will, I'm sure, for if any one can make him happy, you can."

"I?" catching her breath, and beginning to laugh a little hysterically.

"What's the matter, Kate? You are looking white."

"Oh," cried Kate, her voice broken between a sob and a laugh, "won't Harry and Lily enjoy this?"

Ranald gazed at her in fear as if she had suddenly gone mad.

"Lily?" he gasped.

"Yes, Lily," cried Kate; "didn't you know Lily Langford, Harry's dearest and most devoted?"

"No," said Ranald; "and it is not you?"

"Not me," cried Kate, "not in the very least."

"Oh, Kate, tell me, is this all true? Are you still free? And is there any use?"

"What do you mean?" cried Kate, dancing about in sheer joy, "you silly boy."

By this time Ranald had quite hold of her hands.

"Look here, old chap," burst in Merrill, "your train's going. Oh, beg pardon."

"Take the next, Ranald."

"Merrill," said Ranald, solemnly, "tell the fellows I'm not going on this train."

"Hoorah!" cried little Merrill, "I guess I'll tell 'em you are gone. May I tell the fellows, Kate?"

"What?" said Kate, blushing furiously.

"Yes, Merrill," cried Ranald, in a voice strident with ecstasy, "you may tell them. Tell the whole town."

Merrill rushed to the door. "I say, fellows," he cried, "look here."

The men came trooping at his call, but only to see Ranald and Kate disappearing through the other door.

"He's not going," cried Merrill, "he's gone. By Jove! They've both gone."

"I say, little man," said big Starry Hamilton, "call yourself together if you can. Who've both gone? In short, who is the lady?"

"Why, Kate Raymond, you blessed idiot!" cried Merrill, rushing for the door, followed by the whole crowd.

"Three cheers for Macdonald!" cried Starry Hamilton, as the carriage drove away, and after the three cheers and the tiger, little Merrill's voice led them in the old battle-cry, heard long ago on the river, but afterward on many a hard-fought foot-ball field, "Glengarry forever!"

AFTERWORD

BY ALISON GORDON

I never knew my grandfather, who died several years before I was born, but memories of the Reverend Charles William Gordon were at the heart of some of the best tales of my childhood summers.

Of course, in the family legends, he wasn't Rev. Gordon, the distinguished clergyman, or even Ralph Connor, the pen name under which he wrote his twenty wildly popular novels. He was Grandfather Gordon, or, to my father's six younger sisters, simply "Daddy."

Our family spent every summer at "Birkencraig," an island in Ontario's Lake of the Woods, five miles by boat from Kenora, the nearest town. My grandfather had bought the island in 1906. He wrote many of his books sitting in The Lookout, a little octagonal tower, one room on top of another, which was attached to the sprawling main house. From the top room, isolated from his large and lively family, he was able to see down the lake for miles while keeping his eye on the occasional passing canoeist.

Birkencraig is where the family kept the legend's flame. The cousins learned to paddle a canoe and chop wood the way

Grandfather Gordon did. We ate porridge every morning, cooked the way he had liked it, and walked through the paths he and his generation had cut to get to the other side of the island, paths that to this day are cleared each year. We didn't play cards on Sunday until well after my grandmother died in the early '60s, and Sunday card-playing still doesn't feel quite right to some of us.

I remember one day, when the morning's project (there is always a project at Birkencraig; we're Presbyterian stock, remember?) was cleaning a back room. A bathrobe hung on a nail in a corner. The aunts avoided it until it was the last thing left.

"It was Daddy's," the youngest aunt, Alison, finally explained, folding it over her arm and smoothing the old plaid wool.

The in-laws and cousins looked off into the middle distance and tried not to laugh. The man had not been around to need the robe for, easily, thirty years. Finally, regretfully, it was thrown away. (At least I think it was. It may be lurking in a trunk somewhere still.)

Such was the power of my grandfather's personality, and the love and respect with which he was remembered.

The first of his legacies of which I was aware was the most frivolous. Meals at Birkencraig were eaten in the dining room, the large corner of the screened verandah nearest the kitchen with its wood-burning stove. The table was large enough, at a pinch, to seat two at each end and eight or nine on each side, depending on the size of the eaters.

In the summers of my youth, the table was covered with an oilcloth that hung down eight inches all around. The highlight of every season was the appearance of guests unfamiliar with our family ways. In the middle of the meal, a couple of the cousins would nudge each other and surreptitiously fold up the edge of the oilcloth to make a little trough. Those adjacent would be let into the gag until the trough ran down the length of the table, ending just above the lap of the visitor, who was being diverted by conversation at his or her end of the table. The cousin at the top of the trough would take a glass of water and pour.

Usually, the victim would leap up, toppling the chair and, occasionally and *most* gratifyingly, swear. Sometimes, amazingly, there would be *no reaction at all*: a wonderfully Presbyterian pretence that nothing was out of the ordinary.

Whatever the outcome, by meal's end, several of the cousins would be banished from the table, sent away to control fits of giggling, but the punishment never diminished our glee.

The water trick, as we called it, was invented by my distinguished grandfather. It is said that he played it himself on visiting parishioners.

I was in my early teens when I first read the Glengarry books. I don't recall how I answered my relatives when asked my opinion, but I'm sure I lied, because, in truth, I was terribly embarrassed by the books. They were so old-fashioned! There was all that praying and people talking funny. Who cares about a bunch of hokey old pioneers anyway?

I was on the shady side of forty-five by the time I read the Glengarry books again. In the meantime, I had written some novels myself. I had also discovered that my grandfather had been extraordinarily popular in his day, the best-selling author in the English-speaking world. His first three novels, published around the turn of the century, sold five million copies. I, with sales figures somewhat more humble, decided it might be time to go back and read my illustrious ancestor again.

The writing surprised me: clean, matter-of-fact, and Presbyterian in its simplicity, but evocative despite its thrift.

The descriptions of the landscape, the forests and rivers that gave Glengarry its living, made me wish I'd seen it before we whipped the wilderness into our shape.

I was intrigued by the details of daily life in the lumber-camp and the manse and rivetted by the action sequences. I could see and hear the wolves at the heels of Mrs. Murray's pony during the chase to the Macdonalds' cabin in the night. I could see, hear, and smell the horse teams in the competition at the logging bee, lathered with sweat, eyes blazing, and nostrils flaring for the final pull.

This time through, I didn't mind the dialect. In the first few pages of the book we meet LeNoir, "de boss on de reever Hottawa! by Gar!", Murphy, with his "Hiven bliss ye," and Black Hugh Macdonald, who allows that "It is a fery goot evening, indeed," and the book's rhythms are established. Dialect is a device I would be embarrassed to use, for fear of seeming to mock the characters, but that was never my grandfather's intent, and in the context of his time, it is very effective.

The biggest surprise I had in re-reading *The Man from Glengarry* was the importance of women to the story. Men, it seems, aren't the only muscular Christians.

In his autobiography, *Postscript to Adventure*, written at the end of his life, my grandfather wrote: "It is one of the tragedies of literature that historians fill their pages with the doings of men and leave unsung the lives of the heroines of the race. . . . at times when I begin to lose my faith in the nobler qualities of the race, I let my mind wander back to the wives, mothers and sisters of the pioneer-settler of Glengarry and find my faith revive."

Mrs. Murray, around whom the novel revolves, was based on my great-grandmother, Mary Robertson Gordon, who, like the character, turned her back on a genteel, cultured life in Sherbrooke, Quebec, to follow her husband to the backwoods to minister to the lumberjacks. "A gay and gallant saint," her son called her.

If there's a problem with his portrayal of Mrs. Murray, it's that he made her too perfect. Surely she had doubts, occasionally. She must have chafed at her role in the family and the community. Did she never tell her husband to put a sock in it (or the nineteenth-century equivalent) when his evening prayer ticked past the forty-five-minute mark? She had to get crabby once in a while. But we never see that private face, perhaps because Mary Robertson Gordon never showed it to her son.

Mrs. Murray is a woman of intelligence, compassion, and humour, a good foil for the dreadful and pretentious Miss Frances St. Clair. My grandfather's description of her is devastating: "She supposed, of course, there must be people to carry on the trades and industry of a country – very worthy people, too – but these were people one could not be expected to know."

To Mrs. Murray's great sorrow, Miss St. Clair is the strongest influence on Maimie, the niece they share. Despite the values she learned during vacations spent at the manse, Maimie grows up to be a deeply shallow woman.

Her friend Kate Raymond is another story. Even though her modern independence breaks with Mrs. Murray's traditions, the older woman admires her spirit, and considers her, finally, a worthy partner for her beloved Ranald.

(Permit a small digression. When I named the heroine of my mysteries Kate Henry, I had completely forgotten about the Kate in this book. When I met her again, to say I was astounded by the coincidence would be to understate dramatically. My Kate, too, is independent-minded, iconoclastic, basically decent and caring, and full of spirit. Surely she's kin to Kate Raymond.)

In the later decades of the twentieth century, history began to judge harshly the Scottish settlers in Canada. It was pointed out that we stole land from the aboriginal people who were here first, and ruined it. Then of course, we went on to run the banks and foreclose people's dreams.

We haven't got any really good ethnicity, especially if you're not fond of tartan and bagpipes. And let's not even mention food.

Add all of the above to the Presbyterian guilt that flows through our veins, and it's no wonder we slink about apologizing half the time.

But the fictional people of Glengarry have changed that for me, even if they do live on "the Indian Lands" and make their living cutting down the wilderness as fast as it grows. As portrayed by the man who was a boy in Glengarry, they are decent, strong, hard-working people of great courage, who care for each other and respect the land around them. They look beyond a person's clothing or manner to see the character underneath. They have dignity and strength as well as those traits their minister found most noble – "endurance and patience."

Among the scenes I find most moving in *The Man from Glengarry* are those around the death of the lumberjack Mack Cameron. The news of his drowning is received with restraint, and the community rallies round his family and the girl who loved him, with compassion and grace.

The torch-lit scene as his comrades carry him home along the concession roads, past the neighbours, makes my hair stand on end, like a bagpipe wailing in the distance. By the time his mother, tears streaming down her face, says, "Come in, Malcolm; come in, my boy. Your mother is waiting for you," I can't see the print for my own tears.

The Man from Glengarry is my grandfather's greatest legacy: an understanding of what is inside my bones. My specific bones, in this case, but also the bones of all Canadians descended from the early Scottish settlers.

And they're good bones, after all.

BY RALPH CONNOR

AUTOBIOGRAPHY

Postscript to Adventure:
The Autobiography of Ralph Connor (1938)

BIOGRAPHY

The Life of James Robertson, Missionary Superintendent
in the Northwest Territories (1908)

FICTION

Black Rock: A Tale of the Selkirks (1898)
The Sky Pilot: A Tale of the Foothills (1899)
The Man from Glengarry: A Tale of the Ottawa (1901)
Glengarry School Days: A Story of Early Days in Glengarry (1902)
The Prospector: A Tale of the Crow's Nest Pass (1904)
The Pilot at Swan Creek and Other Stories (1905)
The Doctor: A Tale of the Rockies (1906)
The Foreigner: A Tale of Saskatchewan (1909)
Corporal Cameron of the North West Mounted Police:
A Tale of the MacLeod Trail (1912)
The Patrol of the Sun Dance Trail (1914)
The Major (1917)
The Sky Pilot in No Man's Land (1919)
To Him That Hath: A Novel of the West of Today (1921)
The Gaspards of Pine Croft: A Romance of the Windermere (1923)
Treading the Winepress: A Tale of Glengarry (1925)
The Runner: A Romance of the Niagaras (1929)
The Rock and the River: A Romance of Quebec (1931)
The Arm of Gold (1932)
The Girl from Glengarry (1933)

Torches Through the Bush: A Tale of Glengarry (1934)
The Rebel Loyalist (1935)
The Gay Crusader (1936)

HISTORY

The Cape and Its Story, or The Struggle for South Africa (1902)

SCRIPTURAL HISTORY

The Angel and the Star (1908)
The Dawn by Galilee: A Story of the Christ (1909)
The Recall of Love (1910)
The Friendly Four and Other Stories (1926)
He Dwelt Among Us (1936)